DEADLY TIES

**Center Point
Large Print**

Also by Vicki Hinze
and available from Center Point Large Print:

Forget Me Not
Crossroads Crisis Center Book One

CROSSROADS CRISIS CENTER
BOOK TWO

DEADLY TIES

VICKI HINZE

CENTER POINT PUBLISHING
THORNDIKE, MAINE

This Center Point Large Print edition is published in the year 2012 by arrangement with Multnomah Books, an imprint of The Crown Publishing Group, a division of Random House, Inc.

All Scripture quotations unless otherwise indicated are taken from the Holy Bible, New International Version®. NIV®. Copyright © 1973, 1978, 1984 by Biblica Inc.™ Used by permission of Zondervan. All rights reserved worldwide. www.zondervan.com. Scripture quotations marked (KJV) are taken from the King James Version.

The characters and events in this book are fictional, and any resemblance to actual persons or events is coincidental.
The text of this Large Print edition is unabridged.
In other aspects, this book may vary
from the original edition.
Printed in the United States of America
on permanent paper.
Set in 16-point Times New Roman type.

ISBN: 978-1-61173-278-8

Library of Congress Cataloging-in-Publication Data

Hinze, Vicki.
  Deadly ties / Vicki Hinze.
    p. cm.
  ISBN 978-1-61173-278-8 (library binding : alk. paper)
  1. Mothers and daughters—Fiction. 2. Human trafficking—Fiction.
    3. Private security services—Fiction. 4. Americans—Mexico—Fiction.
    5. Large type books. I. Title.
PS3558.I574D43 2012
813'.54—dc23
                                                        2011035871

To Dr. Samuel Poppell
Thank you for using your gifts
and saving my eyes.
There aren't enough words.
With heartfelt gratitude and many blessings,
Vicki

ACKNOWLEDGMENTS

Watching an idea take concrete form and grow into a novel is an amazing thing. Contributions come from many (flaws are all mine), and each is significant to what becomes the story. I'd like to express my deep gratitude to:

Bobby Threlkel, who encourages and willingly brainstorms in the dead of night.

Debra Webb, Kathy Carmichael, and Marge Smith, three of the most nimble minds at interpreting the complexities of the human heart.

Cheryl Mansfield, my assistant and right arm (and often, also the left).

Julee Schwarzburg, who goes the extra mile . . . and then another and another.

Steve Cobb and Ken Petersen, for their thoughtful support and kindnesses.

Alice Crider, Pamela, Ashley, Amy, Chris, Tiffany, Staci, and the others on the WaterBrook Multnomah team who work so hard on behalf of my books and do so with elegance and grace.

Kelly L. Howard, for creating awesome covers that take my breath away.

Allen Wyler and Julie Korenzenko, whose efforts above and beyond make this woman one very happy veep in performing her board duties for International Thriller Writers, Inc.

Jim, David, William Olsen, and Aaron Schuster.

You make me think—even when I'd rather not—and I'm grateful for that. It's such an honor to call you my friends.

To my Dear Ones, members of RWA PRO, for keeping me on my toes and permitting me the pleasure of sharing your joys and successes.

My family—hubby, kids, and grands. Thank you for knowing my every flaw and loving me anyway. I'll love you forever and ever—and that's a promise.

And to my mother, Edna Sampson, the inspiration for Annie, who loves with her whole heart.

To all of you: You enrich my life in ways I can't begin to explain but for which I am ever grateful. I see you and know I am blessed.

Prologue

The child is not; and I, wither shall I go?
GENESIS 37:30 (KJV)

July 1987, Seagrove Village, Florida

It was an ordinary day. Bad things aren't supposed to happen on ordinary days. Only normal things.

Annie Harper looked at her reflection in the entryway mirror. Her hair was a wreck. The dark circles under her eyes looked as if they'd been drawn on with markers and then smudged. And her nails were a disgrace. Haggard and beaten down. That's how she looked. And she felt worse.

"There should be universal rules about this," she told her reflection. "When a woman is body slammed, she can only take so much without breaking under the pressure."

Gathering a full head of steam, she frowned and jabbed her finger in the air. "Life should go easy on you then." *That would be humane. Civil.* "And if bad things have to happen, there should be warning signs so there's time to brace and prepare for them."

She dipped her chin and glared into her own eyes. "Especially if it's too horrific to wrap your mind around—and it happens not to you, but to someone you love."

Pain shot through her heart, leaving her chest hollow and empty. "But there aren't any rules and there weren't any signs." She shifted her gaze to the ceiling. "Why, God? Why didn't You send me at least one bad feeling? An intuitive flash? Couldn't You spare me even one piddling stomach flutter?" Tears stung her eyes. "I've been loyal, obedient. Why didn't I get *something?*"

No edgy nerves. No hitch in her chest. No whispered warning in her mind like, *Annie Harper, you listen to me, woman. Trouble's coming. Summon your faith and gird your loins because every mother's worst fear is about to knock on your door.*

Fisting her hand, she rested it on the gleaming wooden table beneath the mirror. *But did You? No.*

She glared at the vase of freshly cut white roses. The scent was heavy, cloying. "Women's intuition?" She picked up a bud, plucked a petal, and dropped it on the spotless marble floor. "No, I failed."

Tore off another petal. "Mother's intuition?" Tossed it down. "Failed."

Jerked at another petal. "God?" Thrust it. "Failed."

Her breath caught in her throat. *"Everything* failed."

She reached for more petals, but she had stripped the rose bare. All that remained was its stem and thorns.

Like me.

Outrage and agony ripped her soul. *Oh, I resent this and I wish I had someone to blame. But You didn't even give me that. Why?*

She staggered into the living room and collapsed on the sofa, curling her knees to her chest to keep the pain bottled up inside. If she let it loose, she'd never recover, and anyway, there was nowhere to dump it.

It was just an ordinary day.

"Take me back," she cried out, her face tear-soaked. Cradling herself, she rocked back and forth, seeking comfort where there was none. "Just twenty-four hours. Please, take me back."

"Annie?" Miranda Kent came in from the kitchen, clipping an earring back onto her lobe. Not a strand of her auburn hair was out of place. Loose curls framed her face. Her nails, like the rest of her, were perfect.

She snagged a tissue and passed it to Annie. "I've put on a pot of coffee. The church ladies were meeting at the club, but I told Nora about Charles. She said they would be here in a flash."

Annie nodded, pretending to care. She wanted two people in her house. Two. And neither of them would be coming. "Charles and I were at the club night before last."

She and her beloved husband had enjoyed dinner with the mayor and forty or so close friends at Somerset House on the Bay. They feasted on

11

salad with baby artichoke hearts and spears of cucumber, then ate honeyed baby carrots and blackened grouper caught fresh that morning in the Gulf of Mexico. Grouper was Charles's favorite. She swallowed hard. They'd never dine there again.

"We were with you, remember?" Miranda clutched her flat stomach. "I know better than to eat a heavy meal that late. I was up all night."

Annie and Charles had slept like rocks. After they got up and ate breakfast, Lisa and he went on their way.

Miranda sat beside Annie and crossed her ankles. "Is Lisa seven or eight now? I can't remember. After thirty, the years tend to run together."

"Seven." Annie's voice cracked. Lisa was bright and beautiful inside and out—at times all sweetness and innocence, and at others wise beyond her years.

"She told me she wanted to be a doctor like her dad. We were at Nora's birthday party, I think."

Pain twisted in Annie like hot wires coiled tight. "It's what she's always wanted." Lisa idolized her father. "She has a stronger stomach for medical procedures than I do, and she never complains about Charles's long hours at the office and hospital." Annie sniffed and dabbed at her eyes. "His practice takes him away from us so much, but Lisa always defends him." Oh, how Annie wished he were at the office now. That Lisa were here with her.

"They left early yesterday, didn't they?"

Annie didn't answer.

"Annie? They left early yesterday, right?"

"If this shows up in the *Village Log*, I'm going to cut off your fingers, Miranda."

"Not a word without your express permission." She crossed her heart.

Annie believed her. "Yesterday. At the crack of dawn." Seagrove Village was up in the Florida panhandle, and getting down to Orlando for a trip to Disney World would take a solid eight hours. "Charles wanted to beat the tourist traffic." She'd been so proud of him for finally taking a break from work to spend some quality time with Lisa. Charles was brilliant and committed to his patients, but he rarely took time off.

"Highway 98 is a nightmare during the season." Miranda shifted on the white sofa. "I'm sure Lisa was excited."

She was their only child, their miracle baby. "Beyond excited."

"Why didn't you go with them?"

"It's my month to chair the charity function. I couldn't beg off, and rescheduling would have been a nightmare for Charles's staff and patients." Now she wished she had gone. That she hadn't, she'd regret forever.

"Just as well." Miranda stood. "If Charles is

13

anything like my Paul and you'd been there, he would have spent the entire week on the phone with his office." She walked to the kitchen.

Dishes clanged in the kitchen, and Annie resented the racket almost as much as she resented Miranda's being right. Charles would have used Annie as a buffer, and Lisa didn't need him just being in the same room; she got enough of that already.

Miranda returned with a tea tray and the puzzle from the *New York Times*. "I saw this on the counter and thought you might want a diversion."

"I don't work the puzzles. I saved it for Lisa. She loves them." Annie took a cup and saucer Miranda extended to her. "From the cradle, she couldn't resist a mystery of any sort." She was good at solving them too.

"Obviously that's from Charles's side of the family."

Annie nodded. "They want to know and fix everything." If they could fix this, Annie would never complain about that again.

But they couldn't. God help her, no one could.

Miranda poured tea into her own cup. Steam lifted from it. "Interesting family dynamic. The Harpers are into everything, and you avoid everything."

"I don't." Annie took exception. "I face what I have to face to survive."

"Exactly." Miranda waved. "You only worry

after you've prayed and done all you can do. I've always admired that about you."

Annie didn't want or need admiration. She wanted and needed her family.

She stared through the sheers out to the lawn. It was a glorious summer day, much like yesterday when Miranda and Annie had skipped the fashion show and played nine holes of golf. The club's courses were the best in northwest Florida, and Miranda's game was far better than Annie's, but then it should be. Annie dabbled. Miranda hit the links nearly every day.

Ordinary.

The doorbell rang.

"I'll get it." Miranda set down her cup and got to her feet. "You just relax. Shall I bring the church ladies in here?"

"Yes." Annie stood. "I'm going to my room for a few minutes to compose myself."

Miranda nodded. "Good idea." Pity shone in her eyes. "I'll keep them busy until you're ready to see them."

Annie walked through to the master suite, shut the door, and then flung herself across her bed. If this were yesterday, she'd be in the hammock out back facing the cove, enjoying the salt-tanged breeze, lost in a good book. Even as night had fallen and the clock inched toward eight, she hadn't been antsy.

Lisa had promised to phone every night at eight

for a virtual tuck in. She'd outgrown it but indulged Annie because it was her favorite daily ritual, not that Annie ever dwelled on how much it meant to her. She learned early in life not to want or need anything too much. That could make you do crazy things. But the truth was, it was just too scary—the risks of wanting those things and not getting them. She'd worked hard on that, but life lessons instilled young were as hard to break as bad habits.

Was that just another latent gift of being orphaned and raised by a series of foster parents? Maybe so. Two were good people, but more than two should have been in jail. Yet more likely, she avoided those risks because until she'd married Charles, she had to claw her way through her whole life just to survive.

She scrunched her pillow and wadded it under her ear. The lavender smell reminded her of the roses. She tossed the pillow aside and tugged over Charles's. His scent clung to the pillowcase. Gripping wads of the fine linen in both hands, she held on tight and buried her nose deep. Yesterday, those early days had faded from her life.

Yesterday, she had a good husband, an amazing daughter, a beautiful home in the village, and more stuff than anyone could want, much less need.

Yesterday.

Yet even then, the fear of being hungry never

went away. She could tell herself anything, go through all the therapy in the world, but down deep she still feared being hungry again.

Annie always had kept money stashed away for a rainy day. At least she had until a month ago. Lisa came home from Sunday school and said an orphanage in Haiti needed a roof to get the kids out of the rain.

Images of those children soaked to the skin burned in Annie's mind now as they had then. She hadn't slept a wink. It was a fierce battle, but on the third day she forfeited her stash. She wasn't hungry, and the kids were suffering. They needed to get dry.

Charles was indulgent and Lisa was ecstatic, lavish with grateful butterfly kisses and twinkling sparkles in her dancing blue eyes. She had no idea Annie had virtually been on her knees ever since, praying she hadn't set herself up for starvation.

Ordinary.

"Take me back twenty-four hours," she mumbled into the pillow. "Let me live them just once more." She wept openly, begged without shame. "Just once more."

The picture formed vividly in her mind. Twenty-four hours ago she had walked down the tiled east wing to Lisa's room. Rex, her two-year-old yellow lab, lay parked right in the middle of her canopied bed. He seemed so sad that Annie lacked the heart to fuss at him. "You miss her too, eh, boy?"

Rex wagged his tail. She crawled up beside him and scratched his ears. Without Charles and Lisa, the house was far too big and empty. Rex felt it too. His bottom line was that he wanted Lisa and Annie in the same space. Anything less and he just wasn't happy. Truthfully, neither was she.

At straight-up eight, the phone rang. Rex barked and Annie snagged the receiver. "Hello."

"Mom?"

Lisa. "Hi, darling." Annie smiled. "Did you make it down okay?"

"We're not in Orlando. We went to Disney, but Daddy messed up the hotel reservation. He made it for tomorrow, not today."

"Oh no." She should have double-checked that. Charles was lousy with the mundane. One of the quirks Annie adored about him. "So where are you guys?"

"In a motel by a big hat. It's loud here, but the resort man couldn't find us anywhere to stay, so we drove around until Daddy found this place."

July Fourth weekend. Not an easy task to find a room with all the tourists in town for the holiday. An incredible amount of racket in the background hurt Annie's ear. She pulled the receiver away. "Where is Daddy, darling?"

"In the shower. Scrubbing off road grime."

Rex pawed at her thigh, nudging her to keep scratching his scruff. "So you guys are settling in for the night, eh?"

"Yes, but Daddy isn't happy about the music."

"Oh, that's not the TV?" Annie sank back against the pillows and scratched Rex's ears. The dog was nearly as spoiled as Lisa.

"It's off."

Annie frowned. "So what's making all the noise?"

"There's a place across the street that's got an orchestra."

A band. Hard rock, from the sounds of it. Charles would definitely hate that. Annie grinned. "Why do you sound winded?"

"Oh, that man's back, knocking on the door again." Lisa sounded more annoyed than scared. "Mom, he's got a spiderweb drawn on his hand."

"A tattoo?"

"Uh-huh."

Wait. The man was *back?* Alarmed, Annie sat straight up. "Lisa, do *not* open that door." She tried to keep panic out of her voice, but her throat was clenched-fist, white-knuckle tight. "Go get Daddy, darling."

"Just a second. The man is saying something to me through the window."

"What?" Rex perked his ears, lifted his head from her lap—a terrible sign. "What's he saying?" Was there a fire in the building or something?

"It's time for you to become a shrub." Lisa sounded baffled. "What does *that* mean?"

Become a shrub? Definitely a nut case.

19

Whatever was going on sounded bad and felt worse. "Go get your dad. Do it right now, Lisa Marie!"

A loud crackle ripped through the phone. Something cracked. Splintered. Scuffled. Shattered.

Lisa screamed.

"Lisa!" Annie jumped out of bed. Growling and baring his teeth, Rex barked. "Lisa, answer me. Lisa!"

The line went dead.

Annie's blood ran cold.

Yesterday was no longer an ordinary day.

1

July 2007, Iraq

Mark Taylor hated sand.

He'd hated it before coming to the desert for the tenth time in three years, but now buried in it, he really hated it. It got into everything, everywhere—in his boots, along with the scorpions; in his eyes; in his ears. Its grit was always clinging, chafing his skin.

As irritating as it was to his team, the sand was even harder on their equipment. Every man in his unit and Jane, the lone female attached as mission essential because she was a subject-matter expert, protected their weapons as best they could. Their lives depended on it.

Sensitive equipment repairs were left to other experts. When they had their heat source–detecting equipment and it worked, they ruled the night. Unfortunately, they had arrived, the equipment had not, and the honchos had classified immediate action critical. Under direct orders, they'd left the Green Zone without it to do the impossible on sheer guts, determination, and a wing and a prayer.

They'd succeeded at taking out the terrorist cell and gathered data that could help Intel save lives. Overall, execution of their plan had gone smoothly. But five klicks from their rendezvous exit point, they hit a snag. A big one.

Two Humvees of hostiles sped toward each other down the road the team was to follow.

"I thought this road was abandoned," Joe said.

"Obviously not," Tim whispered. "Gentlemen, scatter."

Mark tapped his lip mic. "Six, where are you?"

"Three-Point Charlie," she said. "On point, sir."

Jane was on schedule, the other men had disappeared from his sight, but Mark's luck ran out. The hostiles halted about fifty meters in front of him.

He dropped back, well out of the beam of their headlights, dug in, and prayed they hadn't seen him. Even his breathing seemed magnified, echoing across the desert floor. Stealth movement when digging in yourself and a sixty-pound pack didn't go hand in hand.

He waited, shallowing his breath, watching . . . Noting no signs that they were aware of him, he stilled, his heart thumping against his ribs.

Long minutes later, Mark adjusted his lip mic and whispered, "Delta Three, you read me?"

"Loud and clear, bud," Sam responded. "Where are you?"

Seven minutes and two klicks short of where he should be. "Detained." Mark craned his neck and squinted to see. Weak moonlight was to his advantage, and he was grateful for it. Both Humvees had .50 cals mounted on them. Outgunned, his team needed all the help it could wrangle to get out of this alive.

"Two vehicles. Parked fifty meters off the tip of my nose." He didn't dare check his watch for the GPS coordinates. The Humvees faced each other on the road. One man inside each vehicle stood, and they talked back and forth between them. He couldn't make out their words, but they didn't seem anxious or excited.

"Window's closing, bud."

"Routine patrol. Eight hostiles. Dug in." Mark was out of position and late. The chopper would arrive in minutes. It couldn't linger; it'd be spotted for sure. "Is Six clear?"

He'd met Jane in advanced intelligence training four years earlier, and she'd become the little sister Mark never had, a spitfire with attitude and the smarts to back it up. He loved her, pure and simple, not that he'd ever told her. She loved him too as a brother, not that she'd ever told him. They'd just drifted into a makeshift family. Natural, considering her birth family ranked about as low on the lousy scale as his.

"Not yet," Sam said. "Everyone else is still on the move."

Worry streaked up Mark's backbone, stung the roof of his mouth. "Last report?"

Had she run into trouble at Three-Point Charlie? Mark unclenched his muscles, forcing them to relax. Fear had a distinct smell. It carried on the wind, and anyone who'd been in combat conditions longer than a week recognized the scent. Jane knew how to take care of herself. She was capable and competent.

Please, let her be all right.

No answer from Sam.

He was worried too. It'd been too long since her last report. She was overdue verifying clearance, and Sam didn't want to tell Mark. But his silence said it all.

Mark's worry grew more urgent. He diverted his focus to calm down. Not staying calm under any kind of pressure wasn't an option; it invited mistakes. Mistakes on covert missions infiltrating enemy territory assured death—your own if you were lucky. Your own and others if you weren't.

Mark inhaled the night air, blessedly cool

compared to the day's scorching hundred twenty degrees and relentless sun. He was supposed to meet Jane at Three-Point Charlie ten minutes ago, then they were to make the rendezvous point and join the others for their ride home.

He glared at the men in the Humvees. *For pity's sake, move it.*

The hostiles had become adept at spotting men in the night desert. Mark had become better at evading them. On his stomach, buried in sand, they'd have to be hunting him to see him. They still weren't. That was good news.

He and the team had managed to avoid detection the entire mission and execute their orders. While they all had been trained to kill, whenever possible they avoided it. Just slipped in and out under the radar, and often under the hostiles' noses.

"Six reporting in," Jane's voice sounded through his earpod. Her tone was shrill, rushed. "One, what's your ETA? Company could be coming."

Mark checked the Humvees. No movement yet. "Dug in. Need a diversion."

No response.

Mark tried another. "Four?" He waited, but Tim didn't respond. "Five?" Where was Joe?

"Off point," Joe said. "Heading to Three-Point Charlie."

"Two," Mark tried Nick, then Tim again, "Four, I need a diversion—now."

No answer.

Mark's skin crawled. "Three, where is everybody?"

"Communications are up, bud," Sam said. "Two and Four activated radio silence. I'm out of reach. Five's hauling it to back up Six. Diversion presently impossible."

If communications were up and a diversion was impossible because Nick and Tim weren't in a position to speak, then they were either hiding or dead. With the bean counters giving the team a forty percent success-and-survival rating on this mission—with the right equipment—and their being without it, they could be either.

"One, they're closing in on me." Jane's breathing sped up, turned tinny and crackled static. "Closing in—fast. Digging in. Not going to make it. Oh God, help me."

If Mark didn't move, Jane would die. If he did move, they both would die. Yet this was Jane. *Jane.* Mark had to try. Every muscle in his body tensed, preparing to move. He lifted an arm, cleared the sand.

"Stay put, One," Sam ordered, knowing Mark well. "You hear me, bud?"

Gunfire erupted in Mark's earpod.

"Aw, no. No." Joe's voice cracked.

Sam cursed.

And then came silence.

Mark's throat went tight, his chest tighter.

"Six?" He forced his voice to work. Tears streaked down his face. "Six?"

Jane didn't answer. *Please, please, please.*

"Think steel, bro," Joe said. "Nothing we can do to help her now."

No. Joe had to be wrong. "You sure?"

"I'd give everything I've got not to be."

Mark swallowed hard. *Oh, Jane.*

"Lousy shots." Joe grunted. "Gunfire pattern was random."

"You mean they were just shooting to be shooting?" Sam sounded as galled as Mark felt.

"No rhythm or rhyme, bro."

Sam cut loose a string of curses.

Mark interrupted. "Are they coming after her?" If targeted, they would definitely verify whether or not she was dead.

"No. The rats are departing the fix. I don't think they even saw her."

Jane. Killed by a random shot. It took everything in Mark to hold his position. But Joe was right. It was too late to move. Only God could help Jane now. Mark mourned. *Think steel. Think steel. Think—*

"It's not your fault, One." Joe's deep voice sounded cool and controlled.

It was his fault. His mother's death, for which his father and brother blamed Mark his whole life, hadn't been his fault. She died giving birth to him. But this . . . *this* was Mark's fault. He wasn't where he was supposed to be. Random or deliberate, Jane suffered the consequences. It was that simple.

Finally the Humvees sped off. One went in the direction it had been facing, away from the Green Zone. The other looped a U-turn on the road and fell in line behind the first one.

Mark shoved at the sand. "Moving out." He ran full speed toward Three-Point Charlie, adrenaline pumping through his veins, screams boiling deep in the back of his throat. Sweat dripped from his brow and stung his eyes. His lungs burned, his side stitched and settled into an ache. He buried the pain deep and kept running.

"Four." Tim reported in. "Quarter klick from rendezvous point."

"Two. Arrived at rendezvous," Nick said. "Chopper is two minutes out."

Tim and Nick were on point. A stream of half-formed phrases and stilted, shuddered words said all that needed saying about Jane. Mark checked the GPS on his watch. Another minute.

It was the longest minute of his life. But finally he arrived at Three-Point Charlie. Joe and Sam heard him approach and spun toward him, their weapons raised. When they recognized Mark, they lowered their barrels.

Jane lay between them at their feet.

Sam wept.

Regret burned deep in Joe's eyes. "I'm sorry, bro. I tried but I couldn't get here in time."

"My fault. I should have been here." Mark dropped to his knees beside her, huffing, struggling to even out his breathing. He pressed his fingertips to her throat, checking her carotid for a pulse.

"There isn't one." Joe swiped at his face with his sleeve.

Mark knew it, but he had to check anyway. Gunshot wounds peppered her entire chest, soaked it in blood. Jane had died before she hit the ground. Mark's heart split in two. He lifted her into his arms. "Let's go."

"You can't take her, bud." Sam touched his arm. "Despite what Joe said, they had to know she was here. They're suffering a bullet shortage. They're not going to burn thirty rounds just for kicks. They're just lousy shots. If they don't find her body, they'll come after—"

"I am not leaving her." Mark glared at Sam.

Calm as always, Joe stepped between them. "She's coming home. Move it—now."

They started running across the desert floor, made it to the rendezvous point, and met up with Tim and Nick. Within seconds, the thump of chopper blades split the dark silence, then the craft hovered just beyond them, kicking up sand that salted bare skin and even through camo stung like fire. A shadowy soldier stood in the side-door opening, scanning the area with his weapon.

The team jumped onboard, and the chopper lifted.

"Let me have her, sir. Maybe it's not too late." A medic took Jane to the open area behind them, and Mark started to follow.

A second medic stepped between them. "Take a seat, sir. We've got her now."

Mark sat, keeping an eye on the medics. They both worked hard to revive her, and they did it knowing as well as Mark that their efforts were a lost cause. Did they try for Jane or for her team?

Either way, it was too late. Jane had bled out in seconds. She hadn't had a chance.

Tears stung Mark's eyes. The back of his nose burned, and an ache cinched his heart in a tight fist. He'd never hear her laugh again. Never hear her introduce him to her friends as her favorite big brother. Never look into her eyes and see her looking back at him with affection.

I can't stand this. God, why did You let me love her and fail to protect her? I can't take—

"You okay, bro?"

Mark glanced from Jane to Joe. Of all the guys, Joe and Mark were closest. Sam, Nick, and Tim all sat staring at them. They too had red-rimmed eyes. "No, Joe, I'm not okay." Jane was gone. Dead. He'd killed her. "I'm not okay, and I am never doing this again."

Barely thirty, Tim swiped a hand at his temple, ruffling the premature gray salting his brown hair, and leaned forward. "Don't make rash decisions. We're all hurting right now. Give it time."

No amount of time would fix this. "I wasn't there and she's dead." His throat thickened. He swallowed hard. "When the chopper hits the ground, I'm putting in my papers."

The guys studied one another, and then Sam shoved off his helmet and hung it on his knee. "You realize that leaves our team two short. The brass isn't going to drop a guy in, bud."

Mark wouldn't be replaced. The team would be expected to function short. The Shadow Watchers were an elite, highly specialized unit, and its members' skills were cumulative. It'd take at least two years to get a new man qualified to take on their kind of missions and cleared by Intel to do them. And that's if they put the new recruit on the fast track, learning the systems they created and destroyed.

"Sorry. I'm done. I won't risk killing another one of you."

The chopper blades' steady *whap, whap, whap* filled the silence.

Tim stared beyond the group to Jane, paused a long time, and then swerved his gaze back to Mark. "It could have been any of us. Nick and I weren't in a position to help her either."

"I was her primary backup." Mark dangled his helmet between his spread knees, swinging it by its strap.

"We're a team, bud," Sam said. "We all watch each other's backs."

"I failed."

"Yeah, you did." Joe cut through the clutter. "Due to circumstances beyond your control, you failed. So did the rest of us. We all risk failing each other every time we go out. You know it. Jane knew it. We all know it. She's gone, and we have to live with it." Joe softened his voice. "She was like your little sister. I get that. But you don't get exclusive rights on the guilt, bro. There's plenty to go around."

Mark opened his mouth to object.

Joe lifted a hand to halt it. "We're sorry we lost her, Mark. If we could change it, we would. But we can't."

"Dang right." Sam shoved his fist into their inner circle.

One by one they all bumped knuckles, then Tim said, "You had to hunker down. That's how these missions go. Stuff comes up. We deal with it as best we can. Sometimes we get lucky. Sometimes we don't. Jane's regular team goes through the same thing."

"We'll have to tell them." Mark hated the thought of it, but he couldn't let them find out through official channels, especially Omega One. They were close.

"When we get to the Pentagon, we'll tell them together." Joe stared at the back of the guy manning the side door. The dread on his face was as fierce as Mark's.

31

Tim stared at Jane a long minute, then resolve slid down his lean face. "I've had enough of this too. We've done our share and then some."

Nick mumbled, agreeing and disagreeing. Sam and Nick went back and forth a bit, and then they all fell silent.

Mark had no idea what position Nick had taken, but Mark had his own problems to worry about. He slumped back, doing his best to absorb what had happened.

Deep inside the Green Zone, the chopper started its descent at headquarters. Tim glanced from man to man. "Gentlemen, it's time for us to go home and get ourselves lives."

Seated beside Joe, Sam jerked. "Whoa, bud." He had helmet head. His hair was smashed in places, ruffled and on end in others. "Two short, we no longer have a viable team. Mission selection will be the pits." He rounded on Nick. "Figured out your final call yet?"

Nick shrugged, then his body tensed. "I don't like the way things are shaping up. They'll never let us run two short, much less three. They'll disband the unit." He leaned back, crossed his outstretched legs at the ankles. Sand sprinkled off his boot. "The team's the only reason I've hung in here. If you're gone, it's gone, so I'm gone."

"That's it then." Sam rolled his shoulders. "We're just moving up the timetable on them before they move it up on us."

There'd been high-level talks of breaking up the unit. The work would continue to be essential, but the political climate didn't currently welcome it. So the unit would be formally disbanded and informally re-formed elsewhere by others under a different covert umbrella.

Joe crossed his arms over his chest, seemingly at peace with their decision. "None of us planned to make this a career. Duty called with 9/11. We answered. Now we're done."

One by one, they all nodded. But none returned Mark's gaze. All eyes were on the medics. Both pulled back from Jane's body, and one made the sign of the cross. "Sorry, sirs. Nothing more we could do."

Mark moved and squatted beside Jane. Her pasty skin was cool to the touch, but without her warm expressions, her vibrancy, she didn't much look like herself. That should have helped. She was at peace now. But it didn't.

I already miss you, Jane. You needed me and I wasn't there. I won't ask for forgiveness—I haven't earned it. But I'll regret failing you every day of my life. Tears washed down his face. *I'll never forget you.*

With a trembling hand, he closed her sightless eyes and then lifted the sheet over her beloved face.

2

Kill order Alpha 24733." The woman's voice didn't falter. "Execute it immediately, Lone Wolf." Male or female, when issuing a kill order, most hesitated or showed some emotion, but not Raven.

"Yes ma'am." Karl Masson stared through the darkness to the target: a young woman, midthirties, brown hair, thin face, seated on her patio. Definitely her, though he wasn't crazy about killing a woman sitting in her own backyard. It raised concerns about his own wife and her safety while he was away on business. But orders were orders.

He lifted his rifle, sighted in until her left temple was dead center in his scope's crosshairs. Then he pulled the trigger.

She jerked, then slumped.

It was done.

Why her husband hadn't just paid her alimony, Karl had no idea. Some men were tough to figure. They were crazy in love one minute, and when they weren't the next, they suddenly got greedy. The man was done with her, and she was disposable.

There was no need to double-check the body.

Fired at this distance on that trajectory, the bullet had penetrated her brain. She was as dead as dead gets.

Karl tucked the rifle under his long coat and held it close to his body. It was a rainy night, so anyone spotting him would assume he was wearing a raincoat. He made his way along the hedge to the sidewalk and then down the empty street. Lightning streaked a jagged path through the sky and thunder rolled, making far more noise than his weapon had. The woman he'd just killed had to be pretty miserable to be sitting out on her patio in the rain.

He cut through the yards to the next street over, paused on the sidewalk to look through a wide window, and watched a woman stir a pot at her stove. He loved glimpses of domestic life. Made him less homesick.

At the curb he got into his car, stashed his rifle, then drove away. After he cleared the subdivision, he phoned the boss.

"Raven."

He reported the mission code, the kill-order authorization code, and then added, "Complete."

"Excellent. Any problems?"

"No ma'am." If there were, he wouldn't tell her. Raven didn't react well to bad news. He'd clear it up and then report.

"Excellent. You've quickly become my go-to man."

That was his goal. "Whatever you need, ma'am."

"Thank you." Her tone lightened. "Raven out."

Not so much as a flicker of compassion for the dead woman. That was a common trait for NINA—Nihilists in Anarchy—members in general, but especially for high-level ones, and Raven was as high up as Karl knew existed. Words like *mercy* and *compassion* were not in her vocabulary.

NINA was an international organization, and its members were dedicated to making money. Governments, terrorists, private individuals— NINA did whatever to whomever for the right price. And Raven alone determined what that price should be. She sat on NINA's throne and chased money with such a single-minded focus, it wouldn't surprise Karl to discover her blood was tinted green.

He drove a couple of miles down the road, then lifted his phone from its console cubby and tapped *Angel* to speed dial home.

"Hello."

Karl softened his voice. "Hi, Angel."

"You're calling early tonight. Everything okay?"

"Everything's fine." He accelerated and headed north out of Atlanta. "I finished my business ahead of schedule, so I'm coming home. Tell the motorcycle gang they have to go."

"Oh, shoot. I was having such fun with them."
She laughed, lusty and deep. "You'll make it in for
Brent's game, then?"

The motorcycle gang was a longstanding joke
between them that never seemed to get old.
"Wouldn't miss it." Love swelled in Karl's chest.
Family was everything. "Did you see the doctor
today about that lump?"

"We'll talk about it when you get home. Did you
explore any of Atlanta while you were there?"

"Not this time. Too homesick to linger."

"Twenty years and I still have it, huh?"

"Baby, you'll always have it." He smiled, but it
was strained. "Did the doc give you bad news
today?"

"That can wait. I'd rather hear you tell me how
adorable I am."

"You're adorable. Now tell me what the doc
said. Otherwise, I'll be worried sick about you all
nine hundred and ninety-seven miles."

"It's fine, Karl."

"Don't lie to me, Angel. I can hear it in your
voice."

"Pull over and stop, and then I'll tell you."

Karl whipped onto the shoulder of the road. His
mouth went dust dry. He licked his lips and
stiffened, bracing for whatever she might say.
"Okay, I'm parked."

"It's cancer, honey." She sniffed. "Malignant,
I'm afraid."

"No."

"I'm so sorry."

"What are they going to do about it?" Cut it out? Chemo? Radiation? He didn't care what they did as long as she lived. She *had* to live.

"I go in for surgery tomorrow morning. My mother is here with the kids."

"Surgery? And you didn't call me?"

"I didn't want to tell you this over the phone."

She was holding back. As awful as this was, she wasn't telling him everything. "What else?"

No answer.

"Angel, tell me."

"It—it's probably too late."

"Don't say that. Don't even think it. They've made significant advances, you said so before you went. All you need is a fighting chance. That's all you need."

"Yes."

"That's right, yes. Just a chance. That's all it'll take."

Silence fell. Angel broke it. "You're going to have to accept this, you know. You can't protect the kids and me from everything. I know you want to and you try, but this is . . . different."

"Doctors don't know. Not until they're in surgery and can see for sure. There could be a chance."

"Karl, no." She sobbed. "It's my body and I know."

38

"What do you know? You have a lump. Just a little lump."

"It's too late, honey."

The finality in her tone chilled him, drained away his rebellion. And sitting in the rain on the side of a road too far away from their home in Syracuse, Karl stared through the spotted windshield into the darkness and sobbed with his wife.

"Do the kids know?" Angry lightning slashed the night sky, and thunder clashed, reverberating in his ears.

"I've told them."

"How are they taking it?"

"Brent's better than Shelley. She's dazed."

At seven, she would be. She'd been shielded from death and as much else as possible. How would he work with the kids? He kept his mind busy, avoiding the question he didn't want to ask because he didn't want it answered. He wasn't that brave or strong.

"Mom's offered to move in so she can help with the kids."

"Angel—" He cleared his throat. "I don't work without you."

"You have to, Karl. The kids will need you. And I need to know you'll all be okay."

That hit him like a sucker-punch to the gut. *So brave. So strong.* But she needed reassurance too. "How long?"

"Three months if things go well tomorrow."

He blew out a sharp breath. She'd be gone before Christmas. *If things go well.* "And if they don't?"

"Please don't make me answer that."

"Okay, baby." He cranked the engine. He needed to get home. Before she went into surgery, he had to see her. He pulled back onto the highway. They talked and soothed and sobbed some more, and finally, somewhere near Roanoke, Virginia, he accepted the truth.

There would be no chance.

His beloved Angel was dying.

3

The path of the righteous is like
the first gleam of dawn,
shining ever brighter till the full light of day.
—PROVERBS 4:18

Present Day

Get up on the balls of your feet." Lisa Harper walked across the Crossroads Crisis Center exercise studio to Kelly Walker. "In that position, he'll attack you from the left. You need to be able to pivot and get your arm up. Then when he does attack, you twist and bring your arm down. That will break his hold." She hiked her leg and feigned a kick to Kelly's right knee. "Pop his kneecap and he's down. You can get away."

Sweat-drenched, Lisa dabbed at her face with her sleeve and shoved strands of damp hair that had escaped her ponytail away from her eyes. She addressed the twenty-four students in her self-defense class: all women-in-jeopardy from people who wanted them hurt or dead. Her chest went tight. "Everybody got that?"

Some mumbled, Kelly nodded, and Melanie Ross, the Crossroads Crisis Center receptionist, groaned. "Not me," Mel said. "Not yet. Can you show us again?"

If it would help, Lisa would show them fifty more times. "Sure." Movement from the door caught her eye, and she glanced over just as Mark walked in with a man she didn't recognize. She ignored a little flutter in her heart and smiled. "Ah, good. Mark. Come help me demonstrate."

The man with him took a seat on the bleachers, and Mark walked out to where Lisa stood before the class. He nodded a greeting to the women. "What are we doing, Lisa?"

"Self-defense tactics. Level one."

For the next fifteen minutes, Lisa and Mark demonstrated escape-and-evade tactics. Winded and worn, they wrapped up. The class applauded.

Mel got to her feet. Dressed funky as usual in lime green and hunter orange, she rubbed her neck. Her hair stood in short, gelled chocolate spikes that hadn't moved an inch during the entire class. "It'll take me a year to learn all that, but if Mark's helping you teach it, I'll gladly invest the time."

The class laughed.

"You're adorable, Mark Taylor." Mel batted her eyes, flirting and clowning around at the same time.

"Back off, sister." Lisa smiled, but she meant it. Why she should feel so proprietorial toward Mark she had no idea. But she always had. She peeked over at him. He winked at her and something in his eyes softened. She loved his eyes. Dark gray, flecked with deep blue and hints of gold. Intoxicating. "Sorry, Mark."

"No problem." He grinned at Mel. "If you were ten years older, we might have something to talk about, sweet stuff. Until then, consider me your big brother."

Mel pouted. "Just what I need. Another over-protective relative."

Lisa laughed because she *was* overprotective. She tried to watch herself, but she didn't always succeed. "Here we go. One more time." She lifted her arms and signaled Mark. "Come on. I'm ready."

"Are you?" A spark lit in his eyes.

Her breath escaped. "Give it your best shot."

"Seriously?"

She nodded, motioned him to bring it on.

He sidestepped, then came in at an angle, moving fast. Lisa feinted left, moved right, and caught him on the ribs with a jab.

He shifted his weight and her fist slid off, doing no damage. Before he could counter, she ducked low and tight and went for his instep.

He rotated his foot and countered, catching her by the throat and holding her out of reach. "Never, ever let your opponent get his hands around your throat," he told the class. "If he's taller, he'll probably have a longer reach. Combine the two, and he'll just lift you off the ground, and you'll be done."

"Unless you do this." Lisa jumped up and wrapped her legs around his waist.

He automatically caught her.

Solid. With a square jaw and light stubble that so appealed. Always tender and gentle with her. That tenderness set Mark apart from other men because it took effort on his part. He was large, strong inside and out.

She blinked hard and held his steady gaze. How in the world had she missed the full-force magnetism in his eyes for so long? Magnetism and mirth. *Potent combination.* Unsure what to do, she pecked a kiss to his cheek. Not because she wanted to, but because she had to or she'd kiss his lips, and that would be a huge mistake.

You're acting like a love-starved crazy woman, Lisa Marie Harper.

Love starved, maybe. But not crazy. She just didn't expect being this close to him would affect her this way. It was a sensual assault. No part of her was unaware of any part of him. That's what's crazy.

He mumbled softly so only she could hear, his breath warm on her face, mirth still in his eyes. "You can do better. I know you can."

Assault. Assault. Assault. Only one way to counter this kind of attack. She wrinkled her nose at him. "Absolutely, I can. But will I? That's the question."

Before he could respond, she addressed the class. "I, um, don't recommend kissing your opponent under ordinary circumstances, but it might surprise him enough that he lets you go."

Mark dropped her right on her bottom. "Like that?"

Stunned, Lisa tilted her head back and saw the twinkle in his eye had spread to his mouth. "Yes." She clasped his extended hand, rose to her feet, and rubbed her smarting bottom. "Like that."

Kelly and Melanie started giggling. "Pretty entertaining watching you two." Mel swayed side to side.

"But this is also serious business." Mark glanced at Lisa. "The point is for you to use whatever tactics or weapons are at your disposal. The unexpected can be the one thing that saves your life."

"Mark is exactly right." Lisa put her hands on her hips. "You have to always think. Always assess. Never pause for a moment. The bottom line is to do whatever it takes to protect yourself."

"I'll still be here next January trying to learn this stuff." Mel dragged her hands through her hair. "If I'm lucky . . . and I'm not or I wouldn't be here."

"Be determined, Mel. The important thing is you will learn it. You all will." Lisa waved. "Same time next week. Remember to practice every day—and, oh, don't forget the party tonight at Three Gables. You're all coming, right?"

Kelly Walker tapped Lisa on the upper arm. "Everyone in the entire village will be there." The amusement drained from her face. "Well, except for he-who-shall-remain-nameless."

Dutch. "We can but hope." If there were a way to mess up the celebration of Lisa's getting her medical license, Dutch would do it. Since the day her mother had married him, he always messed up anything that made Lisa happy, and gauging from his attitude and past exploits, he always would.

Chatting, the women returned Mark's killer smile and filed out of the studio. The blond man, wearing tight jeans, a white shirt, and sunglasses, who'd come in with Mark, stood at the bleachers, then walked over to join Lisa and Mark.

"Lisa, this is Joe, a friend from my military days." Mark lifted a hand. "Joe, Lisa Harper, a doctor here at the center."

No last name. No information about him. Clearly he was one of Mark's spy friends. Not that Mark ever had admitted being a spy, but everyone close to him had just sort of figured it out on their own when Benjamin Brandt, who owned Crossroads, hired Mark as the chief of security for the center and his home, Three Gables.

Lisa extended a hand. "Hi, Joe. Welcome to Seagrove Village."

"Thanks." He shook her hand and smiled. "It's nice to finally meet you. Mark talks about you all the time."

Surprised, she glanced at Mark, but he looked away. No sense getting excited and making more of it than it was, probably just social chatter. "Mark is very kind. My mother and I owe him a lot." That would win her the grand prize for understatement of the year. Without Mark, she wouldn't know if her mother were alive or dead. Dutch made sure of that.

Joe was about Mark's age—thirty or maybe a little older—and in great shape, solid, maybe five-ten. He was a great-looking guy who had that ease of being comfortable in his own skin, but he lacked Mark's "total package" curb appeal. Even Joe's lazy charm didn't fare well in a direct comparison to Mark—tall, tanned, broad shoulders, and black hair that curled ever so slightly on his neck. Simply put, inside and out, Mark Taylor was gorgeous.

Gazing into Joe's eyes, she didn't feel that total command and complete confidence Mark exuded. How many times had they talked about everything and nothing and she'd longed for just a touch of his confidence? Just a touch of his certainty he could handle whatever came his way?

"One day, I hope to belong, Lisa. I want a family. A real home. A simple life where I'm wanted and not just needed."

When he'd finally confided those things to her in one of their many walks on the beach, it resonated with her down to her bones. She wanted exactly those things, yet when he said them, there had been a wistfulness in his tone, as if he knew his wishes were a pipe dream. She'd hated that. And she'd prayed about it every night since, that God would touch Mark's heart and show him it was okay to want and wish and that pipe dreams could come true.

"You owe me nothing." With a deftness she'd come to expect from Mark, he shifted the topic. "My old team is in town for a reunion."

"How fun."

"We've planned it a long time. A little golf and deep-sea fishing. You know, typical guy stuff."

Now why did Mark sound defensive? Maybe because this wasn't a reunion so much as a summons for reinforcements, which could mean that Mark expected trouble. Maybe trouble from her nut-case stepfather. Heaven knew she expected it, and Mark had become her mother's and her self-appointed guardian. Yet she could be making a mountain out of nothing but her own fears. Maybe this was just a reunion. Though the odds of their scheduling it at the same time as her party seemed a bit of a stretch. If Mark expected trouble, surely he would have said so. He'd always been straight talking and up-front.

Lisa, get a grip. His whole life doesn't revolve around you. Could be about Kelly Walker or something else entirely.

Right. Exactly. Grip gotten.

"How long have you been into self-defense courses?" Joe parked his sunglasses atop his head.

Very nice eyes. Not exactly green or blue but somewhere in between—and full of secrets. "Most of my life." She could have been more explicit. Since she was seven years, four months, and twenty-one days old—and she hadn't started classes young enough.

"Lisa's been teaching since she was seventeen," Mark added. "She got an early start."

"That explains it, then." Joe folded his arms across his chest. "Your skills are impressive. Anytime you need a sparring partner, I'm available." He winked.

"Mark takes it easy on me."

"Even so, you've got good technique." He stuck a stick of chewing gum into his mouth. "Sorry. Trying to quit smoking."

"Chew away." She encouraged him. "My mother insisted I needed the skills and that I practice them. I should be great, so I've still got a ways to go." She attempted a smile but her heart wasn't in it. "Unfortunately, the women taking my classes need excellent skills—now."

"Sorry to hear that." He stuffed the gum wrapper into the back pocket of his jeans.

"We work in a crisis center. That makes these situations common." Lisa lightened her tone. "Joe, why don't you—the whole team—come to my party tonight?"

Joe slid Mark an inquisitive glance, and he responded with a nod she would have missed had she not been watching for it. "That would be great. Thank you, Lisa."

"Wonderful." Excitement bubbled in her and overflowed. She tried to tamp it, but she hadn't had a party since her father died, and she couldn't help herself.

Mark turned to Joe. "I need a minute."

"You got it, bro. I'll check in with the guys." Joe stepped away.

"He seems nice."

Mark frowned. "He's a woman magnet."

She bit back a smile. "I see that potential." When Mark's frown deepened, she added, "Of course, I'm immune. But other women would drop at his feet."

"Why are you immune?"

She shrugged. "He just doesn't do it for me. We could be friends, but it'd never go beyond that."

"Good." Mark looked like he hadn't meant to say that aloud. "Stepping over the broken hearts can be a pain, but we're close."

"You're not jealous of him?" No way. Joe didn't have a thing on Mark.

"No. But try playing a game of volleyball at the beach or even shooting hoops. He's distracted by women hanging all over him."

Lisa worked hard not to laugh. Mark was totally sincere, and Joe probably loved the attention. "That would be a pain."

"Yeah, but what can you do? I trust him." Mark cleared his throat. "I need to tell you something."

Lisa inwardly groaned. *Not bad news. Please. Not today.* She summoned her courage and made herself ask, "What?"

Mark stuffed a hand in his pocket. "Don't call your mom's cell."

Tension flooded her. "What's happened?"

"Dutch found the phone and crushed it with a sledgehammer. You can bet he tagged the number first and is tracking calls to it."

Lisa stiffened, barely resisted the urge to grab Mark's sleeve. "He didn't hurt her—"

"No, she's fine. He hasn't gotten that stupid yet."

They both knew it was just a matter of time. The closer Lisa had gotten to her license, the tighter

Dutch pulled the reins on her mother. Now he was doing any and everything he could to avoid forfeiting control of her. But unless God was napping, Dutch's days of riding ramrod over them both would soon be over. As of today, Lisa had her license, and her first full-time paycheck was a week away. The minute it hit her hot little hand, she would march up to her childhood home—a place where she had not been welcome since she was sixteen—get her mother, and move them into the beach cottage Lisa was going to rent from Kelly Walker.

Then Dutch Hauk's reign of terror would finally be over.

"Kelly would let you guys move in early." Mark glanced toward Joe, who paced a path near the bleachers while talking on his phone.

"She's offered, but Mom won't do it. She agreed to stay with Dutch until I was self-sufficient."

"It's a week. Not a month. Why did she do that?"

Sometimes a week seemed a lot longer than a month. "Because he asked." She tilted her head. "When they met, she was in a bad place. Her life was like it had been before she married my father—just awful. Dutch was there when she needed him, so when he asked her to stay until I was self-sufficient, she agreed."

"Okay, now you're self-sufficient. A week is splitting hairs."

"To Dutch, it's a big deal," Lisa surmised. "To her, it's a bigger deal. She lives by the letter of God's law. She made vows, Mark. It's taken a long time to get her to even consider leaving Dutch. Everyone who manages to steal a few words with her tries."

"What does she say?"

"That I'm overprotective."

"You are. Don't glare at me. Mel says the same thing all the time. Considering your mom's circumstance, I don't see being overprotective as a bad thing."

"Mom doesn't either. But about Dutch, the best I've managed is for us to agree to disagree." Lisa lifted her hand. "Divorce is a very big deal to a woman of faith."

"Of course it is." Mark paused and then tried again. "An advance on your pay—*something*— should satisfy this self-sufficient agreement. I'd feel a lot better if she was out of there now."

"Believe me, I've suggested everything. The rest of the world might hedge or fall apart, but Annie Harper lives by her word."

"But she did agree to come live at the beach with you?"

"Finally. Just to live there. She hasn't agreed that he'll be out of her life."

Mark slumped. "She won't divorce him?"

"Never. You have to understand . . . after my dad died, my mom learned their money had been swindled away, there was no insurance, and everything was mortgaged to the hilt. She had a heart attack over that. Afterward, she had a weak heart and a daughter to house and feed, and she was terrified of being hungry again. Of me being hungry. Dutch rode into her life like an adoring white knight."

"And after they married, he turned into a nightmare."

"Yes." Lisa held off a sigh. "But she'll stay married to the nightmare because she gave her word—no, wait." Lisa stopped cold. "It's not Dutch; it's God she's honoring." Lisa slapped at her spandex-clad thigh. "How did I miss that? It's so obvious."

"Don't look at me. I don't think God would want a woman to stay with an abusive man."

"Me either, but what we think doesn't matter. The Bible says divorce is outside of God's will, and she's trying to be obedient."

"Obedience doesn't require taking abuse."

"No, it doesn't—in our view." Guilt streaked through Lisa. She'd failed to protect her mother, failed to make her understand that difference earlier. "I thought she stayed to keep her word to him, but I was wrong. I can't believe I was so blind."

"You see now. That's what matters, and she's finally agreed to leave him. That's a good start."

Lisa nodded.

"You were wrong about something else too."
Mark's voice softened. "You said once that
principles, honor, and integrity are all your mom
has left, but it's not." He lifted his gaze from the
floor. "She has you."

Lisa clenched her fist at her side. "Yes, and
Dutch used me against her."

Mark's mouth flattened even more, and a
muscle in his clenched jaw ticked. "Did she
discuss her situation with Ben?"

"No. I mentioned it, but she wasn't interested.
It's even more complicated. She was recovering
from the heart attack, still mourning and worried
sick about everything, and Dutch came in and was
so kind to her. He seemed to know just what she
needed. He told her not to worry about losing the
house. He'd take care of it. She was so relieved
she cried. He asked her to marry him, and she said
yes." Lisa recalled it all so vividly. "I think she'd
have done anything to keep that house, Mark,
including marrying a man she barely knew."

"Why? It's just a house."

"Not to her. It was our home, and she and my
father were happy there. She's had a lot of
unhappiness in her life. She'd lost my dad, and I
think she was afraid if she lost the house, she
would lose her memories of our life with him too.
There'd be nothing to prove that that time had
been real."

"Except you."

"I'm different." Lisa shrugged. "It's hard to explain, but I understand why she did what she did and why she feels as she does. But I also agree with you. Dutch is a dangerous man."

"The incident he pulled at your apartment last year proves it."

It did. He'd nearly scared Lisa out of her skin, and when she'd asked, the judge hadn't hesitated to sign the restraining order against him. Lisa shuddered. Nora, Ben's Scots housekeeper, had agreed to Ben and Lisa's request and moved into the Towers apartment with Lisa back when she was sixteen so she wouldn't have to live alone, and she'd just stayed. Thank goodness she hadn't been home when Dutch showed up. Nora might be up in years and nearly bat-blind, but she acted as if she were neither and went toe-to-toe with anyone whenever the need arose, and sometimes when it didn't. Against Dutch, Nora would've lost. A chill rippled through Lisa. By the grace of God, Nora had been detained at her ophthalmologist's office that day.

Mark shoved a hand in his pocket. "I'm worried Annie doesn't really get how dangerous Dutch is."

"Oh no, she gets it." Her mother had seen the truth when Lisa was sixteen. That's why she put Lisa in Ben's wife's care. Annie Harper Hauk had loved her daughter enough to forfeit her to keep her safe and out of Dutch's clutches. "She does what she can, then puts it on the altar."

"In God's hands, eh?"

Lisa nodded. "But between you and me, I still think she sleeps with one eye open. At least, I pray every day she does for her own safety."

"That's a tough way to live."

"Yes, it is." Lisa tugged at a thread on her sleeve. It was tough for both of them. "But what is just is, right?"

"Right." Mark gave Lisa's shoulder a gentle squeeze. "I took her a new phone right before coming here."

Lisa's nerves crackled and hissed. "Dutch didn't see you?"

"Of course not." Mark smiled. "She's going to call you at first chance about the party tonight."

"She's coming?" Lisa clasped her throat, unable to hide her shock. Dutch had forbidden her mother to have any contact with Lisa. There's no way he'd allow her to come to the party.

"You didn't invite her?" Mark's surprise mirrored Lisa's.

"No, I didn't." She couldn't hold his gaze. "It wasn't that I didn't want to—I'd love for her to be there."

He appeared confused for a second, and then understanding dawned on his expression. "Dutch wouldn't permit it, Annie wouldn't go against him, and then she'd feel guilty for letting you down."

Lisa nodded, fighting a lump in her throat. She

hadn't wanted to put her mother in the position of having to refuse. Heaven knew Annie had enough troubles without Lisa deliberately adding to them.

"I hope she can come," Mark said.

"It's okay either way. I've learned to expect nothing." Lisa said what she'd trained herself to say and feel, knowing the pain that came with it shone in her eyes.

"Yeah, me too." He looked away. "Fewer disappointments that way."

Disappointments she could handle. She had handled them by the bucketfuls most of her life. This went deeper. "It's essential to survival without going nuts about it inside."

"Exactly."

Their conversation would have sounded strange to anyone else, but they understood in ways she wished neither of them did.

"Mark?" Joe walked up, still chewing, his shoes silent on the wooden floor. "Sorry to interrupt, but the guys are about to lose the reservation, waiting for their guest of honor to arrive." He looked at Lisa. "It's Mark's birthday. He gets to buy us lunch."

"Some honor, eh?" Mark grunted.

He was happy about it. His mother's death in childbirth had always cast gloom over any birthday celebration. At least, according to Lisa's mom—apparently the two of them talked often. Spending your birthday alone didn't make for much of a celebration.

"Oh, so today is your birthday, is it?"

"Yeah." He gave her a sheepish grin. "Just another day, only these characters use it to soak me for lunch."

"Nice friends." His birthday was circled in red on her calendar, and she had a reminder countdown set on her computer for three days in advance. Of course, he didn't know any of that. Just as he didn't know he had become increasingly important to her while helping her stay in contact with her mother.

When Dutch had pulled "the incident" in the hallway outside her apartment last year, he threatened to hurt her mother unless Lisa did what he wanted. Mark put a stop to it. He'd gotten there before the police, and Dutch discovered quickly he wanted no part of Mark Taylor. Afterward, Mark helped her file the police report with Detective Jeff Meyers, calm down an outraged Nora who had arrived home, and then helped Lisa get the restraining order.

Dutch went nuts. But he hadn't hurt her mother, and he hadn't dared to cross the line with Lisa after that. He went right up to it, annoying her, but so far he hadn't crossed it. *So far.*

"Well, you guys have a great time." Tonight was a joint celebration. His part of the party was a surprise, and she couldn't wait to see his face when he realized it. According to her mother, Mark never had a birthday party or a cake. That was about to change—and as long as Lisa drew breath, from here on out, he'd have at least a cake every birthday. Mark was special. He needed to know it, and even more, he needed to feel it.

"Thanks." Mark watched her gathering her things. "Where are you running off to?"

She wiggled her fingers at him. "Manicure—and I'm cutting it close."

"Manicure?"

"I'm splurging. My mama says"—she put a heavy southern twang in her voice—"a lady never attends a social gatherin' without a proper manicure." She blew on her nails. "Mine shall be Passionate Pink. Fingers and toes."

Joe smiled. Mark nodded. "Okay, then. I'll see you and your fingers and toes later at the party."

"No, here at the center first."

"Right. Tradition. At the center."

She gave him a wide smile and batted her lashes. "I'll be the dazzling lady in blue."

"With Passionate Pink nails."

"Fingers and toes."

"Perfectly manicured, of course."

"You betcha!" She giggled.

The humor faded from Mark's eyes, and his expression sobered. "You watch your back today. Dutch knows you can take care of Annie now, and he'll do anything to keep you away from her. You're at higher risk now than ever."

He was worried. Maybe he did care more for her

than in the general, woman-in-trouble kind of way. Her mom said he did, but Lisa hadn't seen signs of it until maybe this moment.

She bit her lower lip. "I don't understand the man, but I believe in his own sick and twisted way, he loves her."

"He thinks he owns her. And no one takes what belongs to Dutch Hauk. Understand, Lisa. The restraining order never stopped him from pushing at you or her, and it won't now. If anything, it'll be less effective."

Really worried. Her heart beat harder, faster. "It hasn't, it won't, and it will be less effective. He's desperate now. I understand."

"Wait." Joe, who had stood silent, stepped in. "This guy's under a restraining order and he's still bothering you?"

"No words on a piece of paper change what's written in a man's heart, Joe, or the evil he's put in his mind." A shiver snaked through her veins, heated her blood. "The truth is, Dutch hates me, but now that I have my license, he's on a deadline."

"A deadline?"

She nodded at Joe. "Dutch hates anything he can't control, and he has to win."

"Win . . . *how?*"

"By getting me out of commission before I can get my mom out of his clutches." Shame heated her face. "Embarrassing to admit, but he'll do

60

anything to avoid losing. If that means killing me, he'll kill me."

Joe blinked hard, stopped midchew, and looked at Mark. Understanding passed between the men.

Lisa expelled a staggered sigh. This battle was inevitable and had been since she was sixteen. Now it must be fought. And while it terrified her, she was every bit as determined that Dutch lose as he was to win.

Help me, Lord. I can't save Mom or myself on my own. Please, help me.

4

There's been a slight change of plans." Dutch cut across the thick green lawn, holding the phone to his ear. He stared out across the sun-spangled water in the cove. The tang of salt stung his nostrils, and he twitched his nose. "You'll have to take down Annie earlier than planned."

"Why? We're all set up to go at Three Gables and then make the grab at—"

"Trust me, Karl. You don't want to hit anything at Three Gables." What was wrong with him? Karl Masson knew Benjamin Brandt's estate was heavily guarded by Mark Taylor and his security staff, that Taylor's old military buddies were in town, and that he was Annie and Lisa's self-appointed protector.

Dutch swatted at a bee buzzing the jasmine.

Killing that man would be pure pleasure. Of course, first Taylor had to fail to protect Dutch's women, and then he could die. *Utter humiliation, then death. Nothing less would be enough.*

The man was long overdue at learning to keep his nose out of other people's business. Especially Dutch Hauk's. But Taylor would get the message soon enough.

"Why not?" A hard edge grated Karl's voice. "You know how the boss feels about changing plans on an active mission."

"Yeah, I do." Overhead a gull screeched and then dove for a fish. It missed. The water splashed and then settled into a ripple, and the bird flew on. "But the place is a fortress. Brandt upgraded security when the boss was after Kelly Walker. You remember her, don't you?"

Dutch knew Karl wouldn't forget the woman who had seen him conspiring with Gregory Chessman and his whacked-out sidekick, Paul Johnson, on Chessman's terrace. After botching NINA's operation smuggling bioterrorists into the country, she had NINA freaking out. That landed Johnson and Chessman in jail and spurred a serious crackdown on NINA's local operations. Kelly Walker also gave the FBI a sworn statement that slapped an artist's rendition of Karl Masson in the number-three slot on its Most Wanted list.

NINA typically functioned in stealth mode, quiet and behind the scenes, under Homeland

Security's nose but also under its radar. Exposure was the last thing NINA wanted.

"Don't be flip," Masson said. "Of course I remember Kelly Walker. She's the reason I personally took on this job."

Interesting. NINA's notorious cleaner, who removed obstacles and made worries disappear, was going rogue to take out Walker himself. NINA didn't like rogue actions, but in Walker's case, it would make an exception.

In Karl's position, Dutch would do the same thing. Without Walker's testimony, the feds had no case. If the heat hadn't been on full force, NINA probably would have already eliminated her. But the heat was scorching hot, and Walker and the man in her life, Benjamin Brandt, had loads of money and Mark Taylor, and that gave them the ability to keep the heat on for a long time to come.

"Yeah, well don't let your personal business interfere with your job. I'm paying good money for priority handling on this bit of business."

"Not a problem." The sounds of Karl swallowing came through the phone. "I'll avoid the fortress."

Dutch glanced back toward the house to make sure Annie hadn't come outside. Most afternoons, she liked to read in the hammock. A pang of worry rippled through him. Karl would knock her around a little, but she'd be fine in a week or two. And she'd know the consequences of not doing as she was told. It was her fault. He couldn't have her ignoring his orders. "Where are you going to do it, then?"

"It's better that you don't know."

"But—"

"Leave my job to me. You have your alibi in place?"

Dutch glanced from the empty hammock back to the house. *No Annie.* Probably still packing his clothes. "I'm leaving for Georgia in a few minutes." He checked his watch. Nearly three o'clock. "Checking on my stores up there."

Dutch owned a chain of thirty-seven convenience stores that ran from Georgia across the south and down to the Texas-Mexico border. None of them made much money, but that was insignificant. His income stream was staggeringly high regardless of the economy *and* mostly tax free. He smiled. Recession, depression, and inflation proof.

"Sounds good. Just forget everything and go to Georgia. The bottom line is, nothing can interfere with the shipment," Karl said. "Anything goes wrong here, it goes wrong all the way down the line."

"I know." Dutch toed a lump of grass. "The boss wouldn't like it."

Karl's cackle held no humor. "You're talking a loss of roughly ten million. Uh, no. The boss wouldn't like it."

Heads would roll, including his own. "Do what you have to do, but try not to kill Annie." Dutch hated the weakness in his voice. Stupid. Loving a woman who can't stand the sight of him. "I mean, if you have to, then do it, but if you don't, then let her live."

"I understand."

"Do you?" Impossible. Dutch didn't understand his own conflicting thoughts about Annie.

"Of course. It's simple really. You hate your stepdaughter more than you love your wife."

The line went dead, and Dutch slipped his phone in his pocket. Karl was wrong. He did love Annie.

Annie. Dutch would never forget the night Charles Harper had brought him into his home for dinner. Even then Lisa had been a brat, whining about not wanting to dress for dinner for a man she didn't know. Annie had defended him.

"He is our guest, Lisa Marie, and you will treat him with respect."

Dutch had known right then Annie was different. She'd given him a chance. No woman in his life had defended or respected him. He'd made up his mind on the spot not to just take Harper's money, but to take his life and claim it for his own—his money, his life, his wife, and his respect.

Unfortunately, Lisa Marie came with Annie. And after the way Annie had grieved for Charles, killing the brat was out. Annie would never get over it. So Dutch had settled for getting the kid out of the way and then keeping them apart before Lisa could remember anything. If she ever did remember, he would know it and could handle her before NINA did and held him responsible.

All that extra trouble just for Annie. Not that she knew the pains he'd suffered for her. But he had loved her as much as he could. It was hard for a man who'd been told from birth he was evil and had it beaten into him until he believed it. Annie was good to him, but she'd never loved him. She honored their vows because she made them.

And because if she didn't, Dutch would come down on her and Lisa like a hammer.

The key to respect was money. That's why he'd hooked up with NINA. All he had to do was let them run people—all kinds of people—through his stores and launder a little money now and then. It cost him nothing and he'd made a fortune, enough to buy Annie's respect if not her love. Respect meant more. It lasted longer. She had respected him out of necessity and then out of fear. Not for herself, for the brat. But that would change. Soon.

Lisa Marie Harper would learn that she had picked the wrong man to mess with—and she'd have an entire lifetime to regret it.

Killing her was too easy. He wanted her alive . . . And suffering.

5

Mark set out snacks for the guys, then dusted his hands. "Ready?" He lifted the remote while the guys positioned themselves in his media room. "Hit the lights, Joe."

The lights dimmed, and the first slide filled the wall screen. In it, a smiling couple stood near a bench nestled between moss-laden oaks. In the background, a three-story gray stone house rose like a stately tower. Somehow it retained the warm appeal of a home and not a museum. "This is Three Gables. The couple is Benjamin Brandt and Kelly Walker."

"I thought he'd be older. He's our age?" Tim asked from his seat on the sofa, looking stylish enough to have stepped off the pages of *GQ*. Not a strand of brown hair out of place, not a crease daring to wrinkle his brown slacks.

"Early thirties. Same as most of us. You kind of remind me of him, Tim," Mark said.

"We don't favor each other."

"You're the only two guys I know who can look sophisticated in fatigues."

"Oh, he's one of us?" Tim's interest piqued.

"No, you both just have that same sense about you."

"What sense?"

"Perfect, rich, and probably useless," Joe cut in.

Mark lifted a hand. "I didn't say that."

"Just needling you, bro. You and Brandt have it all together. Now that you've gotten your ego stroked, can we press on?" Joe never minced words. He ditched his chewing gum and sat at a bistro table. "I have a feeling I picked a lousy time to quit smoking."

"No such thing. Any time's a good time for that." Sam snagged a chair opposite Joe, spun it around, then straddled it. An Alabama boy, Sam looked a lot like Larry the Cable Guy with his goatee and trucker hat. Yet there was a lot more to him that he didn't let many people see. He was extremely smart, if not brilliant, and he had uncanny senses. The man never quit.

"Just don't get any ideas about my pipe," Tim warned Sam.

"Keep it outside, bud. Smoke wrecks my sniffer." He tapped his nose, and the ragged edges of his T-shirt sleeves clung to his arm. He tugged his cap down low on his forehead, shadowing his eyes. "Shoot, Mark."

"Give me a napkin," Nick told Tim while dragging a carrot through the ranch dressing.

Tim passed it over and Nick took it. Their lanky friend was a loner. Even with the team, he had his chair slightly apart from the others. Nick prized privacy, respecting it in others and demanding it for himself. Lightening up a little could benefit him. But there was nothing light about Nick. His hair and eyes were as dark as his typical thoughts.

Anyone who didn't know the team would consider them all relaxed, maybe even bored, but Mark knew them well. They were all highly trained, diversely skilled and experienced, mentally alert, and totally engaged.

Sam made a get-on-with-it circle with his hand. "Three Gables, the knockout Kelly Walker, and Tim-like Benjamin Brandt. Got it. Go."

Mark bit back a smile. "As some of you know, Ben owns Crossroads Crisis Center. Kelly came here after a run-in with Gregory Chessman and NINA."

"Our NINA?" Sam gulped down a large swallow of drink.

"The Nihilists in Anarchy NINA," Mark said. NINA's involvement in all kinds of illegal behavior made it familiar to everyone in the intelligence community. Prevailing thought was that NINA intended to destroy the country from the inside out using a combination of criminal activities to fund its ideology and political manipulations. "Our archenemy. *That* NINA."

"That's what I meant." Sam grunted. "Wait, I remember these two." He waved a finger at the people on the slide. "NINA meant to hit Walker but killed Brandt's wife instead, right?"

Mark felt the familiar stab of Ben's grief. "Just over three years ago."

"What was the wife's name again?"

"Susan." Tim scratched his ear. "But it wasn't NINA. Edward Johnson and his partner, Harry, made that hit."

"Yeah." Sam exaggerated a nod. "I remember now. There was confusion on it because Gregory Chessman hired Johnson, and Chessman was a high-level NINA operative."

"That's right. He's in jail now." Mark looked at Sam. "Edward and Harry killed Susan and her son, Christopher." Collateral damage. Losing them had devastated Ben, and when he discovered his family had been assassinated by mistake, it nearly killed him.

"Despicable, hitting a kid." Tim sniffed his disgust.

"Aren't both of the Johnson men dead now?" Joe spoke up.

"Maybe." Sam shrugged. "They were reported dead."

"False report?" Tim asked Mark.

"Not totally. One of them is dead. Edward." Mark motioned with two pointed fingers to his own eyes, signaling he had seen the body firsthand.

The whole situation had been kept pretty hush-hush to avoid jeopardizing the case, but Mark wasn't surprised the team knew as much about it as they did. Once you were inducted into the intelligence world, you might leave it, but you were never really out of it. The reality of black ops and covert operations just didn't work that way. You know too much, and too many continue to come after you to find out just how much you know. "The other Johnson, Paul, is in jail with Chessman."

"Gregory Chessman. Now there's a piece of work." Tim cleared his throat. "I challenge anyone to name an illegal activity he wasn't involved in."

"There isn't one." Joe dragged a chip through the bowl of salsa. "Jerk's corrupt to the core. He was even working with the mayor's wife."

Darla Green. Mark nodded. "She and Paul Johnson killed the mayor. Chessman thought his secret partner was the mayor, but it was his wife. Now she's in jail too."

"For how long?" Nick asked. "She probably got a slap on the wrist. Don't look at me like that, Tim. She had money, connections, and a local judge. Of course she got a slap on the wrist."

"Unfortunately, Nick's right." Mark didn't like it any better than the rest of them. "She got five years. Normally a third would be cut off, but I hear there's something in the works to get her down to time served."

"Sickening."

"Predictable, Tim." Sam downed a swig from his glass and hiked his chin to the screen. "Those two seem pretty chummy."

Ben and Kelly had been through a lot together. Trial by fire can do that. "They are close." Mark moved to block the glare streaking across their faces and studied the slide. "One day they'll end up married, but it's going to take some time to work through their issues."

"I can see where it would." Nick stroked his thin brown mustache. "She looks just like his wife."

"Kelly and Susan do resemble each other, but they're different. The more you know of them, the less alike they seem."

"How?" Sam asked Mark.

"Susan was softer, gentler, and more reserved. Kelly's stronger, blunt, and takes big chances. I think a lot of them both." Mark advanced the slide.

A grainy image of Annie appeared on the screen. In her midfifties, she had a head full of gray curls. Her weariness etched lines into her face that dragged at the corners of her mouth. "This is Lisa's mom, Annie Harper Hauk." His voice went husky. "She's a good woman in a bad situation."

Sam slid Mark a sidelong glance. "Well, why haven't you gotten her out of it, bud?"

"Tried. She refused. Still trying." It was complicated, and he didn't want the guys to bog down on this, but they needed to understand the complexities to grasp the threat. "Lisa's dad was a doctor, and they were supposedly well off. Good Christian family. Everyday average Americans. But when Lisa was seven, she heard about this orphanage in Haiti that needed a roof. Charles went down to tend to the kids and help out. In short, he fell off the roof and broke his neck."

"He died?"

Mark nodded at Tim. "The second he hit the ground, gone."

Sam looped his arms on the back of his chair. "So if they were wealthy, what's the deal? Why's Annie in a bad situation?"

Mark rubbed the back of his neck. "They really weren't wealthy—at least not at the end. Charles lost everything in a Ponzi scheme. He borrowed against his life insurance policies to stay afloat."

"He doesn't sound like the kind to be suckered in. What happened?" Nick asked. "Drugs? Gambling? Women?"

Leave it to Nick to go down the dark road. "Nothing like that. He just fell for a con with a slick tongue and no conscience." Mark grabbed a handful of Sam's pretzels. "He left Annie and Lisa penniless and crippled by debt."

"Oh man." Sam groaned and stared at the ceiling. "Annie got jammed into marrying the jerk."

"In a way. She's got a weak heart. Working was out. All she had left was the house, and it was about to go into foreclosure. Dutch had plenty of money but no respectability. Seagrove Village is a close community. Dutch wanted land for his convenience stores. He's got over thirty of them. No respect, no land sales for stores. Annie was respected in the village, so he courted her, they married, he took care of her and Lisa. And Annie got him the respect in the community he wanted."

Nick took a long swallow of his soda. "So what's bad in that situation?"

"He turned mean. She's a virtual prisoner." Mark chewed the pretzel.

"Wait a minute." Joe grabbed a bottle of juice from the fridge. "You said Lisa has been living at the Towers since she was sixteen. Why?"

"Something happened. I'm not sure what— neither Lisa nor Annie will say. But it was bad enough that Annie got Ben's wife, Susan, to intercede. That's when Lisa moved into the Towers. Ben owns it too."

"And Dutch just let Lisa go?" Tim stretched out his long legs.

"He tried to stop her," Mark said. "But Annie had already signed over custody of Lisa to Susan and refused to revoke it. Dutch and Susan got into it, and she told him to take them to court. The Brandts are seriously loaded. Dutch couldn't outspend them, and Susan vowed she'd use every dime she had to keep him away from Lisa."

"Hmm." Tim slid an arm over the back of the sofa. "I'm surprised he didn't go after Susan."

"It wouldn't have done him any good. Annie named Susan *and* successively the entire board of directors of Crossroads Crisis Center as Lisa's legal guardians. He'd have to have gone after them all and then their replacements for the rest of his life. Well, until Lisa was of legal age, anyway."

"The center we were in today?" Joe dragged a hand through his short blond hair. "It's not that old."

"The building isn't. They broke ground for it three years ago. But the organization's been around for a lot of years."

"What's the scope of their work at the center?"

Mark turned to face Tim. "They deal with the usual abuse, homeless, interventions—pretty much any kind of crisis that comes into someone's life. They've also helped people disappear, handled stalkers, cybercrime, and the incident last year intercepting NINA terrorists being brought into the country to launch attacks."

"A little different from your typical crisis center." Tim rubbed his chin.

"They do what needs doing to help people in trouble. The center was Susan's dream," Mark said.

"You didn't mention it"—Joe stood and stretched—"but they've got a decent medical facility too."

Mark nodded. "The hospital here is good but small. It needs the help, especially during tourist season."

"Good to know," Tim said. "So Dutch was hamstrung and backed off Lisa—until now?"

"He pulled a few legal stunts but got nowhere. Everyone in the village knew he was up to no good with Lisa and he had no legal standing."

"So his hands were tied but, man, this sounds bad for Lisa." Empathy deepened Nick's tone. "She's grown up pretty much alone."

"Like you, eh, Mark?"

"Not really, Sam." Mark was grateful for it. "She's had Susan and Ben and their housekeeper, Nora; Peggy Crane, the center's director; and its chief psychologist, Dr. Harvey Talbot. They've been a strong surrogate family to Lisa, so she's had people who care about her in her life."

"You've had us, bud. What are we, chopped liver?"

"We came later, Sam," Tim said.

"Why the Towers?" Joe planted his elbow on the table and pressed his chin into his hand. "Why didn't Lisa live with Susan and Ben at Three Gables?"

"She refused," Mark said. "Dutch was capable of anything, and if he did something awful, she didn't want it to be anywhere near them."

Nick frowned. "There'd be no one left to help her."

Mark nodded. "Later on they had Christopher too, and Lisa worried about him getting caught in any cross fire."

"But she was a kid," Tim said. "What kind of judge agreed to her living on her own?"

"She didn't live on her own." Mark hadn't mentioned that? "Nora moved in with her at the Towers."

Mark advanced the slide to a photo of Peggy Crane. Round and affable, she smiled directly into the camera, still wearing her hair in a bob. "Don't be fooled by this one's soft looks. Peggy has a will of steel and a backbone to match. She'll take on anyone short of God. Him, she serves with her whole heart."

"Doesn't everyone at the center?" Joe asked. "I saw the chapel. It's well used."

"It is. Everyone working there is a believer."

"So Peggy Crane is a vintage southern woman," Nick said. "I've always liked southern women."

Good news. Nick actually liked something. "Then you'll love Peggy. But be warned. Do not engage in evasive tactics, and do not cross her. She'll get meaner than a junkyard dog." Mark swiveled around. "Sam, scrub your language."

"Sam, not curse?" Nick snorted. "You've got to be kidding."

"Not even a little." Peggy would take serious offense and, as Nora puts it, blister his ears.

Joe parked his arms on his knees. "You could end up with jalapeño pepper juice in your iced tea."

"No way." Sam cast a doubtful look at Mark.

He didn't deny it.

"Seriously?" Nick asked.

Joe shrugged. "She warned me first, but I slipped."

"I like this woman." Nick almost smiled. Not quite, but closer than Mark had ever seen.

Tim laughed. "Bet you haven't slipped since."

"My mother isn't from the south," Joe said. "But on some things, moms are universal. When they set a rule, it's set. Break it and you suffer the consequences."

"But she's not your mother and you're not a kid."

"No, I'm not." Joe sent Nick a level look. "Which means I should've had an adult's self-discipline and respect." He rocked back and parked an elbow on the edge of his chair's back. "If I'd been a kid, I'd have gotten a few drops, not a full ounce."

Tim slapped his thigh. "I like this woman too."

"I hate jalapeño peppers." Sam groaned like the dying. "Party manners are officially on."

Nick harrumphed. "I'll believe that when I see it."

"Believe it." Sam stiffened, a pretzel hung midair to his mouth. "In thirty years, my mother has never heard me curse." He grinned. "She doesn't use pepper juice, she uses hot sauce. Three drops break you into a sweat and burn your gut out for the better part of a week."

Tim leaned forward. "Is she from the south too?"

"You know it, bud." Sam tugged at the brim of his ball cap. "Alabama born and raised."

"Roll Tide, roll." Joe lifted his glass, citing the ball team's familiar mantra.

Mark advanced the slide. "This is Nora." Old, bent, and wrinkled, yet there was something defiant in her Mark couldn't peg. "She takes care of Three Gables for Ben and mothers us all, including my security staff."

Tim sat up straighter. "She's long in the tooth for that kind of job, don't you think?"

Some would mistakenly think so, gauging just by her age. "Actually, she's half blind, Scots, and as opinioned as a heart attack. But she runs the place with a cast-iron fist."

"Velvet glove?"

"No glove, Tim. Just the fist." Mark narrowed his eyes. "Do not mess with her. No exceptions."

Tim slid Sam, Nick, and then Joe a quizzical look.

Joe answered. "She's his surrogate mom, and if you think crossing Peggy is bad, it's only because you haven't yet ticked off Nora. Everyone in this village will come down on you like a ton of bricks."

"Got it," Nick said.

"No, you really don't." Mark couldn't resist feeling a little proud. "But once you meet her, you will. With just a glance, Nora can filet you like a fish and have you begging her pardon and thanking her for doing it."

"So who's that old guy with Nora?" Sam pointed to the slide. "Her husband?"

"No, but they're always together." Mark glanced back to the photo projected onto the screen. "Clyde Parker is a widower. Supposedly retired, but he does odd jobs at the center. Kelly Walker and he are close. Neither of them has any family left, so they've kind of adopted each other." *Like Jane and Mark.*

"Very cool." Leaning forward, Joe nodded. "I'd opt for handpicking my family."

"I guess you would. Your family is a nightmare."

"Watch it, Nick." Joe stiffened. "Mine is no worse than anyone else's. They might be drunks, thugs, and thieves, but they're mine."

Mark stepped in. "Can we get back to Clyde Parker?"

"No offense, Joe." Nick laced his hands behind his head and stared at the screen. "Proceed."

"Clyde rebuilt a beach house Kelly Walker inherited from her aunt. Lisa plans to move into it in about a week."

"With Annie?" Astute as always, Joe checked Mark for signs of confirmation.

"With Annie." It couldn't come soon enough to please Mark, even though it meant Lisa would go into hyperprotective mode. She was already protective, but knowing Dutch would do all he could to cause trouble, she'd be worse—and even more afraid. He hated Lisa's fear.

"Good security?" Nick asked.

Mark crossed his arms. "I designed it."

"Enough said."

Mark advanced the slide. The man on the screen could as easily have been a professional athlete as a doctor. Tall, muscular, lean like a distance runner. "I mentioned Dr. Harvey Talbot. He's Lisa's immediate boss. Harvey's a good man. Divorced, which eats him up. Otherwise he's about like the rest of us."

"If it eats him up, why did he get a divorce?" Joe asked.

"He didn't. His wife did. She was gone before I got here, so I don't have deep background, but Harvey's a workaholic—most at the center are—and supposedly his wife got tired of him putting his job first." Mark turned to the men. "It's kind of the same for them as it was for us. The staff can't put victims in crisis on hold—they need help now—so they put everyone and everything else on hold to help them."

"I hear that." Nick dragged a carrot stick through the bowl of ranch. "So is Harvey hot for Lisa or what?"

"No. He's strictly a good friend."

"Friends can hook up, bud." Sam studied the screen and chewed on his lower lip. "Man, I wouldn't want him as my competition. Too easy on the eyes, and women like those gentle doc types."

"He isn't competition. We're on the same side, Sam." These men knew him better than anyone else in the world. They wouldn't buy his sidestepping tactic, though they might let him slide by on it.

They all laughed.

Guess not. "Jerks," Mark muttered.

Tim walked over and slapped Mark's shoulder. "Look, buddy, we've never had a reunion, and you wouldn't have called us for one now—too many people out there would love to see us all dead, and you'd never lump us together and make it easy for them. Not unless your back was against an impenetrable wall you couldn't blast through on your own."

"Yeah." Joe stood. "One of my sources confirms NINA could be active here again, but I strongly suspect this summons is more personal. And nothing puts a man's back against an impenetrable wall like a woman."

"Correction," Sam said. "Not just *a* woman. *The* woman."

Joe pointed with a chip. "Actually, loving *the* woman."

"Scratch that." Tim paused until the others fell silent. "Nothing puts a man's back up against an impenetrable wall he can't blast through like trying to protect *the* woman he loves who is in danger."

Mark wasn't the least surprised they'd

recognized the reunion for the help-me summons it was. And Joe had seen far more at the center with Lisa today than he'd let on. Mark had never admitted his feelings for Lisa to himself much less to anyone else. It felt scarier than infiltrating the terrorist cell in Iraq.

Tim smiled. "So what's up?"

This is where things got touchy. "One of our former friends sent me a video. Fifteen seconds long. It's of two women fighting."

"You called us here because of a cat fight?" Sam grunted. "Man, go to Hooley's Bar at home any night of the week—"

"It's not just a cat fight, Sam. Reportedly NINA controls the fighters, and they fight to the death."

Nick cleared his throat. "I heard they were into prostitution but not fighting. Did you see the death?"

"No."

"The cartels do both and have for years," Tim said. "Guess NINA saw income potential."

Mark agreed. "They apparently need more funding to carry out their agenda than they're getting through their normal channels. Word is they've joined forces with the criminal culture to get it."

"That's pretty much what my source said," Joe told him.

"Consider it confirmed, then."

"Why wouldn't NINA do that? Money is its

primary objective. It doesn't care about the source." Tim sat forward, braced his arms on his knees. "Iran's been working on infiltrating the Mexican cartels for a couple of years. Seems logical NINA wouldn't want to miss that opportunity."

Nick raised his forefinger. "What does this have to do with the princess in peril who's stolen your heart?"

"I don't know that it has anything to do with it. My source says the same thing as Joe's. There's chatter NINA is active again in this area. If so, odds are good they're coming after Kelly Walker. She can tie one of their bigwigs, Karl Masson, to bringing terrorists into the country. If they come, I need help I can trust to protect her. So I summoned you."

"You run the video through official channels?" Joe asked.

Quantico. "Redundant. I did ask a friend here, Beth Dawson, to see if she could study the tape and pinpoint the source or the location."

"You went to an outsider?" Sam sounded horrified.

"Beth's not an outsider. She's volunteered at the center for years—and don't sneeze at that. The woman happens to be one of the leading computer experts in the country. She co-owns a killer software firm."

"Unnecessary risk." Nick wore his objection on

84

his reddened face. "If our guys can't find it, why bring her in?"

"Because when our guys are stuck, they go to her for help. They've tried to recruit her, but they can't afford her." Mark cut to the chase. "What she does for them she does out of duty. What she does for the center she does out of faith."

"You trust her?" Joe called the question, but they all waited for Mark's response.

"Yeah."

"Okay, bud. Enough said. Let's see your princess." Sam motioned with his pretzel. "Where's her picture?"

Mark advanced the slide. His breath caught, hitched in his chest. She stood on the church lawn in a flowing dress, her head thrown back, her long blond hair loose to her shoulders lifted by the breeze, laughing, a wide-brimmed hat dangling from her hand at her side. "This is Lisa."

Sam whistled. "Whoa."

"Enchanting," Tim said.

"Wow." Nick's brows shot up. "No wonder you're nuts about her. She's beautiful."

"The picture doesn't do her justice." Joe offered his opinion. "Trust me, I've seen her. She can kick his backside in hand-to-hand too. Fights dirty to do it, though."

Sam scrunched his shoulders. "That's not good."

"Sam . . . Sam." Tim shook his head. "How

often must it be said? Ask the right question." Tim focused on Joe. "*How* does she fight dirty?"

Joe grinned. "She kisses him."

The guys got a good laugh out of that one. "Enough, Joe."

He cut his glance to Mark. "Uh-oh. This isn't the brotherly kind of love like you had for Jane. You're *in* love with Lisa."

"Oh, man." Sam whacked his thigh and expelled a sigh so deep it lifted his linebacker-sized shoulders. "Another bachelor bites the dust."

"Not hardly. Not yet, anyway." Lisa had no idea he was romantically interested. With the demands on her and her schedule, it had to be that way.

"Well, well." Tim studied her image a bit longer. "I've wondered for years what kind of woman it'd take to captivate you."

"Enough have tried." Nick pulled out his wallet and pushed a fifty toward Tim. "You cost me, Mark. I bet you were immune."

"Sucker bet. No man is immune." Tim shoved the fifty into his money clip, then put it back into his pocket. "I have to say, she is stunning. You've got great taste."

"I wish I could take the credit, but my tastes have nothing to do with it. If they did, I'd have nixed my feelings for her a long time ago."

Tim's eyes gleamed. "Now that's interesting."

Sam agreed. "Nix her? You nuts? She's a knockout."

"Ordinarily, I prefer brunettes," Joe said. "But for her, I'd make an exception."

Mark slid Joe a killer glare.

"Easy, bro. I picked up on your claim." Joe sent Mark a lazy smile, then told the guys, "She talks straight too. I like that. You won't believe the things she gets away with."

Sam turned to look back at Joe. "Like what?"

"She touches him unexpectedly, and he doesn't swing first and ask questions later."

Sam's jaw dropped. Nick's brows shot up. Tim cocked his head and softly chuckled. "Imagine that."

Mark shifted uneasily on his feet. "We were demonstrating self-defense techniques."

"Not after class. They were just talking." Joe glanced at the guys. "She touched him. Repeatedly."

"Impressive." Nick fanned an arm on the back of the sofa.

"Wow." Sam stared at Mark. "You're finally getting over the first-strike thing, then."

"It's just with her," Joe said.

"It's a start," Nick said. "Mark's taking control."

"Control?" Joe strutted to the fridge, then back to the table. "He was a total yes-man. She wanted, and he fell in line. I wasn't sure the guy standing next to me was Mark. 'Course, she is seriously hot. I might be tempted to say yes a lot to her myself."

Sam rolled back his eyes. "Sure. I can just see it. Mr. Cool sacrificing himself at a woman's feet." Sam cracked up. "When pigs fly."

"I'm not sacrificing anything anywhere." They'd had their fun and Mark'd had enough.

Tim sniggered. "That's how it goes. They steal our hearts and then lead us around by the nose."

"Not true." The tips of Mark's ears warmed.

"I saw it, bro." Joe pointed two fingers at his eyes, signaling eyes-on.

"What you saw was her leading me by the nose because I let her. It's still my nose. I choose." The problem was, Lisa was just too cute to resist. He loved seeing her being playful, and between her work and studies, she seldom was. For more playful moments, Mark probably would let her lead him anywhere that didn't get them killed. And just how she'd made that happen, he had no idea. He didn't totally like it. "Look, she's different."

"Different?" Tim flicked at a speck of lint on his slacks.

Mark struggled. "She has every reason to be hard and jaded, but she's not. She's kind and compassionate, and there's something pure about her that just gets to me." Why didn't he shut up? He should shut up. "She's subtle too."

Joe choked on a drink. "About as subtle as a sledgehammer."

"To others, yeah. But nobody sees her like I do."

Nick grunted. "You mean through the stars in your eyes?"

"No, Grim Reaper, I mean she doesn't show anyone else what she shows me. To her, I'm different."

"I always said that about you, bro." Joe faked a toothy grin. "You see me through stars too?"

"Another crack and you'll be seeing stars."

"Touchy, touchy." Tim leaned forward, clasped his hands atop his knees.

"I'm trying to be serious here." Mark's take on Lisa rattled him enough that he wanted to get their insight because he lacked his own. Now he wondered why. "The fact is, I'm floored by her purity."

"Um." Sam tugged at his cap's brim. "Can't say that's an asset I generally seek in my women."

Mark frowned. "I mean inside, moron."

"Huh?"

"Sam, you're hopeless." Flustered, Mark gave up.

Tim walked over. "Tell us what you mean, buddy."

He was sorry he'd brought it up. But he couldn't undo what he'd done. "She's got this innocence about her, and she believes in other people. She sees the good in them, even when you really have to look hard to find it."

Tim dipped his chin. "That's nice. But not what this innocence is about, is it?"

Mark opted for the truth. "No. It's about the way she is with me."

"How's that?" Joe asked.

"Tender. I love that. She's protective of Mel and the others—most of the time overprotective—but she's not tender with them like she is with me. I don't know. I can't figure it out, much less explain it."

"None needed." Tim assured him. "I think of Mandy and know exactly what you mean."

"Well, if you've got any sense, you'll hightail it outta here, bud." Sam sighed. "Otherwise you're gonna end up hogtied, dragging a pure ball and chain."

Mark looked Sam straight in the eye. "Hers? I should be so lucky."

Tim clapped Mark on the shoulder. "Don't worry, buddy. Their turns will come." Tim lifted his chin. "Sometimes being led by the nose must be experienced to be appreciated—like classical music and opera."

Sam harrumphed. "I'll stick to country."

Mark swung his gaze to Joe, who held up a staying hand. "Sorry, bro. I'm a jazzman. Why pick a woman with that kind of power?"

"I didn't exactly pick her." Mark shrugged. God had picked her for him. "The first time I saw her, I just knew she was it. I don't know what I have to do to earn her, but whatever it is, I'm in. She's worth it."

"Earn her?"

"Well, yeah." Mark grunted. "You know. You never get something for nothing. I'm just saying, whatever the cost, I'll pay it."

"Well," Joe confessed, "I've been giving you a hard time, but if she looked at me like she looks at you, I'd know it too." Joe turned to the others. "She teaches self-defense to at-risk women. Even during med school."

"Wait a second." Nick lifted a hand. "Did I just pay my fifty by mistake?"

"How would I know?" Mark glared at Nick and Tim. "I *was* the bet. I don't know the terms you goons put on it."

Nick stayed Mark's objection. "From your own mouth, are you or are you not in love with her, man?"

Mark bit the bullet. "I love her. Always have, always will. But she doesn't know it."

"You haven't told her?"

Mr. Refined sounded stunned. "No, Tim, I haven't told her. She's had enough to deal with without my complicating her life even more."

Joe rubbed his chin. "So you just do what you can to help her and her mom out and keep the rest to yourself."

"Pretty much, yeah." Mark searched for condemnation in their eyes but saw none.

"Smart move," Tim said. "Especially under these circumstances."

"I have to agree." Sam swiped his teeth with his tongue. "She's had her hands full, and relationships are messy."

"Like you'd know."

"Yeah, Nick, I do know." Sam grinned. "I have a relationship every couple months. Then they get *the look,* and I run. Fast."

Nick snorted. "Coward."

"Hey, I'll dodge bullets anytime. But I don't want to be anywhere near a woman with *the look.* I'm not that brave."

Tim grunted. "Someone sharing your life and caring about you . . . Yeah, being loved is a real hardship."

"Not all women are like Mandy, okay," Sam said. "If they were, all you doofuses would be engaged."

"Buddy, you don't have to tell me she's a rare find. I know it."

"Well, I know I'd welcome *the look* from Lisa." So far Mark's odds for getting it appeared slim to none, though when she'd surprised him jumping into his arms today . . . Of course, he'd blown it, dropping her on her backside like that. What had he been thinking? *Moron.*

Joe snatched one of Sam's pretzels. "Maybe now that she's practicing, she'll have time for a life, and you'll have the chance to get her used to the idea."

"Just tell her, Mark," Nick said. "She talks straight, she'll hear straight too."

"Absurd." Tim returned to his seat, then went on. "A man never just tells a woman anything. It's suicide, Nick. You should know that." Tim cut his gaze to Joe. "Step in any time, Romeo. It's obvious your expertise is needed."

Joe did have a way with women. "Normally I wouldn't reveal my secrets, but you guys are way too lost to ever be found. The answer is simple, bro. Charm. Clean and simple."

"I'm charming." Nick scowled.

"Me too. So's Tim and Mark." Snarling, Sam swiveled on the stool. "You saying we're not charming?"

Joe lifted one hand. "I'm saying there's charm," he said, then lifted the other, "and then there's *charm*. The secret is sincerity. Charm isn't telling her she has a nice body. Or pretty teeth."

Sam stood. "He's talking about that little waitress down at Ruby's Diner—and she did have pretty teeth."

Nick gave it up and cracked a smile.

"Joe?" Mark prodded him. "Sincerity about what?"

"Seeing into her heart and validating her dreams."

"What the spit does that mean?" Sam twisted his cap, as if deciphering that puzzle had fried his brain.

"It's an incredible insight." Tim nodded and slapped his knee. "That's it, Mark. Charm her. Sincerely."

Just looking at her made it impossible to think straight, and he was supposed to charm her sincerely? Man, he could take down terrorists, but was he up to this? "I'll give it my best shot." Serious doubts crept in. "No, I'm going to be myself. It's who I am, and it either works for her or it doesn't."

Still, fear burned in him, and he let the guys see it in his eyes. "Really, it's just going to depend."

Joe frowned. "On what, bro?"

Mark met and held his gaze, unflinching. "Whether or not we can keep her alive."

6

S he's here!" From the receptionist's desk at Crossroads Crisis Center, Melanie shouted to the others. "She's parking the lemon at the curb."

Mark smiled. Mel had abandoned her preference for seriously funky and worn a simple black dress. It matched her nail polish and worked with the neon-green streaks in her hair. She'd gone all out for Lisa, and that endeared her to Mark—and apparently to Sam. Mark gave him the two-finger "eyes only" signal.

"She's over twenty-one," Sam whispered. "College student, right?"

"Touch her and die."

Joe relaxed into a cool smile. "That's our Mark.

Cutting to the bottom line. The lady is hands off, Sam. Got it?"

He frowned, clearly disappointed. "I got it."

Nick dropped his voice. "What's the lemon, and why are we here? We're supposed to be at Three Gables for a party, right?"

"Praying together here first is a tradition—for Lisa in her practice—and the lemon is her car. Well, the car she drives. Someone donated it to the center a couple of years ago. The gray Pontiac." Mark nodded past the bank of arched windows to the curb. "Everybody calls it the lemon." He nudged his tie.

Nick grunted. "Always breaking down, eh?"

"Get real, bud," Sam said. "Mark wouldn't put up with that. Not her car."

"Sure he would." Joe chuckled, a twinkle in his eye. "Or am I wrong?"

Mark didn't answer.

"Ten says you're not." Tim slid a knowing glance from Joe to Mark. "Why do I sense you're behind these breakdowns?"

"Because I am," Mark confessed. "They're a cover to facilitate communications between Lisa and Annie. Otherwise they'd never get to talk."

The light dawned in Tim's eyes. "Dutch knows the car is a lemon."

"Of course. He hears she's broken down, tries to intervene, Lisa and Annie talk while I'm intercepting him. It's not slick but it works."

"That's what matters." Joe shrugged.

Tim stepped away to answer a call on his cell. From his expression—a little dazed, a little dreamy—he was talking to Mandy. *Love looks good on him.*

Mark caught movement from the corner of his eye and turned. Kelly and Ben walked into the reception area, their hands linked. *Nice progress going on there.* Nora and Clyde and Harvey soon joined them.

"Mrs. Crane, you're gonna miss her!" Mel shouted out.

Peggy came rushing down the short hallway and half stumbled into the reception area, bumping her elbow against the wall and knocking her glasses askew. "I was on the phone with Beth Dawson. Someone's tried to hack into our computers."

"What?" Ben asked. "Were they successful?"

"Against Beth Dawson?" Peggy snorted. "Absolutely not. She's putting in some new code to add another layer of protection. I didn't understand it exactly. She says to think of our firewall having a firewall."

"Whatever it is, dearie, Beth will handle it." Nora patted her arm.

"Just tell me I'm not late." Peggy craned her neck.

"Cutting it pretty close, but you're okay." Mel chided Peggy. "She's five feet from the door."

Lisa walked in smiling and wearing a pale blue gown that swished around her calves. Her long blond hair was swept up, and thin, curly strands fell loose and framed her glowing face. Had he ever seen her this excited? Mark couldn't recall it. His insides warmed.

Sam sucked in a sharp breath. "Whoa, Joe. You were right."

"Of course." He looked at Sam. "About what?"

"The picture didn't do her justice. She could be a model on one of those runways or something."

"Maybe from heaven," Tim said. "Definitely looks angelic."

"Breathe, bro," Joe whispered to Mark. "Just breathe."

He tried. Lisa laughingly accepted greeting kisses from all the staff. Mark couldn't seem to move, and the guys deliberately hung back and watched everyone else interact. *Old habits die hard.*

She paused to say something to Mel, who frowned. "Will you quit worrying about me, Lisa? This is your night."

Lisa whispered an unheard response, and Melanie gave her a warning. "You've got to let me scrape my knees so I learn, okay? Otherwise, I'm going to crash and scrape my nose."

"Okay. Okay." Lisa nodded. "I am trying."

"I know," Mel said. "That's why I adore you."

Lisa wrinkled her nose. "Me too."

"What's she holding?" Sam asked. "Hey, it's got a bow."

"Are you that dense?" Tim tugged at the tip of his bow tie. "No, wait. Don't answer that. I put my life in your hands too many times. If you are that dense, I don't want to know it."

Nick thumbed his cuff link. It caught the light, winked. "Our princess has obviously brought herself a present to her party." He turned to Mark. "Is that a southern woman thing too?"

"We're lucky to be alive," Tim told Joe. "Alabama and New York, both sides of the Mason-Dixon, and they're as dense as dirt."

"From the neck up, dead stumps." Joe shrugged. "But they are pretty good at blowing things up."

Tim, the only one of them classy enough to be totally at ease in a tux, sighed. Mark, Joe, and Nick had settled for dark suits, and Sam, well, they were lucky to get him not to wear his cap, though someone—probably Nora—had wrangled him into a tie. Its knot hung loose halfway down his chest.

Lisa scanned the room and stopped on Mark. He smiled. She smiled back, and it flooded her deep blue eyes, stealing his breath all over again.

"Mark." She rushed over and flung her arms around his neck. "Bend down so I can kiss you."

Mark bent and offered her his cheek.

Lisa laughed, cupped his face in her hands, and planted a solid kiss on his lips. "It's my party, Mark Taylor. No kiss on the cheek for or from you tonight."

Surprise rippled through him. What did he say or do? Having no idea, he just stood there, hoping he didn't look as dopey as he felt. *Sincerely charming. Right.*

She kissed him again, looped her arm through his, and then nodded a greeting to the guys. "Joe, I'm so glad you came—all of you, welcome."

Joe introduced her to the others, and a twinkle sparkled in his eyes. "Wouldn't miss it. We don't often get to see Mark speechless."

"It is a wondrous thing, isn't it?" She teased and passed the package to Mark. "Happy birthday."

"For me?" He tried to control his voice, but she'd stunned him and knocked him off guard twice.

She nodded. "It's not much."

Money was tight for her. A lump swelled in his throat. "Thank you, Lisa." He could count on one hand the number of times he'd been given a gift by someone other than Nora or Annie and have fingers left over.

"Well, open it."

"Now?" He gazed at her, at the crisp white paper and big blue bow. "No, I'll wait. Tonight is your night."

"It's your night too." Lisa smiled and motioned to someone behind him.

Peggy Crane walked forward with a cake. Candles flickered atop it, and the group broke into singing "Happy Birthday."

Mark nearly lost it. This was a first for him, and the tenderness in it had his eyes stinging.

"Blow out the candles, my boy." Nora stepped closer, her eyes shining, her bright red lipstick creasing in her wide lips.

Mark breathed in the smell of hot wax, blew out the candles, and watched the smoke plumes rise, taking in every detail and committing it to memory so he could relive it again.

The group applauded, and Tim and Joe shared a knowing look. They understood what this meant to Mark.

Sam started to say something, but Nick shoved an elbow in his ribs. His words dissolved into a grunt.

Finally, Mark had a birthday with a celebration: A birthday where no one mourned or blamed him for his mother's death. One where guilt that Jane was dead and he was alive yet another year didn't eat him alive. And he had not one but two kisses from Lisa.

Life didn't get much better than this.

To a gentle roar of laughter, he opened gifts from the others, and from the guys, and then from Lisa. His big hands fumbled on the bow. Inside he was shaking, eager and hesitant.

"It's a rock." Sam sounded befuddled. "I wait all this time to see what it is and it's a rock?" He rolled his eyes.

"That's not a rock, genius," Tim whispered. "It's

a sand dollar. Obviously one that means something to them."

Mark pretended not to hear them and stayed focused on Lisa. "You kept this?"

"I've carried it with me since you gave it back to me." She smiled up at him much as she had on the beach the night they'd found it.

"Why?"

"I gave it to you, and you kept it because it meant something to you. And then you gave it to me because you knew I needed to know I had value." Her smile faded.

"So does this mean you don't want it anymore?"

"Oh no." She clasped his arm. Her mother's ring on her right hand caught the light and gleamed.

"I don't understand." He scrambled but remained lost. "You want me to carry it?"

She nodded. "Barring emergencies, until my birthday. Then you can give it back to me."

A bubble of joy burst in Mark. "And then on my birthday, you'll—"

"Give it back to you, yes." She tilted her head. "What do you think?"

"I don't get it." Sam's voice carried to them.

"You don't need to; they do," Tim told him.

"This is sincerely charming?"

"Zip it, bro." Joe glared at Sam. "He needs work, but he's nailed the important part."

Nick edged closer. "What?"

"Are you morons looking? listening?" Joe shook his head. "He's seeing into her heart."

Mark was, and he was praying Lisa couldn't hear the morons. But maybe he was making too much of this. She could just be setting up the terms of their ongoing relationship. That didn't mean it was a romantic thing. It could be more of what they already had—coffee now and then, walks on the beach, a picnic here and there, and the connections between her and her mom. That sounded far more likely.

The old guilt and shame and unworthiness crept up from the dark places where he kept them buried. *Don't forget who you are. Don't delude yourself. You? Loveable? Come on, Mark. You know better. Outside of God, that ain't gonna happen. Not after Jane. Not ever. Women want to feel safe and secure. Who's going to feel safe and secure with you? Not Lisa, that's for sure.*

Disappointment hit him hard. He tried to shake it off. *Think steel.* Of course he was wishing more into this than she intended. Lisa needed to feel safe and secure more than most.

Have a little faith. Just a little. Ask her.

Asking her anything would be stupid. He'd be setting himself up to crash and burn.

Ask her what she means, what she wants.

The urge burned strong. He tried to squash it, but it wouldn't go away. Maybe he could earn a little of her love. Not too much, but maybe just a

102

little. That would be enough for a man like him. Any would be more than he deserved.

Yet the hunger for just a little love spread and seeped into his bones. His mouth went dry, and the muscles in his throat quivered.

Will you just ask her?

When she leveled him, it was going to hurt. He stiffened, preparing himself for the impact. "Um, how long will we do this, do you think?" He motioned back and forth between them. "Pass the sand dollar?"

"That depends."

"On what?"

She gave him an enigmatic smile.

"Oh, man, she's got it." Sam warned Joe. "See, there it is."

"There what is?" Nick asked.

Tim smiled. "The look."

"She's in love with him?" Joe couldn't believe it, glanced at Tim for confirmation.

He nodded. "Oh yeah."

"Did I tell you or what? Man, I know the look." Sam sighed. "He's a goner."

Joe crossed his arms. "I got a twenty that says they're passing that sand dollar back and forth for about fifty years."

"If her stepfather doesn't kill her."

The others glared at Nick.

He shrugged. "I'm just saying."

"Twenty, huh?" Tim studied Mark and Lisa for a long moment. "He still thinks he has to earn his way on everything."

"That'll include her heart." Joe worried his lip with his teeth. "I understand why, but it isn't going to work."

Tim nodded. " 'Course not. But she's into him, so I'm predicting he'll figure it out or she'll just tell him. Either way, I'm not taking that bet."

Peggy Crane cleared her throat. "I know you're not standing here gambling when we're about to walk into the chapel."

"No ma'am," Joe said. "No one would take it."

She gave him her best straighten-up-right-now look. "Come this way, Joseph."

"Joseph," Nick whispered. "If I were you, I'd make Sam taste-test my tea for a while."

Joe nodded. "Yeah, I will."

The group filed into the chapel, and, standing in front, Lisa held out her hand. "Come here, Mark. It's your night too."

He took a place at her side and faced the group, hoping his face wasn't red.

"Thank you all for coming." Lisa smiled. "I think we surprised Mark with our joint celebration."

"More than I can say," he admitted. "Thank you all very much."

Lisa's delight bubbled, and then she stilled and

sobered. "After we say Mark's birthday prayer and before we head over to Three Gables, I want to thank you for all you've done for me. It's a blessing to be a part of the tradition, praying for me in practicing medicine. I need God's wisdom, guidance, and direction." She let out a nervous little laugh. "He hears all of you in ways I'm not sure He hears me, and I need all the help I can get."

Ben stepped forward. "Our prayers and love are always with you both."

Lisa and Mark sat in the front pew, and as Ben began to speak, Lisa clasped Mark's hand, twined their fingers, and held on tight.

It was the best night of his life. *Thank You, Father. You said to be still and wait. To be patient. Well, it's taken a long time, but You were right.* If ever there was a time to ask, tonight was it. Never had he felt more favored.

Bless her, Lord, in caring for others and herself. Protect her. And, please, please help me keep her and her mother safe. Don't let me fail either of them.

He'd never survive killing another woman important in his life.

7

Karl Masson shifted in the front seat of his Lexus and tapped his sun visor. Just after six o'clock on a Friday night, and traffic was heavy. It was already dark, and the glare from oncoming headlights was giving him a headache. Half a block up the street, Annie Hauk came out her front door dressed to the nines.

Dutch had figured she wouldn't miss Lisa's party, and unfortunately for Annie he'd been right.

A man paying to have his wife worked over when she was a respectable woman scraped at Karl's sense of decency, but the orders came down, and his choices were limited. Follow them or die.

Since he wasn't yet ready to die, he'd follow orders—at least until he got rid of Kelly Walker and wasn't reliant on NINA's goodwill and protection to stay out of jail. If he went to jail and wasn't there to care for the kids, Angel would never forgive him.

He dialed his cell phone, waited.

On the third ring, the boss answered. "Yes?"

Raven. "Lone Wolf." Karl identified himself. "Verification request on Shifter, Target Number Two."

"Transfer is complete. Target is approved."

Annie Hauk was bought and paid for. That left only one thing. "Authorization code?"

"Stand by one, Lone Wolf." A pause, then Raven came back on the line. "Alpha 263891. Target Number Two. Kill order."

Karl double-checked the code written on a cigarette butt in his ashtray. It matched. But a *kill* order? "The client personally requested that, if possible, the target survive."

Static filtered through the line, and then finally she responded. "That was not a mutually agreed-to term in the original contract."

NINA was huge on sticking to contract terms. No one at headquarters liked unnecessary changes on active missions. Least of all Raven, who had a reputation for ruthlessness that gave even hardliners like Karl the shakes. "Is that an official refusal to comply with the client's wishes?"

Another pause. A longer one. "Not yet, no. Was the request made to you firsthand?"

"Affirmative."

"Why does the client want to alter the contract terms? There will be no price reduction."

Only Raven would conclude the client wanted a discount on a murder. "He didn't mention money, ma'am."

"What did he mention—specifically?"

"He's decided he loves the woman, and if possible he wants her to live. Provided her living doesn't negatively impact our orders on Target

One or in any way hinder the overall mission."

"How very kind of him." Raven's voice turned to steel. "He should know better."

"He does." Karl pinched the ache at the bridge of his nose and then checked to make sure no neighbors were watching. He didn't see a soul except Annie. "The problem is, she's his wife."

"Hmm." Raven paused, then added a sigh. "Well, I guess we can't expect emotional stability from a man making these types of purchases for his wife, now can we?"

"I guess not." Karl waited. Raven alone would make the call, and what it would be Karl wouldn't hazard a guess. She was just as apt to order Karl to kill both targets and the fickle client. One never knew exactly what to expect from her. That made her effective, mysterious, and dangerous.

So far no one in NINA knew Raven's decision-making criteria. Just as no one below Raven knew the full details of any operation. Operatives like Karl knew what he needed to know, when he needed to know it to perform his assigned duties. No more, no less. That made for great security but also for totally unpredictable decisions above and below.

"It's imperative that the target be immobilized until the shift is made. If you can do that without killing her, fine. I'll authorize the contract revision. If you can't, then kill her. And, Lone

Wolf, be warned. If she hampers the shift in any way, she and the client won't be dying alone."

Karl broke into a cold sweat. "Understood."

"Raven out."

Karl hung up the phone. Raven out, all right. And if his judgment proved anything less than perfect, he'd be out too.

Popping his phone onto its dash mount, he glared out the windshield at Annie walking up the street. He didn't much care for being threatened, but NINA was NINA. It protected itself above all else, and if push came to shove, to spare herself or NINA, Raven would sacrifice every cleaner and operative in the entire organization in a finger snap.

Annie was halfway down the street, leaving her cove-front cul-de-sac on foot rather than in her car. Dutch must have taken her keys. The guy was sick in the head, treating his wife as he did. Too bad she'd ended up with him. Her first husband, the do-gooder doctor, really messed her up dying when he did. "Sorry, Annie. You're a pretty woman, and you make a mean pot roast."

He cranked the engine of his car, wishing she didn't remind him of Angel. Wishing he didn't know what she'd endured to protect her daughter. His own daughter still missed her mom. Lisa would miss Annie too. With what was to come, much more so and far more often.

He shook off their similarities. There was no

help for it. This was just a job. He didn't care what happened to their family; he cared about his own.

"Bottom line is, I can't risk something going wrong. Raven doesn't make idle threats. That means it's you or me."

Annie paused to pluck a weed out of the crack on the sidewalk.

"Don't worry, Annie. Angel will be there to meet you."

The calendar might say it was January, and it might be six o'clock in the evening, but it was still hot and muggy.

The snowbirds that flocked to the village to winter in the south likely loved the heat, but Annie Harper Hauk had been here through a sweltering summer—all of them, actually, for her whole life—and she needed a cool-weather reprieve.

She wiped the sweat from her brow, silently seething. The next-door neighbor who spied on her for Dutch had seen her leaving her yard and had the nerve to ask if she needed anything.

That annoyed her, but no more so than finding a strip of tape on her right rear tire. If she moved the car an inch, Dutch would know it. If she opened the garage door, he would know that too. But she was onto his tricks, and it would take more than silly pieces of tape to catch her. He relied on her weak heart keeping her confined. But when he was gone, she walked every day, inside where she wouldn't be seen. Lap after lap around the house until she'd walked a mile, and then two. Now she was walking five miles every time he left home, which was most days. She had to be ready for days like today, when she needed the strength to get where she needed to go.

It was a shame she would be all sticky and sweaty in her delicate peach-and-cream dress when really seeing her daughter for the first time in twelve years, but Lisa wouldn't mind, and it sure didn't matter to Annie, though she'd worn the dress for Lisa and it would have been nice if it had remained fresh. Lisa had always loved peach and cream.

Twelve years of distant and stolen glimpses of her daughter were enough to get Annie through the separation, and for the last three years, thanks to Mark, getting to talk with Lisa on the phone. But all that ended tonight. Tonight Annie would see and talk to Lisa.

She swallowed hard, her vision blurred. That, not being hot and wilted, mattered. Finally. Finally, she would get to hug her daughter again. Oh, but she'd hung on to that hope for years. And she was a mere hour from realizing it. *Thank You, God. Thank You so much.*

Her heart suffered a squeeze. All the years away . . . missing out on so much in Lisa's life. Annie had done what she thought she had to do to protect her child, but, oh, she had been so blind.

Why in the world hadn't she trusted God to provide for her? Marrying a man she barely knew. A horrible, horrible man. Tears burned the backs of her eyes and she blinked hard. She would not see Lisa Marie with streaked mascara.

Annie had made the mistake, and Lisa, her beautiful Lisa, had paid the highest price for it. They both had sacrificed so much—all because Annie had been so afraid of starving that she refused to trust in herself and in God. Regret pumped through her, pounding deep inside, swelling in every nook and cranny.

She stiffened against it. Why things had to be this way, only the Lord knew. Losing Charles so suddenly and then losing her baby, too, was a lot for one woman to take. But it was less than Job had lost. God saw far more than she did, and He deeply loved them both, so He surely had His reasons. It made sense in her head, though in her heart she still had a hard time day to day, but she learned her lesson. And she grabbed tight and held on to trust enough to get through this.

One more week and then it'll be over. She had made it all these years. She could make it one more week, and then finally the healing could begin. She wouldn't divorce Dutch. That would be an even bigger mistake. The Bible was very clear on the matter, despite what Lisa said. God didn't want women abused, that Annie had finally come to believe, and it was why she was willing to leave

112

Dutch. But divorce? Never. Never! He would kill Annie and Lisa both. There was no doubt in her mind, and even Mark Taylor couldn't protect them against a determined Dutch.

At Highway 98, Annie paused. All the excitement wore her out and her heart raced. On the other side of the highway, hotels and restaurants speckled the sugar-white beach, and beyond the sand was the Gulf. Seas looked three to five feet today. Breaking pretty close in. To her left was the harbor. A lot of the boat slips were empty, and a fleet was lined up waiting to come in through the pass. The harbor was unusually busy for the off-season. Must be having some kind of fishing rodeo or something.

Her heart calmed after her rest, so she turned right, stepping onto the sidewalk, and saw one of Dutch's stores. Parched, she debated stopping in to get a cool drink, but no, best not. Someone would surely tell him. A cold drink would be heavenly, but it wasn't worth the risk. She'd get a drink at the party.

She could call someone there to come and pick her up, but it was better not to get anyone else involved. Not that they'd mind. Mark, Lisa, Clyde, Nora, Peggy, or Ben would gladly come and get Annie, but if word got back to Dutch that she was at Lisa's party—and chances were pretty good that it would—then Annie wanted his anger restricted to her. He could be a mean and spiteful man, and he would be to anyone who helped her in any way. She couldn't deliberately turn him loose on someone else. She alone had made the deal with the devil, and she alone would take the brunt of his worst. That was only right. Besides, she'd endured since the day they had married, and she would endure this last week.

Then she would never have to endure again.

The thought had her giddy. Pulling a tissue from her purse, she dabbed at the sweat beading on her brow, sliding down the sides of her face and soaking her throat. Oh, but she was thirsty. She stared back longingly at the storefront but again decided against it. This was a special day, and if she went in there, she'd have to look at those horrible human-trafficking signs Dutch always taped inside the front window.

A chill raced up her spine, set the roof of her mouth to tingling, and an image of Lisa at seven filled her mind. "God, please don't let her remember. Please *never* let her remember."

Yet Annie never forgot anything from that dark time. But today was not a day for bad memories. It was a fine, excellent, extraordinary day for Lisa, and that's all Annie would remember.

Shoving hard, she buried the bad memories deep and put them under lock and key in a distant place like the therapist had suggested all those years ago. Then she turned her thoughts to Lisa: her courage, her trials, and this fabulous triumph. In spite of everything, with the unstinting support of Susan and Benjamin Brandt and Mark Taylor these last few years, Lisa had reached her dream and become a doctor.

Pride spread through Annie. Her baby had done it. She'd done it! Charles would have been so proud. And Susan too.

"Annie," a man called out.

She swung toward the voice and saw Karl behind her on the sidewalk. For the life of her, she couldn't recall his last name. Had she ever heard it?

"What a surprise." What was he doing here?

"I thought that was you." He smiled and caught up to her. "Why are you walking down the highway? Did your car break down?"

"My garage door wouldn't open. I think there's a short in the opener. How are you, Karl? I haven't seen you in some time."

"Oh, I'm staying busy, like everyone else." He let his gaze slide down her. "You're all dolled up. Pretty dress. Going someplace special?"

"Thank you." What did she do now? She'd never been any good at lying, and she really hated doing it. But if she told him the truth, he'd burn up the phone lines calling Dutch. "It's our regular church ladies' monthly meeting night." That was true enough, but they had canceled the meeting to attend Lisa's party. Still, many of the church ladies would be there.

"Ah, well let me give you a ride. It's way too hot and dangerous for you to be walking out here on the highway."

"I've lived here all my life. The village has a very low crime rate. I'm fine."

"I insist." He held out a hand.

"I'm not stranded." Annie smiled. "I don't want to put you to any trouble." How was she going to get out of this?

"It's no trouble at all." He clasped her arm.

Out of excuses and backed into a corner, she gave in. Not that she had much choice. The only way to get away from him would be to pull away, and that would be rude.

Don't do it, Annie.

That small, quiet voice inside her sounded loud and clear.

Something's not right. Don't do it.

"You go on, Karl." She patted his arm and pulled away. "I missed my treadmill walk this morning. The exercise will do me good—and it's just a few more blocks." Spotting his black car on the opposite side of the road, she got inspired. "I'll be there before you can get your car turned around. But thank you so much for offering."

He looped their arms. "Now, Annie, what kind of man leaves a woman stranded on the street? My wife would be appalled." His smile didn't touch his eyes. It chilled her.

Danger, Annie. Danger!

The alarm blaring in her mind set her to trembling. "No. Thank you, but no. I need the exerc—"

His fist came up fast, and a hard blow struck her jaw.

Pain exploded in her face. She staggered, dizzy. Fumbling, she reached for her cell phone, but before she could open her purse, he hit her again. And again.

And again.

Unable to lift her head or arm, she stared at the street, bits of dirt and concrete digging into her face. Cars zoomed by. She couldn't see them for the cluster of trees blocking her view, but she heard them and silently begged one to glimpse her and stop. Just one of them. *Just one!*

But none did.

She begged and begged, then an excruciatingly hard blow slammed into her head.

And she couldn't beg anymore.

Her heart stopped.

Karl stooped low and checked her pulse. Gone. He hesitated, darted his gaze around to see if anyone had taken notice, but covered by the trees that prompted him to intercept her in this spot, the cars sped by and no pedestrians were in sight on the sidewalk or outside any of the nearby condos.

Give her a chance.

His instincts rebelled against it, but she so

reminded him of Angel. All Angel had needed was a chance. She hadn't gotten it. All Annie wanted was a chance to know her child. After begging for a chance for Angel, could he deny Annie one?

Raven will kill you.

Some things were worse than death.

Help her and you're crazy. Raven kills you, what about your own kids?

Brent and Shelley had their grandmother. If he didn't give Annie a chance, he'd never again think of Angel without seeing Annie's face, without believing Angel was denied a chance because of him and the decisions he made. This decision. His hands shook. His whole body shook. *I have to do it.*

He started CPR and pumped her chest. Sweat dripped from his brow onto Annie's dress, splatted, and left a wet stain. "Come on, woman."

He kept pumping . . . pumping . . . and then he felt it. A beat.

He waited a few seconds and then pressed his fingers to her throat. Weak and thready, but the thump against his fingertips was there.

"Okay, Annie. You've got your chance."

Unfortunately he couldn't say the same for her daughter.

8

Three Gables never seemed more beautiful.

Breathless, Lisa stood and just soaked it all in. Lanterns hung in the trees and on the landscaped islands, and the fat squatty bushes beneath them sparkled with tiny twinkling lights. A huge tent had been erected on the grounds behind the house.

"Mark, look. Twinkling lights, bubbles in the fountain, and rose-petal trails all along the walkways. Isn't it beautiful?" Lisa swallowed a lump in her throat. "Ben went to so much trouble."

"Actually, Nora and Kelly took care of most of it."

Kelly lived in one of the two cottages on the estate, so that didn't surprise Lisa. Still . . . she turned to Mark, the skirt of her gown rustling. "I know Nora and Kelly didn't do all of this. Some of the lanterns are hung fifteen feet high."

"The guys and I lent a hand, mostly following instructions."

Touched that he and his team would go to so much trouble for a woman they didn't even know, Lisa glanced up at Mark. "Thank you. I don't know . . ." She shook her head.

"What?" Mark clasped her shoulders. "I know you like it, so what is it?"

"I love it. I'm just overwhelmed, I guess." She looked away. "I don't say it often enough, Mark, but I am very grateful to have you in my life."

"I'm the lucky one."

Finally, he's letting me know I'm important to him personally too. She'd feared the day would never come. "I was thinking. This is a special night for both of us." Lisa had wanted to do something for a very long time, but it carried consequences. Ones she wasn't sure she was willing to pay. Did she dare risk losing him?

"What?"

Too risky. You could lose what you have. "Never mind."

"I hate it when you do that," he said without any heat in his voice. "Just say what you want to say."

"Okay, but I'd better not regret it." Daring, she took a leap of faith. "Do you think two people can be friends for a long time and then realize what's between them has become something more than friendship? Or maybe that it has the potential to become something more?"

Mark tensed and studied her. "I guess it depends on the people, but why not? I suppose they can."

A little flutter leapt inside her. "Do you think if they tried to see if there could be something more between them and discovered that there couldn't, they could still be friends?"

His brows knitted, and the smile faded from

120

his eyes. "That would definitely depend on the people."

"Oh." At a loss, she wasn't sure what to say. Friends were too rare to risk squandering even one. Now he appeared suspicious. Had she said too much to go back?

"I know you're a puzzle queen and mental pretzels are fun for you, but I'm lousy with them. Show a little mercy and just tell me what's on your mind." Mark lifted a hand from her shoulder to her chin, raising it to see her eyes. "You can trust me, Lisa. No matter what you say, it'll be okay."

She waited for a couple to greet and then walk past them. When they were near the tent and out of earshot, she steeled herself and dared to say what she really wanted to say. "You've been such a friend to me and my mother. I wouldn't want anything to jeopardize that."

"Is something jeopardizing that?"

"I don't know. That's what I'm trying to figure out." Unable to hold his gaze, she dipped her chin, focused on his chest. "It's just that lately things have slowed down. I've had time to think, and I've been noticing things and thinking a lot."

"Such as?"

She made herself meet his eyes. "You've become really important to me, Mark."

His expression gave nothing away. "Don't confuse gratitude with something else. I haven't done any more or less for you than anyone else."

Apparently he didn't feel the same way, and she'd made him uncomfortable. But something was there. Something that urged her not to give up, to push a bit harder. "I know the difference between gratitude and . . . what I'm feeling. I've depended on others since I was sixteen. Without Susan, who knows where I'd be? Without Ben's generosity, I wouldn't be a doctor. I would have been homeless or worse, stuck living with my mother and Dutch. I am grateful, but I'm not confusing what I'm feeling for you with gratitude."

"I'm glad your life is getting calmer." Hunger flashed through his eyes, and the gleam in them went serious. "But I don't know if—"

But. Not good. Disappointment bit her hard. *No, not tonight. Not during her party.* "You know, I was wrong to bring this up." She shrugged. "Let's just forget it."

Forget it? Not a chance. Mark had waited nearly three years for this moment, for her life to get in enough order so she had time to notice more than work and study. He wasn't yet convinced she had her feelings straight about him, but he wanted to be. He wasn't forgetting anything.

"Look, Lisa, you've always been able to talk to me. We've shared everything with each other since day one." He'd even talked to her about

Jane, something he'd never spoken of to anyone other than the team. "Don't clam up now."

The wind stirred, rustling through the leaves, setting the lanterns to swaying and casting streams of light across the walkways and lawn. "This is hard."

"Why?"

She took Mark's hands in hers. "Because I don't want to lose you. Ever. I don't want to mess up what we have for what we may or may not get."

Behind her, on the other side of the lawn island, the guys huddled near a bench. Lisa had no idea they were there. But from their expressions, they were hearing every word of the most intimate conversation Lisa and he had ever had, and Mark didn't like it, but he didn't want to say anything. She could back away and clam up for another three years. Mark turned and signaled with his hand for them to depart the fix.

Not one of them budged.

He lifted her hand, studied her nails.

"What are you doing?"

"Checking out your Passionate Pink." He grinned. "You mentioned it. It stuck with me." Boy, had it. He'd imagined her long, slender fingers, colored a thousand shades.

"What do you think?"

"It's rich. Deep." Mark swallowed hard, met her eyes. "Promises the kind of passion that lasts."

Did she realize he was no longer talking about her nails?

She wrinkled her nose. "So, do you like it?"

"Oh yeah."

The hint of a smile curved her lips, also tinted passionate pink. Her mouth took his breath away and didn't give it back.

She tilted her head, little wisps of loose hair soft on her face. "May I kiss you?"

That snagged the one thread of his attention she hadn't already captured. Had he heard her right? "Excuse me?"

"I was hoping not to have to ask twice. It's taken me a long time to work up the guts to do it once. But I can't stuff the proverbial genie back in the bottle now." She paused, then set her chin. "This is a big night for me and it's your birthday and I've wanted to do this for a long time, so if you wouldn't mind . . . may I kiss you?" She lifted a hand and stroked his jaw. "Not a peck like at the center, though those were nice too, but a real kiss."

"Why?" Mark inwardly groaned. Everything in him shouted yes, but he had to know what it would mean.

Don't make more of it than it is. You're not lovable. You're needed. That works for you. Don't you dare forget this is Lisa. Lisa. *She can break your heart. She can make you believe in fairy tales and pipe dreams.*

He stiffened. He wanted her in his life, couldn't imagine life without her. But he was way ahead of her on this relationship between them, and if he scared her off . . . Well, a broken heart he did not need. Not when in his whole life his heart had never been whole. When he'd made peace with constantly being blamed for his mother's death, Jane had been killed. That *was* his fault. He didn't dare to dream, especially not about Lisa. He'd fall so hard he'd never recover.

"Why?" She frowned. "Well, why not?" Lisa let out an exaggerated sigh, clasped her arms around his neck, and tugged him down to her. She brushed her lips against his, testing him. Slowly pulling back, she looked into his eyes, and then kissed him again. Harder. Deeper. Longer.

And shaken to the core by this unexpected but welcome turn of events, Mark kissed her back.

The guys waited until Lisa's and his lips parted, then started whistling and laughing, teasing. They startled Lisa. "Knock it off, guys."

"So sorry. It does appear we're interrupting, gentlemen." Tim cleared a choked chuckle from his throat. "Apologies, Lisa."

She feigned a frown. "Uh-huh. I can see your regret all over your faces."

"Couldn't resist, dear heart." Tim urged Sam to pass him on the walkway leading to the tent. "Carry on. We'll see you two inside." He motioned the guys toward the tent.

Mark watched them go, and Sam's voice floated back to him on the gentle night breeze. "She's definitely got the look."

"She's does, bro." Joe patted Sam's shoulder and leaned in to stage whisper, "But so does he."

Mark wanted to crawl into a hole.

Lisa laughed. "Look at me, Mark."

He couldn't make himself do it.

"Please."

Forcing himself, he turned his gaze.

She studied him critically. "You *do* have the look."

"What do you know about the look?"

"I know you've got it." She beamed. "You like me."

He loved her. "You're usually a very likable person—except for maybe right now." Nudging him, making him dare to hope when he knew that was foolish, maybe even an insane thing to do.

"No." She let her hand float down his sleeve. "You *seriously* like me."

This was no nudge; it was a full-force push. Decision time. Dare to tell the truth and risk being a brokenhearted fool who would never recover, or stay silent and safe? He'd been safe. Safe was . . . well . . . safe, not content. Just once, he'd like to feel content.

Leap, Mark. Go on and leap. I won't fail you.

God or wishful thinking? With his emotions in riot mode, it was hard to tell.

"Maybe a little." Man, he hoped he didn't regret this.

Lisa stepped into his arms. "I maybe like you a little too."

A shield inside him crumbled like a pile of rocks. It was done, out in the open. He wanted to rebuild the shield, to believe the voice inside telling him to have faith was just wishful thinking, but he couldn't. The rubble remained. He did believe. He did hope.

Weak. Stupid. You're setting yourself up for a big, big fall.

I'll carry you, son. Trust Me.

The battle within raged.

I know your fears. I love you, and I'm here.

Love. It *was* God. No one else had ever said *love* to Mark Taylor. Calm settled in. "I'm glad to hear that, Lisa."

"Good." She licked her lips, seeming nervous. "I can't believe I missed this bond between us, but maybe I didn't. That first night on the beach. That was special."

"When we had coffee at Ruby's too."

She nodded. "How long did we sit there and talk? Three hours?"

"Nearly five." He clasped their pinkies. "I enjoyed every minute of it."

"Me too—and all the times we met there afterward, just talking about our days. Everything and nothing. That meant the world to me."

"Really?"

"Surely you knew."

"I'm glad to know it now." Maybe her feelings for him were further along than he thought. Talking, she had let him look into her heart, and he had validated her dreams. She'd done the same for him too. Why hadn't Joe mentioned that part? *Charm her sincerely.*

"Good. It's settled then."

He'd leapt too far and missed a step. "What's settled?"

She wrinkled her nose and smiled up at him. "We're officially more than friends."

They always had been. He fought it, still wasn't confident in how to earn even a little bit of her love, but a part of him had been waiting and hoping she'd catch up. "Officially, yes." He clasped her arm. "Now let's get to your party before it's over."

They walked to the edge of the canopied tent, then stepped inside. Tables stood draped in white linen, and at the far end of the tent on the stage, the band began playing a new song. Music filled the air, and couples danced and sang along, having a great time.

Lisa scanned the crowd. Something dark flashed in her eyes.

"What's wrong?" Mark asked.

"My mom called and said she'd be here, but I don't see her. Something must have happened."

She wanted Annie with her tonight to celebrate. Getting her license was a huge moment, and she'd been denied too many huge moments with her mom.

"I'm sure she'll be here soon, unless Dutch somehow found out."

"He's in Georgia, checking on his stores." She dropped her voice. "I'll be so glad when she's out of that house."

"You're worried."

Lisa clutched at her stomach. "So much I can barely breathe."

Mark wished he could reassure her, but he couldn't. He pulled out his cell and checked for messages. "She hasn't called."

Lisa checked hers as well. "Me either. Something's wrong, Mark. I feel it."

She could be overreacting. With Dutch on the attack, that would be justified, but it wouldn't really be typical. Lisa took things in stride, even very bad things. Her training and life experience demanded it. Otherwise, she'd always be rattled.

"Detective Meyers is keeping an eye out. Let's dance one dance, and if she isn't here by then, I'll go check on her myself."

"Can you check on her without getting caught?"

"I do it every night."

Lisa stopped on a dime. "Since when?"

"Since I started working for Ben."

"I didn't know that."

"Annie and I have a system. She puts a candle in the window. It's not lit. That'd be too obvious. Just on the windowsill. If the candle is there, she's okay. If not, then she needs help."

Tears brimmed in Lisa's eyes. "So Ben did this too? Taking care of me, med school, and my mom?"

"Um, actually, Ben doesn't know about the checkups on your mom." Mark's ears burned.

"I don't understand. Who pays you to do that?"

"No one." He looked away. Penance for Jane, for Lisa because she couldn't do it. "I like her."

Tears trickled down Lisa's face. "I think I might like you more than a little bit, Mark Taylor."

He thumbed the tears off her cheeks. "Glad to hear it, Dr. Harper, but if that's the reason, it's definitely gratitude and it isn't necessary."

"Not because I owe it you. Because you're the kind of man who thinks to do something like that."

"Oh."

"You're . . . special."

A lump settled in his throat and wouldn't go down. *Special.* He was special.

Beside him, Joe approached Beth Dawson. At her back, he bent over her shoulder and spoke softly, but his voice carried. "Tell me some man didn't put that snarl on your face."

Beth whirled around, her green dress clinging to

her waist and falling free at the hem. "Actually, one did."

"Point him out. I'll make him regret it."

Beth smiled. "I appreciate it, but I can't. The jerk happens to be married to my best friend and business partner. I'd love to see him flattened, but it wouldn't go down well with her."

"That does make the matter complicated."

"Boy, does it ever."

"Then forget the insensitive ingrate and dance with me instead."

Charm in action. Mark bit back a smile.

Lisa followed Mark's gaze. "Ah, Joe's discovered Beth Dawson. She looks like Demi Moore with her hair long like that. I love it."

She did look pretty. Very different from the sweats and shorts she usually wore. "They look good together." Joe was partial to brunettes, and Beth's hair was a warm brown with gold streaks. He'd like that.

"Striking." Lisa hiked her shoulders, smiling.

Joe was a pretty big guy, nearly as tall as Mark and a lot better looking by Mark's measure, and Beth had bright eyes to go with that long brown hair. She was a good five inches shorter than Lisa. Probably about five foot five. She cleaned up pretty good.

Lisa leaned closer to Mark. "I hope they have a great time tonight."

"Why?"

"Why not?" Lisa shrugged. "I like Beth, I like Joe, and"—she nudged Mark—"I want everyone to be as happy as I am—officially."

Mark let his fingertip slide down Lisa's face, cheek to chin. "Then I hope they do too."

Mark also hoped Joe didn't address the object of Beth's snarl. Seagrove Village was a close community. Everyone knew everyone's business, and it was no secret that Beth's partner, Sara, had married a social-climbing moron with expensive tastes and tons of arrogance.

"Before we mingle, may I ask for one more thing?"

Mark gave Lisa his full attention. "Sure."

"Kiss me again."

Lisa wanted his kiss, his touch. He curled his arms around her and kissed her soundly, swearing he wouldn't stop until she was dazed, he was, or both.

Lisa stood in the crowded tent. Ben and Kelly swirled on the dance floor, so did Nora and Clyde, and Harvey was on its edge, teaching Mel the rudiments of the Viennese Waltz. Her frame needed work, but she had great lines.

"Mark," Lisa whispered. "Check out Mel. No green spikes in her hair and a sophisticated little black dress—she's gorgeous."

Mark smiled. "She had green spikes at the center. I distinctly remember them."

"Well, she doesn't have them now."

"No, she doesn't." He paused to study her. "To tell you the truth, I miss her funky look. It suits her."

Peggy Crane joined them. "I agree. Funky is uniquely Mel. But she's worried she's not being taken seriously at college, so she's toning down her appearance. It's been planned for weeks that she'd debut her makeover here tonight, which is why you saw green spikes at the center and not here."

Lisa smiled. "I'm honored." She also wished Mel would just be Mel. She was special and unique and adorable exactly as she was.

Talking with Nick, Sam cursed.

Peggy stiffened. "Excuse me," she told Mark and Lisa.

Mark sighed. "I warned him."

"He won't forget again," Lisa murmured. Peggy took Sam by the arm and led him out of the tent. Lisa staved off a giggle. "Ready for that dance?"

"More than ready." Mark gave her his most charming smile. "I hate dancing, you know. But if it gets you into my arms, I'll do it and be grateful for it."

"Straight talk. I love it." From the corner of her eye, she saw Tim speak to the lead singer. The music shifted to a slow ballad. Lisa shot Tim a thumbs-up and smiled at his acknowledging wink.

Mark's team was always aware. To have a group so attuned to you was something else. They'd depended on one another to survive, and now they watched over one another to make sure they lived well. Bonds like that were lifelong. Special and rare.

"Cutting in." Nick tapped Mark's shoulder.

"It's our first dance."

"Yes, I know."

Mark scowled. "Well, can't you wait for the next one?"

"I could." Nick's expression stayed sober. "But I'm not going to."

Mark's scowl deepened. Lisa shrugged. "You guys are a package deal."

Mark backed away, allowed Nick to replace him, and watched them dance his dance.

"Mark's a good man," Nick told Lisa. "He hasn't caught a lot of breaks, so if you're planning on ripping out his heart and feeding it to him— don't."

Ah, the protective bears were already laying down the law. It sure hadn't taken them long. "No ripping in my plans, Nick. I've had my share of tough breaks too."

Another shoulder tap and Tim stepped in. Nick grumbled at him but released her.

"Ignore Nick," Tim told her. "He's a great guy, but if there's a dark side, he's going to wallow in it. It's his nature."

Lisa let her arm relax against Tim's shoulder. "I see."

"No, but with time you will." He dipped her and then lifted her up in perfect time with the music. "So are you serious about Mark or just playing around?"

"I don't play around. Never learned how, see no sense in learning now."

He studied her eyes, then a twinkle lit in his. "Fabulous."

Moments later, Joe tapped Tim's shoulder. Lisa moved into his arms, laughing. "You guys are something else."

"Definitely," Joe said. "You know Mark's been kicked around his whole life by everyone but us and a few of you here, right?"

Her chest tightened. His father she'd known about. But all his family? "Actually, I didn't know that."

"What about Jane? Has he told you about her?"

Lisa nodded. Her heart ached. What would it be like to be loved by a man like Mark Taylor? Even as a sister?

"I figured as much, which is why I'm telling you if you treat him right, he'll be the best thing that ever happened to you. If you don't—"

"Then I'll have to contend with all of you."

"Well, yeah." Joe shrugged. "I wouldn't have phrased it that way, but it works for me."

She should be insulted, but she couldn't be. They weren't against her; they were just for Mark. And from the way his family had treated him, it sounded as if he needed someone on his side. Someone besides her.

"So you know, Mark is already one of the best things to ever happen to me, Joe. I haven't seen my mother in twelve years. I hadn't talked with her for nine of them. Her husband forbade it. Then three years ago, Mark shows up at the center and hands me a phone. 'When it rings, answer it,' he said. Then he turned around and walked out. I didn't know what to think."

"The caller was your mother."

Her vision blurred from her glistening eyes. Lisa nodded, too moved to speak.

"Vintage Mark."

"Yes, vintage Mark." She kept one eye on the tent door. Mark stood near it, talking on his cell phone. He glanced at her but didn't smile. His tension radiated to her. "I was right. Something is wrong."

Joe didn't miss a step. He swirled her in a circle, seemingly checking everywhere at once. "Relax. We're good."

"No, we're not good." Lisa stopped dancing. Worry pounded off Mark in waves, nearly knocking her to her knees. "Something's wrong with my mom." She backed away from Joe and hurried over, hearing him follow behind her.

Weaving through the people, she stepped off the dance floor and up to Mark. "What is it?"

He held up a wait-a-second finger. "I

understand," he said into the phone, letting his gaze slide past her to Joe, who immediately turned and summoned the others.

The tension built in Lisa so fast and tight she feared she'd explode. *God, please. Please.* She clenched her hands into fists at her sides.

"We're on our way." Mark closed the phone, tucked it away.

"What is it?" Lisa couldn't stand not knowing another second.

A whisper rippled through the crowd, and the jovial tone dimmed. Ben and Kelly, Harvey and Mel, Nora and Clyde and Peggy all circled around.

"Will you please tell me what's wrong? It's my mother, isn't it?"

"Yes. That was Detective Meyers on the phone." Mark stiffened and clasped Lisa's hands. "Annie was found on Highway 98. She was badly beaten, Lisa."

Lisa sucked in a sharp, staggered breath. "Is she . . . ?" Her voice faltered. She feared the answer but tried again. "Is she—?"

"She's alive but critical." Mark softened his tone. "Jeff says we need to get to the hospital right away . . . just in case."

Dutch, what have you done? Inside Lisa screamed, *What have you done?*

Karl pulled into the hospital parking lot and cut the engine.

It was dark now, which annoyed him. He had planned on taking Annie to a more remote location, but Seagrove Village was a tourist town. People were there for fun and sun, to enjoy the deep-sea fishing and sugar-white beaches, not to witness crimes that would require them to return later to testify. Taking her down in full view wasn't as risky as it might seem, and he could make up some time—or so he'd thought. An astounding number of cars passed before one stopped. Rather than the moments he'd expected, it had taken a solid twenty-six minutes for a good Samaritan to surface.

NINA would not be pleased. Raven wouldn't be happy to have to report it to the powers that be, which meant Karl certainly would not be happy. Had their schedule been impacted? It couldn't be that tight, could it? Not knowing for certain had him sweating bullets.

He stared up at the lighted hospital building, then again checked his watch. Just enough time to touch base with Dutch before phase two kicked in. Pulling out his phone, Karl dialed.

Before the first ring ended Dutch answered, clearly eager for a mission-status update. "Is it done?"

Karl frowned. "Have you lost your mind, answering the phone like that? Anyone could have been calling—and don't give me that caller ID nonsense. What if I'd been compromised and someone was tracking the numbers in my phone?"

"Sorry. But now that it's clear you are you and I am me, is it done?"

Karl choked the leather steering wheel. "Mostly. I'm at the hospital now, waiting."

"Is Annie—?"

"She was alive when I left her. Whether or not she is now, I don't have a clue."

"Can you find out? She's got a weak heart, you know."

And you had her worked over? "Nothing I can do at the moment. I'm not finished here, remember?" Karl plucked a piece of lint off his slacks, grateful kneeling on the concrete hadn't ruined his suit. "And don't you dare call the hospital and ask." Dutch Hauk was arrogant enough to do it.

Until Mark Taylor had interceded, Hauk believed he could do anything. Well, except with NINA. Even he wasn't arrogant enough to put Raven to the test, not that they had much, if any, direct contact. Hauk was an organizational peon.

"Where are you, anyway?" Karl asked.

"Near the state line."

Great. Just great. Karl sipped from a steaming cup of aromatic coffee. "You're behind schedule."

"I had a flat tire."

Unavoidable, but any more bad breaks and the mission would be in a heap of trouble, which meant Raven would be gunning for Karl and his men. "Okay." Karl went into damage-control mode. "I'll handle your cover at the hotel. The room key will be near the closest fire alarm. Get there as fast as you can." Karl watched a familiar blue SUV pull into the parking lot. *Taylor and Lisa Harper.* "I have to go. The target has arrived."

"Lisa's there? At the hospital?"

Dutch was beyond arrogant—and not half as untouchable as he thought he was. How he had survived this long was beyond Karl. Rather than answering, he hung up. If Karl wasn't careful, Hauk would get them both killed—if not by cops then by NINA.

Putting his phone back into his pocket, Karl watched his targets walk inside. When the automatic door shut behind them, he flashed his headlights.

Across the lot appeared a responding flash.

Ah, right on time.

9

R ose." Seeing the back of a nurse she had worked with often, Lisa rushed through the ER over to where she stood between a scale and a crash cart. "Where's my mother?"

Tall and lean, Rose stilled. Her thin face pinched tight. "Oh, thank goodness. I'm so glad you're here." She paused to nod at Mark. "They've taken her up to ICU."

"How is she?" Lisa hiked her purse strap on her shoulder. "What happened?"

"If I were you, I'd get up there right now. They barely got her through the door before she lapsed into a coma." Pity flashed through Rose's eyes. "I—I don't know, Lisa. I just don't know."

Mark intervened. "Did she tell anyone who attacked her?"

Lisa opted to be blunt. "Was it Dutch?"

"When I saw her, she was already comatose. Detective Meyers rode in with her. Maybe he knows something. She was conscious on the ride in."

"Where is he?"

"I don't know, Mark."

"Talk with him later." Lisa moved down the hallway toward the elevator. "ICU first."

"Definitely." Rose glanced back over her shoulder at Lisa. "I'm sorry about your mom and your party."

The party was nothing. But her mother . . . Lisa's throat cinched tight. Swallowing hard, she rushed to the elevator, then staccato-punched the button three times. When the elevator failed to appear, she took off for the stairs.

"Slow down," Mark warned her. "Breaking your neck to get up there isn't going to help her. It's one flight; it'll just take a minute."

"You don't understand." Lisa didn't slow down. "She might not have a minute."

Shoving against the stairwell door, Lisa pushed through, took the steps two at a time, and then hurried down the hallway to the nurses' station. "Where's my mother?" she asked the nurse whose back faced her.

The nurse turned around.

"Jessie, where's my mother?"

"Calm down, Dr. Harper, and I'll let you in to see her. She's been through the initial battery of tests. Broken ribs, left arm, right leg. Her kneecap is shattered. Her face is banged up, but they're bruises and breaks that will heal, okay?"

Lisa nodded, holding her silence for fear Jessie would stop talking.

"She took a bad blow to the head. The brain was swelling, so we followed normal protocol on that."

"What does that mean?" Mark asked.

"They drilled a hole in her skull to relieve the pressure." Lisa darted her gaze to Jessie. "Rose says she's in a coma."

"Yes." That same pity she'd seen on Rose she now saw in Jessie. "It doesn't look good, Lisa. Be prepared."

"What do you mean?" She couldn't wrap her mind around it.

"We're still evaluating, but what isn't broken is bruised and swollen, and we think there's some internal bleeding. Waiting on lab results and scans for that now. Don's running her labs—he's new but really good." A frown settled on Jessie's face, wrinkling the skin between her eyebrows. "We don't have all the results we need to prove it, but she's definitely critical. We'll know more when we hear from Don."

Lisa absorbed the shocks one by one and locked her knees to stay upright. *Critical. Now? Now, when the end is in sight? Oh, God, why? We've waited so long and worked so hard.* "I want to see her."

Jessie motioned across the hall. "Mark, the ICU waiting room is right there. You're welcome to wait for Dr. Harper. It's family only in with Annie."

"He is her family. Put him on the list."

"Lisa, I can't—"

"Do it, Jessie. He's been a son to her. When she regains consciousness, she'll tell you so herself. Until then, I'm telling you. Put him on the list."

"Okay. But you're signing off on it."

"No problem." Lisa moved toward the heavy double doors to the unit.

"Is this the only door in?" Mark asked Jessie.

When she nodded, he ended the discussion on letting him inside. "I'll find out what I can from Jeff Meyers. You go on, Lisa. Annie's waiting."

She sent him a searching look that said everything and nothing. "Mark?"

He lifted his chin, waited.

Her voice dropped to a whisper. "I'm scared."

"I know. Me too." A lump in his throat bobbed. "Be strong now, and go see about your mom."

Lisa turned and pushed through the heavy doors, then disappeared into the dark hollows of the Intensive Care Unit.

Mark watched her go, his whole body in revolt. If anything happened to Annie . . .

Why didn't you watch her yourself?

Dutch was gone. In Georgia.

Maybe. That could be a lie. You knew it, or you wouldn't have made the arrangements with Jeff Meyers. You didn't watch over her yourself, and now she's critical. She needed you and you weren't there. You failed again, Mark, and now Lisa could be left devastated and Annie dead.

Dutch couldn't be in Georgia. He had to have done this. No one else would want to hurt Annie.

That made Mark sick. What manner of man would rather see his wife dead than away from him?

In the waiting room, he kept one eye on the heavy doors into the unit and called Jeff.

"Meyers." He answered the phone sounding breathless. "Talk fast."

"Jeff, it's Mark. What happened?"

"Man, I am so sorry. I know we agreed I'd watch over Annie until she got to Three Gables, but I got an emergency call. There was a brawl down at the marina on the pier. I had to take it."

Mark leaned against the door frame, punching his shoulder against the wood. "Why didn't you let me know?"

"Totally my fault. I saw Dutch leave. Annie told me herself he was going to Georgia. I thought I'd just be a minute and she'd be okay. Now she's . . . I'm so sorry." The timbre of his voice crackled. "I don't know what else to say."

"It's my fault." Mark sighed, understanding exactly how responsible and guilty Jeff felt because he felt it too. "Done is done. We can't change it. Let's focus on what we can change." Before Jeff could revert to wallowing in guilt, Mark went on. "Jessie says you rode in with Annie and she was conscious. What did she say? Did Dutch assault her?"

"Boy, I wish I knew. She was conscious, but I couldn't get her to talk to me. She was in a lot of pain, Mark."

"Did she say anything at all?"

"Yeah. Over and over she said, 'God, don't let him hurt Lisa. Don't let her remember.'"

Mark waited for an orderly to roll a gurney down the hallway and get out of earshot. "Remember what?"

"I have no idea. I asked several times, but Annie didn't answer. It was like she was in her own little world."

"So all we know is her attacker was a man and she doesn't want Lisa to remember something."

145

"Yeah, that's it."

Mark stared at the blank television screen in the corner. "Her fearing he'd hurt Lisa sounds a lot like Dutch."

"I thought the same thing, but she never said his name, so it's supposition."

"Tell me you're looking for him, Jeff."

"I am. He's not home or at the store. I left word with his employees that Annie had been injured. They're trying to find him too."

"He was supposedly going out of town and his employees didn't know it?" Odd behavior for a control freak, and Dutch was definitely a control freak.

"The clerk said he disappears without a word all the time, so they never know when he might drop by. He says it keeps them on their toes. So when I mentioned Georgia, they didn't think a thing about it."

That kind of logic fit the twisted way the man's mind worked. Dutch owned a string of convenience stores all the way from Georgia down through Florida and across the south to the border between Texas and Mexico, and he did periodically check on each of them.

"He must be in a dead zone or have the battery out of his phone," Jeff said. "I'm having no luck tracking his cell. We have no clue where he is right now."

Convenient. Mark frowned at a man walking

down the hall in a hospital gown, tugging at the back flap. "What about witnesses?" Highway 98 was a major thoroughfare. Someone had to have seen something.

"My guys are checking, knocking on doors, but so far no one saw a thing."

"Maybe we'll get lucky." Mark said it, but he didn't store any faith in it. These days, people just didn't want to get involved.

"I'm still trying to figure out why she was on Highway 98 on foot. Her car was in the garage at her home, and it started right up. So why was she walking?"

That mystery Mark could solve. "Dutch uses markers so she can't leave the house without his knowledge. He puts them everywhere—on doors, drawers, windows, even on cabinets in the kitchen. If the tires on her car roll an inch on the garage floor, he knows it."

"What about phones? We didn't see a single one in the house. Just empty jacks."

"When he leaves, he takes them with him so she can't call anyone, and he empties her wallet so she can't call a cab."

"Good grief."

"She keeps a private money stash, though. She's always got cab fare." Mark had made sure of that.

"I can't believe she puts up with that and stays with him." Jeff caught himself. "Sorry, I shouldn't have said that."

"No need to apologize for saying what I've been thinking for years." Mark checked the clock— nearly ten thirty—and then the heavy doors. The harsh light glinted off the metal push plate. "Annie has her reasons."

"It's her life," Jeff said. "We have to respect her decisions."

"Yeah, whether or not we like them." Ben and Kelly walked into the ICU waiting room. Nora and Clyde came in behind them. Over their shoulders, Mark saw Harvey stop at the nurses' station. "Listen." Mark tipped the phone closer to his mouth and dropped his voice. "Keep me posted, and I'll do the same with you. Remember that my old team is in town. They'll help in any way they can." He reeled off Joe's and Tim's cell phone numbers.

"You're a step behind them. Joe's already been in touch. They've been recruited to work in ways that won't cost me my badge. With the budget cutbacks, we just don't have the manpower we need to cast a wide net on finding witnesses."

"You're keeping my security team active at Three Gables, correct?" It wouldn't surprise Mark to discover Dutch lurking in the woods on the reservation land adjacent to the property, looking for a way to wreck Lisa's party. He would want to punish Lisa for Annie's defying him and going over anyway. Hurting Lisa would most hurt Annie.

Twisted. Sick. Mark had been skeptical of this Georgia trip from the start and so was Jeff, which was why, when Peggy said Annie was coming to the party, Mark and Jeff agreed that since Jeff had the authority to make arrests, he would keep an eye on Annie until she got to Three Gables, and then Mark would take over.

"If Annie's condition changes, let me know," Jeff said. "Should I put a guard on her, or will you be there?"

"I'll be here." After Jane, Mark would never again be anywhere other than exactly where he was supposed to be. He put a bite in his tone. "I'm telling you right now that Dutch Hauk isn't getting within a mile of her."

He'd protect Annie as intensely as Lisa would protect her. He'd been loved as a friend—Jane, the guys did that. But the possibility of being loved as a man . . . He craved it, and he'd do anything that didn't dishonor God to get it. He had no pride. Not when it came to earning Lisa's love. She filled his empty heart. Only Annie really understood that.

"You might want to get the judge to sign a restraining order to that effect now, because whether or not you have one, Jeff, if he shows up here, I will keep him away from her."

"Just don't kill him, okay?" There was no humor in Jeff's tone.

"If it can be avoided, I'll avoid it. But protecting her is my first priority."

Jeff sighed. "I'll get the paperwork started."

Mark hung up. The group of Crossroads Crisis Center friends all started talking at once, rapid-firing questions.

He answered as best he could. Midsentence, he saw the heavy door leading into the ICU burst open. Lisa ran out, tears streaming down her face, and rushed straight into Mark's arms.

Closing them around her, he held her tight, cradling her head in his hand. "It's okay, honey. Shh, it's okay." He led her away from the others so they could speak privately.

"It's not okay." She rocked back, her chin quivering, voice quaking. "Harvey says . . . I have . . . to be strong. She . . . she probably won't . . . live through . . . the night." A deep sob burst out.

A lump lodged in Mark's throat. "Lisa, don't. No. Don't think it, and don't believe it." He swayed gently with her. "Only God knows, honey. You know that. She's in His hands."

Her eyes red-rimmed, her face damp, Lisa glared up at Mark. "Well, I hope He's paying closer attention now than He was when she got beaten to a pulp."

Mark could have responded to that, but Lisa was hurt and angry and scared. So scared she wasn't thinking straight, and God made for an easy target. He opened his mouth to say—something. He had no idea what she was ready to hear.

"Don't." She lifted a hand. "Just don't." Agony dragged at her mouth, flooded her eyes. "She's struggled her whole life. She's lived with that monster, put up with all his abuse, and God's watched." Lisa thumped her chest. "He's allowed me to be banished, stuck without her and my dad." She sniffed. "I can't figure out what God's doing or why He's letting these awful things happen to us, Mark. Every time I think things can't get worse for us, they do."

She swiped at her face with a soggy tissue. "Mom and I have been crawling on our knees in a dark tunnel our whole lives. Believing but seeing good things happen to everyone else while we're stuck, forgotten in the dark. Finally—finally—we see the end of the tunnel, and we're so ready to step into the light, and then this happens."

Her frown deepened, turned stony. "So no platitudes. No preaching to me about God's goodness. He is good and I know it. I see it all around me—I always have. But that goodness is always for everyone else. Not for me, and certainly not for my mother."

Mark understood. He'd lived stuck in the dark tunnel too. Unforgiven by his family about his mom, having to keep secrets during his time as a Shadow Watcher, which wrecked any chance of a relationship with anyone—when you keep things from women, they know it and imagine all kinds of personal infractions when the secrets you hold are professional but you can't explain.

"Everything you said is true. I've been there too. But we do believe, Lisa. And, okay, we haven't had the family relationships we wanted, but we've had other relationships, and they've been good ones."

"What are you saying?"

"Let's don't throw the good out with the bad. You've had Nora and the folks at the Center. I've had my team and for a while Jane. We haven't been forgotten. That's all I'm saying."

"It just hit me." She snatched a fresh tissue from a box on a table. "You know what we are, Mark? We're fumes-of-faith Christians. We go through the motions, trying to hang on. But when you get down to it, we've got nothing more than fumes. We get the dirty work, and other Christians get favor and blessings and peace." She dabbed at her eyes. "Is it so wrong to want favor and peace for us too?"

He rubbed a little circle on her forearm. "No, it's not wrong. But we don't see the big picture. Don't glare at me like that. It's true. And I guess that's where faith really comes in. We can't see it, so we have to choose to have it or—"

"I've had faith. I want peace. I see it in Kelly and Ben and Peggy, and I want it so badly, at times I can barely breathe. But I'm not feeling it, Mark. Just more of the same—fumes and do for others. I love serving, but I'm so weary of that being all there is I can't think straight anymore."

"Stop it. Now." He was grateful the others had moved outside the waiting room door to give them even more privacy. Still, he lowered his voice to keep the conversation between them. "You don't need to think, Lisa. You need to remember."

"Remember what?"

He softened his expression. "For everything we've gone through, Annie's gone through more. Daily, Lisa. And she still believes there's a reason and purpose for every season. I believe that too. Okay, so maybe we don't know what it is. Maybe we are Christians going through the motions and hoping for more, living on fumes of faith. But maybe that's exactly what we're supposed to be doing right now."

"Why?"

"I don't know why. But the Lord does." Mark squeezed her shoulders. "Listen, if Annie can endure all she does and keep believing, then I can too. One day, all those fumes are going to come together, and then I'll have what others have. God's got a plan, and I'm going to trust Him to execute it. Will it be easy? Not for either of us. But we can handle the tough stuff. We've trained for it our whole lives."

Lisa didn't shrug his hands off her shoulders, didn't dispute him or fire back a hot retort. She stilled.

153

A long moment later, she swiped at her eyes with the soaked tissue, and her expression mellowed. "Okay. I'll try. I really will." She stepped closer, wrapped her arms around his waist, and sank against him.

"We both will." He rubbed circles on her back, planted a kiss at her crown, and prayed hard that God would spare Annie and help Lisa through this—whatever in the end this turned out to be.

Fumes of faith. Like the mustard seed.

She shuddered, her whole body quaking, then pulled back and looked up at him. "I've got to get back in there. Will you be here—?"

"I'm here for as long as you need me."

She swiped her hair back from her face and licked her lips. "I've accepted a lot in my life, and I've tried to ask only for what I had to have, never for what I've wanted. But I want something, and I'm asking you for it."

"What do you want?"

"Find him, Mark." She lifted her chin. "Find him and make him pay for doing this to my mom. This time, I need justice."

Dutch. She didn't have to say it. No good would come from mentioning Dutch might not be guilty. There would be a time for reason, but this wasn't it. Not with Lisa facing the news that her mother could die tonight. "Jeff and my team are searching for him."

"No, you find him. You're better than anyone at this."

She still had faith in him? Humbling, especially considering he'd just failed to protect her mother. "Joe and the rest of the guys and Jeff and his crew are on it. They're exceptional. My place is here with you. Dutch will be found. You have my word on it."

"Thank you." She sniffed, pressed a kiss to his cheek, then moved toward the door where everyone stood grouped in the hall. "Thanks for being here, guys."

"We're with you, Lisa," Kelly said.

"Whatever we can do." Ben patted her shoulder.

"Don't you give up on Annie, dearie. She's a fighter." Nora elbowed Clyde. "Isn't that right?"

Clyde flinched and rubbed his ribs. "That's right."

"Absolutely right," Harvey agreed, keeping his distance from Nora.

Mel snorted. "She survives the creep, she can survive this. Believe it."

"I'll hold those thoughts." Lisa's expression turned tender.

Mark felt more than saw her love for them all and how much their support meant to her. And they were right: Annie was a fighter. But even the best fighters lose sometimes and can't defeat death. Through Christ, yes, but not the physical act of dying.

God would give them the strength to handle whatever came, but Mark hoped it wasn't borderline unbearable. *We're not perfect, God, but we try to serve. Please, please let this be once when Lisa is served. She's in spiritual crisis and needs Your mercy and grace. Help her out of that dark tunnel.*

Lisa went back inside the ICU, and the big wooden doors swung closed.

Mark swallowed hard. God would do whatever He deemed best. And Mark feared that would require he and Lisa to combat Dutch's worst.

Mark dialed Joe. "What do you think?"

"I think I picked a lousy time to try to quit smoking."

Keeping one eye on the ICU door, Mark darted a glance at the others. "If Dutch did this . . ."

"Of course he did it." Peggy Crane said what was on all their minds, her chunky jewelry clanging. "He's the only one who would ever hurt a gentle soul like Annie. What we have to figure out isn't *if* but *how*—and then nail him for it."

"That's right." Kelly nodded. "The only places Annie goes without him are church, the grocery store, and to have her hair and nails done. Who there would do this to her?"

"What about brunch at the club with Miranda Kent and the church ladies?" Clyde Parker asked.

"Where have you been, man?" Nora slid Clyde

a sidelong glance. "Dutch Hauk put a stop to those outings years ago."

Peggy sniffed. "Making the victim totally dependent on the abuser is common, Clyde. Annie has no typical friends anymore."

"Maybe Dutch didn't do it. This could have been a random attack." Ben shrugged. "Sorry, Kelly, but it's true. Your attack was deliberate, and I still believe random attacks are the exception not the rule, but it is possible."

"Random doesn't work for me," Kelly shot back. "If I were in that hospital bed, it'd be because Karl Masson put me there, not because of some random act."

Kelly slid Ben a look Mark totally understood, considering her experience with Masson, NINA, and Gregory Chessman's goons. Only Masson was still on the loose. Having gone through that and fearing Masson's return every minute of every day, how could Kelly relate to a vicious personal attack like this being random?

"Okay, yes, I think Dutch did it," Ben said. "But until we can prove it, we have to keep an open mind. Otherwise, the person guilty of attacking Annie could go free."

"Logical and reasonable, but I'm with them." Harvey motioned to Kelly, Peggy, and Nora. "Dutch has been building up to something like this for a long time." Harvey leaned against the door frame. "It's way past time he paid the piper.

Annie's been his prisoner for twelve years. So has Lisa. Does anyone here deny it?"

No one did.

Mark felt like the rest of them, but his gut warned him there was more going on and Annie's incident wasn't as simple and straightforward as it seemed. "Ben's right. Odds are Dutch did this, but we need hard evidence to prove it or he'll walk. He's as slippery as a snake."

"As slimy too." Nora hitched her purse up on her folded arm. "Bless his heart." Scots but southern woman to the core; they made bluntness an art form. "All the more reason we need irrefutable proof."

"Well," Clyde said, slow and easy, rubbing his arthritic shoulder. "As Christians, we should give the man the benefit of the doubt."

Nora smiled sweetly. "The law calls for benefit of doubt, dearie. I'm opting for using the gift God gave me—common sense. Dutch did it, I'm thinking, and that's the view I'll be holding until I know I'm wrong. If I'm right and Annie survives, he'll be back to finish what he started." Nora pursed her lips. "It's safest for Annie—and I would remind you she's not able to protect herself right now and she's a Christian too."

Nora had a point, Mark conceded. "Fair, I suppose, and erring on the side of caution."

"Absolutely." Nora nodded.

He glanced from person to person, surveying

158

them all. Everyone agreed. Because they were struggling to be fair, he addressed his hunch. "What else is going on here?"

"I don't know." Ben answered first. "But something." He swung his gaze to Kelly.

"No idea, but I feel it too."

Nora faced Mark. "Karl Masson is still out there, and you can bet he ain't forgetting a thing."

Mark rubbed his neck. "Masson would come after Kelly, not Annie. He and Annie don't connect." This leap from Annie to NINA didn't make sense.

"Maybe he don't, my boy, but maybe he does," Nora said. "I think you and your spy friends need to be finding out for sure."

Surprise streaked up Mark's back, lifted the hair on his neck. "My *what?*"

"Sorry, dearie." She covered her mouth with her hand. "I meant your old team of friends. I don't know why I said that."

They all knew Mark had been assigned to Special Operations. They didn't know—couldn't know—about his Shadow Watcher assignments. And yet none of them was meeting his eyes.

How had they found out? Mark couldn't ask, and his glare at Peggy, who was most apt to have discovered the truth through unofficial channels, offered him nothing.

"Pity's sake." Flustered, Nora enlightened him. "Remember two years ago when you had the flu and that high, high fever?"

He nodded.

"The church ladies took care of you, if you'll recall."

They had for three full days. Well, the last two days Nora and Peggy had, but they were part of the church ladies auxiliary group. Again he nodded.

"When a man's half out of his mind with the fever, he says things."

The blood drained from Mark's face, and he broke out in a cold sweat. "What did I say?"

"Nothing Peggy or I would dare repeat to anyone, including you." Fire burned in Nora's eyes. "Never have, never will."

Treading on dangerous ground—anything said, he'd have to report—he turned the topic back to Annie and Dutch and Lisa. "We don't know of any connection between NINA and Annie."

Kelly frowned. "We didn't know of any connection between Susan and me either until we found one. Just because we don't know it doesn't mean a connection isn't there."

"So everyone feels there's more to what's happening here than Dutch's coming down on Annie for coming to Lisa's party."

"Oh yeah." Ben loosened his tie.

Kelly nodded emphatically.

"You bet I do, dearie," Nora said.

Clyde rubbed his neck and muttered, "I reckon so."

"Definitely." Peggy nodded to Harvey.

"Yes." He glanced at Mel.

"Duh, yeah. It's a no-brainer." She rolled her eyes. "He's a creep, but he keeps his dirty work hidden in the dark. You know, like a rat."

Abusers did typically do that. And Mark knew instinctively it was true about Dutch. The warning inside stretched and yawned, pulsed stronger. What more would be revealed? He didn't know.

But every honed instinct in his body cautioned that whatever it was, it would be really bad for Annie and Lisa.

10

Dutch sat parked on the street in front of Gregory Chessman's Seagrove Village estate, confident Karl Masson believed he was nearly to the hotel in Georgia.

Dutch had to watch. He had to see Annie get exactly what she deserved for not doing what he'd told her to do. Oh, he'd heard all about Lisa's party at Three Gables; everyone in the village was talking about it. And Miss Too-Good-For-Him Lisa hadn't invited him or her mother to attend. Taking out a restraining order against him. Ignoring her mother like that. He had heard way too much. Then that busybody Peggy Crane had called and told Annie it would mean the world to Lisa for Annie to be there, but Lisa wouldn't ask because she didn't want to cause trouble between Annie and Dutch.

Ha! All Lisa Marie Harper had ever caused between Annie and him was trouble.

And that hoity-toity center director, Peggy, sticking her nose in where it didn't belong all the time. She was just as bad as Lisa, if not worse.

He'd seen the battle going on inside Annie since Peggy called, and he knew she would crack. He'd warned her. Specifically told her not to leave the house. If she'd listened to him, she'd have been fine. But did she listen to him? *Noooo.*

That'd teach her to defy him. She got exactly what she deserved. If she lived, she lived. If she died, she died. And that snooty daughter of hers would still get what she had coming.

Dutch gripped the steering wheel and stared through the darkness up at the streetlight-silhouetted mansion.

Once Chessman had been the most respected philanthropist in all of Seagrove Village. He built a wing on the hospital, contributed to every charity within fifty miles, and he'd even stood in for the absent mayor at groundbreaking ceremonies. Then Chessman had gotten sloppy, and now he was in jail and soon to be convicted on more than thirty counts, including smuggling terrorists into the country. Even worse for him, a situation far more dangerous than treason had also been revealed: Gregory Chessman was a NINA frontman.

He and Dutch had a lot in common.

Until the truth came out, Dutch had envied Chessman. He had been respected, welcomed into all the best homes by all the best people. Dutch had been tolerated by some people in some of those homes but only after he married Annie. Before then, he hadn't been welcome anywhere in the village.

Yet that was then and this was now. And now, Dutch wanted Chessman's house.

The federal government had seized all of Chessman's assets, but some flaky Florida homestead law had the house tied up. Dutch wasn't sure exactly how all that worked, but word from his Realtor was Chessman intended to sell the place to raise money for attorney's fees. The minute the house landed on the market, Dutch's Realtor would put in an offer and let him know. Then he would own it.

And finally, after all these years, he could move out of the house that belonged to the good doctor and Annie and into the home where Dutch belonged. Oh, not the way the home was now with weeds peppering the lawn and encroaching on the cobbled sidewalk, the bushes all spiky and untrimmed, but manicured and as perfect as it had been when Chessman lived there.

If Annie survived and they lived in this house, maybe then she could respect him the way she did the good doctor. Crazy woman loved Charles

Harper more dead than she did Dutch alive. Maybe if she saw him as rich and powerful and a do-gooder—Annie liked that—then she wouldn't resent being married to him so much. Maybe he'd even go inactive with NINA, actually try being the kind of man everyone thought Chessman had been. Annie had respected Chessman, and she'd taken his fall from grace pretty hard.

Dutch stared longingly through the windshield to the estate. If he did all that, then maybe she could love him.

Someone rapped on his passenger window.

Startled, Dutch jumped.

A man in his midsixties backed up and lifted his hands. "Sorry. Didn't mean to catch you unaware."

Terrific. He'd been spotted. If Masson caught wind of this, he would have a cow. But the old man seemed harmless enough, wearing a baseball cap with the Seagrove Harbor emblem on it, jeans, and boat shoes. He was a local. Dutch could handle him. He tapped a button and the window slid down.

"You need help or something?" the man asked, his voice gruff.

"Heard the house is for sale. Just looking."

"In the dark?"

It was after eleven o'clock at night. The man had a valid point and reason to be wary. "I've seen it in the daylight. Haven't seen it in the dark." No sense lying about it. The man didn't come across as well-off enough to live here, but people dressed relaxed in Florida. You couldn't tell a thing about them by their clothes. "I've always liked it."

"Yeah, she's a beauty—or she will be once I get her whipped back into shape."

"Yours?"

"No sir. When the economy hit the skids, it took everything I had with it." The man's smile faded. "Name's Tack Grady. I had a mom-and-pop diner down by the harbor."

"Tack's." Dutch recalled the hole-in-the-wall place. A lot of local honchos met there for breakfast on weekdays.

His face brightened. "You remember it?"

"Sure. Used to come in pretty often. I wondered what happened to you."

"Lost it all when the economy tanked. Now I'm a caretaker here for the new owner." He shrugged. "It's a living."

"There's a new owner?" Dutch's heart sank. "Gregory Chessman sold the place?"

"Not exactly." Grady's disdain shone on his face. "He lost the tangle with the government. It got control about a week ago and sold it to a widow lady."

"A widow lady?" Some widow bought Dutch's dream house?

The man nodded. "She owns a lot of property around here."

The only woman who owned a lot of property in the village was in jail. "Who is she?" He couldn't be talking about—

"Darla Green. She used to be married to the mayor, before she got accused of killing him." Tack Grady crossed himself. "May the good Lord spare his soul and he rest in peace."

Darla Green. Dutch couldn't believe it. "I read about that in the paper." Why would she buy Chessman's house? *Accused* of killing Mayor Green? "I thought she was in jail for his murder?"

"She was." Tack lifted his cap, then swiped his brow with his forearm. "Turns out she didn't do anything wrong."

That was crazy. She'd killed him; Dutch and Masson had talked about it. What was going on here? "I hadn't heard."

"It hit the papers today. I've known about it for a few days because I hired on." He hooked a thumb toward the house.

"It's hard to believe she got off. Thought they'd nailed her." Dutch grunted. "You're sure about this?"

"Sure as sundown. About two weeks ago, Paul Johnson—he used to work here for Gregory Chessman—confessed. Said she was innocent all the way around and she didn't know anything. The mayor and he put the deal together, and then Johnson got rid of the mayor himself."

"Now why did he admit that?" Surely no one was foolish enough to believe Johnson. Darla was up to her eyeballs in everything, including John Green's murder. John was the innocent one. Poor slob didn't have a clue anything was going on—which is exactly what happened when a man didn't keep a tight rein on his wife.

"Johnson said prison was hard. Too much time to think. He needed to clear his conscience."

Paul Johnson had no conscience. "This is all fact—her release and buying the house?"

"Far as I know. The Realtor hired me to spiffy up the place and maintain it. Johnson's confession was on the news last night. Heard it myself."

"So Darla's been released?"

"Not yet." Tack swatted at a mosquito buzzing his face. "Paperwork. The Realtor says her lawyer's bringing her home in the morning, which is why I'm out here cleaning up the front yard tonight." He checked to make sure no one else was around.

The street was empty.

Tack stepped closer to the car. "Megan over at Ruby's Diner told me Hank's having a fit."

"Hank?"

"The coroner, Mayor Green's brother. He comes into Ruby's for coffee every morning."

"What's ticked him off? If she's innocent, you'd think he'd be glad to know it."

"They never did get along. He says there's no

way John did anything wrong; it had to be her. But what he's upset about is John's boy."

Hank was right about his brother. What was John and Darla's son's name? That's right. "Lance is in high school now, isn't he?"

"Basketball player. A good one. He don't want to go back to live with his mother, but she's insisting. Everyone down at Ruby's figures they'll end up in court."

At Lance's age, a judge wouldn't make him go with his mother if he didn't want to—well, maybe he wouldn't. Darla being deemed innocent might make the judge insist the boy give her a chance. Lance Green probably knew his mother killed his father, and she scared him out of his socks. "Sounds like he blames her for his dad's death anyway."

"I figure he must." Tack nodded. "Can't blame the boy. A grown man gets something like that in his mind and it's hard to let go. He's a kid, and I figure it's settled in."

Dutch chewed at his inner lip. "Yeah, word is Lance and John were tight."

"Oh yeah."

"Well, I hope it works out for the boy. He's been through a lot." Dutch didn't give a flying fig whether or not it worked out, but some social conventions were necessary evils. Wouldn't do to let word get out at Ruby's Diner that he didn't care, should Tack at some point recognize him.

Everyone in the village would know it by dark the same day.

So Darla Green was getting out of jail. There could only be one reason. NINA bought her out. Couldn't happen any other way. Dutch bet it cost them a fortune, so the honchos surely had a specific reason for doing it. He smiled. Whatever they had paid, it would cost Darla double. Hers would be the forever-after kind of fortune. That was NINA's way—and it served her right for buying Dutch's house out from under him.

"Glad she's been cleared," Dutch told the man. "Awful, being accused of something you didn't do."

"Frankly, most folks at Ruby's never thought she had the smarts to do what they said she'd done, so they were more surprised to hear she had than to learn now she hadn't."

She was good. Really good. Her trophy-wife persona had served her well. Even Chessman used to call her an airhead. At least, he had until he discovered she'd outwitted him. Dutch smiled. "Well, thanks for the info, Tack. Guess I can forget about the place now."

"Sure." Tack backed away. "You have a good night, er—"

Dutch thought fast. He'd be remembered if he just took off. "Mark. Mark Taylor."

Might as well set up the jerk for a little grief. He'd brought Dutch plenty.

"Night, Mark. Enjoyed talking with you."

"Same here." With a nod, Dutch drove around the circle at the base of the cul-de-sac and then headed out of the neighborhood. It was past time for him to get to Georgia.

What exactly was NINA up to with Darla Green? Dutch braked for a red light, then took Highway 331 and headed north. Maybe when he talked to Masson, he'd ask him about it.

Odds were good he knew.

They were also good he would pretend he didn't.

Either way, Dutch would find out. One way or another he was going to get that house.

If Annie was dead, he could marry Darla for it. Possible, but the woman was too independent and too crafty. He'd have to watch his back for her attacks the rest of his life.

Not interested in that, he sought another solution and found one. Maybe he'd just have her killed and buy the house off her estate. Far less messy, though he'd have to keep NINA in the dark about it. She owed them and now they owned her. She wasn't any good to them dead.

Dutch braked at a stop sign, then hung a left. That wasn't much of a problem. People taking on hits were a dime a dozen. Annie wouldn't be happy about moving, but after getting the stuffing knocked out of her, she'd do as she was told.

Provided, of course, she lived.

· · ·

Tack Grady stood at the curb outside the Chessman estate and made his call.

"Hello." Someone answered but didn't identify himself.

"Shifter," Tack said, checking up and down the street. All was calm, still. Quiet.

"Verification code?"

The person's voice was so muffled he couldn't tell for sure if it belonged to a woman or a man. He reeled off the code number.

"Go ahead."

"I need Raven."

A long moment of dead air and then a response. "Raven. Talk to me."

"The client is not in Georgia."

"Where is he?"

"As of five minutes ago, he was parked in front of the old Chessman estate."

"So the cleaner lied?" Anger deepened her voice.

"I expect the client lied to the cleaner." That remark might just save Karl Masson's life, not that he'd know it.

"Is that it?"

"Yes ma'am."

"Thank you."

The line went dead.

Soon, Tack feared, Dutch Hauk too would be dead.

· · ·

At 11:30 p.m. Dutch's phone rang.

He grabbed it from the console and then answered. "Hauk."

"I just picked up some news on the police scanner I thought you might find of interest."

Karl Masson. "What's that?"

"She's alive."

"Good." Dutch told himself it didn't matter, but his body betrayed him, quivering with relief. "I understand circumstances have changed with Chessman's house."

Masson didn't answer.

"I want to buy it."

"I'll inform the powers that be."

"I'll pay double the fair-market value."

"Why?"

"I want it." No way was he explaining his reasons to Masson. He was a thug—a high-ranking one in NINA, skilled in murder and making problems disappear, but still a thug. He'd never understand matters of the soul.

"Where are you?"

"Just crossing the tracks. State line is less than ten miles up the road." The lie rolled easily off his tongue. Across the highway, amber lights shone on the cars parked in the Seagrove Village Community Hospital's lot. Dutch glanced up at the building where light dotted the windows.

"Nearly there, then."

"Nearly. Still riding on the spare. Nothing's open where I can get the flat fixed." Dutch shifted the topic, worried Masson might pick up on background noise or something else that betrayed Dutch's true locale. "What about that other business of ours? Is it done?" He avoided using Lisa's name. Lone Wolf had lost patience with him once on that already. Wouldn't do to mess up again.

"Occurring as we speak."

"Excellent. Thanks for the update." Dutch smiled into the night and hung up the phone.

Annie would be home in no time. She'd never divorce him, but with Lisa out of the way, she'd eagerly stay put. With her weak heart, she'd have no choice. "Well, Lisa, finally you get yours." He glanced into the rearview mirror and preened a little. "Never mess with Dutch Hauk, little girl. One way or another, you lose."

In her case, for life.

11

Five beds circled the center-hub nurses' station in the Intensive Care Unit. Only one bed was occupied, and only the steady beep of Annie's heart monitor broke the still silence.

From her mother's bedside, Lisa noted Jessie standing at the hub's edge charting something. Clearly, she was still waiting for lab results and diagnostics.

Be patient, Lisa. Just be patient.

Soft light shone down on her mother and reflected off the white sheets, making her look more gaunt, her bruises a deeper purple, the swelling more disfiguring and grotesque. Her poor face was scraped from concrete and knuckled fists, her arms were twice the size they should have been, and she had a wicked bruise in her kidney area. Lisa hoped there wasn't internal bleeding associated with that, but there had to be serious organ bruising.

She glanced over at the monitor, checked her mom's respiration and oxygenation level. The numbers fell well within the normal range. The steady beep reassured her. The pressure on her mom's brain had been relieved, and there were no signs of excessive fluid. Emotion welled and overcame Lisa. The back of her throat clenched, her eyes burned. *Please, don't take her. Not now. Let me be with her just for a while. Please.*

"She okay, Dr. Harper?"

Lisa glanced back at Jessie. "Stable. Results back yet?"

"Not yet." Jessie returned to her chart.

Lisa bent low and whispered to her mother, "Mom? Mom, please wake up." Tears blurred Lisa's eyes. "If you want to live, you have to fight. Please, fight." Her voice cracked and she swallowed hard.

Nothing. No response, no reaction.

Lisa clasped her mother's hand and stroked her fingers. "I love you. It's been so hard being away from you, and I know it's been hard for you too. We both hated it, but it had to be done." Careful not to jar the clamp monitoring her oxygenation, Lisa hooked their fingers, pinkie-to-pinkie, as she had when she was little.

"Mom, please don't leave me." She let the tears flow down her cheeks unchecked. "Not when we can finally be together again." She swallowed a sob. "It—it's my fault. I should have done something else. Something faster. I shouldn't have become a doctor. It took so long. I'm sorry, Mom. I'm so sorry I didn't get you away from him right after high school. If I'd known your agreement then—"

"Dr. Harper?"

Startled by a strange and deep male voice, Lisa glared back. Two men in white lab coats stood behind her. She sniffed and swiped at her eyes. "Yes?"

The older one spoke, his balding pate shiny in the light. "I'm Dr. Edmunds and this is Dr. Powell. We're consulting on your mother's case."

Harvey must have called them. Powell was gray haired, wore glasses, and had two chins. "You've gotten the test results?" Lisa cleared her throat.

"Yes." He swiveled to Annie, then refocused on Lisa. "We need to speak with you privately."

That was never a harbinger of good news. Good

news, he would share bedside. Bad news, he didn't want her mother to hear. Lisa didn't want to hear it either, but she had no choice. "Okay." She released her mother's finger and turned for the door that led back to the waiting room. The private office for family-member consults was right beside it. She braced herself, glad Mark would be close by, and started toward the door.

"No." Powell clasped her arm, led her in the opposite direction. "This way."

"But that's a restricted area, just for doctors."

Dr. Edmunds smiled. "You have hospital privileges here now, Dr. Harper."

Being on staff at Crossroads, she did apply for and get hospital privileges. "Jessie, I'll be right back. If there's any change at all, page me."

She nodded, casting a quizzical look at the two doctors. One of them must have bathed in cologne. The sickly sweet smell was overpowering.

"I'll tell Rose. She's on her way up," Jessie said. "I'm done for the day—unless you want me to stay."

"No, you go on home." Jessie had two kids waiting for her, and the administrator already had called her in early. A lot of the staff was out with the flu. Everyone was pulling extra hours and shifts. "Tell Rose, then."

Lisa walked out into the hallway. Dr. Edmunds followed her and then Dr. Powell. The door closed and locked.

How had they gotten into the unit? She didn't have a key. As far as she knew, no one had a key to enter through the back hall. Yet to walk up on her unnoticed as they had, they couldn't have entered through the main door.

An alarm went off inside Lisa. "This is obviously going to be hard to hear. Let me run get Mark, and we'll meet you in the consult room across—"

Edmunds shoved the nose of a handgun into her side. "No, Dr. Harper. No running anywhere to get anyone."

Lisa instinctively jerked back, tried to throw her weight to bang against the door. Powell shifted, blocking her. She tried to run.

Edmunds grabbed her, spun her around. "Stop."

The warning in his eyes terrified her. She'd seen it before. In Dutch, the night she'd left home.

"One way or another, you're coming with us." Powell glared at her over the top of his glasses.

"No, I'm not." Who were these people, and what made them think she'd go anywhere with them with her mother at death's door? Where did they want her to go, anyway?

"Yes, you are."

"Edmunds, don't argue." Powell stepped forward. "Come with us without incident, and I won't kill your mother. Fight us and she dies. Make the call, Dr. Harper."

Lisa stared at him a long moment. He didn't flinch. Didn't blink. And he didn't waver.

Frantic, she searched for an alternate solution but slammed into the same dead ends. There was no way to contact Mark for help. No way out of this predicament that would end without her mother being murdered.

God, please. I don't understand. I don't understand.

But she did understand. Once again, she had been sacrificed. Yet at least this time it was for her mother.

The worst of it was in not knowing why. Who were these men? Why were they doing this? Did they even know her mother?

They know enough to be willing to kill her.

But killing her wasn't their objective. Getting Lisa to go with them was their objective. Which meant only one person could be behind this.

Dutch.

Every muscle in her body tensed. Her nemesis, of course, causing her still more challenges and trials—and this time doing it with hired gunmen. She swallowed hard. "I won't give you any trouble, provided you leave my mother alone."

"Fair enough. I'm glad to see your black belt in karate isn't choking off your sense." Powell linked arms with Lisa and they began walking.

Where were they so eager to take her? She had no idea, but it was away from her mother. That's what mattered. She'd get an opportunity to defend herself. Mark would discover she was missing and come after her, and his team would help him. Provided these thugs didn't drive to the nearest patch of woods and shoot her in the head, she had a chance of survival *if* she got them away from her mother.

How much of a chance?

Not knowing, she waited until they took the elevator down. When they stepped out into the hallway, she asked, "So are you planning on killing me or what?"

Edmunds grunted.

Powell glanced her way as they moved down the hall toward the outside exit. "That too is your choice."

A man came bolting out of the lab pushing a cart of blood vials and zoomed toward them. "Sorry."

Red hair, early twenties—Lisa didn't recognize him. Must be the new guy. *What is his name? Dan? Denny?* "No problem, Don." Maybe since she responded, he would remember seeing her later.

Edmunds spoke softly. "Another word to anyone, and you won't live to see the far end of the parking lot."

Jessie's strange look at these two flashed through Lisa's mind, and now it made sense. She had assumed Lisa summoned them. Lisa assumed Harvey brought them in on a consult.

They both had been wrong.

Lisa hoped she didn't have to pay for that mistake with her life. "I know these people. If I don't acknowledge them, they're going to think that's strange."

"Far end of the parking lot," he repeated. "Your choice."

"My choice?" She leveled a frown on Powell. "Sorry, but with your gun in my back, I don't have much of a choice about anything." She couldn't let them get her into a car. If she did, odds were astronomical that she'd end up dead.

"I suppose you don't." He shoved a hand into his pocket. "How's this? Unless you get out of hand, you will live. The plan isn't to kill you, Lisa."

Truth or lie? Powell's body language said he was telling her the truth, but Harvey and Peggy were better at spotting liars than Lisa. Should she trust her own judgment? "What is the plan?"

"I have no idea. I only know we're not to kill you unless you're uncooperative."

"What does that mean? You're passing me off to someone else?"

They stepped outside, into the inky black night. A white box truck pulled up to the curb and stopped. The driver jumped out and opened the back end.

Her heart beat hard and fast. *Oh no. No. Three of them?* There was no way— and they'd brought the vehicle to her. No chance to lose them in the parking lot.

Powell grabbed Lisa's arm, dragged her in that direction.

"I am not getting in that truck!" *God, help me. Please, help me. Don't leave me in this tunnel.* "Let go of me." She screamed and kept screaming.

They tussled and Powell grabbed her left arm. She spun and popped him hard in the knee. He doubled over, dropped down. Lisa broke free, turned to run for it—and rushed straight into Edmunds's flying fist.

Pain exploded in her jaw, radiated down her neck and up her face to her eye. Reeling, she fought to regain her balance. He slammed the butt of the gun against her skull. Stars floated in white spots before her eyes. She rocked and swayed and went down on one knee.

All three men attacked full force. *Too fast. Too fast. Too many of them.* She couldn't fight them all at once. Her only option was flight. She had to somehow get away.

Looking for an opening, she saw the glimmer of one and prepared, but Edmunds feinted left and landed a solid punch to her stomach. It took her breath away. All three moved in close. She folded over, head spinning, staggering, totally unable to defend against the constant barrage.

Edmunds grabbed the back of her dress, jerked her off her feet, and tossed her into the truck.

She landed with a hard thud against the wooden subfloor.

Pain pounded through her body; she fought to stay conscious. *Don't black out. If they close that door, your odds of surviving are cut in half.*

In her mind she sang the 4-H song. Bizarre; she'd never been a member of 4-H. But she started singing it when her mom told her that her dad had died, and ever since, when hyperstressed, she went back to it.

She slid over the plywood truck bed on her stomach, too weak to lift herself. The door was too far away.

The man who'd jumped out of the truck slapped a metal cuff on her wrist and snapped it shut. "Got her."

She collapsed and stared at it. A computer chip? What was that thing? Fear proved stronger than her leaden arms. She shoved and rolled toward the door. The man who had cuffed her jumped out and grabbed the left door.

Too late. She rolled right, thrust toward the opening. The hinges creaked, and a rush of air whistled past. The door smacked against her shoulder, and she fell onto her back.

It slammed shut.

The sound reverberated, echoed inside the truck, inside the chambers of her mind. Darkness and still air settled over her. Lisa stared sightlessly, helpless and hopeless.

Click.

A lock slid into place.

Once again she'd been forgotten in a dark tunnel. And this time, she was as good as dead.

Across the parking lot, Karl Masson watched the scuffle.

Lisa Harper couldn't win, fighting three men at once. But a flicker of admiration lit in him; she had given it her all.

Fortunately for Karl and his men, her all wasn't enough.

He waited until the driver got back into the truck and Powell and Edmunds—not their real names, of course, but NINA friendlies all the same—got into their car. The truck left the lot with the docs following behind. Karl hung back and brought up the rear.

When the truck turned onto Highway 98 and headed west, he gave the signal to the docs, flashing his lights.

At the next intersection, they turned right and headed north. He'd pulled them in via New Orleans, but where they were from, he had no idea. NINA friendlies never relayed non-mission-essential information.

At the edge of the village, the truck disappeared around a curve. It was in the clear. Karl's breathing slowed. Now he could take a break long enough to attend to a piece of private business.

He should phone Dutch and let him know that Lisa was on her way to the future he'd bought for her. But he could wait. Going after strangers was one thing, but your own wife and her kid, especially when the kid had left you alone for years? That was just weak. Lisa had showed more strength in fighting off her abductors than Hauk had in anything. Besides that, he'd lied to Karl, and for that, he'd have to pay.

In due time.

His phone chirped.

Karl answered it. "Hello."

"Is my shipment on schedule?"

Raven. "Yes ma'am."

"Excellent."

The line went dead.

Karl closed his phone. Not much spooked him. He'd been in this business too long. But every time he spoke to Raven, he got knots in his stomach and every nerve ending in his body went on alert.

Of all the people he'd had contact with at NINA, she was hands-down the one you never wanted to disappoint.

She tolerated no errors. Accepted no excuses. And with her everything held the urgency of a detonating nuke.

Fail, and you only failed once.

The Crossroads folks had settled inside the ICU waiting room. Clyde sat listing in a corner chair, dozing, with Nora beside him. Ben and Kelly were on a small sofa, whispering softly, and Peggy sat across from them in a wing chair, nodding off, jerking awake, then nodding off again.

Everyone had been running full out all day preparing for the party, and now it was nearly midnight. Exhaustion had set in.

At the door, Mark stared across the hallway past the nurses' station to the heavy wooden ICU doors.

Harvey, who had ditched his tie and put on his lab coat, walked over. All the center docs had hospital privileges at Seagrove Village Community. "You okay?"

"Fine." Mark didn't shrink away. "It's just that she's been back there a long time."

"Lisa hasn't seen her mother up close since she was sixteen, and she's terrified she's going to lose her. She probably won't surface until Annie's able to walk out of ICU on her own."

"I don't know, Harvey." Mark hated to give his fears voice, but this one was pulsing through him like blood courses through veins. "Something feels strange."

Harvey clasped Mark's shoulder. "Being anxious is normal. Annie's just been the victim of a violent crime."

It wasn't that. It was Lisa. Inside, he felt her screaming. And inside, she probably was. Her mother was clinging to life by a thread; of course she was screaming.

185

Rose walked up the hallway, heading toward the unit. "You guys need anything?"

"We're fine," Mark said. "I thought you and Jessie were headed home."

"Short-handed. Flu's sweeping through the village, and the hospital's been hit hard. Everyone able-bodied has been called in or is staying over."

Mark nodded. "How is Annie? Is Lisa holding up?"

"I've been down in the ER, so I'm not sure. But I'm relieving Jessie now. She'll be out in a second, and you can ask her."

"Thanks, Rose."

"Sure." She smiled and then disappeared behind the doors.

Minutes later, Jessie came out, dragging her feet, weary and haggard.

Mark stepped into her path. "How are they?"

"Annie's hanging on. No significant change, but that's good news. The longer she's stable, the better."

"And Lisa?"

"Sad, crying, scared—everything you'd expect." Jessie looked next door to the family-member consult room. It was dark and empty, and she frowned. "I thought she'd be here and you'd be with her."

"What do you mean?" Mark asked.

"She went out the back door—"

"Back door?" Mark's voice elevated, startling

Clyde awake. "You said there was only one door."

"There is, for general use. The one in back is 'doctors only.'"

Great. Just great. "Why did she go out it?"

"To talk to those doctors she called in to consult."

Fear burst in Mark. Ben jumped to his feet. Everyone stood and Harvey shot forward. "No one called in any consults."

Jessie seemed baffled. "There were two doctors, Powell and Edmunds. They evaluated Annie, checked her chart, and went over their findings out back. Lisa came in, and a few minutes later, they returned and asked her to step out back to talk. That was the last I saw of them."

The Crossroads group gasped and grumbled.

"When was that?" Mark couldn't believe what he was hearing. "How long ago, Jessie?"

"About half an hour—maybe a little more. I was about to leave, but Rose got tied up downstairs, so there was a delay. Yeah, probably forty-five minutes or so."

Everyone started talking at once.

"Stop." Mark raised his voice, turned, and held up his hands. "Peggy, get in touch with my team. Tell them what's happened." He rounded on Ben, who was dialing his phone.

"Detective Meyers," Ben said.

Mark nodded. "Harvey, check with everybody in the building and see if anyone saw Lisa or the men she was with. Mel, help him." He swiveled his gaze to the nurse. "Jessie, write down clear descriptions of Powell and Edmunds. Detailed and specific, as close as you can get."

"Mark, don't you think you might be overreacting?" Kelly asked. "Jessie knows Dutch. It wasn't Dutch, was it, Jessie?"

"No, it wasn't Dutch."

Nora stepped forward and told Harvey, "Check the building, dearie—now."

"Page her," Jessie said. "Lisa told me if there was any change to page her, so she's got her pager with her."

He hadn't seen a pager or a cell, but Mark jumped on it. "Do it—and call security and issue a code. Lock down the facility, Jessie. No one comes or goes without a security check."

"I can't do that. It's premature." She shrugged. "They might just have gone down to the cafeteria for coffee."

"Do it or I'll pull a fire alarm." Something was wrong. Mark knew it—just as he knew now was too late; she wasn't here anymore.

Pain shattered inside him. Fear rode hard on its heels. He stiffened, clenching and unclenching his fist at his side. "Peggy, when my team gets here, tell them to review the security tapes. I want every corner checked and everyone quizzed. Someone had to see something—and get Beth Dawson over here. See if she can figure out how they got into the hospital's security system." They had to breach it to pull this.

Peggy nodded. "Calling her now."

"Don't just stand there, Jessie." Mark motioned with a swinging hand. "Move. Call the code."

"Okay." She started toward a phone hanging on the wall. "But tell me why I'm doing this before we even check the building? Because that's the first thing security will ask me, and I don't have a good answer."

Mark fought panic, buried the guilt and regret and shame swamping him. Still, he was shaking so hard he could barely speak. "Because unless every instinct in my body is dead wrong, Lisa has just been abducted."

12

The waitress plunked down a steaming mug of coffee.

Karl reached for it, spinning the steaming mug around to grab its handle. Just as he lifted it to his mouth, his cell phone rang. He checked caller ID. *Dutch.* The man was a nuisance.

"Hey." Karl crooked a finger, summoning the waitress. "Can you put this in a to-go cup for me?"

"Sure can." She spared him a smile.

He answered the call. "Hold on."

Dropping the money to cover his bill on the counter, he took the cardboard cup from the waitress, nodded his thanks, and then made his way out to his car.

Safely inside, he set the cup into a cup holder and went back to the phone. "You there?"

"Yeah."

"Where are you?"

"Waiting for the flat to be fixed. The spare's shot."

Lying. Again.

"I still haven't heard from the hospital."

"You probably won't for a while." Karl spotted the I-10 sign. Two eighteen-wheelers pulled into the roadside café and parked. "They're pretty busy right now." Taylor would reason his way out of checking on Lisa for a time, but by now that time surely had expired and he had everyone in the place hopping to find out what happened to her.

"So the cargo is in tow, then?"

"Yes." Karl sipped the hot coffee. "An associate handled the hotel. You're in room 222. Key's under the mat—there wasn't a fire extinguisher close by. Your alibi is in place."

"What about the patient?"

"ICU. In a coma."

"She's in a coma?" Dutch shouted, then lowered his voice. "Tell me I'm not going to be stuck taking care of a vegetable."

"Out of my control. She hit her head on a concrete marker."

"I can't believe it." A pause, then Dutch added, "So is she going to recover or die?"

That was the best he could muster for someone he loved? Karl had run into some cold ones, but Dutch Hauk put them all to shame. "Too soon to tell."

"When will they know?"

Karl's patience snapped. "How should I know?"

"Well, can't you have somebody ask?"

"Think about it. That would be a serious tactical error. I don't make tactical errors." Karl took another sip of coffee. Man, he hated dealing with amateurs—especially ones who considered themselves professionals. "In light of this unexpected development, do you want to cancel the cargo portion on your contract? If the patient survives and she is a vegetable, someone needs to take care of her. Or do you plan to do that yourself?" That was the best Karl could do to give Lisa Harper a fighting chance. With this moron she deserved one. Besides, Angel would have liked it.

"No way. The patient either fully recovers or dies."

"So it's full-steam ahead?"

"Absolutely." Dutch grumbled. "I didn't pay for a vegetable, and I am not dealing with a vegetable."

"Hope she makes it, then."

"Why?"

"I like her." Annie hadn't known Karl, but she had welcomed him into her home as Dutch's guest with dignity and grace. She reminded him so much of Angel. His heart squeezed. How long would it take to stop missing her? Likely a lifetime. If she'd just had a chance . . .

"The cargo shipment is not about Annie. It's about that sniveling brat of hers. She's a problem, she's always been a problem, and I'm going to stop her from ever being *my* problem again."

What the man was doing to Annie was bad, but what he was doing to Lisa . . . He didn't just resent the girl, he hated her. "If your wife recovers, what's happening to her daughter will kill her figuratively, if not literally. But of course you realize that."

No answer.

"If you didn't, you might consider your actions a little shortsighted. Just something to think about."

"Keep your advice and just do your job. I'll handle my wife and her daughter."

Karl thumbed the black plastic tab to seal his cup. Its snap echoed through the car. "Very well." He lifted his hand and studied the spiderweb tattoo between his forefinger and thumb. "But don't say you weren't warned."

Mark, Harvey, Joe, and Grant Thurman, the fiftyish, potbellied head of hospital security, huddled in Thurman's office, waiting for him to get off the phone with Jeff Meyers.

Mark took the opportunity to confer with Joe. "Where are we?"

Joe dropped his voice. "Tim is on point at Annie's bedside. Nick is running a third review on the security tapes. Harvey's interviewing employees. Kelly's talking with folks down in the ER who might have seen something, and Mel's working the owners of all the cars parked in the lot. Sam, Ben, and Clyde coordinated with Meyers and are working Annie's assault, talking to potential witnesses, her neighbors, and Dutch's store employees. Basically, they're scouting for anyone who might have seen or knows something about the attack. Nora and Peggy are calling in volunteer reinforcements and people from church to help canvass the condos, restaurants, and the marina—everything facing Highway 98 where people might have seen something. Beth Dawson and her partner, Sara, are working on the security breach from the center."

"How's she checking the hospital computers from there?"

"Thurman gave her clearance and a remote-access code."

"Good." Mark let Joe see his worry. "They're working the assault. We need to focus on Lisa."

Joe gave Mark a level look. "They're connected. We have to work them both, bro. Yeah, Lisa's position is unknown and Annie's here getting care, but one of those connecting threads could be *the* one we need to find Lisa."

"You're right." Mark sank his teeth into his lower lip. "It's just—"

"You love her and you're freaking out."

Mark blinked, then blinked again. "It's my fault, Joe." *Just like Jane.*

"You got faulty intel on the doors."

"I should have checked myself."

"You can't be all and do all. That's not fair, bro. Look, you know the drill. We control what we can, knowing we can't control everything."

Mark nodded.

Thurman hung up the phone and turned to Mark. "Jeff's put out an APB on Dutch and his car."

That could easily be justified by Annie's condition. Anything related to Lisa would require special authorization. Without some evidence of foul play, she couldn't be designated as a missing person for forty-eight hours.

"We haven't found anything on the tapes," Grant Thurman said. "One minute Lisa was inside the unit, the next she was gone. Your man and mine are going over them again, just to be sure nothing was missed."

If there was anything to find, Nick would find it. "Is the camera covering that hallway functioning?"

"We thought it was, but it turned out to be a loop. The lens was destroyed."

Mark glanced at Joe. He returned it with the same certainty in his eyes Mark felt down to his bones.

"That's evidence of foul play, isn't it?" Harvey asked Thurman.

"Against the camera but not against Lisa."

Harvey frowned. "What is it, Mark?"

He hated thinking it, much less saying it aloud, but truth was truth. "Dutch didn't do this—well, he might have paid for it to be done, but he didn't execute it. It's obvious the two doctors were complicit in getting Lisa out of the hospital."

Harvey shrugged. "Anyone who's ever watched a crime show can destroy a camera, even Dutch."

"Yeah, but not everyone can hack into the hospital's security system and upload a film loop."

"Joe's right," Mark said. "Powell and Edmunds are professionals."

Thurman lifted a hand. "They don't have privileges to practice here, and we can't find anything in the directory on them being on staff or having privileges anywhere else in the area either."

Definitely professionals and apparently not doctors. "Are Edmunds and Powell working directly for Dutch, or is this part of something bigger?"

"Bigger?" Thurman looked at Mark, who nodded.

Understanding passed between them. "We'd better get Jessie busy viewing photos." Thurman clearly knew Mark's Special Operations past and knew or intuited it was time to stop asking questions.

"After she gets her descriptions down. We don't want to muddy her memory." Jeff Meyers would agree on that. "Grant," Mark said to Thurman. "How did these two clowns get into your ICU as docs?"

"They said Lisa called them to consult on Annie."

"That's all it took?" Surely not. That would be beyond bizarre in a post-9/11 world.

"Yeah." Thurman flushed. "Believe it or not, we don't have problems like this. There was no reason to doubt them, especially with Dr. Harper having privileges here. It wasn't logical that they'd be here under false pretenses."

"Well, they were, so you'd better develop a different policy." Heat flooded Joe's voice. "You've got this kind of problem now, and the media is going to chew you up and spit you out for a week on it—and that's *if* Lisa is found safe. If not, you might want to spruce up your résumé."

Thurman took exception to that comment, and he and Joe barked back and forth.

Mark ignored them and prayed Lisa would be found safe. *She's accomplished at self-defense. She's sharp. She's determined. She's a survivor.*

She'll do something to help us help her. Somehow, she'll do something.

In the meantime, Mark would keep looking. He walked out of Thurman's office.

Harvey came up behind him. "While they're arguing, I'm going back downstairs to continue interviewing employees."

"Good idea. I'll walk down with you." Mark interrupted the argument. "Joe, I'm going to take a look at the parking lot."

He acknowledged with a quick nod, then lit into Thurman again. Mark should have put a stop to it, but the truth was, Thurman had it coming, and as pointed as Joe was being, he was calm and cool. Mark wasn't.

Harvey and he took the stairs down and then entered the corridor. "I have a whole new empathy for what Ben went through, not knowing who was behind the incident with Susan. All the possibilities that keep running through my mind— they're making me crazy."

Harvey looked over, the tail of his lab coat lifting behind him. "But remember that Lisa isn't Susan. This is a different situation, and Lisa's trained in defense. She'll find a way."

"I'm counting on it." *And praying harder than I've ever prayed in my life.*

"If you hear anything—"

"I'll let you know right away."

At the cafeteria, Harvey peeled off.

Mark kept walking, went out the sliding door, and then turned right. Most people automatically turned right on entering or leaving someplace.

He glanced at his watch. One in the morning. Crisp and dark, except for the amber light cast from tall streetlights in the lot and lining the sidewalk. He scoured the concrete. Found loose gravel, two old cigarette butts, a scrap of paper with tire-tread marks on it, and a wad of chewing gum. He turned back, passed the door, then walked down the left. Nothing.

Frustrated, he trotted over to his SUV, grabbed a flashlight, and then rechecked the sidewalk.

Nothing.

Went back to the right of the door.

Again nothing.

Sinking deeper and deeper into despair, he swung the light and turned for the door. This was a waste of time and ener— The beam fanned onto the street and something glinted. Mark stopped.

He stepped off the sidewalk and bent down for a closer look. A ring.

Lisa's ring. Actually, her mother's thin gold band from her marriage to Charles. Lisa always wore it. To take it off her finger, she had to be desperate.

Chills swam up and down Mark's torso. He examined the pavement. Black scuff marks discolored the concrete. Etched lines—drag marks from her high heels. And a scrap of pale blue fabric. God help him. It was the same color and fabric as Lisa's gown.

A pager rested near the curb. Jessie's words echoed through his mind. Lisa had said to page her.

His worst fears confirmed, he whipped out his phone and conference called Jeff and Joe. "I need forensics in the main parking lot."

"What did you find?" Jeff asked.

Mark squeezed his eyes shut, hating the words he was forced to say. "Proof that Lisa was abducted."

Dutch drove slowly past the Stateline Hotel's office door. In the window beside it hung a paper flier. He stopped to read it. Lost puppy. Mixed breed. Call Nina . . .

Smiling, he drove on. It paid to do business with friends.

Five minutes later, he lifted the edge of the mat outside his door and spotted the key. Masson might be an interfering, opinionated jerk, but he was a gifted cleaner and had made good on his word.

Inside, the place smelled musty and moldy. Annie would never put up with that; she kept a fine house, even if he hated living in it. Twitching his nose, Dutch turned down the thermostat, forcing the air conditioner on to blow out the stench. He messed up the bedding, tossed a couple of potato-chip bags he'd brought with him into the trash can, then snagged a soda from the minibar. Walking into the shoebox-size bath, he poured the drink down the sink, dumped the can into the trash, and messed up three towels washing his hands. Leaving on the light, he returned to the bed area. A few more minutes' work, and the room appeared as if he'd been in it for hours.

Satisfied, he grabbed the remote and clicked on the television, and then he waited. The hospital had been calling about every fifteen minutes for the past hour. He checked the clock; 1:35 a.m. shone on its face in bold, red numerals. Still had a few minutes to go before they called again.

After dropping onto the bed, he cranked back on the pillows and closed his eyes. A catnap wouldn't hurt. It'd be a good thing to sound as if he'd just awakened.

He slept like the dead.

The blasting-horn ringtone he'd installed startled him. Dutch sat straight up, grabbed his phone from the nightstand between the two double beds, then fumbled it open. "Yeah." His voice was thick with sleep. He rubbed at his eyes to clear the blur and checked the clock. Two o'clock, straight up. He must have slept through the 1:45 attempt to call.

"Mr. Hauk?" a woman asked.

"Yeah." He cleared the fog from his throat. "This is Dutch Hauk."

"This is Rose Paxton. I'm an RN over at Seagrove Village Community Hospital."

"Yes?" *She would be the one to call.* He bit down on frustration and rolled out of bed ready to go. Leaving the room lights on to signal a hasty departure, he walked out and let the door slam shut behind him.

"I'm afraid that your wife is with us. She's in our Intensive Care Unit."

"Why? Who is she visiting?" *Nice touch—to not assume she was a patient.* He took the elevator down, stared up into the security camera mounted in the corner of the ceiling. *There's your proof I was here.*

"She isn't visiting anyone, sir. I'm afraid she's our patient."

"Annie?" *Good job on the shock. Played just right.* "What for? She was fine when I left home this morning."

"She was assaulted. The police found her on Highway 98." Regret laced the nurse's tone. "Mr. Hauk, you need to know your wife is in critical condition. We've been trying to reach you for hours."

"I—I'm in Georgia on business. I guess I've been out of range." *Nice touch.* "Annie's critical? What's wrong with her?"

"She has a lot of cuts and bruises and some serious internal swelling, but as far as we can tell, she's not bleeding internally."

"That doesn't sound critical."

"I'm sorry, sir. It's been a bit hectic. Your wife suffered a blunt-force trauma to the head," Rose said. "She's in a coma."

Outside now, Dutch rushed his steps to the office door, opened it wide, and hurried inside. "Just a second, please."

A droopy-eyed clerk appeared from a door behind the desk, wearing a tattered sweater and his glasses parked up on his forehead. Rather than wait for him to ask what Dutch wanted, he said in an urgent rush, "I'm checking out. Here's my key. It's an emergency. My wife has been attacked. She's critical."

"I'm so sorry, sir."

Before the clerk could shove paperwork at him, Dutch headed out the door and returned to the nurse on the phone. "Like I said, I'm in Georgia, but I'll be there as soon as I can. Is Lisa with her? She's her daughter—a doctor there." Rose Paxton knew that, of course. She'd known all the Harpers for years. *Couldn't resist a little jab, pretending not to know you, Rose.*

"Not at the moment." Rose hesitated. "But some of your wife's friends are here."

"What friends?" Annie didn't have any friends. Not anymore. Was she slipping around with Miranda Kent and her church cronies too?

"People from her church and Crossroads Crisis Center."

"But Lisa is not there?" Was Rose going to tell him anything about Lisa or not?

"No sir."

Apparently not. "Well, has she been called?"

"She was notified, yes."

Cagey. "Typical." He heaved a sigh. "Well, if she shows up there, you keep her away from my wife. Annie doesn't want to see her. You got that?" Dutch said what he'd be expected to say, folded himself into his car, and then cranked the engine.

"I've got it." Rose paused. "I'm sorry to bring you bad news, but I have to get back to my patient."

Nothing more on Lisa coming from that end. Was that hospital policy or Taylor putting a lid on it? "It'll take me a couple of hours to get there." Dutch pulled onto the highway and hit the gas. "Please, take care of my wife."

"We'll do our best, Mr. Hauk."

Dutch felt sure they would. Tight-mouthed Rose Paxton had been Charles's nurse when he was practicing. She'd take it personally to let his wife die from anything but natural causes.

Even now, he couldn't wrench Annie away from Charles Harper or her past.

Muttering, Dutch dodged a pothole. Well, maybe he couldn't. But he'd sure gotten Lisa.

Content with that and with knowing Masson wouldn't leave Dutch stuck with a vegetable, he leaned back in his seat and let his tires eat up the miles.

13

A breathless Rose rushed to the entrance of the ICU waiting room and leaned hard against the doorframe. "Dutch is in Georgia."

Consulting with Ben and Kelly, Mark glanced over. "You're sure?"

"Relatively sure. I guess it could be faked, but he told someone on his end of the phone that he needed to check out, and from the sounds, I got the impression he was at a hotel. Didn't sound like a store. I heard the other man's voice too."

Mark processed that in context. Everyone was reporting in and impatiently waiting for Jeff and his forensics guy to finish up in the parking lot. Sam was assisting since that was his area of expertise. If anything else was out there, Sam would find it. He had a better nose than a bloodhound when it came to sniffing out evidence.

"Where's Joe?" Mark sought him but didn't find him.

"He's tracking the call."

Surprised Rose had been the one to answer him, Mark focused back on her.

"He set up a tracer, and then we kept calling Dutch until I finally got him. He said he'd report in as soon as he's verified Dutch's location."

"It'll be in Georgia." Mark had no doubt about that. Establishing his alibi was the intent of the trip, removing him as a suspect or a person of interest. Had to be.

"So he didn't do this to Annie?" Kelly smoothed her hair back from her face.

"I think he had it done." Mark should probably reserve his opinion, but Lisa was missing. The sooner people structured their thinking in the right direction with that in the equation, the sooner they might make the connection needed to find her. "The evidence is leading us in that direction."

"Professionals?" Rose shot an incredulous gaze to Mark. "Targeting Annie Harper, er, Hauk?"

Annie and Lisa. A paid hit? Or something else? Mark didn't know, not definitively—yet. His instincts were buzzing, yet lacking concrete proof gave him no choice but to hedge. "After Sam's reviewed the evidence, we'll have a firmer grip."

Harvey walked into the waiting room with a red-headed man in his early twenties wearing black scrubs and a white jacket. His eyes stretched wide, and his pockets bulged with medical paraphernalia. The end of a tubing band dangled from the left one.

Everyone fell quiet.

"Mark, this is Don Barnes. He's a tech down in the lab and he saw Lisa—"

"I don't know for fact it was her," Don cut in, "but I did see a woman walking out with two docs. She greeted me by name—that's why I remember her. I'm new here. Not many know me."

"Describe her," Mark said.

"Pretty blonde, wearing a fancy blue dress. The men might not have been docs, but they had on white lab coats like Dr. Talbot's."

Mark whipped out his wallet, then flashed it open. "Is this her?"

"Yeah." Don checked again. "That's her, all right."

"So you saw Lisa leave with two men in white lab coats?"

"Yes sir. Well, not exactly. They were headed toward the exit together. I didn't see where they actually went." He backed up a step. "But they fit the descriptions of the men Dr. Talbot gave me."

"I had to describe them, Mark. The cameras didn't pick up pictures of them anywhere in the hospital." Harvey frowned, then shrugged. "Wise of you to get Rose's descriptions down. She nailed these two all the way to the tattoo on Edmunds's hand."

"I definitely saw that," Don told Mark. "It was a spiderweb." He stretched his fingers and pointed to the fleshy part on his hand between his thumb and forefinger. "Right there."

"That's right." *What doc had a spiderweb tattoo on his hand?* "Was Lisa fighting them?"

"To tell you the truth, I was running and just caught a glimpse of her. But the men weren't hauling her out kicking and screaming or anything. She was walking between them. They were moving close together. With her calling me by name, I figured they were all staffers. Like I said, I'm new and nobody knows me. I just moved to Seagrove Village from Fairhope."

Word of someone new on staff passed down the grapevine fast. Of greater interest was that the men walked closely on each side of Lisa. "Thurman," Mark told the head of hospital security, "if they were close and she wasn't fighting them, then they had a gun on her. You've got a problem there too."

"They got a gun into the hospital?" Grant Thurman lifted his hands. "How?"

Joe entered the waiting room. "Well, since you didn't check them because they were supposed to be doctors, I expect they just walked in your door armed." His voice carried heat, threatening to rekindle their earlier argument.

Thurman swiped at his brow. "We blew it, okay, Joe? I admit it. We've never had any trouble here or any reason to expect any and—"

"You got lazy." Joe jabbed the air with a pointed forefinger. "Well, Lisa's paying for that, and you've got plenty of trouble here now."

"Yeah, we do. I'm taking responsibility, okay? You can't make me feel any worse than I already do." Thurman blew out a long breath. "And I'm sure the board isn't going to like it either."

"You can bet on that." Joe folded his arms across his chest.

Kelly whispered something to Ben. Now why was she panicking? It was written all over her face. "I don't like it either," Mark said.

"A gun?" Don frowned, wrinkling the smooth skin on his freckled forehead. "Whoa. I didn't say that. I didn't see a gun." He jabbed a pen back into his pocket, thumbed its clicker repeatedly. "She didn't look scared. If anything, she looked ticked off."

"She would be." Mark shared a look with Joe, who silently agreed.

"I didn't think a thing about it," Don said, "until Dr. Talbot said you guys were looking for her."

Nora brought over a photo of Annie and Dutch and showed it to Don. "Was this one of the two men, dearie?"

"No ma'am." Don checked again, then shook his head. "Definitely not. Never seen that one before."

"Ben, stop shushing me. I'm not being paranoid; I'm being cautious—and I am going to ask him." Kelly fished a packet of photos out of her purse, sifted through, pulled one apart from the stack, then showed it to Don. "Was this man one of them?"

Mark guessed who was in the photo before Don flipped it around and looked. It was a snapshot of the artist's rendition, all right. Karl Masson.

Masson wanted Kelly dead because she could

tie him directly to Gregory Chessman and Paul Johnson, crimes bringing terrorists into the U.S.—NINA crimes. She had good cause to be afraid—they'd nearly killed her several times—and to carry Masson's sketch in her purse for identification purposes. Kelly lived every day of her life with the fear of knowing he'd be back for her. So did Ben. And so did Mark.

"No, that's not him." Don's eyes darted back and forth rapidly, as if he was trying to slot something in his mind.

Ben sighed. "I told you so."

"You did, dear. And now I can forget about it." Clearly relieved, Kelly reached for the photograph.

Don held on to it. "Wait a minute." His rapid eye movement stopped. "I saw this guy."

"Oh no." Kelly tensed.

"Where?" Mark asked. "When?"

"A few hours ago—before Dr. Harper went missing. I was coming in from a break, and he was in the parking lot, sitting in his car. He might have been on the phone. I can't remember for sure. But it was him. I'm sure of that."

Kelly gasped. "Oh, Ben. He's back."

Ben circled her with a protective arm. "Why would Masson be sitting in the parking lot here, Mark?"

Good question. Why would he show up here on the very night during the very time Lisa was being abducted? There was an unfortunate and obvious reason, and it chilled Mark to the bone. "NINA has Lisa."

"Why? She can't identify any of them." Kelly groaned. "Oh no. Oh, please tell me they didn't make a mistake and grab her instead of me." Tears spilled down Kelly's face. "I can't be the reason for another woman being—"

"They didn't get her by mistake, Kelly," Mark reassured her. "Getting Lisa was the goal. Annie was the bait to get her here so they could snatch her." Away from Three Gables and its topnotch security to a place where she was vulnerable.

And their plan had succeeded.

Harvey's expression went from worried to terrified. "Why? What will they do with her? She's not a threat to NINA."

"I don't know." A sinking feeling settled in Mark. How could he help her when he had no idea why they'd taken her? His own worry reflected in Joe's eyes. "I just don't know."

Joe signaled Mark over, and he stepped away from the others. "What?"

"What's the plan, bro?"

"Developing. She'll contact me here. That much I know."

"So you'll be staying put."

Mark nodded. No way would he be anywhere else. Lisa would look here first. He'd be here.

Lisa was not going to be another Jane.

• • •

"Wake up." A woman tapped Lisa's face.

"Don't hit her. She's banged up enough."

A different voice, another woman. Jarring. Bouncing. The steady hum of tires on the road. She was riding—the truck. She'd been abducted.

Lisa struggled to open her eyes.

Two women sat on the plywood truck bed looking at her.

"Why is there light?" Lisa looked around. There were no windows, just big doors that had been locked.

"My mini-Mag," the first woman said. She was a redhead. Pretty and petite. "I hate the dark. Everyone laughed at me for stuffing a mini in my, er—next to my heart in my clothes—but I'm glad I did or we'd be in a blackout right now."

"Who are you?" Lisa's jaw throbbed. She touched it, her fingers trembling. Swollen.

"Gwen Baker," the redhead told her. "And this is Selene Gray."

"*The* Selene Gray? The singer?" She was a superstar.

"Yes, I sing." She shifted her weight to give Lisa room to sit up. "Or I did. I just canceled my contract."

"Which is probably why you're here." Gwen deflected the light so it wasn't shining in anyone's eyes.

"Indirectly, maybe. My manager loves money

and he was very upset. If I'm no longer alive, my work is very valuable, and I fear I did a stupid thing."

"What?" Lisa asked.

"I have no family, so I made my manager my beneficiary. If I don't sign the contract, my manager loses about a million dollars. If I'm dead, he inherits about ten million and the rights on all my music."

"But why sell you?" Gwen asked. "Why not just take out a contract on you?"

"Sell you?" Shock rippled through Lisa, but the other women ignored her and kept talking.

"Death benefits pay double in specific circumstances and refuse to pay in others," Selene said. "He has a special kind of murder in mind, I'd say. One that gives him the most benefits he can get."

"That's creepy." Gwen shivered.

"He is a creepy man. But until now, also a very effective manager." Selene looked at Lisa. "You're pretty messed up. Do you think anything's broken?"

"Explain this 'selling you' thing."

"In a moment. We've got time. Let's see if you're okay."

Lisa pulled herself up. Checked her limbs, her torso, frowning at that stupid cuff, and then her face. "Just my pride." Pain shot through her shoulder and she winced. "My name's Lisa, I'm a doctor, and I teach self-defense at a crisis center." Embarrassing how fast she'd fallen. Humiliating.

"Honey, with three men pounding on you, you need a Glock or an army to stop them."

Lisa had little choice but to agree with Gwen on that. "You said sell. Why are we here? What's going on?"

Dark and exotic, Selene lifted a hand. "I was shopping at a mall in Tampa, just about to get into my car. Next thing I know, these three goons grab me and shove me into this nasty truck. I would so love some fresh air."

"Me too." Lisa looked at Gwen. "What about you?"

"Pumping gas at a station in Tallahassee. You?"

"Visiting my mother in ICU."

Selene's jaw dropped open. "They snatched you out of ICU?"

"I had a choice. I could walk out with them or they'd kill my mother. I have a black belt. The goons had a gun."

"That's Draconian." Selene pressed a hand to her chest. "Is your mother . . . ?"

"She's critical." Tears welled. Lisa choked them down. "I hadn't seen her in a long, long time." She shivered. "Stepfather situation."

"Enough said." Selene paused. "No sense torturing yourself. Is she really sick?"

"She doesn't have a disease, but she does have a

weak heart. Her doctor told me to prepare. She's likely to die tonight."

"Oh no. And you're not there." Selene's voice went husky. "I'm so sorry, Lisa."

So was she.

"If she's not sick," Gwen asked, "why is she critical?"

Lisa stiffened. "She was coming to my party—I got my medical license and my friends were celebrating—only someone intercepted her on the way. He beat her up and left her on the side of the road."

"Dumped at the curb like a piece of trash." Selene's expression turned fierce. "These people are animals."

"I don't know that these people are the same ones who hurt my mom, though it's certainly looking that way now."

"You think your stepfather hurt her?" Gwen asked.

"Who else?" Lisa wracked her brain but couldn't come up with another single suspect. "He keeps her under lock and key."

"Which is why you haven't seen each other for a long time."

"Twelve years." Lisa gave Selene an agreeing nod, tried to be patient, but was eager to get back to this selling business. "Why are these people abducting us? Who are they?"

"Oh dear." Gwen shot Selene a look laced with dread.

"She doesn't need more bad news now. Give her a minute."

"We could wait a week, if we had a week. The news isn't going to get any better, Selene." Gwen shrugged.

She was right about that. "Just tell me."

"First, does anyone know you're missing?" Gwen passed the flashlight to Selene. "There's no one to come looking for us."

Mark would know. He and his team and everyone at Crossroads would know. And of course God knew, but she didn't hold out much hope that He'd help her. Use her to help others, yes, but not help her. Things just didn't work that way between them. "A lot of people will be looking for me."

And oh . . . but was she ever grateful that Mark's old team had been spies. None admitted it, of course, but everyone close to Mark had independently drawn the same conclusion. He knew too much about those kinds of things even for a security chief. If anyone could find her, Mark and his team could.

She rubbed the bare skin on her finger. Since the night she'd left home and moved into the Towers with Nora, she'd worn her mom's ring. Not once had she ever taken it off—until tonight. Mark would find it, her pager, and the scrap of material from her dress in the parking lot. She hadn't been able to get out the door before the jerks had slammed it, but when she'd rolled, she released those items. Busy with her, the men hadn't noticed, but Mark would find them, and he'd hold the ring until he found her, and then he'd put it back on her finger. He'd watch over her mother too. He, his team, friends at the center, and their friends at church—they'd all come together to help them both.

"Yes! Did you hear that, Selene? Someone will be searching for her." Gwen clapped her hands softly. "Finally, things are looking up."

"Are you going to tell me what's going on here?" Lisa swept her damp hair back from her face. It was hot in the truck, and the air was stale and stank of sweat.

"We're not positive," Selene said quickly.

"I'm positive." Gwen shushed Selene. "I know what I heard, and you're not doing anyone any favors by soft-pedalling things. Just tell her the truth."

"Excuse me for trying to make it easier on her. She's had her heart broken with her mother, suffered kidnapping and abuse, and now this." Selene waved in a wide arc. "That's a lot to take in, Gwen. I don't care how strong you are; it's hard."

"I know it is. I'm going through it too—"

Lisa's patience snapped. "Will you two stop it, and please just tell me what you know?"

Selene tossed her long and dark curly hair back

behind her shoulder. "Both Gwen and I have heard things. When the men put her in the truck—"

"I fainted." Gwen shrugged, but tears rolled down her face. "Brave and glamorous, huh?"

Understandable, Lisa thought but kept quiet. If she interrupted, who knew how long it would take to get back to this point? More delays she didn't need.

Selene went on, the hand at her throat trembling. "One goon told the other one Gwen was a beauty. Gwen heard more."

"What more?"

"That I'd bring in a fortune," Gwen shrieked.

Lisa dragged in a sharp breath. "You're telling me they're actually going to—"

"Yes!" Gwen grabbed Lisa's hand and squeezed it hard. "We're going to be sold!"

Lisa couldn't speak, couldn't think. This wasn't possible, it couldn't be happening. It had to be a bad dream. Any second she would wake up and discover none of it was true.

"We don't know who they are, but that's what they said they would do."

Selene frowned. "I'm so naive; I thought maybe I was being abducted for ransom. But no." Her voice went shrill. "Can you believe that? Sold?"

As absurd as it sounded, being held for ransom appealed more than the thought of being sold. As the shock settled in, Lisa found her voice. "So they just snatch women they think they can sell somewhere?"

Selene looked at Gwen, clearly seeking reinforcement. That she didn't want to be the bearer of more bad news didn't alarm Lisa. Already she had revealed herself as a gentle, protective type. But Gwen, straight talking and blunt, returning the look, alarmed Lisa immensely. "What are you not telling me?"

"We aren't holding out. Honest. We just haven't gotten to it yet."

"Well, get to it, Gwen."

"All right, already." Gwen worried her lip with her teeth. "Selene told you she refused to sign her new recording contract. Her manager didn't take the news well. He warned her that her label would ruin her."

Selene hiked a shoulder. "Pure rubbish. They wouldn't. They're good people. He, on the other hand, was very upset. He said he'd earned the money by negotiating a fair deal and if I refused to sign, he would sue me for his share of it. He can, but he'd lose. I checked with my lawyer, and I told my manager so."

Now, evident from her mercurial expressions, Selene was rethinking the wisdom of that. "He is more apt to do this to me than my label. They totally understood I needed time to myself for a while to recharge. It's essential to creativity that an artist take time to feed her muse."

Selene paused, giving Lisa time to digest that, but before she could string together her thoughts, Gwen hooked a thumb toward Selene. "What she means is after a year on tour, she was exhausted and couldn't take it anymore. She was fried head to toe and needed a break to get human again."

"Precisely," Selene said. "Crass but unfortunately accurate."

"Honey, truth is truth. No sense dressing it up. It works fine just as it is." Gwen sniffed. "Making the jerk her beneficiary gave him a direct route to her money and her copyrights. That's the straight skinny on Selene."

Gwen touched a fingertip to her chest. Her metal cuff banged against her arm. "Me, I'm in the middle of a very messy and expensive divorce. Derek, my moronic and soon-to-be ex, and I have been haggling over the settlement for seven months with no end in sight. If he could make me disappear, it would save him a fortune. No division of marital assets, no divorce. He takes it all."

What they were saying penetrated the fog in Lisa's mind. "You're saying these abductions aren't random?" How could they not be random? Human trafficking was well documented, but were there really that many sick people out there? "Are you telling me that your husband and your business manager have paid to get you out of their lives for giving them problems?" Good grief, there had to be a mistake.

Fifty percent divorce rate. More single than married households for the first time in the history of the nation. Maybe it wasn't a mistake, but no one with any business sense would build a trade around an anomaly. Could there really be enough men like Dutch to support a trade?

For money? There's always someone willing to do anything for money, Lisa. You've seen too much to deny that.

"Deliberately. Intentionally. On purpose." Gwen nodded.

Horror slithered through her, set her pulse to pounding in her temples. "Someone paid money to have this done to me?"

"My guess is yes. No one is going to snatch any of us off the street or out of a public building unless someone is paying him to do it."

"They might, Selene." Gwen fanned the beam of light across the bed of the truck. "Remember, they're selling us on the other end. So they might."

"Don't be absurd. No one involved in this kind of sick, nefarious activity would miss the opportunity not to double their money. If they can be paid twice, they're going to get paid twice."

"She has a point," Lisa said, really thinking it through. "I see this same kind of mentality at the center. To the professionals, it's not personal. It's business. They couldn't care less about our lives. To them, it's all about money, control, and power.

Get paid to get rid of the problem, get paid again when selling the problem. One job, two payments."

"See?" Selene lifted a hand. "Exactly my point. It's always about greed."

"Makes sense," Gwen admitted. "Even if it does scare me to death and tick me off."

"Be scared and ticked off later." Lisa forced her own anger and fear to take a backseat. "If we want to live through this, we need clear heads."

"Exactly. We're all scared, but we need to keep our wits to help ourselves."

"Selene's right." So Gwen's husband and Selene's manager paid for their disappearances. And Lisa's? Dutch. *Of course, Dutch.* Which meant her initial reaction had been right. He'd had her mother brutalized to guarantee Lisa be in a specific location at a set time. *Staged.* Her stomach sank. *Despicable. Twisted. Evil.*

"You okay, Lisa?" Gwen asked.

"No." Her stomach hurt, her head throbbed, and if she didn't get some fresh air soon, she was going to be sick. "Wait. Yes, I'm okay." She steeled herself. "I'm just fine." She had to think. Think. "Who are our buyers?" Even trying hard, she could barely wrap her mind around this kind of evil. "Do we have any idea?"

"Not yet." Gwen sounded as vexed as she looked. "All I've heard Frank say was I would bring a fortune at auction."

Frank. "Which one is he?"

"Dirty. Long hair, grimy T-shirt. He was driving. I don't know if he still is or not."

"So is this Frank auctioning us off?" The sickness inside Lisa swelled. *Auctioned and sold?* Dutch must have thought for years about the worst thing he could do to her to pull her into something this seedy and disgusting. How did he sleep at night? How did any of them sleep at night? Did they have no consciences? No spark in their souls they hadn't corrupted?

Evil exists. You know it does. This is one of its many faces.

It was an ugly one. The truck hit a bump, jarring them. Pain shot through Lisa's hip and back. "What else do we know?"

Selene lifted a hand for Gwen to speak.

"They stop every two hours and let us go to the rest room."

"What else?"

Gwen frowned. "These men are Spiders, Lisa."

"What does that mean?" Lisa hated spiders. She was terrified of them and had been for as long as she could remember, though she had no idea why.

"Spiders get rid of problem women."

Spiders. She'd never heard of them. Gangs and traffickers and drug cartels, yes, but Spiders had eluded her and her professional community. Were they that good that they could function under everyone's radar? And if they were, what did that mean to her and the others?

"So they're going to sell us and then what? Prostitution?"

"Worse," Gwen said. "They're going to sell and then kill us whenever they're ready—or have us kill each other so we get to live another day. They call it the kill-or-be-killed game."

"It's true." Selene pulled a face mirroring Lisa's disgust. "Frank has asked about our fighting skills."

"Kill-or-be-killed. Like some sick sporting event where depraved people bet on the outcome?" Lisa's head throbbed. "I can't do that. I'm a doctor. I took an oath to heal people, not kill them."

Gwen grunted. "None of us wants to kill. But all of us want to survive."

"Like that?" Dangerously close to losing it, Lisa wrestled for control. "I couldn't stand it."

Gwen dipped her chin. "Which is probably why your stepfather chose it for you."

The truth in that stole Lisa's breath. She massaged her temples and prayed for the fear and turmoil churning inside her to settle enough so she could think straight. Think at all. "Sold and then murdered or forced to commit murder to survive by some unknown group that has Spiders find their victims. Unbelievable."

"Oh, believe it." Selene passed the flashlight back to Gwen. "They've all been preening about the fights since they threw me in this truck. Frank especially." Her hands on her face shook. "Watch out for him. He's as mean as a rattlesnake." She pointed at Gwen. "He put that gash in Gwen's head. It's bleeding again, by the way."

Gwen tore her slip, folded a ragged piece of the fabric into a makeshift bandage, and then pressed it to her forehead.

Struggling to absorb everything, Lisa rubbed her temples again, then her stiff neck.

Dutch, I knew you were capable of horrific things, but this kind of evil scorches even your charred soul.

14

Karl borrowed the convenience store's facilities and then did a little reconnaissance. The women's rest room reeked of pine cleaner and had a window. He'd put one of the men out back in case any of the cargo decided to try to crawl through it. Satisfied, he got a fresh cup of coffee, then returned to his car to wait for the truck.

The man he'd retrieved from the airport, now sitting in his passenger's seat, didn't say a word.

His silence didn't surprise Karl any more than his not snatching the car and taking off. No need not to keep the engine running and the air conditioner going. Juan wasn't going anywhere. The reason was simple. Give a man more to lose by running than by staying, and he would stay and do exactly as he was told.

Karl shut the door, then tapped the vent to blow cold air on his face. "Why does anyone live in the South?" he asked Juan. "Three in the morning, and it's still hot and humid. I walk from here into the store and break a sweat." He'd already removed his suit jacket and tie.

Juan spared him a glance. "You get used to it."

He couldn't get back home fast enough. "You're clear on your instructions?"

"*Sí, señor.*" He looked out through the windshield, his expression drawn and tense, his voice muted. "Drive the truck where I'm told and keep my mouth shut."

"Good." Juan was scared, shaking. The man at least had sense. He should be terrified.

The white truck pulled off the road and into the store's parking lot. Karl watched it swerve around a pothole. Frank sat in the driver's seat. As he pulled alongside the building, he kept the nose of the truck free of obstacles. If Frank had to depart quickly, all he had to do was throw the gearshift into Drive and hit the gas.

Pleased, Karl told Juan, "Time to move."

Juan squeezed his eyes shut. "*Dios,* forgive me for what I am about to do." He opened the door and stepped out.

He'd whispered but Karl had heard. No man liked to act against his own will, and while Karl didn't lose sleep over the cargo—the chosen ones generally gave as good as they got—it grated at him to give another man a job he didn't want. He'd been in that position early on and hated it. The Spiders were ignorant subcontractors out to make a buck. But Juan was being forced to act. Raven wanted him involved. That was more than enough.

Frank hopped down out of the truck and waited beside his open door.

As Karl and Juan approached, Karl lifted his right hand, stretched his fingers, exposing his tattoo for full view.

Frank flashed his and looked over at Juan.

"He's not one of us." Karl took the truck keys from Frank. "He'll be driving."

Frank's jaw tightened and his expression darkened, clearly objecting to having an outsider aboard on his run, but the dark circles and bags under his eyes proved he needed a relief driver. "Who authorized this?"

"Chessman ordered it."

Gregory Chessman had remained active in some NINA operations, even from his jail cell. Not as high up in the food chain as he once was, but high enough. Karl, who had been NINA's point of contact for the Spiders, had gotten himself promoted to Chessman's old job, and now Chessman worked under him and Karl ran the Spiders, which is why Karl had pegged Chessman and not Raven with issuing the order. Frank might or might not know Raven existed.

Neither Frank nor anyone else knew more than they needed to know about Karl's promotion or about Karl. It was safer for him. Blend in, be indistinctive, the guy everyone sees and no one remembers. He had always hidden in plain sight; it was part of his job and what made him effective as a cleaner, mopping up soured operations.

When he'd first started over a decade ago, NINA assigned him to Europe, where he perfected his skills. His ability to fade into the background and his attention to detail were essential assets, and he prided himself on providing exceptional work—whatever, whenever, and wherever NINA needed him. In Europe and in the States, he'd made it his business to become their top go-to man. They wanted it, they got it, and it got done right. He served NINA well, and it rewarded him, promoted him right up through the ranks.

Surprise lit in Frank's eyes, and he rubbed his jaw. "How long's he going to be with me?" He jerked his head toward Juan.

"Until the cargo is delivered."

Frank blinked hard, shifting his body weight, uneasy and not bothering to hide it. He stared at Karl with open suspicion. "Project?"

He and Karl had worked together on many occasions, yet Frank was still verifying. *Good man. Excellent.* If their positions were reversed, Karl would be doing the same thing. "Shifter."

"Code?"

"Alpha 263891. Supplemental Executive Order."

That woke up Frank. "An SEO? Seriously?"

Even Juan picked up on Frank's surprise and tensed. Executive orders rarely trickled this far down the chain. Karl nodded.

Frank cleared his throat, outwardly nervous. "Raven?"

So he did know about her. "Yes."

"All right." Frank slapped his thigh. "That's that, then."

"There's more." Nothing stirred. Karl still scanned their surroundings. Isolated. No unknown cars in the lot. Just them and normal night sounds. He lowered his voice anyway. "They've added a cargo pickup in Jackson, Mississippi."

Frank glowered into the woods abutting the ramshackle store. "That'll add another four hours to the schedule."

"A little more than that, but our orders are to adjust the schedule. I've taken care of it down the line."

"Fine." Frank grimaced. "I hope the client at least got soaked on the contract."

"Paid triple the normal fee." Karl had no idea if that was fact or fiction, but it was the word he got from Chessman when they last coordinated on the schedule.

"Whoa, baby. Now you're talking." Frank guffawed, clearly pleased that he'd get a piece of that profit. "Is she royalty?"

"Who cares?" It didn't pay to share information you weren't required to share. A man never knew when something he revealed would turn up in some jerk lawyer's hands and he'd toss a man down in a deal.

Of course Karl knew the cargo's history. Information was valuable, gave a man bargaining power. But he wasn't revealing it. Especially not to a disposable gopher lowlife like Frank who had brawn but was a penny-thinking lightweight. "Cargo's cargo."

The woman was a witness on a federal investigation that would put an influential businessman in prison a minimum of thirty years for cooking his books. She couldn't testify—it wasn't in NINA's best interests—and she was scheduled to on Monday.

"Do we intercept her too?"

"The cargo is already in custody." Her guards were dead, and she had been relocated. "Pick it up in Jackson and resume your normal schedule."

"Sweet."

"Thought you'd appreciate that." Karl smiled. "You'll be notified where at the appropriate time."

"Fine. That it?"

"That's it."

Frank studied Juan. "Don't think about being a

hero or giving me any trouble. I don't give warnings. You do anything other than drive and you're a dead man."

"*Sí, comprendo.*"

Karl stepped back. "He won't give you any trouble. Juan's got a strong incentive to cooperate."

"Good. We understand each other then." He sighed. "Let's get the cargo out and run them through so we can get back on the road."

"The cargo is a them?" Juan asked. "What them? Run them through what?"

Frank landed a solid punch to Juan's jaw.

He staggered back and thudded against the side of the truck. Catching his balance, Juan righted himself and clutched his face.

"No questions." Frank warned him with a pointed finger. "You do what you're told when you're told."

"My fault, Frank. I'm afraid I gave Juan the impression we were moving drugs." A little chuckle escaped Karl's throat. "I'm sure he was wondering what we were going to run them through."

"Our cargo is women." Frank parked his hands on his hips. "And we're running them through the john, unless you want to hose them down and clean up the stink."

"You're shipping women?" Juan paled.

The question had been directed at Karl, who deigned not to respond.

Juan turned green. He quickly made his way to a patch of grass, bent over, and vomited.

"Oh, great." Frank blew out an annoyed sigh. "Pull that in my truck, and you'll be riding in back with the cargo."

Juan heaved again, then straightened, wiping at his watering eyes.

"I'll leave you to it, Frank." Laughing, Karl returned to his car.

Juan, the poor slob, hadn't had a clue. Karl almost wished he could be around to see the man's reaction when he figured out the whole truth.

He'd totally freak.

Unfortunately Karl would have to miss it. He had other plans for a certain young woman in Seagrove Village.

A woman out of chances who needed to die.

The truck sat idle.

Something thumped against its side.

Lisa frowned at Gwen and Selene. "What was that?"

"Dunno," Gwen said. "Too light to be a car."

Lisa started shaking. "What's going on? Why are we stopped?" They'd been still too long for it to be a traffic light.

"We must be at another one of those stores." Gwen aimed the flashlight at her wrist and checked her watch. "Three o'clock. That's what it is." She pulled her blouse down over her hip,

231

then turned off the light. "Potty-break time."

Selene scooted back. "Don't touch the door. Frank gets very angry if you're close to the door."

Lisa moved back. "How many men are with him?" Three had abducted her, but that didn't mean there were three now. As the door was closing, she'd seen Edmunds and Powell getting into a car in the hospital parking lot.

"Who knows? The only one we ever see up close is Frank." Gwen dabbed at the cut on her forehead. It was still bleeding.

"Keep pressure on it," Lisa said.

Gwen pressed the bandage back into place. "That's why you don't look at anybody. The store will probably be empty, but if not, don't trust anyone, and do not ask for help. You can bet they're working for the people doing this or Frank wouldn't be stopping here. Trust me on this, Lisa. Been there, done that, and all it got me was a head wound."

If Frank was alone, Lisa might be able to take him down. If an opportunity presented itself, she would take it.

The lock clicked, and the door swung open.

A man with bags and dark circles under his eyes and stringy blond hair that hung loose down to his shoulders stepped forward with the gush of fresh air. He wore jeans and a dirty white T-shirt, had bulky muscles and no flab—not a good sign for an easy takedown.

"Here are the rules," he said to Lisa. "You walk in the door, straight back to the bathroom, take care of business, walk straight out of the store, and get back into the truck. Understand?"

He waited for each of the women to nod. Lisa did, and though she was tempted to ask questions, she sensed this was a good time to be quiet and fade away. Then if she did attack, it would be more of a surprise.

"Don't talk to anybody. Don't look at anybody. That bracelet you're wearing is a tracking device. If you run, I will find you. Break any of these rules, and this will be your last stop."

The hard, cold shards in his eyes warned her it wasn't a scare tactic; it was a statement of fact.

Lisa followed Selene out of the truck onto the asphalt. Straightening her legs had them stinging. Being folded for so long had cut off her circulation. Lisa rotated her feet to get the blood flowing and stop the needle-prick sensations shooting up and down her legs. She was sore all over and used the brief pause to visually investigate.

Shabby convenience store with a half-torn-up parking lot surrounded by woods. No other businesses, no other cars, and no lights shining in the distance signaling nearby houses. The only sign in sight was one for the Interstate 10 on ramp. *Totally remote.* Not a single clue as to what state they were in, and nothing pointed to anyone assisting Frank. Apparently he was working this leg of the operation alone. That carried a spark of hope that her next thought dashed. He and his cohorts could have split up.

Frank lifted his cell phone to his ear. "Yeah." He held an outstretched arm to keep the women from moving. A long moment later, he said, "Got it." He shoved the phone back into his pants pocket. "Juan!"

A short Latino man in his late forties came around the side of the truck to the back. He didn't look at them or say a word.

"Go around the side of the building." He jerked his head to the right. "Guard the window in the women's rest room. If anybody comes out it, shoot 'em."

Juan crossed the lot and then disappeared around the corner of the cinder-block building.

"Remember the rules." Frank gestured for them to move.

They walked inside. An elderly woman sat on a stool behind the counter near a cash register. She hurriedly lifted her newspaper to hide her face. Clearly she didn't want to see or be seen. Lisa strained to read the title on the front page, hoping to get an idea of their location, but the print was too far away and the woman's hands were shaking.

That telltale shake proved she knew exactly what was going on, and she wouldn't do a thing to stop it.

On the way to the rest room, Lisa snagged a tube of Neosporin off the shelf. *Forgive me for stealing, Lord. Gwen needs it.*

After shoving it into her top, Lisa entered the rest room, washed her face and hands, and checked the mirror above the sink.

Her face was swollen, and she had a few scratches on her jaw. Her ribs, legs, and arms were muddy with bruises, but nothing that wouldn't heal. The men had tried to avoid hitting her in the face. Now she knew why. *Auctioned. Sold!*

Fear crackled inside her. Her hands shook. She shook all over. Was her mother still alive? Would Lisa see her again? And what about Mark? He'd feel guilty and was probably chewing himself up. She hated that. He deserved so much better. So much good.

She just had to make it out of this. Mark would spend the rest of his life looking for her, and he'd never forgive himself for failing her. He hadn't failed her, of course. She'd been foolish, taking the backdoor exit from the ICU. But Mark wouldn't see it that way—not looking at it through eyes that failed Jane. Yet even if her mom lived and by some miracle Lisa made it home, would she and Mark work past this? Would she or her mom ever again feel or be safe?

How could Dutch do this? Cruel and vicious and malicious barely began to cover it. How could any human being do this to another human being? Her mother could be dying. *Dying*. And Lisa wasn't there with her.

Tears threatened, clogged her throat. Lisa fought them, repeatedly swallowing hard, and turned away from the sink and mirror. Facing the wall, she squeezed her eyes shut.

God, help me. Give me the wisdom and strength to survive this. It's too big for me. I can't do it alone. And help Mark find me. If an opportunity comes for me to help myself and these other women, I'm so scared I'll miss it. God, please make sure I see it. Thank You.

Gwen and Selene stood waiting at the door. "Do you do that often?"

"Do what?" Lisa had no idea what Selene meant.

"Pray?"

"Yes, I guess I do."

Selene sounded almost shy. "Does it help?"

Lisa checked her eyes, expecting mockery but seeing genuine interest. "Honestly? Not always the way I would like, but things usually work out."

Gwen dragged her fingers down her face. "I used to pray all the time. I'm not sure why I stopped. I'm not even sure when it happened. I just stopped."

"It's like anything else," Lisa said. "You let it slide, and next time letting it slide is easier, and one day you don't think about it anymore."

"I guess so." Gwen sighed. "Maybe now would be a good time to start again, huh?"

Easy, Lisa. No pressure, no force. "Couldn't hurt. All I know is, for me life's too hard without it." Lisa smeared salve on her fingertip, wrote *Lisa needs help! Call,* and then added Mark's cell number.

"Clever." Gwen gawked at her reflection in the mirror. "But who's gonna see it? That woman out there?"

Selene harrumphed. "She's not calling anyone."

"Someone has to shop here." Lisa turned away from the mirror, tore off a hand towel, and then wiped her hands.

"We can hope."

Lisa tossed the crunched towel into the trash can.

"Pray on that too, Lisa." Selene looked down. "I don't pray. Not many who walk in my world do."

Lisa knew what it was to feel like an outsider. Selene lived in a world of people where faith largely stood apart from daily life. Lisa lived in a world of people immersed in faith and felt largely separated on the inside. Everyone had her own path to walk, and they all had trials to face. "Your world doesn't really matter. You either believe or you don't. It's a personal choice we all make."

"True." Selene scrunched her nose. "I'm just not that holy, you know?"

Lisa had heard that a hundred times in her first

month at the center. "Who is? We all just do the best we can."

Gwen tilted her head toward the door. "We'd better get back out there before Juan or Frank gets testy. I'm not up to another beating—none of us is." She grabbed the door handle. "Ready?"

Lisa eyed the window. She could take Juan, unless he started shooting the second she bobbed her head through the window, and with Frank's orders, that's what he was apt to do. Wiser to wait for a better opportunity. "Yeah."

"No." Selene pouted, wrung her hands. "But what choice do we have?"

"At the moment, none. But hope springs eternal." Lisa walked out behind the other two.

Frank waited just outside the door.

No one had come into the store; still just the woman on her stool, hiding behind the newspaper. She couldn't identify them; she had made sure of that. Lisa worked hard not to judge her. She could be under as much duress as they were or even more. Lisa glanced out through the front windows. Still no other cars in the parking lot and none at the gas pumps.

Disappointment bit harder and sank deeper, but she expected it. She never could catch a break, not even with two hands and a net.

Gwen shoved open the door, and they filed outside.

Bringing up the rear, Lisa closed the door

behind her—and saw a sign taped to its glass. *Human trafficking is a crime. If you are a victim or know of a victim, call . . .*

Chilled to the bone, she ignored the number. No way would she have the opportunity to call anyone, and nothing in the store had cued her as to where exactly they were—not that she had much opportunity to look with Frank hovering like a shadow. But the sign chilled her for another reason.

It was just like the one that hung in Dutch's store.

A flier posted in the window near the sign caught her eye. *Lost puppy. Black and white mixed breed. Call Nina.* Weird. There was no phone number.

"Move it, woman." Frank grabbed her by the arm and tugged her toward the truck.

Where was the other guy—Juan? If Lisa took on Frank, Gwen and Selene wouldn't be prepared. The delay could be costly—he was armed—but if Juan didn't intercede, they might make it to the woods. The distance back into the store was shorter. They could make it in and lock Frank out. He'd have to shoot his way in. Surely that'd give one of them time to call police. Lisa didn't see Juan anywhere.

Two more steps and the window of opportunity would be closed.

"Got that water yet?" Frank shouted.

"Sí, I have it." Juan came into view from the far

side of the truck, carrying three bottles of water. He walked over to Frank but didn't pass out the bottles.

"Get in." Frank motioned to Lisa. "You first."

The opportunity was gone. Let down, Lisa shunned her disappointment. The time hadn't been right. But in two hours, when they stopped again, she'd have another chance, and next time, she and Gwen and Selene would all be ready.

Hiking her hem, Lisa stepped onto the wide bumper and then pulled herself up into the truck. From the corner of her eye, she glimpsed the store clerk peering out at them from behind a sign at the window. She definitely knew what was going on and wasn't going to lift a finger to help them.

Maybe she can't.

Lisa frowned. *Sorry. I tried to give her the benefit of the doubt, but "can't" just isn't good enough. Anyone can make an anonymous phone call. You want her forgiven, God, then You'll have to forgive her. I can't do it. I'm not that holy or that strong.*

When Selene and Gwen were seated on the floor of the truck, Frank tossed two bottles of water toward them. When he got to Lisa, he paused. "I know about your black belt. I'm not impressed. Pull any of that martial-arts stuff on me, and you won't be going inside or getting water again." The imprint of his gun tucked into his waistband bulged, stark and menacing.

"Figured that." She leaned forward to reach for the bottle—and saw the spiderweb tattoo on his hand.

Jerking back, she fell onto her bottom, thumping against the truck bed. "Lost my balance," she said, hoping to cover her reaction. She took the water bottle and sat back, locking her muscles to keep from cringing at the image flooding her mind.

A misty, fuzzy image of her as a young child, fiddling with the peach-and-cream ribbons on a barrette she and her mother had made at a craft workshop. Sounds of her voice filled her ears, a telephone conversation with her mother, but the voices were distant, muffled by hard-rock music, the words inaudible.

Lisa locked on to the image, forced it to her, and in her mind's eye she saw a man beating on the window of her room. He shouted at her through the glass. *It's time for you to become a shrub.* Her repeating that to her mother, asking what it meant. Her dog Rex's snarling coming through the phone, her mother's panicked, *Do not open that door. Go get Daddy, darling . . .*

What door? Where was she?

Inside her mind, something snapped. She heard a crash. Wood splinter and crack. The door caved in, and her father shouted from behind her. Something flashed, exploded. Lisa screamed and screamed.

And screamed.

15

Mark stood near the nurses' station outside the ICU.

Detective Jeff Meyers stood next to him, his suit a little snug. He'd put on a couple of pounds over the winter, but tourist season always took it off. He'd be rail thin by its end. Passersby gave them a wide berth. Everyone working with them had scattered inside the hospital and out in the village, trying to scare up or run down leads.

So far, they all came up dry.

"Brought you some coffee from Ruby's." Jeff set a cardboard tray holding two paper cups on the ledge of the counter. The distinct scent of Ruby's strong coffee filled the air.

Jeff's pug nose twitched. "It's pretty obvious Dutch is behind this. But it's just as obvious that he didn't act alone. It'd be easy enough for him to hire a couple of thugs to help him, but hacking into the hospital's security system . . . None of the thugs around here is that smart and neither is he."

"Dutch definitely had help. When Rose finally got him on the phone, he was in Georgia. Joe verified his location."

"Where exactly was he?" Jeff pulled a cup free from the carton and passed it to Mark.

"In a hotel just across the state line." Mark thumbed the tab and drank through the lid. "We faxed up a photo, and the clerk positively identified him."

"So he hired professionals to assault Annie and abduct Lisa. Is that what you're thinking?"

"Yeah." Mark covertly scanned the area to be sure they wouldn't be overheard. This was the first chance they'd had to talk one-on-one in person, and what he was about to say wasn't the kind of thing you trusted to the phone. "I'm afraid it isn't just professionals he hired, Jeff. It's NINA."

"NINA?" Jeff pulled his own cup from the holder and sent Mark a confused look. "Why?"

"I don't know." Boy, those were hard words to admit. "But Karl Masson was in the parking lot when Lisa was abducted."

"Whoa." Jeff scowled. "Think he's back in the village for Kelly Walker?"

"Maybe, but I don't believe that's all of it. Why would he leave the hospital with Kelly still inside? Why abduct Lisa instead?" Mark couldn't answer those questions with any degree of certainty, but the scope of this had to be wider than Masson's killing Kelly. "I'm sure Masson wants Kelly neutralized, but this has to be a multipurpose visit. Taking Lisa was a deliberate act."

Leaving the coffee untouched, Jeff stared off at the wall, then snapped his gaze back to Mark. "Had to be or Annie wouldn't be here."

Two orderlies walked by complaining about runny eggs in the cafeteria. Waiting for them to move out of earshot, Mark glanced over at a painting hanging on the wall. It was a serene landscape. Calm and tranquil—the antithesis of all he was feeling inside. He wished he could crawl into it and absorb some of its calm. Maybe if he got some of the knots out of his gut, his focus would get off of what could be happening to Lisa and on to finding her. "If Masson was here on behalf of NINA, what are they doing and why?"

"Good questions. Unfortunately, I can't answer them." His eyes red-rimmed from the lack of sleep, Jeff rubbed his neck. "Man, it just doesn't make sense. These kinds of crimes are way outside NINA's profile."

They were alien to NINA's *existing* profile. "I have reason to believe NINA has expanded its operations."

"I see." Jeff sobered, leaned against the counter ledge. "What do they want with Lisa?"

"I don't know."

"You're confident they didn't make a mistake?" Jeff rubbed his jaw.

Mark grunted. "With Annie in ICU? The hospital computer hacked and the security camera destroyed? No. They didn't make a mistake."

"Masson had to be here under orders. No way would he come on his own for anything that didn't involve killing Kelly. But it's a big organization. Assaulting a woman and kidnapping her daughter seems too small a thing for NINA to take on."

"I wasn't asking you if they had expanded, Jeff. I'm telling you they have."

Jeff muttered a curse under his breath. "Why did they take her?"

"Nick's been digging deep. Most obvious reason would be human trafficking for prostitution." Just saying it sickened Mark.

"Sex trafficking isn't chump change. Drugs, they sell once. People, they sell over and over again."

The video clip Mark's buddy had sent over of the two women fighting stuck in Mark's mind. The women who survived fought over and over again. What if those were connected to Lisa? Mark hadn't permitted his thoughts to go there. Now he had no choice.

Mark's cell rang. He paused to answer it. "Taylor."

"Omega One." Jane's former intelligence buddy. "Yes?"

"Check out this URL." He rambled it off. "Got it?"

"Yeah." Mark tensed, stared at Jeff. "Reply?"

"Absolutely not."

"Thanks."

Mark ended the call, then brought up the Internet and keyed in the URL on a secure laptop Beth Dawson had brought over when she'd warned them off using the hospital's system until she could run analytics.

"Need some privacy?" Jeff asked.

"No, you need to see this." Mark turned the screen so they could both view the clip.

A rambunctious crowd cheered, pumping their fists. Two women faced each other in a boxing ring, dressed in evening gowns and high heels: one in red, the other in black. It was an absurd sight. The crowd, too, was dressed in formal attire. This was no cut-rate, low-cost operation. A bell rang. The women locked together, fists flying. They fought and fought hard. By the time the bell rang, they were both bloody. Then came round two and three and four.

The woman in red cracked the one in black with a right cross that sent her reeling. She staggered back against the ropes. The woman in red lunged, grabbed the other by the throat, and yanked her down to the mat, choking her. The woman on the bottom kicked and flailed, but the other didn't let go.

The crowd jumped to its feet, shouting so loudly their words created an indecipherable din. Then they chanted, "Kill. Kill. Kill."

And they kept shouting it until the woman in black moved no more.

A collective hush settled over the crowd. The woman in red checked her opponent's bloody throat for a pulse. She stood, stared down at the mat, her expression haunted.

Thunderous applause erupted.

The woman in red covered her ears, trying to block out the sound.

The woman in black was dead.

The clip ended.

"She killed that woman—and they're cheering." Jeff looked from the screen to Mark. "I've seen some cold stuff on the force, but this is—"

"I know. I need a minute." Mark's stomach roiled. He touched the screen on the laptop. It went black. He pulled out his phone and conference called the guys. When he had them, he said, "Everyone on secure computers?"

Everyone reported that they were, and Mark added, "Something you need to see. Here's the URL."

"Got it, bud."

"Me too, bro."

"Hanging on or reporting back?"

Tim. "Neither. Just new information to add to the initial."

"Connected?" Joe asked.

"I don't know, but it's looking more like it all the time." His voice husky, Mark ended the call.

Jeff turned down the static-ridden radio clipped to his hip, then rubbed his neck. "That's no small-time operation."

"No, it isn't."

Mark's cell rang. Expecting it, he stepped away from Jeff, then tapped the computer screen. The film reappeared. Then Mark lifted the phone to his ear. "Taylor."

"Omega One."

"I've seen it."

"The woman in black was one of ours—civilian side, undercover."

"My sympathy to her family."

"Yeah." Jane's friend hung up.

Jeff frowned, his eyes clouded with trouble. "What's really going on, Mark?"

He checked for others within earshot and saw none. "That was the second fight video I've seen. The first one was fifteen, maybe twenty seconds. When it ended, the women were still fighting. In this one, the woman dressed in black—"

"Yeah?"

"She was an FBI agent who had infiltrated the operation."

"Why are you getting—?" Jeff suddenly stilled. "This is related to Lisa?"

There's no other reason Omega One would have risked sending it to him. "Someone thinks it is, but I have to know. When I got the first video, it was an alert that NINA was active in the area again. I thought they were coming after Kelly Walker."

"So you called in your buddies for backup."

"Yeah. But now I'm thinking this isn't about Kelly at all."

Empathy flashed across Jeff's face. "This stuff is way over my head. I don't have the manpower or the resources to take on NINA. It's time to pull in some power from outside sources. Maybe you and your friends could do the same."

"Joe's already put in some calls." Mark tumbled Lisa's ring inside his pocket, flipping it over, rubbing its smooth, worn surface. "He has more connections than the rest of us put together."

"I'll make some calls too. Highway patrol hasn't picked up the truck. If we had a tag, maybe."

"I know it's a long shot." Mark was glad they were beyond the missing person's requirements, now that they had evidence a crime had been committed and they could call in outsiders to help. But he wasn't surprised. Jeff was no fool, and he'd gone up against NINA before. Even aided by the FBI, it'd been all they could handle. NINA played hardball—and it played to win. "Did you get that restraining order to keep Dutch out of here?"

"Yeah. I delivered it to Grant Thurman and dropped off a copy at the administration office on the way up here."

"Thanks. Keep me posted." Mark frowned. "I need to go check on Annie."

Jeff set down his cup and stepped away from the station. "I know I've already said this, but I am sorry, Mark. If I could change places with either of them, I would."

"I know. Me too." Mark didn't have to pretend to understand how Jeff felt or act as if he didn't see the tormented look in the man's eyes. The nearest mirror would reflect the same look in his own.

Jeff got a call and left. Mark headed to the elevator, spotted Joe coming upstairs.

"I hear you're not eating or sleeping, bro."

"After watching that latest video?"

"Point taken." Joe glanced down the hall. "However, you're a risk to the rest of us right now, and I won't have that. You said you were too involved, so you put me in charge. My responsibility is to the team. For the team, go get some food and then hit the rack for a while."

Mark glowered at Joe. "You know what could be happening to her."

"I know." Joe lowered his voice, stepped closer. "And I know it scares you out of your skin—as it should. But this isn't your fault. She's not Jane."

Anger flashed through Mark, hot and furious. He stiffened. "I *know* that." He took a few steps, whipped around, and came back. "That agent was killed. *Killed,* Joe. You think I'm out of control? You're lucky I'm not at HQ pounding heads."

"So are you. Leavenworth isn't much fun, and you'd be totally worthless to us or Lisa in there." Joe pointed to an empty room. "Go to Ruby's. Eat. Sleep. Clear your head. I've got it covered, okay?"

"Okay." Mark headed toward the elevator. The sag in his shoulders was heavy, familiar. Guilt was a heavy load.

• • •

Ten minutes later, Mark slid into a booth at Ruby's Diner and ordered eggs and toast and a mug of coffee. In another thirty minutes, the place would be hopping. Ruby's was just as busy on Saturday as it was on a weekday. For now, only he and two other nonstaffers were inside.

Outside, dawn cracked the night sky and weak sunlight spilled through. Arrogant of the sun to shine such soft pinks and yellows when everything that most mattered to him was in danger. The sky should be striped with jagged slashes of red.

Something in his pocket stuck into his thigh. Keys? He reached in and pulled out the little box, then opened it. Lisa's and his sand dollar.

Memories assaulted him. The warm breezy night at the beach when she'd first given it to him. Nora had called and insisted he go to the annual singles' event at church. He'd refused until she mentioned that she had insisted Lisa take a break from studying and go. After she left, Nora was worried Dutch might find out and give her trouble. He seemed to know where Lisa was all the time.

That's all it had taken. Mark went. He flipped the shell over in his hand, studied it. Now he was so glad he had. Lisa had looked amazing in the moonlight, her face glowing from the heat of the bonfire. But as he approached, he could see she was wary, watching the crowd, checking back over her shoulder . . .

She spotted him, and her wariness disappeared. "Mark. I'm surprised to see you here."

He shrugged. "It's a nice night. Want to go for a walk?"

"Sure."

At the water's edge, Lisa held on to him, removed her sandals, and let them dangle from her crooked finger. He took his shoes off, and they let the incoming waves curl over their feet.

They'd walked for miles and talked the entire way. He told her about Jane—something he'd never told anyone outside the team who had lived through it with him.

"I'm so sorry." Lisa dropped her sandals, nudged him to drop his. When he did, she laced both their hands. Her eyes were luminous, large and wet with unshed tears. "You loved her."

"Yes." He lightly squeezed her fingers until their palms pressed flat. "She was the best friend I've ever had."

The wind teased Lisa's hair, blowing it back from her face. "You weren't a couple?"

"No, no." He lifted a strand caressing Lisa's cheek, let the backs of his fingertips brush against her skin. *So soft.* "She was the little sister of my heart." *Did that sound silly? Probably. But it was true.*

"Did she feel that way too?"

252

"She did." He nodded, too emotional to say more.

Lisa brought their joined hands to her face, held them tightly to her. "I'm so sorry, Mark."

"Me too." He swallowed hard, rebuffed the urge to turn for safer, less charged ground.

Lisa must have understood. With gentle strokes of her thumb, she soothed his hand, stepped closer, and hugged him.

Mark's heart thundered against her ear. She smelled like he imagined heaven would smell: sweet and pure, fresh and clean. Traces of the fire's scent lingered and mingled with that of the tangy salt water. But they blended and faded, and her scent was the only one noted. Familiar and good, and uniquely Lisa.

She smoothed the back of his shirt in long arcs that burned his skin beneath the cotton fabric. Caressing that sank deep into his skin and beyond through flesh and muscle until its tenderness touched his heart. He'd never felt such care or comfort in a woman's hands. Hands that could heal wounds he couldn't see but carried with him every day of his life.

"Jane was a lucky woman." Lisa lifted her chin, sincerity shining in her eyes.

"I killed her, Lisa."

"No, you didn't." She pressed a kiss over his heart. "You loved her and you were stuck. Sometimes people we love get into situations where they're just stuck, Mark."

"I wasn't where I was supposed to be."

"For good reason. You were pinned down." Lisa cupped his face in her hands. "If you'd gone to her, what would have happened?"

"We'd both have been killed."

"And what purpose would have been served in that?"

"I wouldn't feel . . ." He couldn't say it. Wouldn't.

"Guilty?" Lisa studied his face, and compassion burned in her eyes. Finally, he nodded and she went on. "I feel the same way about my mother. But I know I can't be all and do all; I'm human and I have limitations. So do you."

"I should have tried."

"You'd be dead." Lisa hugged him hard, as if trying to take his pain into her and relieve him of it. "You couldn't die then because if you had, you wouldn't be here now." She pulled back, picked up a sand dollar, dusted the sand from it with her fingertips, and then passed it to him. "Whenever you think about this, I want you to think about me holding this shell. When I do, it'll be because I'm scared or worried."

"I don't want to think about you being scared or worried, Lisa."

"I wasn't finished." She tapped his chin. "Think about me holding this and it reminding me that you're here, and because you are, I'm not so scared. I'm not so worried. I'm not alone—and neither are you."

It was more than he dared to dream he'd receive from her. Far more. "You'll be there for me?" He tried but failed to keep his surprise out of his voice.

"Yes." She sounded as breathless as he felt.

He wanted to kiss her. Needed to kiss her, and she looked as if she wanted to be kissed, but— He hesitated, weighing the costs. He didn't dare.

The moment was gone.

She bent down and lifted her sandals. He got his shoes and they walked on.

Two steps, and Lisa reached over and clasped their pinkie fingers.

He looked at their joined hands and smiled. "This is new."

She smiled over at him, a little bittersweet. "It's special."

"Meaning just for me?" he asked, then kicked himself for it.

"You and my mother." Her voice softened even more. "From the time I was little, it was our way of saying we were there for each other."

Touched, he stopped and stroked her face. "I'm here for you, Lisa. I'll always be here for you."

"Hey, Mark, are you okay?"

Startled, Mark jerked himself from the memory and looked into Megan's questioning eyes. "What?"

Smacking her chewing gum, she tilted her head. A riot of red curls sprang out in all directions. She was about Mel's age, but they were nothing alike. Megan thrived on gossip. "I said do you want a refill on your coffee?" She motioned with the pot.

"Um, no. Just the bill."

She fished it out of her pocket and pressed it down on the table. "I was real sorry to hear about Annie and Lisa. How are they doing?"

"No news."

Megan nodded, frowning. "Keep us posted. Everyone's waiting for word."

"I will." Mark paid the bill and covered the tip, then slid out of the booth. On his way to the door, he dropped the sand dollar back into its box, then pocketed it. When had the place filled up?

He nodded to those he recognized, then left Ruby's and headed back to the hospital.

Back on the second floor, he spotted Joe in the hallway. "I'm fine," he said before Joe could ask.

Joe dipped his chin and glared at him. "You're not resting."

"I need to check on Annie first, then I will." Mark stepped around the edge of the station desk, dumped some trash from the car into the can, and then headed for the big wooden doors to the unit.

Rose stood inside the hub with one hand on the emergency buzzer. When she saw Mark, she relaxed and went back to entering something in her computer.

Glad to see her on her toes, Mark glanced over. Sam stood beside Annie's bed, his cap low over his eyes, his back to the wall. Annie lay still on the narrow bed. Battered and hooked up to machines with tubes and wires everywhere, she seemed so small and frail. What kind of man could justify hurting a woman like that?

Pity and rage warred in Mark, and he had to get his emotions under control. They didn't go down easy, but when he sealed them up, he walked over to her bedside.

"No change." Sam kept his voice just above a whisper.

"Take a break and get some breakfast. I'll stay until you get back."

"Any word yet on Lisa?"

Mark shook his head. "None I care to repeat."

"Think steel, bud. She's tough and smart. She'll help us find her. Joe's working the phones, calling everyone short of the president. If there's info to be had, we'll get it."

Sam meant well. Thinking steel was good advice. Getting emotional during crises led to mistakes. Mistakes led to deaths. But this was about Lisa, the woman who held his heart. And he wasn't sure he'd want to be the kind of man who under these circumstances could follow that advice anyway. But he kept those thoughts to himself. "Thanks, Sam."

"You bet, bud. Back in fifteen." He clapped Mark's shoulder and then left the unit.

Mark studied Annie, praying Sam was right and

they'd get a break. He pulled Lisa's ring out of his pocket. "I've got your ring, Annie. Lisa left it for me to find. She's smart, you know. Sam's right. She will find a way to help us locate her."

As he searched her pasty, still face, a fresh wave of regret washed over him. It seeped deep inside and soaked his bones. Lisa's voice sounded in his mind. *"My mama says a lady never attends a social gatherin' without a proper manicure."*

Annie's nails were cracked. Several were broken down to the quick until they had bled.

She'd fought and fought hard.

"You were counting on me to keep you both safe, and I let you down." His throat went thick, his voice hollowed. He blinked hard and fast. "I'm sorry, Annie. If I had come after you myself, we wouldn't be in this position. What's happened to you and Lisa—it's my fault."

A tear trickled down his cheek. "I love your daughter, you know. I've been in love with her since the first time I saw her. She was at the center, and a guy came in demanding to see his wife. Mel called Lisa, and she came out of her office. He gave her a hard time and took a swing at her. Before I could get to her, Lisa had cleaned his clock and I'd fallen in love."

The memory burned bittersweet. "I love you too, Annie." He lightly skimmed her short gray curls, careful not to bump the tubes jutting out from her body. "They say you have a weak heart, but your heart is the strongest one I've ever seen. It was strong enough to protect Lisa when it meant giving her up. I don't know how you stood that, but I know you did it for her, to protect her from Dutch. And loving her as much as you do, I'm sure you've cried a lot of nights."

He studied the thin gold band, his blurred vision distorting it. "I promise, I'll find her, Annie. If I have to spend the rest of my life looking for her, I will. I'll never give up. Never. You have my word on that."

Needing the reassurance of touch, he crooked his little finger and clasped it with Annie's. "Lisa loves you, you know. At the party, for the first time I thought maybe one day she could love me too. Now the odds of earning even a little of her love, well, they're shot." His big body quaked. He rolled his shoulders, stretching to absorb the pain pounding through him in waves.

He cleared his throat, his anguish billowing. "I don't know why I fail the women I most care for and destroy their lives, Annie—Jane, Lisa, you." Guilt slumped his shoulders. "But I will bring your baby back to you. So help me, I will." Another tear leaked from his eye and splashed on his cheek, then rolled down his face. "You have to do your part and be here, okay?"

He bent low, whispered close to her ear, "Remember how strong your heart is. Annie, wake up. Please, wake up and tell us what happened to you. I need to know what you don't want Lisa to remember. Don't you dare give up, you hear me? You have to fight for you and Lisa."

He looked down at their hooked fingers. "And don't die, Annie. Please, don't die on me too. I'll never forgive myself, and Lisa will live every day of her life believing she's to blame." Mark whispered that with the authority of one tormented by living it. "She'll hate me forever, and I'll have lost all of you." *Oh, God, please.* Mark sniffed, forced strength into his voice. "Your days as Dutch's prisoner are over. You can live your life any way you want. You're free now."

Her finger bumped against his.

Startled, he jerked up straight. "Annie?" He stared down at their hands. Hers rested against the white sheets so still. Had he imagined the movement? God knew he wanted it, begged for it, prayed for it. Maybe he imagined it. "Annie, did you move your finger?"

He waited. And waited. "Annie, please. Please."

Again, the tip of her little finger curled and touched against his.

Relief burst inside him. He swung his gaze toward the nurses' station and called out, "Rose, come quick! Annie moved!"

16

Dutch drove south on Highway 331, looking for someplace to stop to eat. There wasn't much in the way of choices this far out in the sticks at the crack of dawn. Everything he came across between the long stretches of thick and twisted pines was closed.

Finally, he spotted a mom-and-pop café with its lights on and pulled into the loose-gravel parking lot. He parked right outside the door. A red neon OPEN sign in the front window reflected off his hood.

He should call the hospital and check on Annie. Naw, he would wait. If he called and she was dead, it'd only mess up a decent meal.

He went inside and sat in a small green-vinyl booth, then ordered coffee, sausage and eggs, hash browns, and the homemade biscuits he'd smelled as soon as he walked through the door.

The waitress wasn't much to look at, but she was efficient and that was enough, considering the hour and his mood. "Refill," he called out, waving his cup.

Annie wouldn't have liked that. Her face would have turned red.

He liked embarrassing Annie, not that she'd ever dare say a word, but he always knew, and that she kept her tongue still about it showed she knew who was boss. A man could never forget to remind his woman who was boss. Mayor John Green sure found out the costs of failing to do that. Now his widow had bought Dutch's house. She'd have to find out he was the boss too. That woman was not keeping his house.

The waitress hurried over with the coffeepot and refilled his cup. "Getting an early start this morning, huh?"

"Late night," he said, solidifying his alibi. This waitress needed to remember him. "I was up in Georgia on business and got a call from the coast that my wife had been mugged. She's in ICU—critical, the nurse said. So I'm rushing back to see her."

"You want your food to go, then?"

"No, I'm too upset to try to eat and drive. Safer for everyone else if I just eat and then get back on my way."

She gave him a sympathy-laced look and touched his shoulder. "I'm so sorry for your trouble, and I hope your wife recovers. Hope they catch whoever hurt her too. People can be so mean these days."

"They sure can." He cast his eyes down at the table as if overcome. "She's just got to recover. I can't imagine life without my Annie."

The touch on his shoulder turned to a pat. "If you need anything else, you just let me know."

"Thank you." She'd remember him, all right.

This sympathy thing felt pretty good. After eating his meal, he called the hospital and got through to the ICU. "This is Dutch Hauk. How's Annie?"

"I'm sorry, sir. I'm not at liberty to release that information."

Rose. Only now the good doctor's former nurse was all business and not at all friendly. What was up with that? "Why not? She's my wife, Rose; of course you can tell me how she is."

"No sir, I can't."

He stilled. "Why not?"

"Let me transfer you to the administrator's office, Mr. Hauk. They'll explain. I'm not at liberty to say anything more than that, sir."

Dutch clamped his jaw and ground his teeth. Somebody had been up to no good—probably that jerk Mark Taylor. Well, it didn't matter. Dutch wasn't having it. Nobody had the right to keep him uninformed about Annie. Nobody.

"Mr. Hauk?" A man came on the line.

"Yeah, who's this?"

"This is Grant Thurman, the hospital security chief."

"I got nothing to say to you. I want to know how my wife's doing."

"I'm sorry, sir. The hospital is under a court order not to release that information to you."

"A court order?" He saw red. "Her daughter did this, didn't she? She got a court order to keep you from telling me about my own wife?"

"Actually, no sir, Dr. Harper wasn't in any way involved."

"Is she there?" He reacted as would be expected, though of course he knew she was in Masson's filthy truck on her way to hell. "Let me talk to her."

"Dr. Harper isn't here, sir."

"Well then, get me somebody who can talk to me, and do it right now."

"There is no one here who can help you, Mr. Hauk. If you want to know anything else, you'll need to contact Detective Jeff Meyers with the Seagrove Village Police Department."

Dutch's blood pressure skyrocketed, setting his temples to throbbing. "Give me his number."

"I'm sorry but I don't have it, Mr. Hauk."

"You have it. You can get it. Grab a phone book, man, and look it up. I'm on the road, trying to get back to see Annie."

"I'm sorry, sir. I can't help you. Hospital policy is explicitly clear when it comes to court orders. I'm authorized only to tell you to contact the detective."

Dutch nearly exploded. "Thurman, right? That's your name?"

"Yes sir."

"Fine. I'll deal with you when I get there."

"It isn't in your best interests to levy a threat against hospital security. I'll have to report it, of course. Regardless, you can't come to the hospital, sir."

"Excuse me?" Dutch fisted his hand on the tabletop.

"I said you can't come to—"

"I heard you, moron. I just can't believe what you're telling me."

"I'm telling you, sir, that you can't come within a mile of the hospital unless you're in a life-threatening situation, and in that case, it must be your own life that is in jeopardy and you must be accompanied by a police escort."

Dutch let out a foul stream of curses. "Thurman, you have no idea how much you're going to regret this."

"I'm just a working stiff doing my job, sir." Thurman paused. "You are aware that you've just threatened me again, right? And that all calls into hospital security are recorded for quality assurance purposes? I'll be contacting Detective Meyers immediately."

"Kiss my—"

"Thank you for calling, Mr. Hauk," Thurman interrupted him. "If I can be of further service, please let me know."

The line went dead.

Dutch stared at the phone, too furious to even breathe.

No respect. None. Daring to treat him like this—someone was going to pay for it. They'd gotten a court order to keep him away from his own wife? Only one person would dare.

Mark Taylor.

Dutch growled low in his throat. *Say good-bye, troublemaker. I don't care if it costs me a million dollars. I'll pay whatever it takes. You're a dead man.*

"Are you okay, Lisa?" Gwen flashed the light against the side of the truck near Lisa's head. "You look like you've seen a ghost."

Lisa wasn't sure what she'd seen. Maybe she'd imagined the whole motel-room scene. The door being knocked down, the man with the spiderweb on his hand crashing in.

"You're worried about your mother, aren't you?" Selene shoved her damp hair away from her face. Poured a little water in her hand and patted it against Lisa's forehead.

"Yes. I need to be there with her." Lisa pulled out the tube of salve. "Gwen, put this on your head before that gash gets infected."

"You pray *and* steal?" The petite redhead took the tube. "Now that's a surprising combination."

Lisa grimaced. "It was an emergency. I'm a doctor and I'm seeing signs of infection. It's my duty to help."

"You haven't mentioned your father." Gwen passed Selene the flashlight. "Was theirs a messy divorce?"

"They didn't divorce." Oh, how she wished he were with her mother. This would be so much easier to bear. "He died when I was little." That was her fault too. If she hadn't begged for that roof and told him about the plight of the children in the Haitian orphanage, he wouldn't have gone down there and fallen.

The motel room flashed in her mind. His shouts reverberated and echoed off the walls of her heart. Why couldn't she make out what he was saying? Something exploded. Why couldn't she see what happened in that room after that?

It must not have really happened. If it had, she would remember it. Surely something that important, she'd remember vividly.

"I'm sorry." Selene let out a sigh. "Losing someone you love is never easy, but when you're a child, it's so much harder."

Lisa tried to focus on the conversation, but the images of that room, the man rushing in, her father coming out of the shower wrapped in a towel, his scream—wait a minute. Wait. Wait . . .

If this was a real memory and he was there, then he hadn't died in Haiti. He couldn't have. She clearly saw her barrette in that room. She and her mother had made it at a craft workshop *while* her father had been in Haiti.

"See, Daddy."

"It's beautiful, honey."

"Mom and I made it. It's the only one like it in the whole world . . ."

He'd seen the barrette—*after Haiti.*

Confused and afraid, unable to sort it all out, she grabbed at her throbbing temples and rubbed hard. "Something's not right."

"A lot's not right." Gwen smeared the ointment on her head. "You need to be a little more specific."

Lisa told them about seeing the tattoo on Frank's hand, the images it had triggered in her mind. "They were so real."

"Do you think it actually happened?" Gwen screwed the cap back on the tube of salve. "That's a pretty big thing to forget, Lisa. Maybe your mind's playing tricks on you."

"Maybe." She took the tube from Gwen and offered it to Selene. "Treat that scrape on your knee."

Selene took it. "What happened after you screamed? Was your father still shouting?"

In her mind, Lisa heard the explosion. She involuntarily jumped, her ears ringing. Watching herself, she saw herself cover her ears with her hands, bury her face against the wall, and stare down at the floor.

"Oh no. It's real. It happened." A deep sob lodged in her soul broke loose and pealed, piercing her ears. "It happened."

Selene scooted over and hugged Lisa. So did Gwen. The three of them rocked back and forth, back and forth while Lisa cried.

After long minutes, Selene asked, "What happened in that room?"

Lisa lifted her head from Gwen's shoulder. "My dad didn't die falling off the roof in Haiti. He was shot. A man broke into our motel room and shot him dead. He—he grabbed me and took me out—took me . . ." Lisa tried and tried but couldn't remember. "I don't know where he took me, but my dad died in that room."

"Now I understand why you didn't remember." Selene smoothed Lisa's hair and pressed her cheek against Lisa's crown. "I'm so sorry."

She straightened. The spiderweb. It was the same men. *Impossible. They were too young.* Ones with the same tattoo, then. *Spiders.* No wonder she had always hated them. Could these Spiders really be connected to that one, to what happened back then?

She sniffed and wiped her face with her sleeve. "The man who shot my dad had a tattoo like Frank's."

"A Spider?" Gwen groaned. "Oh, this doesn't sound good. Who was it? Do you know who he worked for?"

"No idea." Lisa shrugged. "I'm only now remembering this at all." Her hands shook. She laced them in her lap. "I—I guess I suppressed it. Trauma can do that, you know."

"It can, and you were very young." Selene squeezed Lisa's shoulder. "I know it's hard and you're hurt and stunned and these aren't the best circumstances, but you've got to keep it together and try to remember where the man took you. It's a long shot that it's the same place, but you could remember something that will help us."

"Give her some time, for pity's sake. This is a big shock."

"I know that, Gwen." Selene shone the flashlight on the truck's wall near Gwen. "But think about it. We need to know all we can to avoid an even bigger shock. This is no time to fall apart. None of us has that luxury. Whatever happened happened, and she survived it. Now if we all want to survive, we have to do what must be done to make that happen. It's that simple."

"You're right. We don't have the luxury of falling apart." Gwen sobered. "When you can, Lisa."

Lisa agreed with Selene. To survive and reclaim their lives, remembering quickly was critical. "I'm trying. Really."

Shoving past the pain, she sank deeper and deeper into her past. Planted herself back in that hotel room. The Spider lifted her off her feet, tucking her under his arm like a football, and then ran outside . . .

"It was a van," she said. White. No windows in back. "He put something over my mouth." She covered her lips with her fingertips. "It was silver. Duct tape. He bound my wrists behind my back with it too. He dumped me in the back and then drove away."

"Was anyone else with him?" Gwen asked.

"No. Just him and me. I—I couldn't move." Panic burgeoning, her chest heaved and fell rapidly, her breathing blasted fast and furious. Hyperventilating, she blinked hard, wrapped herself with her arms and fought to control it. "He murdered my father and abducted me," Lisa told them, her voice cracking. "And God help me, now it's happened again."

"I thought she was coming out of it." Mark had prayed Annie was coming out of the coma.

Rose sent him a sympathetic look. "It happens sometimes. Patients twitch. It's an automatic response."

"But twice?" And twitching at precisely the right time? There had to be more to it. Annie heard him. He felt it in his bones.

"Excuse me." Jeff Meyers claimed Mark's attention. "You need to get out to the waiting room. Peggy Crane has uncovered something you'll want to see."

"Sam?" Mark glanced beyond Annie to the other side of her bed.

"Right here, bud." Sam crossed his arms over his chest. "I'll keep an eye on Annie and Rose. You go on."

Mark left the ICU with Jeff, but Peggy wasn't in the waiting room. "Where is she?"

"Sorry." Jeff motioned to the door on the far side

of the ICU waiting room. "She's in the consult office. Thurman set us up in there right after Dutch called and threatened him because of the restraining order."

"What does Peggy have? Do you know?"

"She wouldn't tell me. She said she wanted you and me together when she broke the seal."

Broke the seal? "What is she talking about?"

Jeff raised his hands. "You know what I know."

When they entered the consult office, Peggy was sitting at the desk, holding a file folder. "Finally. The suspense is making me crazy." Peggy frowned.

"What's this about, Peg?" Mark rounded the desk to face her.

"I went back to the office to check Lisa's old files—the ones Susan Brandt kept on her from the time Lisa first came to her and moved into the Towers with Nora."

"And?"

"And I got the shock of my life." Peggy opened the folder, revealing a large sealed envelope. On it was a handwritten note.

"What does it say?" Mark twisted around so he could read it.

"It's Susan's handwriting. I'd recognize it anywhere," Peggy said. *"To be opened only in case of extreme circumstance directly related to the health and well-being of Lisa Marie Harper."*

Mark's heart beat hard and fast. "You can't get

circumstances any more extreme than these. Open it."

"Jeff, you're witnessing me break the seal."

"I am."

Peggy opened the envelope and slid out a file folder. Her hand shook. On the outside of it CONFIDENTIAL was stamped in dark red ink.

Peggy peeled back the folder front and glanced at the words. "It is indeed a note from Susan."

Mark's knees threatened to buckle. He sat in the visitor's chair. "Read it, Peggy."

She straightened her glasses on her nose, then stared back down at the note. *"Under no circumstances is what I am about to tell you to be revealed to any outside party. I claim medical privilege and retain all rights to the contents of this file. Continuing to read this document attests to your acceptance of these terms and conditions. There are no exceptions I deem acceptable to violate the terms or conditions stated."*

"Can she do that in her capacity?" Mark asked Jeff.

"Unless Lisa killed someone, yes. Murder would have to be disclosed to authorities. Dutch Hauk's alive," Jeff said. "That tells me she hasn't killed anyone. He'd be first on her list."

Mark agreed and dared to hope what Annie had rambled to Jeff Meyers in the ambulance that she didn't want Lisa to remember would be revealed in Susan's note.

Peggy raised her eyebrows. "As director of Crossroads Crisis Center, I am asking both of you if you accept these terms and conditions. If you do, please state so by saying yes."

"Yes."

Playing it by the book. Vintage Peggy. "Yes."

"Here we go then." She adjusted her glasses on the tip of her nose, and then began reading aloud:

When Lisa Harper was seven years old, she witnessed her father's murder and was abducted by the killer during the commission of that crime. Certain specifics in this murder-abduction case were withheld. At the time of this writing, which is nine years after the incident occurred, those specifics still have not been released.

Lisa was missing for nearly two weeks. Despite a massive manhunt, the police had no leads and little hope of ever finding her.

On day twelve, Lisa's mother, Annie Harper, received a phone call from Lisa, who had escaped. The police retrieved Lisa, Annie flew down and picked her up, and they returned home. I was brought in to crisis counsel Lisa, but all of my attempts to assist her were futile. Lisa had no recollection of going to Disney World, of being in a hotel with her father, of his murder or her abduction, or of anything that had happened to her during the time she was held captive. She had no recollection of her escape, the police, or her mother retrieving her and returning home.

Physical examination revealed she had not been sexually abused. She did have bruises and scrapes, but nothing that wouldn't heal. Shortly before Charles and Lisa took the trip to Disney, her father had gone to Haiti to treat the children at an orphanage and help put a new roof onto the building. Soon it became apparent that she mentally substituted what actually happened to her father with something she could emotionally bear. Even today, Lisa believes her father died falling off the orphanage roof.

Over the years, I have attempted many times to convince Annie to seek intensive therapy for Lisa, but Annie consistently refused. She had prayed on the matter and felt strongly that she was to leave it alone. That Lisa was fragile from whatever she had endured, and she would remember the truth when she was emotionally strong enough to cope with it. The matter was kept quiet, and few knew the circumstances surrounding Lisa's situation. The media cooperated, as did the local authorities and those in the know, and Lisa was permitted to forget.

Be advised that in situations of extreme duress, repressed memories can surface. If this happens, Lisa will need professional assistance to cope constructively with the resulting challenges. Historically in these cases, those challenges have the potential to be devastating to the victim.

I have been sworn to secrecy, and I am honoring that request. But Annie has all of the details. Talk to her and, should circumstances warrant it, be prepared to provide extreme intervention.

—Dr. Susan Brandt, administrator, Cross-roads Crisis Center and legal guardian of Lisa Harper

Peggy dropped the page and blinked hard, her jaw dangling loose. "I had no idea."

Jeff sucked in a sharp breath. "I ran a check on Lisa, Mark. We have nothing on any of this."

"Someone sealed the records."

"No," Jeff said. "We'd see that records exist and are sealed. There *are* no records. Not on the kidnapping or the murder."

Peggy looked at Mark. "When Charles was alive, he and the coroner were good friends. They played couples' bridge with their wives."

Mark thought a second. "The coroner wouldn't have access to Lisa's records. Maybe the records of Charles's death, though with that happening in Orlando, at most he'd have a courtesy copy since Charles was a resident here. But there should be a record of Lisa being missing. Something about the search for her."

"Mark's right, our coroner wouldn't be involved at all."

Peggy tucked her chin to her chest and frowned at them over the top of her glasses. "This is a village, okay? We're a close-knit group, and Annie Harper has lived here her whole life. So had Charles. The coroner wouldn't be involved, but his brother certainly could have been."

John Green. Mark stilled. "The mayor could have had the records sealed."

"We'd have an order for that," Jeff insisted.

Peggy sighed. "Now, you would. Back then, John probably called the chief and told him to lose the records, and that was the end of it."

"He was a good man," Mark said. "If John thought it was best for Lisa, he'd do it."

"Yes, he would." Peggy nodded.

"That doesn't help much." Jeff let out a grunt. "Considering John Green's dead and can't answer questions."

Poor Lisa. Hot knives of fear stabbed Mark's chest. To deal with something this awful once was bad enough. But twice? *God, what are You thinking?*

"What do we do?" Mark paced the small office, lacing his hands behind his head. "Only Annie knows the details that could maybe lead us to Lisa, and she can't tell us."

"We know Karl Masson is involved."

"That's presumption, Peggy," Jeff said. "He was here. That makes it likely, but it isn't indisputable proof."

Peggy stood. "Fine, you give him the benefit of the doubt. I'm not. Common sense says if it looks and smells like a skunk, it's a skunk. And if Karl Masson's here and Lisa's been kidnapped, then he's involved. That tells me NINA is behind this. Dutch Hauk's a bully and a coward. He wouldn't dare come after Lisa on his own—and that tells me you two need to be calling in every favor you've got with everyone you know to find out what NINA is up to that could include kidnapping a woman."

"Or a doctor."

"Okay." Peggy flipped the file closed. "A woman or a doctor." She picked up the papers. "We have to be realistic. Annie might not wake up in time to help. Which means we have to do everything we can for Lisa on every other front. When Annie does wake up, I will *not* be telling her that we didn't find her daughter."

"We're doing all we can, Peggy. We're asking the questions. We're checking with resources."

"Well, Mark, I'll leave you to it, then. I'll be at the center. Maybe I can drum up something else on this."

"She's calling in the prayer warriors," Jeff warned Mark.

"Don't be ridiculous, Jeffrey." Peggy walked past them. "The prayer warriors have been in the chapel since we got word Annie was critical, before Lisa was abducted."

The church ladies had immediately activated. Mark watched her go, hoping they had more of God's favor than Lisa or he had. They did have the right idea, going to God first and not as a last resort. He was grateful for that. But honestly he'd have been more grateful if Lisa had been spared. "She's right about Masson."

"Yeah." Jeff looked at Mark, his eyes shining regret. "She is."

Masson had to be neck-deep in this. Because of Dutch or some other as-yet-unknown reason. But Mark was sure of one thing. This new information left by Susan proved Lisa was in double the danger they first thought: danger from her abductors and from her memories, and he dared to wonder . . .

Which would prove to be the more deadly tie?

17

Karl Masson sat in a booth inside Ruby's Diner. He'd changed from one of his usual Brooks Brothers suits to camp shorts, a blue T-shirt advertising Seagrove Village's fishing rodeo, and sandals. Dressed like most other locals, he'd fade into the crowd and go unnoticed. It was as easy to hide out in the open here as it was anywhere else. The key was to look and act as if he belonged. Glancing out the wide window, he scanned the parking lot. The rising sun slanted glints of light on the cars lined up like rows of little soldiers.

Ruby's wasn't a tourist destination. The locals in Seagrove Village came out every morning, some for breakfast, some for coffee, and most for the latest village gossip. This morning the buzz was all about Annie's assault and Lisa's abduction. Sitting alone in a booth with the newspaper, Karl kept his head down, ate slowly, and paid close attention.

Megan, Ruby's friendliest waitress and gossip-in-chief of the village grapevine, refilled Karl's coffee. Her red curls rioted, as if they'd been caught in a stiff storm. "More cream?"

"No thanks." He pretended to be engrossed in the newspaper to avoid looking directly at her.

"All right, then. If you need anything else, just yell."

"Thank you." His cell vibrated against his side. Karl pulled out his phone. "Hello."

"New cargo location is needed."

Frank. He was in Jackson, Mississippi, and ready to pick up the witness.

"Anything else to report?" Karl fished a couple of bills out of his wallet and dropped them on the table.

"No sir."

"Take Highway 49 south back to I-10, then head west. Continue west until further notice."

"Got it."

Spotting the coroner sitting across from a sober-faced teenage boy in the far-left booth, Karl turned away and went out to his car. He'd heard the gossip on them too. The former mayor's brother and son were about to go to court to keep the boy with Hank. They were talking softly about it but loud enough for Karl to hear the boy, Lance, clearly. He was terrified of his mother, Darla Green. Lance told his uncle Hank if the judge made him live with her, he'd run away and stay gone. He had to or his mother would kill him just like she killed his dad. The boy's fear was palpable, and if Karl were Hank, he'd do whatever needed doing to keep the boy away from her.

When a kid was that scared of his own parent, there's reason. Karl knew that firsthand, just as he knew the boy was right. Darla Green had killed John, and Lance would toe her line or she'd kill him too. The woman didn't have a motherly bone in her body. She was every bit as cold-blooded as Raven.

Feeling sorry for the boy, Karl left the parking lot and pulled onto Highway 98, heading west. Nothing he'd heard had him worried that either the pug-nose detective or Mark Taylor and his team had pegged Karl or NINA as being involved. Dutch was getting full credit for Annie and Lisa.

At Gramercy, Karl hooked a right and slowed to a crawl, checking the Crossroads Crisis Center parking lot. Kelly's SUV wasn't in the lot.

He couldn't go after her at Three Gables, not even with half its security force out hunting for Lisa. With Taylor's old team in town, that would be the height of stupidity. But maybe Karl could catch Kelly leaving the grounds. Odds of his being recognized even in Seagrove Village were slim to none. Except by Kelly Walker. All they had was an artist's sketch, and in his opinion, it wasn't a great one.

For the most part, people saw what they expected to see, and few expected to see him on their streets. That's why Karl stayed low-key and hid in plain sight. People ignored him. He used that to his advantage.

Again his cell vibrated. He snatched it up and checked caller ID. Blank. "Hello?"

"Raven. To whom am I speaking?"

Raven calling him unexpectedly? He hoped it wasn't bad news. "Lone Wolf."

"Mission?"

"Shifter." What was she doing?

"Sorry, Lone Wolf. Headquarters has experienced minor technical difficulties. A hundred percent verifications are currently required on all communications."

Karl spit out the mission's authorization code. "Alpha 263891."

"I'd like a cargo status update."

Odd. "We're on schedule, ma'am."

"Excellent." She paused. "And our client is . . . where?"

"On the way to the hospital. They phoned. His wife is critical."

"Critical."

The bitterness in Raven's tone had Karl swallowing hard. If Annie lived and caused problems . . . He'd been warned. He should have just shot her and been done with it. "In a coma."

"That's better."

"Yes ma'am."

"Contact the client and issue a delay order. A restraining order against him has been served on the hospital." She went on to catch Karl up on NINA's reaction to it.

He pulled into a bank's empty parking lot and gave the call his full attention.

"We're taking care of it. Just keep him away from the hospital. Have him get updates from the road."

Something was wrong. Really wrong. Raven wasn't worried about the client. She was worried about NINA. So why would Dutch showing up at the hospital concern her at all?

No matter how he figured it, it didn't make sense. "Yes ma'am."

"Any questions?"

No way was he touching that one. She'd have a

kill order issued on him before he put down the phone. "No ma'am."

"Excellent. Raven out."

Karl hung up, certain he'd just passed the test to determine whether or not he lived another day.

And maybe he had.

Uneasy and shaking, he called Dutch and then waited for him to answer.

Finally he did. "Yeah."

"Stay away from the hospital."

"You've got to be kidding me."

"I never kid anyone." Karl braked for two kids waiting to cross the street on their bikes.

Dutch's sigh crackled through the phone. "As it turns out, I have to stay away. Somebody put out a restraining order against me to keep me away from Annie. My own wife. Can you believe that?"

"The cargo?" Karl guessed Lisa. She had reason.

"No. It happened after the cargo shift."

That could explain Raven's call. Okay, then. Things were making more sense now. Karl watched the cars driving down Highway 98. Morning traffic was picking up. "Working on that. But even if it's dropped, you stay away."

"Why? She's critical."

Karl had told him Annie was critical. Why would he think he didn't know it? *Good grief.* "Let me be clear. Show up there and you won't be leaving."

"I'm the client, remember? Don't threaten me."

"I'm saving your lousy backside, man. Taylor, Meyers, and the entire crew from Crossroads are looking for you. You walk in, and I guarantee you won't walk out."

"Taylor did it. Had to be him. Tell the boss I'm offering a million dollars. I want Mark Taylor dead by dark."

"I'll pass that along." What did Dutch know about Taylor? Couldn't be much.

"Not just wounded. I want him dead."

"I understand. But remember my point. Stay out of that hospital, or you'll be getting buried."

"Taylor's not a killer."

"The boss issued the order. You want to complain, you complain to her."

"The boss? Personally?" Dutch's voice rattled. "What's she got to do with this?"

"You can ask her that too." Karl glanced into the rearview, wishing he'd brought a fresh cup of Ruby's coffee with him. He hadn't stretched out for nearly thirty-six hours. Another jolt of her caffeine would work wonders. "Do what you want, but if it were me, I'd do as I was told. The boss isn't exactly in a good mood."

Dutch paused. "You aren't warning me against Taylor and his apes. You're telling me NINA doesn't want me at the hospital."

Karl laughed. He couldn't help himself. "I just told you the boss said stay away. That's pretty straight talk. What's wrong that you can't get it?"

"No, that's not what I mean. NINA doesn't want me dead. It wants me out of the way in case it wants to take some action at the hospital." Finally, the light dawned.

"If you're told to stay away from the hospital, you'd be wise to stay away from the hospital."

"I'm clear. NINA is everywhere."

Dutch was a sorry excuse for a man.

"I'm supposed to meet with that joker Meyers about the restraining order. I'll have car trouble—again."

"This time, I suggest it be credible trouble. If I hear you're cruising around in Seagrove Village again when you're supposed to be elsewhere, you'll have plenty of reasons to regret it."

"What are you talking about?"

"Don't bother lying to me. I know the truth."

Silence.

Karl laughed. "You were more right than you realized, man. NINA *is* everywhere." Would Dutch figure out that Tack, the caretaker at Chessman's old house, was on NINA's payroll? Probably not for a week or two, if ever.

Call waiting signaled. Karl checked his watch. Seven o'clock. Oh, man. Frank checking in and Karl was late getting specifics back to him. "Follow orders."

"Where do you want me to go?"

That attitude was more like it. "Anywhere but

the village. Wait. Meet me in Opp, Alabama. Usual place."

Without waiting for Dutch's response, Karl took the incoming call. It was Raven. He passed along Dutch's million-dollar offer on Taylor.

"Tell him to wire the funds," Raven said.

"Do I need to stay close pending incoming orders?"

"Continue your scheduled activities. If your orders change, you'll be notified."

"Yes ma'am."

She briefed him on another matter, then abruptly ended the call. "Raven out."

Karl dragged in a steadying breath and then phoned Frank. "How's it going?"

"Routine. Just need directions."

Karl gave them to him, sending Frank to a convenience store on the south side of Jackson.

"I passed that location fifteen minutes ago."

"I got hung up. At the moment, things are not so routine on this end." Karl pulled into a drive-through coffee shop and ordered a large leaded coffee, then pulled halfway around to the window and stopped. "The boss just called. Someone from Seagrove Village PD just called Orlando PD asking for info on Charles Harper's case."

"I see."

A swallow of hot coffee burned all the way down Karl's throat. "Any evidence the doc has remembered anything?" Frank would know he meant Lisa; he'd rather not use her name.

"None. I flashed my web. She didn't react to it."

"Push a little harder. Test her."

"How? You said hands off on this whole shipment unless extreme measures were required. Now it's beat it out of her?"

"No, that won't net the information we want." She might just take Frank in hand-to-hand combat. He had weight, reach, and brute strength, but she was light-years ahead of him in skill, technique, and discipline—and she had the most to lose. "Just watch her for any reaction."

"To what?"

"Call her a shrub."

Lisa sat quietly in the back end of the truck. Gwen and Selene were sleeping. Soon they'd be stopping again, and this time, she had to be ready.

Images filled her mind. Her tied up in the back of the Spider's van, working loose the duct tape binding her arms and then working on that securing her ankles. She left it in place so the Spider couldn't tell.

He stopped and turned a hard glare on her from the driver's seat. "You stay put, you hear me?"

On her side on the floor, Lisa bobbed her head, her heart threatening to punch through her chest wall.

His door cracked open. He got out and she stretched up to see him enter a store.

She ducked down low and stole some of his drinking water and splashed it on her face, then rolled backward so he wouldn't realize she'd moved, getting into place just as he opened the van's back door.

"You're sweating like a pig." He ripped the duct tape off her mouth.

It tore at her skin and her face burned like fire. "I'm sick."

"It's hot out here."

"I—I get sick when I get hot. My mom takes me to the hospital for medicine."

His eyes stretched wide. "Stay here."

That was a silly order for someone tied up.

He went back into the store. She watched from the back window, and as soon as the door closed behind him, she yanked at the loose tape, scrambled to the driver's seat, and slipped out the door. Her bare feet burned on the hot pavement. She bit back a squeal, praying he didn't see her, and ran like the wind straight across the street and into a dress shop.

A gray-haired woman behind the counter saw the dangling tape at her mouth, wrists, and ankles, and her jaw fell open. She rushed over. "Are you all right, sweetheart?"

"No. The man took me. Call my mom. I want my mom!"

"I'll call the police."

"No, he's coming. He's coming! I have to hide!" Frantic, she searched and saw a hole under the counter, then scrambled into it and pulled a curtain at one end shut. Squeezing her eyes shut, she begged. *Please, please don't let him find me. Please don't let him find me. Please.*

"Stay put. No matter what." The lady locked the door.

Lisa heard the click, then thudding. The man beating on the door. Would he knock it down too?

The lady hollered at him through the glass. "Sorry, we don't open until ten."

"My daughter is missing! Did she come here?"

I'm not his daughter. Don't listen. Please, don't listen to him. Lisa opened the curtain and crawled out so she could see the lady. Shaking and shivering, she held her breath. *Don't let him break the glass. Make him too weak.*

"I said my daughter is missing. Have you seen her?"

The lady didn't even glance Lisa's way. "No, but I'll phone the police right away." She grabbed the phone, dialed, and put it to her ear.

He hesitated, then shouted his thanks and ran off. Lisa bobbed up, saw him run to the van, hop in, and take off. His tires churned smoke and squealed on the pavement.

The lady watched to make sure he was really gone, and then she came back to Lisa. "You get down low and out of sight, you hear me? He could come back."

Lisa dropped down, curled her knees to her chest, and crunched into a ball, then held on as tightly as she could and tried not to move, not to breathe too deep. Maybe if she got little enough and stayed still enough, then no one would be able to see her. She could just be . . . invisible, and her daddy would be fine, and everything would be right again.

Invisible. It never happened. None of it ever happened. Daddy's busy at work. He's always busy at work. It never happened. There was no trip to Disney, no motel with the big hat, no barrette, no . . . nothing.

There was nothing.

The box truck stopped short.

Jerked from her memories, Lisa braced herself with a hand to its side and another to the wooden truck bed. Gwen and Selene startled awake.

"What's going on?" Selene's voice trembled.

Gwen turned on her flashlight, checked her watch. "It's only seven o'clock. It's too soon to stop again."

"Maybe we've arrived at wherever they're taking us." Selene sounded as worried as Lisa felt about that.

"We might not have much time. Listen to me," Lisa said. "Next time they take us inside—"

The lock clicked.

Juan swung open the door, and Frank hurled a woman inside.

Her wrists were bound behind her back. Her ankles were banded together, she wore a metal cuff, and black tape slashed an X across her mouth.

She landed with a dull thump and rolled in deeper, colliding with Lisa.

This time, they wouldn't be going inside.

"How's Annie?"

Standing with Jeff and Joe in the ICU consult office, Mark turned at the sound of Ben Brandt's voice. "No change. We thought she might be coming around, but Rose said it was involuntary twitching."

Mark glanced out the window on the far side of the room. Dawn had passed, morning had arrived, and gratitude that Annie was alive tangled with his fear and worry about Lisa. "She survived the night. Rose says that's a good sign. More stable but still critical."

"She's fighting and that's good," Ben said. "Anything new on Lisa?"

"Jeff and Joe were about to brief me." Mark focused on Jeff.

"I've been on the phone with half the county down in Orlando," he said. "Lisa's father was murdered in a motel room down there when Lisa was seven. But she wasn't on scene or mentioned in any of the reports."

Mark didn't understand. "But Susan said Lisa was there."

"And I'm sure she was or Annie wouldn't be worried about her remembering the incident. But Lisa doesn't appear on any of the paperwork. None of it, Mark."

He frowned, sensing plenty was being left unsaid. "That's on the record. Off the record, what's their explanation for that?"

"Unofficially, the detective who reviewed the case file picked up on some odd notes. The bottom line is he suspects the records were recently sanitized." Jeff lowered his voice, dragged a hand over his neck. "I've been thinking about it. Seems logical that before hooking up with NINA, the criminal element expunged anything on Lisa."

"Why do you think so?" Joe folded a fresh piece of gum into his mouth.

"They sure wouldn't want any ties to that incident. It could botch their merger." Jeff shrugged. "That's my suspicion, anyway. But the detective came up with an explanation I can't rule out."

Mark prodded. "What's that?"

"The Orlando police expunged Lisa's records for her own protection."

Surprise streaked through Mark. "Legally expunged her?"

"No." Jeff looked him straight in the eye. "Not legally."

"Mmm." Joe seemed skeptical. "Tampering with official documents? They'd have to have a good reason to take that on."

"Maybe they were afraid she'd be hunted down. She did escape from her kidnappers." Jeff shook his head. "I've been at this awhile, and I read people pretty well. He has a reason for thinking the records were altered. What his reason is, I don't know and I'm not sure it matters. I'd put my money on the crooks' making sure they didn't mess up their merger with NINA. They had to know if the merger failed, NINA would wipe them out. What I'm clear on is that the detective was more afraid of NINA than of exposing anything to us."

"Too scared of retribution to talk openly?"

Jeff nodded. "I'm surprised he told me as much as he did."

"It fits, bro." Joe pulled Mark out of the room and whispered, "Feedback from my sources is loaded. Heavy chatter, some confirmed."

"On what specifically?"

"NINA's formed strategic business alliances with most of the major players here, in Europe, and in Mexico. The Orlando cop's smart to be scared."

NINA chatter was never good news. It was a matter of whether their operations were really bad or internationally lethal. "What kind of alliances?"

"Mostly the trafficking kind."

Which would give weight to Jeff's supposition

about NINA's potential partners' removing Lisa from the record to protect its merger. "Drugs?"

"Worse." Fury burned in Joe's eyes. "Humans. Best our sources can tell, it's relatively new to NINA. Two, maybe three years. But the Orlando thugs have been at it for a long time. They'd target victims who had no families or whose families lacked the resources to fund a search and kick up a media fuss. HQ fears the NINA connection's changed that. Women and kids, bro."

"No." Lisa's first abduction. The cheap motel where Charles had been murdered and she'd been kidnapped. Mark's stomach roiled. His Lisa caught up in that then and again now? "No."

"There's more."

"More?" Mark could barely absorb what he'd already heard.

Joe nodded. "Let's share the rest with the others."

They walked back into the consult office. Jeff stood arms folded over his chest. "Sorry," Joe said.

"No need." Ben shot Jeff a loaded look.

Jeff sighed. "Tell me what you can."

"Masson is directly involved." Joe hiked a hip onto the corner of the desk. "They're abducting women for two reasons. The first is obvious and one we're all too familiar with." He turned his focus to Mark. "The second reason might be worse."

Mark grunted. Selling human beings into prostitution. How could anything be worse?

"Selected women are abducted and auctioned as fighters. To live, they have to fight other women to the death."

The video clip of the murdered FBI agent from Omega One—he'd sent it to warn Mark that they were connected. "You think Lisa was handpicked and abducted because she's strong in self-defense?"

"NINA has a big political agenda. To fund it, they need a lot of money. Human trafficking for various purposes is more lucrative than drugs."

Skills learned and practiced to protect Lisa were to blame for her abduction? It was too sick to wrap his mind around.

"I don't know anything for a fact about Lisa, bro. Just that this is going on, and the clips . . . She could be in even worse jeopardy than we first thought."

He was right. Revulsion swamped Mark.

"She won't do it." Ben slumped, stuffed a hand in his pocket. "She won't fight to kill."

"To stay alive, she might." Jeff turned to Mark. "You know her best. What do you think?"

"It's against everything she believes in." It was a total violation of her faith, morals, ethics, and Hippocratic oath—which is probably why Dutch did it. What would she do?

Fumes-of-faith Christian. Physician.

Would she survive or choose to die?

18

Timing is everything.

And right now, the timing was wrong to get rid of Kelly Walker.

Karl didn't like it. But he hadn't survived and avoided prison his entire career by being stupid.

With minimal muttering, he made a U-turn on Highway 85 south of Crestview and headed north to cross the state line. Highway 9 took him through Florala to Opp, Alabama, and from there, he went north to Frank Jackson State Park where he'd previously parked his RV near the lake.

When Karl arrived, Dutch's car was parked by Karl's RV, and Dutch was sitting in a folding chair beneath a sprawling oak.

Karl pulled into his camping site and glanced down at a white plastic bag on the floorboard. He checked his pocket for the device that had been in the bag, and then parked so he'd have the privacy he needed to do what he wanted done.

The sun was bright and hot. Man, he hated the South. Barely eight o'clock in the morning and it was scorching hot and muggy. In January, no less. Didn't this armpit of the earth ever cool down?

He left his car and paused behind Hauk's, planted the device under his bumper, then walked on out into the open where Hauk could see him.

Hauk tipped a can of beer at his mouth. Drinking before noon? Karl frowned. How Annie put up with the lump of human waste was a mystery. It had to be hard, going from her life with Charles Harper to one with this sorry excuse for a human being. She was so like Angel, and there was no way she would have put up with him. "Surprised you're already here."

Hauk took a long swig. Burped. "Yeah, well, I was headed toward New Orleans, so it was an easy shot."

"New Orleans?"

Hauk's lids lowered, guarding his eyes. "You said anywhere but the village. Figured I'd run down to the Quarter and see what was up."

NINA had active interests in New Orleans that didn't involve Dutch Hauk. Was he trying to insert himself deeper into the organization, or had he just blindly bumbled into NINA's way?

Hauk emptied his can, crushed it with his foot, then tossed it into a small white ice chest beside his chair and pulled out a fresh one. He tugged with his finger and popped the top. His eyes were bloodshot and droopy, his jaw lax. "You handle the Taylor hit?"

"I told you to wire the funds."

"I did. A million, just like I said." He waved a hand. "Better call her and get the code."

"Got it. Just waiting for the green light." Karl had no code, but there was no way he was calling

Raven. She'd been clear. If his orders changed, she'd let him know.

"There's plenty of time. Word at Ruby's is Taylor's staying put at the hospital. He thinks Lisa will contact him there." Dutch chortled and squinted against the sun. "How's Annie?"

The idiot was half snockered already. "How should I know?" Karl retrieved a second chair from his RV and sat near Dutch. "My work with her ended on Highway 98."

"I can't call the hospital. Not with the restraining order out on me. They won't tell me anything."

Was the guy a hypocrite or just nuts? He pays to put her in the hospital or morgue and then acts all upset because she's there? Still, he was the million-dollar client, and at least for the moment, placating him and issuing orders was Karl's best bet for keeping him out of the way and too busy to cause trouble. "She's still in a coma."

"What about Lisa?"

"In tow." Karl got a bottle of water out of his RV fridge, returned to his chair, then unscrewed the cap and fed his curiosity. "You were with Lisa a long time." With her or tormenting her from a distance. "Did you see any evidence that she remembered the incident?"

"You mean the hit on Charles?"

Karl would rather not have used his name, but Charles's murder was exactly what Karl meant. He wished he'd gotten here first. He'd have swept the site to make sure Hauk wasn't wired. If he thought it would benefit him to turn on Karl, he would. The idiot would turn on NINA. Karl nodded.

"None." Hauk set his can into a net holder built into the arm of the chair. "Why?"

"Just wondered." Frank was putting her to the test. A fissure of uneasiness opened inside Karl. What if she recalled the word *shrub?* Karl hadn't wanted to risk doing anything to trigger her memory, but he had no choice. There was a chance going in that the abduction itself could do that, but if she recalled the hit on her father, then both she *and* Kelly Walker could tag Karl for two different crimes. The special risks involved were the reason he'd subcontracted two operatives through his New Orleans contact to come in as Edmunds and Powell. As much as Karl hated adding additional links to a mission, he couldn't have risked snatching Lisa Harper himself.

The minute Dutch had come to NINA with the contract on Lisa that included using Annie to get to Lisa, Karl had gotten a bad feeling. He'd suggested refusing the contract, but Dutch offered big money and Raven moved forward on it. Karl had done little but worry ever since. He hated worrying, but things were working out. Frank would stop shortly and call her a shrub. And her reaction would determine whether she'd make it to her final destination.

"You worried she'll remember?"

Karl frowned at Dutch, sprawled in the chair, his clothes rumpled, his legs stretched out and crossed at the ankles. "You'd be wise to worry too. The intelligence community is involved now."

"Why? She's a nobody." Dutch clamped his jaw tight. "Forget it. I don't care. I've been waiting for this for years, and I'm going to enjoy every second of it. Let her worry." Dutch sniffed. "After all the misery she's put me through . . . she's in for life." He gripped the chair arms, squeezed until his knuckles bulged white. "I want to know she's suffering. I want her to have no control of anything that happens to her. And I want to know there's nothing she can do but put up with it."

"We know what you want. You've been more than clear." Offering her final buyer ten grand a month to post a video of her suffering on a private site . . . Even in a world full of deviates, that was sick.

Hauk's eyes looked glassy, red and rheumy. "So what if the intelligence community is involved? They won't find her, and once she's delivered, she'll never get away. Even if she escaped, there's nowhere to go. She can't cause you any trouble."

Shortsighted fool. Lisa had been seven— *seven*—and she'd caused plenty of trouble. More resourceful than any adult ever snatched and the first and only shrub to ever get away. If she had done that at seven, what could she do as an adult?

The possibilities were staggering.

The truck stopped.

Selene, Gwen, and Amanda walked in front of Lisa toward the convenience store. Lisa saw a sign on it—the same human-trafficking sign as on the other store doors.

A memory she relived often assaulted her. She was sixteen, in Dutch's store cleaning with her mother. He shoved a paper sign like the ones in the windows at her and shouted, "You do what I say or you'll end up just like these people. You hear me, girl?"

Within hours, her mother had turned her over to Susan Brandt, and Lisa's life had changed forever. Her mother had given her up to spare her from Dutch. And, God forgive her, Lisa had been relieved to go.

She skimmed the paper next to the sign. *Lost pet. Call Nina.* No phone number. Just like the others. Nina. Lisa's skin crawled. *NINA!* Dutch was involved with NINA, and so were all these stores on their route. The same NINA that went after Kelly Walker was into human trafficking, and they had snatched Lisa.

Oh, God. Oh, God. What do I do?

"Hurry up." Frank appeared at her shoulder.

Lisa glanced back at the truck, memorized the

tag number, repeating it in her mind, and walked on, hoping her weak knees wouldn't fail her.

The rest room was small but had three stalls. When the door closed behind Lisa, Gwen said, "What do we do?"

"Nothing this time," Lisa said, still reeling and trying to absorb all the information running through her mind. What did she trust? dismiss? What was real and true, and what was borne in fear? "No window, one door. And this clerk is as bad as the woman who hid behind the newspaper. He's not going to help us."

Selene disappeared into a stall. "Obviously the clerks have been bought off."

Another flash. She was much, much younger. In the back of the van. Duct tape. The Spider on the phone, taking bids. He was auctioning her.

How in the world could she forget being auctioned? Riding in the back of that stinky van day and night? One day after another until they ran together like one endless day. One long nightmare.

Her father shot. Murdered.

Being kidnapped. Restrained.

Terrified and helpless. Hopeless.

Trauma could cause her to repress, but her mother surely knew better, and she'd never said a word. Lisa twisted the metal cuff circling her wrist. Why?

"Lisa." Amanda snapped her fingers. "Come on,

we need to move before they come in after us."

"Right." Lisa refocused, rubbing her hands. Hot and yet chilled to the bone. "First chance, I'm going to make a move." In the van, the first time she'd been abducted she'd played sick. It had worked then and, God willing, it would work now. "Just go with what I say, okay?"

Gwen nodded.

Amanda frowned. "Discuss first, then we act."

"Not okay." Selene stood her ground. "You're overprotective, Lisa. This is my life, and I'm not going to just pass control over it to you." Selene, washing her hands, called back over her shoulder, "I did that with my manager and look where it got me. You're nothing like him, but still. I'm never doing that again. It's my choice and my decision to make."

"Sorry. You and Amanda are right." Lisa was working on the overprotective thing, but she had a ways to go.

"No problem." Selene turned to face her. "Right now, any ideas are better than mine so I am listening. I just want to decide for myself."

"Understood." This was touchy. "The more I tell you, the greater the odds we'll get caught. Slips, body language, even rapid-eye movement signals them we're up to something. That's why I asked you to just follow my lead. I'm trained. It increases our odds of success. I wasn't trying to take away your choices."

"Okay. I'm not trained and that sounds reasonable." Selene snagged a towel from a stack near the sink. "But don't take on extra risks for me."

Amanda added, "And don't wait too long to do something. Who knows how many more stops we'll make?"

Wise advice, yet Lisa needed a little processing time. Were all these memories real? How did she tell which ones were and which weren't? How could she be sure?

God, help me. Show me the truth and the way.

If it were just for her, she doubted He'd bother answering. But to spare the others, surely He would.

Someone pounded on the door.

Lisa jumped. So did Gwen.

"Yeah?" Lisa called out.

"Move it."

"Just a second. My stomach is upset. I don't want to get sick in the truck." Her plan solidified. *Prepare the foundation.* "Give me the ointment," Lisa whispered and held out her hand.

She squirted a bit on her fingertip and wrote a message on the mirror to call Mark. *Please, let someone see it who will call him. Please.*

Gwen stuffed the tube down her shirt. "Let's go."

They walked out and Juan dropped his gaze, refusing to look her in the eye. "Are you well, *señorita*?"

Lisa rubbed her abdomen. "My stomach is upset."

"Move it." Frank swept the air with a hand.

They went back to the truck. No one around. No one to signal. *Could we please catch a break? Just one?*

She put her foot on the bumper to hike herself inside.

"Wait." Juan rushed up and handed her a can of 7UP. "For your *estómago.*" He patted his stomach.

"Thank you." She took the can and then got in.

Frank grabbed her arm, exposing the spiderweb tattoo on his hand. "Don't expect special treatment, Harper. You're a shrub now, and don't forget it."

Shrub . . . *"Time for you to become a shrub."*

"Mom, what does that mean?"

Arrows of icy fear streaked through Lisa. Adrenaline gushed through her veins. Shock stole her breath. It took all she had to hide her reaction. *Shrub.*

The man who murdered her father, who kidnapped her from the motel room—he had called her a shrub.

It was definitely all real.

Oh . . . Lord.

And there was more. Much more.

She was in over her head—way too far over to ever get herself, Gwen, Selene, and Amanda out.

I need help, God. I need Mark.

• • •

"How's she doing?" Mark stepped to Annie's bedside and spared Sam a glance.

"No change."

Still comatose. Still small and frail and unmoving. But the steady beep of the heart monitor, the consistent peaks on the screen reassured him. "She's hanging tough."

"You bet she is, bud." Sam stepped back. "I'll be back in five."

Mark nodded. When Sam departed, Mark hooked his little finger with Annie's. He hoped for the tap of her finger against his, but it didn't come, and only the monitors and the steady rise and fall of her chest assured him she was still alive.

"Annie, you have to wake up and help me. I need to know. Is what I've learned what you don't want Lisa to remember?" He plucked a loose piece of lint from her hair. "If it is, Lisa is in trouble. Human trafficking and NINA are involved, not just Dutch. I can't connect all the dots yet, but my gut's telling me I don't have much time. Is Dutch connected to NINA, or did he somehow find them and hire them to do this? There's a connection, and I need you to wake up and help me find it."

No movement, only silence. While he willed her to wake, she stayed asleep. "Don't give up, Annie. We can never give up."

He glanced heavenward and then down at Lisa's mother. "Since Jane, I've never asked anyone for anything for myself. I have no right. You know I accept full responsibility for that. But now I'm begging you for help. Lisa needs me. I have to be there for her. I can't lose her too, Annie. I can't fail again, and I don't know where to look or what to do, because nothing makes sense. NINA and Dutch? What would NINA want with him?"

"Sorry to interrupt, my boy."

Surprised he hadn't noted an approach, he spun around. Nora stood out of striking distance, her eyes clouded, her face lined with worry. "Nora."

She gave his upper arm a gentle squeeze. "Annie would help you if she could, but she can't. Right now, the dearie's got all she can handle to just hang on."

Mark blinked. Where was Nora going with this?

"I want you to stop fretting. There's a time for that"—she twisted her mouth, scrunching her face—"and this ain't it."

"Nora, you don't understand." How could he explain?

"I'm thinking I do. You're scared to death of failing two of the four most important women in your life. You're scared Lisa won't fight like they want her to and she'll be choosing to die herself over hurting somebody else. You've got this weird notion you have to earn her love, when love can't be earned. She's got to give it, my boy, just like

308

Christ Himself's given you redemption by taking on the Cross."

She gave him a healthy nod, then stared at him over the top of her thick glasses. "I understand plenty. It's you who don't understand."

Christ had redeemed him. Logically, Mark knew it. But knowing it and feeling redeemed in your heart were two different things. And try as he might, Mark hadn't figured out the key to the second one. "What don't I understand?"

"Grace, I'm thinking, but that ain't my point."

"What is your point?"

"God understands it all, and He didn't put Lisa through all the hell she's been through for nothing. There's been a purpose to every bit of it. You figure out what that is, and you'll figure out what you need to know to find her."

Mark stilled. Her words resonated, rich in wisdom and full of truth. Lisa standing on her own, enduring trial upon trial, learning to fight, to defend herself, learning to heal wounds— preparing for a purpose. *A purpose.*

Lisa and you.

Yes . . . Lisa and me.

"Figure it out as you go." Nora stepped closer and edged between Annie and him. "Just follow the signs."

"Signs. What signs?"

"There are always signs, my boy." She put her purse down on the floor. "Now, I'll be staying with Annie for a time—until Sam gets back. You need to go to the consult room. Joe and the rest of the boys are there. He's traced Dutch's last call to a cell tower in Alabama. And Nick and Beth Dawson have found something on some security tape they want you to see."

Mark released Annie's fingertip. "You stay strong." No way was he leaving with just Nora and Jessie in the unit. Sam would be back in a minute.

"She's strong as an ox. Gotta be." Nora assured him with a firm nod. "She promised Lisa lunch and shopping and that they'd get their nails done together."

"Those don't sound like life-fighting promises, Nora."

"Maybe not to you, but to a mother who missed those things with her daughter, they're plenty. Annie Harper keeps her word, by gum."

"Yes, she does."

Nora sniffed. "Now go on and see your team—and tell Sam if I see him eating one more bite of junk food before he eats a proper meal, I'm going to blister his ears."

"Yes ma'am."

"The boy should know better."

"I do, Miss Nora." Sam breezed past Mark, tugging on his cap, grinning. "Look, no junk." He held up his empty hands.

She harrumphed. "That's because your gut's already sloshing with the stuff."

"Probably so." He flashed Mark a wink.

Mark walked out of the ICU feeling less helpless and more hopeful. His trials had prepared him for a purpose. *"By grace, not works, we are forgiven."*

He'd heard that just a few weeks ago in the pastor's sermon. Why hadn't it knocked him between the eyes then? Why did he feel poleaxed by it now?

You have ears, but you did not hear.

Redemption is a gift. It couldn't be earned, but it did have to be accepted.

Exactly.

Mark hadn't accepted the gift. How could he? *I want it, God, but I don't deserve it.*

He answered his vibrating phone. "Taylor."

"Hey, bro. What's keeping you?"

Joe. Mark rounded the outside desk near the waiting room and headed toward the consult room's door. "On my way." He was. He had hope, and he had clues.

Signs and purpose.

19

The Opp Public Library was a dark brick, one-story building with a flat white roof located on North Main Street. Glass cases held exhibits of everything from camera collections to porcelain paints and sketches by a local artist.

The man was talented. Karl had an eye for art.

He spotted Dutch Hauk at a table in the center of the room, doubled over a book as if he were reading. Sober, it seemed, and he'd changed out of his rumpled clothes into a pair of brown slacks and a crisp cream-colored shirt that hung loose on his shoulders.

When Dutch looked over, Karl frowned. "The boss is not happy with you." That was an understatement. Raven had been livid.

Hauk checked for bystanders and then asked, "Why? I transferred the money. My part's done." He shrugged. "It's a typical removal."

Karl glared at him. "Typical?"

"Yeah." Hauk shifted on his seat. "I disclosed everything right up front."

"Not exactly everything." Karl leaned over the table and folded his hands, lacing his blunt fingers. "You didn't tell us an army was in the village for a reunion with Annie and Lisa's self-appointed guardian."

"Taylor's friends are there. So what?" Hauk let his gaze rove the shelves of books. "They're nothing. You got the job done, didn't you?"

"Taylor and his friends are Shadow Watchers, Dutch."

A blank look settled on his face. "What's a Shadow Watcher?"

Karl dropped his voice even lower. "Think highly trained, skilled, covert operatives. Think

Special Operations. Think master-level spies who spy on spies. Just think, moron."

The color leaked from Hauk's face. "Taylor is a spy? His friends too?"

"Not anymore, but they were." Karl frowned.

"Taylor? Naw, he can't be. He's worked for Benjamin Brandt a couple of years. Why would a guy with those credentials take a dead-end job for Brandt?"

"He and his friends were a team."

"Okay, so they used to have connections. Is that why the boss is upset? Or does she just want more money for his contract?"

"It's not more money." A first for Raven. "It's them."

"How was I supposed to know they were spies?"

"That we know you didn't is the only reason you're still breathing." Karl waited for a woman clasping a little girl's hand to walk out of earshot. "Look, let me be clear. This is our largest shipment ever—thirty units. If we don't get the cargo out of the country without incident, it'll be because of Taylor and his friends. That happens and, well, don't plan on any more birthdays."

"Wait just a minute." Hauk shut the book, shoved it aside. "Why? Once cargo passes through my stores, I'm out of it. The rest has nothing to do with me."

"Doesn't matter. You brought specific cargo into this shipment knowing that where it goes Taylor follows. And where Taylor follows, his friends will follow. See the point?"

"I see it, but I don't know what you want me to do about it. Wouldn't know 'em if I saw 'em. I can't do anything about—"

"Don't say that," Karl cut Hauk off.

"Why not?"

"Because if you do, I'll have to kill you."

His jaw fell open.

Karl let that sink in, then added, "You made them our problem. The boss refuses to accept it. Her message to you is they're your problem, you fix it." Karl stood. "Don't dawdle. They've been busy since the cargo was removed. The boss is concerned they'll create major challenges for the organization. That makes handling them your number-one priority."

"I can't believe this. My problem? Mine?" He jerked back in his seat. "What am I supposed to do about them?"

"Handle them, Hauk. Otherwise, I have my orders."

"A whole team of master-level spies, and you expect me, a store owner, to handle them?"

"No, I don't." Karl leaned over the table. "Raven does."

"But I'm a client."

He had a point and Karl was at a loss. He sighed.

Hauk licked his lips. "I'll give you a million— five million—to handle it. Between you and me."

314

Cut NINA out? Was he crazy? They'd both be dead before midnight. But it showed the man's desperation. "Look, just stay away from the hospital. Find a hole somewhere isolated, and crawl into it until this is over. You're the connection. If they can't get a bead on you, they can't take their investigation any further. Just disappear until the cargo is delivered."

"I can't just disappear." Hauk lifted his arms. "I have a business to run."

"You can't run anything if you're dead."

Hauk absorbed that with a long, hard blink. "Okay. Okay. I'll disappear."

"Stay in touch with me."

Hauk swabbed at his face with a white handkerchief. His hand shook. "Even now that girl causes me grief."

"Maybe you should have just left her alone."

Fury flashed in Hauk's eyes. "She defied me."

"Yeah, well." Karl hitched his pants up on his hips. "I hope penalizing her for it is worth it."

His eyes glittered. "It will be."

When the videos of Lisa fighting started coming in, and Hauk saw her routinely beaten to a bloody pulp, then he'd be satisfied. *Feeding on her misery. Parasite.* "You know, Dutch, I do terrible things, but they're not personal." Karl saw his own shortcomings clearly, but for all of them, Hauk was worse. If hell had levels, he would be low man on the lowest level.

Hauk met Karl's eyes. "You can say what you want, but in the end, you're no better or smarter or stronger than me, Karl. You might think you are, but when push comes to shove, you're no different. It's always personal."

Wrong. Definitely wrong. "Whatever." Karl pushed his chair back under the table and turned to go.

"Wait."

Karl looked back.

"I still want Chessman's house."

"It's sold."

"I know." Hauk stood. "I want to buy it from Darla Green."

"Are you making a formal offer?"

"Yeah. Tell her I'll give her whatever she paid plus fifteen percent."

"Okay." Karl paused, curious. "You realize if Annie lives, she'll never move out of the house she shared with Charles."

"I didn't plan on asking her." Hauk opened the book he had as a prop and pulled it to him. It scraped on the table. "She's my wife. She'll do what she's told."

"At one time, maybe. But after all this? She recognized me, Dutch. She'll know you're behind what happened."

"Doesn't matter. She'll still do what I tell her."

"Why should she?"

"Because she knows if she doesn't, I'll make Lisa pay for it."

316

"But Lisa's gone."

"Yes, she is." He hiked up his eyebrows. "And she'll stay gone for as long as I choose."

"That's why you want the videotapes. Not for yourself. To control Annie." He'd dangle them before her like carrots, knowing they would torment her. He'd keep her in a nightmare the rest of her life. Karl really wished he'd put a bullet through her head and ended her misery.

"They'll keep her in line," Hauk said. "There's nothing she wouldn't do for her brat. And who knows, maybe after a year or two, I'll buy Lisa back."

"That's not possible and you know it."

He laughed. "Yeah, I know it and you know it, but Annie doesn't."

Bile rose in Karl's throat. "You're sorry, Dutch. No way around it."

"Yeah, I guess I am."

"My old man was sorry too." He had done his best to make Karl's life as miserable as Dutch had made Lisa's. Karl had gotten out young, drafted by a Spider. He'd worked his way up through the ranks on the criminal side of the organization, took on jobs no one else wanted for the political side. He made Raven believe he had ideological preferences, but the truth was, he couldn't care less. Whichever side made him the most money, that's the side he was on.

"Is that why you stay on Lisa? To keep Annie in line?"

"Actually, no. Lisa never did what she was told."

"So you had her abducted for it?"

"She was going to take Annie."

"No, Dutch. I meant the first time you had her abducted."

He lowered his lids, and silence charged the air between them. Finally Hauk said, "I have no idea what you're talking about."

He knew exactly what Karl was talking about, and he was as guilty as sin. "My mistake." Karl gave him the lie and walked out of the library.

Hauk had blown it—huge. Then and now a cleaner wasn't supposed to know the client's identity, yet indirectly he had revealed his connection to Lisa's first abduction.

Everything that had happened then, Hauk had bought and paid for.

His nerves zinging, Karl hustled toward his car, putting everything in its place. Charles and Lisa had stood between Hauk and Annie, and doing what he does best, Hauk hired out his dirty work.

Dutch had set Annie up.

Charles and Lisa too.

Karl dwelled on the matter. Annie was nobody's fool. Maybe, just maybe, she knew it. Maybe Hauk wasn't keeping the reins tight on her to control his wife but to keep his wife from blowing the whistle on him.

Now that put a different spin on the whole situation.

Hauk knew that the minute Annie and Lisa connected, Annie would tell Lisa the truth—or maybe Lisa knew the truth and would tell it to Annie, which meant he had to keep them apart.

Dutch wasn't afraid of losing Annie. He'd never really had her, and he knew it. He was afraid of losing *everything.*

Either Annie or Lisa had the power to take everything.

Question was, which one would do it?

Lisa glanced at Gwen's watch. Ten minutes and it'd be noon. The truck would be stopping again.

Amanda, the witness they'd picked up in Jackson, Mississippi, had shared her story—and her regret that she had agreed to testify. Two men assigned to protect her lay dead in a safe house, and she had been delivered to Frank and tossed in the truck. She, too, was pretty, like Gwen and Selene, maybe Mel's age, early twenties, and scared to death.

They all were. Which is why Lisa wasn't telling them her plan. What they knew, they could be coerced into revealing. It was safer for them all not to know a thing.

In the first abduction, she'd trusted a boy. He turned her in to the Spider, who had nearly beaten her to death. She remembered the lesson if not the specifics, and it was one she wouldn't repeat.

"Your parents don't want you anymore. I'm your family now, and if you tell anyone I'm not your father, I'll kill you. Do you hear me, my little shrub?"

Mr. Phen. She could almost see his face through the veil of shuttered memories, but it slipped away. Yet she distinctly recalled his voice.

"This is your home now. You're safe here. I won't throw you away like they did."

Liar. Liar. Her parents loved her. They wouldn't throw her away.

"Don't move." Mr. Phen left the room.

"I won't." Oh, he was a big man. Big and mean.

Outside, Lisa saw a little boy playing with a soccer ball. She crawled out the window and hit the ground running. The air smelled salty, a lot like it did at home. Running through a green, grassy field, she spotted the top of a distant lighthouse. If she could get there, she could get home. Running toward it, she heard Mr. Phen's voice. "Shrub? Shrub?"

Then the little boy. "She's over there. See? She's running away."

She ran harder, faster, until her legs were so heavy she could barely lift them—and suddenly arms snaked around her middle and lifted her off the ground.

"You'll regret this."

She screamed and kicked, and the more she did,

the madder he got. He tossed her down on the ground and began beating her.

He'd nearly beaten her to death.

For days she lay in bed unable to move, unable to swallow or chew. Parched, she'd dribbled water down her bruised, dry throat. Everything hurt everywhere, and she cried and cried for her daddy to come heal her like he'd healed everyone else.

But her daddy couldn't come.

Then the spiderweb man from the van had come back. He'd put tape on her mouth, around her wrists, her ankles, and thrown her in the van. She'd been bad and was being sold.

And that's when the spiderweb man stopped at the store and she ran to the dress shop and the woman hid her and called the police. They came and asked her about her father, and she told them the truth.

"My daddy's in heaven. He went to Haiti and fell off the roof."

Then there was a blur, and finally her mother was there, and she took Lisa home.

Rex had been so happy to see her. Lisa was happy to see him too. He licked and licked and licked her face.

Her mother didn't ask her anything, just hugged her a lot and cried. *"If you need to talk, we can any time. About anything. Okay?"*

Lisa didn't want to talk. She wanted to sing.

For three solid days, every waking moment, she

321

sang the 4-H song. When she stopped singing, she made up her mind that she never wanted to talk. Never wanted to remember. She wanted to forget, and so she had.

Until now.

NINA. The signs in the stores. No one would help her now. Forgetting was a luxury she couldn't afford, just as Selene said. Lisa had to remember.

Gwen and Amanda talked softly. Selene listened. Lisa frowned. "You sure ask a lot of questions, Amanda."

She had the grace to blush. "This is upsetting. I want to know as much as possible. Don't you?"

"I do." Gwen tapped her chest.

Lisa couldn't dispute Amanda's logic, but something tickled her instincts. Not a warning, more an awareness.

Selene shot Lisa a soft smile. "You have to forgive Lisa, Amanda. Being protective is in her genes. Ask all the questions you like, as will we."

Amanda relaxed. "Protective is good. I'd like about two tons of it right now."

"Wouldn't we all?" Gwen grunted.

"Them selling us doesn't surprise me," Amanda said. "To be honest, I never thought I'd live to testify, so I guess I should be grateful to still be breathing. But I'm not."

"Don't give up." Selene patted Amanda's arm. "Lisa's Mark will find us. He's looking."

He was. And knowing it gave Lisa strength. "True, but we need to do our part."

"What can we do?" Amanda asked. "Our options are limited."

Gwen speculated. "Lisa has figured out her plan."

Amanda's expression proved she expected Lisa to elaborate. Instead, Lisa hugged her knees. "I know we talked about discussing the plan," she looked at Selene, "but it'll help it work if you don't know everything."

"Why?" Selene asked.

"Your reactions will be honest."

Amanda balked. "I'm not okay with this."

Selene studied Lisa. "Get okay with it, Amanda. Lisa will tell us what she can. On the rest, we will trust her."

"Thank you."

"I don't like it." Amanda snorted.

"You don't have to," Gwen told her. "Just do it." She motioned with her flashlight. Its beam skidded over the truck panels. "Go ahead, Lisa."

Grateful for their support, Lisa started. "When we get into the rest room, start vomiting—or make them think you are, Amanda. Pretend claustrophobia or something." Lisa looked from Gwen to Selene. "You two make sure the door stays closed and locked."

"What are you going to do?" Selene swiped her hair back from her face.

"I'm going to try to get us some help."

"That's insane." Amanda grunted. "The minute you try, you'll be shot."

"Maybe not, if we cover for her." Gwen squeezed her arm.

Solemn, Selene touched Lisa's hand. "Be careful. They will kill you."

Lisa stiffened. "Yes, but we all know there are things worse than death."

The truck stopped.

Lisa's stomach filled with flutters. *Give me the courage and wisdom to do this. Carry me.*

Soon Frank ushered them out of the truck and into the store, down the aisle, and to the back. "Two at a time."

Lisa and Gwen went into the rest room.

Frank stuck out an arm and blocked Selene and Amanda, keeping them from entering. "Wait."

Amanda groaned. "I can't. I'm going to be sick." She clutched at her stomach, swiped at her face, and faked a gag.

He beat on the door. "Open it up and let them in. Now."

The door swung open.

Selene and Amanda shuffled inside. Gwen quickly shut the door and turned the lock, and then shot a wild look toward the window.

Lisa was hanging halfway in and out. Craning her neck, she swept her line of sight, left to right and then back again. "Juan isn't out here. Stay put as long as you can."

Worry flooded Selene's eyes. "May God protect you."

She who did not pray, prayed for Lisa.

Touched, she slid out the window and dropped to the ground.

A gas station stood not thirty yards across a lot of tall grass. Hunkering low to the ground, she ran, not daring to look back. Weeds slapped at her calves, her thighs. *I'm looking over a four-leaf clover . . .*

An elderly man in greasy overalls with a crooked nose and grease-smeared hands came walking up front from the rack. "Yes ma'am. Can I help you?"

If he thought it was odd that she was dressed in a crumpled formal, he didn't show it. "I need a phone. Fast."

"We don't have a public phone. No need. Everybody's got cell phones these days."

She darted her gaze to his store door and window. No papers. He wasn't NINA. "It's an emergency. *Please* help me."

He looked at her dirty, tattered evening gown. "Step inside."

She did and he pulled out his phone. "I get free long distance. What's the number?"

Lisa sputtered it to him. "Thank you."

He handed her the receiver. "Don't worry. No man is going to bother you while you're here." He reached behind the counter, pulled out a pistol, and stuffed it in his pocket. "I've got your back."

Tears welled in her eyes. He was about Clyde Parker's age, and his knuckles appeared about as arthritic, but his heart was huge. "Thank you . . ."

"Jed."

"Jed." She smiled.

Mark answered his phone. "Taylor."

Mark. It really was him. The tears threatening spilled. She brushed at her cheeks, forced strength she didn't feel into her voice. "Mark, it's Lisa."

"Where are you? Are you okay?"

"No, I'm not. I was abducted—"

"I know, honey."

"How's my mom?"

"No change."

She was still alive. *Thank God.*

"Where are you now?"

Lisa could breathe again. "I'm not sure. Wait a second. Jed, where are we?"

"You're asking your abductor?"

"He's not my abductor, Mark. I escaped."

"Near Slidell." Jed shot her a worried look.

"Jed is helping me. He owns a car repair shop." Her face went hot. "What state, Jed?"

He wiped his hands on a shop rag, the lines in his face deepening to grooves. "Louisiana. Highway 190, off I-10."

She repeated her location to Mark. "Apparently, they're moving us across country to sell us."

"Us?"

326

"I have to talk fast. There are four of us—at least, so far." She reeled off what she knew about the other women. "There are two men here. Frank and Juan. Frank has a spiderweb tattoo, and Juan—I don't know. There's something strange going on with him." She darted a quick look outside, saw the tip of the truck's front end. "Could you please get help here? They're heavily armed and I'm not."

"Stay put, honey. Joe's already on it."

She reeled off the truck's tag number, model and type, repeated the tag number again. "I have to get back. They'll realize I'm missing."

"*No*. Lisa, don't go back!"

"If I don't, Frank will kill the others. Dutch is behind this, Mark, and NINA is involved. They stop every two hours at a convenience store, and NINA signs are on every door."

"I mean it, Lisa. Stay hidden."

She'd like nothing better than to listen to him, but to live with herself, she had no choice. "You don't understand what they have planned."

"Fights to the death. Auctions. I know." Mark's voice cracked. "What if I can't get to you in time?"

"You will. I'm not Jane. You will get here." She hung up the phone.

Jed's wrinkled face settled into a deep frown. "I couldn't help overhearing. You should listen to your man about this. Don't go back. Let me call the police."

"I can't. The police could be involved." This was NINA. She couldn't risk it.

"Well, at least stay here until he arrives. Then he can help you find the others."

Reasonable. Rational. But wrong. "They'll be dead by then." She headed to the door. "Thank you, Jed."

His phone rang. "You wait. I can help." He answered the phone.

Lisa slipped out the door. There was no way she was dragging him into this.

She checked but didn't see Juan—where was he? He was supposed to be watching the window, but she hadn't seen him coming or going back. She rushed to the convenience store, then wiggled in the rest room window. Someone was beating on the door.

"Thank goodness!" Selene sounded breathless.

Lisa dropped to the floor and closed the window. "Everything okay?"

Gwen, one hand on the lock, let out an expansive sigh. "Frank is getting impatient."

"Amanda, vomit." Lisa motioned with a finger to her mouth.

She crammed her finger down her throat.

Gwen jerked open the door, and Frank witnessed Amanda losing her lunch.

"What's wrong with her?" He looked at Lisa.

Please don't let him see the mud on my shoes. Please.

"I don't know." *I'm looking over a four-leaf clover* . . . Juan had to have seen her. If he hadn't, why hadn't he? If he had, would he tell Frank? If he did, she was a dead woman. Frank would haul her into that field and shoot her in the head. No doubt about it.

"You're a doctor. Take care of her, and hurry up. Man, it stinks to high heaven in there." Pulling a sour face, he slammed the door shut.

Lisa swiped at the mud clinging to her heels and stared at Selene. "Where is Juan?"

"Watching the window the whole time. How did you get past him?"

Lisa frowned. "I didn't see him going or coming."

"He was there," Selene said.

"I saw him too." Gwen looked to the window, then back at Lisa. "Maybe he knew what you were doing and didn't want to stop you."

"That's not likely, Gwen."

"Well, then you explain it, Amanda."

She swished water in her mouth, then spit it into the sink. "I can't." Amanda splashed her face, then turned the spigot off.

Gwen dried her hands on a scrap of paper towel. "Well, he sure let Lisa go and come back, so something's not right with him."

Selene passed a paper towel to Amanda. "Lisa, did you have any luck?"

She nodded. "Mark is on his way."

"Thank God." Gwen smiled.

"Yes." Lisa didn't smile back; she prayed for forgiveness. Because it was all she could do not to ask God to strike Dutch Hauk, NINA, Frank, Edmunds, Powell, and the whole bunch of them dead.

But especially Dutch.

In her heart, she knew he'd put her mother in the hospital in a coma. Just as she knew the only way either of them would ever have peace would be if he were dead.

20

The air crackled with tension.

Walking through the door, Mark felt it. The entire Crossroads Crisis Center staff was moving in high gear.

Mel sat at her desk, working the phones. Spotting Mark, she held up a finger and interrupted a caller, "Please hold." Twice she pushed buttons and repeated herself, and then she spoke to him. "They're waiting for you in the conference room."

"Update?" Here's where Mel excelled.

"Nick and Sam are working the condos. If you want a location on Nick, call Sam. Church ladies are covering the pier, diner, restaurants, and shops. Ben, Kelly, and Nora are with Annie. Clyde's on his way to stay with Nora, then Ben and Kelly are coming back here. Prayer warriors are in the chapel. Joe and Detective Meyers are in the conference room with Dr. Talbot and Mrs. Crane, debating on calling in the FBI. Everyone knows Lisa's called in, but I only explained her circumstances to Joe. I wasn't sure who all you'd want to know."

Smart young woman and very efficient. "Thanks, Mel. Good call." Mark walked through the waiting room. His nerves sizzled like he was wearing them on the outside of his skin. At the conference room, he tapped on the door.

"Come in, Mark."

Peggy. Mel had already let her know he'd arrived.

"Is Lisa okay?" Harvey paced alongside the conference table.

"Holding together. They haven't hurt her." Mark moved to a seat at the closest end of the long wooden table. "So where are we?"

"We've just called in the FBI," Joe said. "Four states are involved, and Sam got word they're actively working an operation that could be connected."

"My ex-wife used to work for the FBI." Harvey stopped pacing. "I'm not sure this is up her alley—she follows money on white-collar crimes—but I could call her. Maybe she knows someone who can move things a little faster."

Peggy twisted her chunky beads. "I thought Roxanne was a forensic accountant."

"She is, but she's also an FBI agent. Or she was." Harvey shrugged. "I'm not sure now."

"Well, find out," Peggy said. "We need to use every asset to help Lisa."

Mark knew that look. The resident Cupid was at it again. Harvey Talbot hadn't wanted the divorce, and Peggy no doubt saw this as an opportunity where Roxanne might be able to help Lisa *and* give Harvey and her a reason to remember why they once loved each other enough to marry.

"She might not take the call, but I'll make it." Harvey left the room.

Peggy sat back, satisfied.

"How long will it take the Louisiana locals to intercept the truck?" Mark asked Joe.

Jeff Meyers answered. "They're not going to intercept it just yet. They said they'd handle it from here."

Mark glanced at Joe and saw his fears confirmed. Must be a mission conflict. Evidently, a serious one. "So when does 'not just yet' run out the clock?" He understood protocol. He understood jeopardizing operations. But he also understood that Lisa needed help now.

Again Jeff answered. "They didn't say."

"Let's go, Joe." Mark stood and moved toward the door.

"On your heels, bro." Joe fell in right behind Mark.

"Mark, wait!" Jeff called out.

"Can't." He let his gaze bounce from Jeff to

Peggy. "We'll call in. Keep tabs on Annie for me, and get someone from my security staff at Three Gables over there to stay with Nora and Clyde."

Peggy nodded. "Be cautious, Mark. NINA plays for keeps."

"That's exactly why Lisa can't wait." Fear knotted in his chest. Three hours. It would take him three hours just to get where she'd been, and who knew where this Frank would have taken her by then? "Get Ben's plane fueled up. Tell the airport I need it right away."

"You've got it. Should we handle the flight plan?"

"I'll take care of it," Joe assured Peggy.

"You fly too?" Peggy asked.

"We all think steel."

Peggy frowned. "Excuse me?"

"We do what needs doing." Mark rushed out of the center.

And they all prayed that what needed doing, they would do in time.

Karl Masson ended the call with Frank and checked his locator screen. Dutch was near Biloxi, Mississippi. Karl had made good time and tracked less than two miles behind him on I-10. More than half tempted to hit the button to blow up Dutch's car, Karl resisted. He couldn't kill Hauk yet. If things went south, he might be needed to take the fall for the entire operation.

A black Toyota Tundra sped by. Driver had to be

going ninety. *Fool.* Speeding this close to a military installation on high alert? Hadn't he heard about monitors being positioned ten miles out in every direction?

Apparently not.

His cell rang. Karl answered it. "Hello."

A male mumbled something inaudible. Karl couldn't get a fix on the speaker. "Sorry, I can't hear you."

"Shifter."

Someone in the loop. He knew the mission name. "Yes?"

"Caged."

Gregory Chessman. Not many prisoners had cell phones or unfettered access to them, but then not many prisoners were NINA managers. "Identify yourself."

"Lone Wolf."

"I understand we've got infected cargo?"

Raven was nothing if not fast, reporting Amanda being sick to everyone in the need-to-know loop. "Yes."

"What's the nature of the infection?"

"We suspect it's viral, but that can't be confirmed without labs."

"No. No labs."

"If the rest of the shipment is infected, the boss will not be pleased," Karl said.

"Neither will those above her, so do what you can to get them well. What does the doc say?"

Lisa Harper. "Nothing without labs. She can't be sure. We've got a testing facility in—"

"No, no unauthorized stops. The schedule's too tight."

It was, considering the Jackson stop to pick up Amanda. "So why are you calling?" Had to be a reason other than to try to order Karl around when he had no right to do so anymore.

"Message from Raven. Have the cargo proceed as scheduled. When it's fifty miles from Houston, I'll issue further instructions. If conditions change or further infestation occurs, call and she'll reconsider."

The stop wouldn't be unauthorized, but Karl would leave that to Raven and Chessman to duke out. The last thing Karl needed was to get caught up in a power struggle between the two of them. But why hadn't Raven called Karl directly? Odd. "The client wants to buy your old house. Fair-market value plus fifteen percent. Formal offer."

"I'll inform the new owner and see if she's interested."

"I'll tell the client." Karl checked his fuel gauge. Half a tank. "Is there an update on the patient's condition?" Chessman would intuit he was asking about Annie.

"An hour ago, there'd been no change. At the moment, we're experiencing a site employee lapse."

Rose Paxton had been their site employee

reporting to Chessman. "Anything I need to know about?"

"Our insider discovered I wasn't the coroner, then recognized my voice and quit." Chessman let out a little laugh.

Laughter? Odd. "Do I need to clean up there?"

"No. She was last seen heading north for parts unknown. She didn't even go back to her house first."

Smart woman. One who obviously knew it was wise to fear Gregory Chessman.

Disappear, Rose. Unless she did, and did so quickly, someone from NINA would take her out.

Chessman might let her go, but Raven would not.

The boss didn't tolerate loose ends.

"It's after four." Gwen turned the flashlight beam from her watch to the wall of the truck near Lisa. "Why hasn't he gotten here?"

Lisa wished she knew. Mark would have had to arrange transport with Ben—there's no way he would have driven when he could fly—but he should have intercepted them by now.

Selene shifted her weight, bumping Lisa's knee. "Maybe he can't find us."

She could be right. Sweating, Lisa wished the smells of sweat and the mustiness of being closed in would pass. She'd love just a few breaths of fresh air only slightly more than she'd love a bath. "He'll find us."

Lisa wouldn't share this, but with NINA's involvement, Mark and his old team could have plans that extended beyond rescuing them.

"I've been thinking about that scratching we heard at the last stop." Selene swiped at her brow. "Maybe it was Frank changing the license plate."

Gwen flicked the flashlight to shine in Selene's eyes. "Don't say that."

"She could be right." Lisa thought back to the sound. It had come from the right place. "What else would he have been doing?"

"Well, if that's the case," Amanda said, "Mark could have driven right past us a dozen times."

He could have. Without the tag, there was nothing to distinguish this truck from any other white box truck on the road, and there had to be hundreds of them. "Good point." Lisa extended a hand to Gwen. "Let me borrow your flashlight."

"What for?"

"I have an idea." Lisa hadn't known this tactic when she'd been abducted the first time, but years of self-defense training had given her dozens of tips she could now put to use.

Gwen passed the light. Its beam flashed across the ceiling of the truck. "There's nothing in here."

"Use whatever tactics or weapons are at your disposal. The unexpected can be the one thing that saves your life."

Mark's words to her class. A memory from the first advanced-defense lesson she'd taken from him flitted through her mind. She'd done the unexpected and such pride had shone in his eyes. Seeing him proud of her . . . She floated for a week.

The reminder infused her with strength, and she doubled her efforts, sweeping the inside of the truck anyway. No tire iron, no nothing. Sighing, she dropped her shoulder as the beam swept over Selene's legs and feet and then snagged on her high-heel burgundy shoes. Twisting, Lisa checked the interior rear-panel taillights. "Selene, give me your heel."

"What for?"

"If Frank changed the tag and Mark is looking for us, we need to signal him. I need your shoe to do it."

"Oh, I saw this on *Staying Alive*." Amanda's voice elevated a notch, grew animated. "Let me help." She scooted toward Lisa.

"Saw what?" Gwen rolled on her hip, letting Amanda scoot by her.

Selene gave Lisa her shoe.

"Oh no. Don't, Lisa. Frank will notice and he'll—"

Lisa swung the shoe like a hammer. The plastic taillight shattered.

"Worry later, Gwen. Hold the light for me now."

"He's going to blow our brains out. I just know it." Gwen took the flashlight and aimed it at the taillight. "I hope my mother never sees my body. She'll be devastated."

"Stop it, Gwen." Selene raised her voice. "No dead talk." Lisa tapped at the jagged plastic edges with Selene's heel until she knocked out enough of the light to fit her hand through the hole.

"Make it bigger," Amanda said. "If Frank hits a bump, you'll sever an artery." She wiggled out of her slip, then shoved it at Lisa. "First, wrap your arm with this for added protection."

"You've done this before." Lisa stated a fact, didn't ask a question.

"No, but I have seen it done."

Where? Not on television. Amanda was trained. Lisa would bank on it. Selene and Gwen went through periods of being scared stiff. Amanda was afraid, but she kept her fears to herself. That took the kind of discipline that came with training. Was she a plant the men had put with them to spy? Anger rushed through Lisa. "Do you work for the kidnappers?" Would she betray them like the boy had betrayed Lisa?

"No. I swear it."

No rapid-eye moment, no avoidance of her eyes. Lisa believed her.

Selene jerked the slip from Amanda's hand and passed it to Lisa. "There's no time for this now. Get on with what you're doing."

Lisa took the slip. The silky fabric was still warm from Amanda's body. "Somebody will see it." She kicked herself yet again for not asking Jed for his phone. "If not Mark, then someone else.

They'll call 911 and somebody will stop this truck."

Lisa resisted the urge to let the slip fly like a flag and took the prudent step instead. She wrapped her arm, then shoved it through the hole where the taillight had been.

"What if Frank sees it?"

"He can't see around corners, Gwen." From the tremor in Selene's voice, Lisa suspected that reminder reassured Selene too. "Shall I knock out the other one?"

"Later, if we have to. We have better odds of Frank's not noticing one broken light. If he does, maybe he'll think a rock hit it or something." Lisa pulled her arm inside and rolled onto her stomach, then peeked out through the hole. The fresh air stung her nose. *Bliss.* Cars lined up behind them in both lanes.

She scrambled to sit up. "There are a ton of cars out there! Someone will see." She shoved her arm back through the hole, waved, and stretched her fingers to snag someone's attention. Hopefully someone would add the digits and pick up her signaling 911 with her fingers.

Please, God. Please.

"I'm glad you know these self-defense things, Lisa."

"Me too." A little tingle spread through her chest. As if Gwen's words held a profound message.

She glanced over, but Gwen didn't say any more, and yet her words stuck with Lisa. Stretching, she got more of her arm outside the truck. With every bounce, the jagged plastic edges stabbed at her slip-wrapped arm. She tried not to wince.

Is this why You had me learn all those self-defense tactics, God? So I'd know what to do now to help us all survive?

Silence.

Maybe that *was* the reason. So she could do what fumes-of-faith Christians do and help the other women.

"Lisa, get your arm in!" Gwen shrieked. "Quick."

Lisa pulled in her arm.

Seconds later, she felt the gravity shift, hurtling her toward the front. The truck stopped suddenly.

21

Outside, gunfire erupted.

"Get down flat." Amanda shoved at Gwen.

The flashlight beam swung wildly inside the truck. Tumbling with the others, Lisa stretched prone on her stomach. Popping noises, muffled but ominous, echoed inside. A pinging noise—a bullet—bounced off the right side panel. Then a flurry of racket signaling a scuffle filled the silence.

Please, let it be Mark. Please.

Shouting. Barked orders. Frantic activity and more yelling . . . but no sirens. No helicopter blades thumping in the air. Then only silence.

And more silence.

"Who is it?" Selene's voice shook. "Do you think it's Mark?"

The lock rattled.

Lisa sucked in a sharp breath. Her heart thudded against the wall of her chest. "We'll soon know."

The door swung open.

He towered in the opening, scowling.

"Mark." Lisa scrambled out of the truck, fighting the skirt of her long dress. *Thank You, God.* "Mark!"

He snatched her up and held her to him, burying his nose at her neck. "Thank God."

Lisa kissed him soundly, trembling, feeling his huge body shake against her, his rough hands pressing hard against her back.

Joe helped the others out of the truck. "You ladies all okay?"

"Okay is seriously relative. We're alive." Gwen clicked off her flashlight. "We were worried you wouldn't find us."

Joe set Gwen onto the ground and reached for Selene. "We've been behind you for an hour, but we weren't sure we had the right vehicle."

Mark pulled back, checked Lisa's arm, and saw the red scratches. "The second I saw that hand signal, I knew it was you."

She smiled. "I'm so glad you're here." A lump formed in her throat and her eyes misted. "I knew you'd find me."

"Or die trying." He kissed her again.

"You look familiar," Joe said to Selene. "Do we know— Oh, wait. You're the singer?"

"I was." She shrugged. "I don't sing anymore, which is why I think I was in that truck."

"I'd like to hear more about that." A woman walked up to them. About thirty-five, she stood a little taller than Gwen. Lean and fit, she had short, spiky blond hair and bright blue eyes. "But first, Lisa, where are the rest of the women?"

"What other women?" An officer had Frank cuffed. He had a bloody lip. Juan lay spread-eagle on the shoulder of the road. A man who had to be with Mark stood over Juan, talking with him. "We're it." Lisa looked from Mark to the woman. "Who are you?"

"I'm sorry." Mark lifted a hand but hung on to Lisa. "This is Special Agent Roxy Savoy. She's with the FBI."

Roxy nodded. "I didn't mean to be rude. It's just that we were expecting thirty women." Her gaze swung to Amanda. "You okay?"

"Yes ma'am."

Alerted by the familiarity passing in the look between them, Lisa glanced from Amanda to Mark, and certainty filled her. "Amanda, you're an agent, and you didn't tell us?"

"I couldn't tell you, Lisa."

"You let me risk getting shot to go to Jed . . ." Anger burned deep, and Lisa glared at Roxy. "You were following us all along?"

"Actually, we weren't. We were supposed to be, but Amanda's tracking device—"

"The watchband broke during the abduction, and I lost it."

Understanding now, Lisa let Amanda brief Roxy and snuggled closer to Mark. "How's my mother? Is she awake now?"

He brushed her hair back from her face with a trembling hand. "No real change, but her vitals are stable. Harvey's encouraged."

She gripped his side. "Get me to her, okay?"

He nodded and dialed his phone. "Nora, tell Annie we've got Lisa. She's safe."

Lisa smiled. She just knew that would help her mom.

Mark's eyes sparkled. "I'll tell you all about it when we get home." He paused to listen to Nora. "Yes, there was gunfire, but so far I haven't shot anyone." He frowned. "You might want to keep the prayer warriors engaged on that. They aren't all in custody yet." Another pause. "Yes, your boys are all fine. We'll be careful. I promise." He rolled his eyes, but appreciation spilled over into his tone. "Don't forget to tell Annie about Lisa." Another short pause. "Okay, but right now I have to go." He finished the call and told Lisa, "She's worried."

"Nora loves you." The conversation between Amanda and Roxy worried Lisa. She took a moment to think it through.

"Yeah, I guess she does." The hint of a smile touched the corner of his mouth. "She loves you too."

"Um, Mark." Roxy glanced from Lisa to him. "I'm glad these women are safe, but dropping this here creates a problem."

"Excuse me?"

Roxy pulled her purse strap up on her shoulder. "According to our source, there are thirty women. We have four. If we interrupt this operation now, the others are out of luck."

"What are we into here?" he asked.

"More than either of us imagined. I've been on this case three years. Human trafficking, criminal activity, drugs, gambling. You name it. It's been a series of nightmares. But we finally got a break. One of the NINA operatives turned for us."

Mark soaked it in. "You're telling me they targeted thirty women like Lisa?"

"No. Only these four were specifically targeted. The rest are random abductions. We have no idea who they are or where they're coming from or where they're going. All we've got is following this truck until it stops and hoping the other women are brought to it, or they meet up. Our guy didn't know the specifics. A decoy inserted, but before we could get her location, she was murdered."

Mark frowned. "How did you get the video?"

"What video?" Lisa asked. Roxy didn't seem surprised at Mark's awareness of it.

"Later." He gave her hand a gentle squeeze.

"We didn't get it," Roxy said. "That same source brought it to us."

"Yet a female agent infiltrated."

"And then was moved." Roxy nodded. "That's all I know. Homeland Security classified the rest." She hiked a shoulder. "You know how it is."

Mark sighed. "Unfortunately, I do."

The agent who had been speaking with Juan ran over to Roxy. They spoke briefly in private, and then she returned to Mark, looking even more stressed and defeated. "There are definitely more women. We've got to keep going."

Mark grimaced. "I know you're not suggesting Lisa and the others continue."

"I'd never suggest such a thing." Roxy shifted on the asphalt. "I can't get civilians involved."

"So you're going to substitute additional agents in their places?" Joe stepped between Selene and Gwen.

"Unfortunately, I can't do that either." Roxy looked from Joe to Lisa. "These four were targeted. If they were random, we could risk substitutions. But handpicked? We can't do it."

"Not just handpicked," Selene said. "People paid to get rid of us, and we were to be sold again." She looked at Lisa. "On both ends, people know exactly who we are."

Twenty-six randomly abducted women. *Twenty-six.* Lisa looked at Gwen and then at Selene. Both of them offered her subtle nods. "We're sticking with it, Roxy."

"No." Mark's lids flattened to a slash. "Lisa, you can't."

She was terrified of going on, but she had no choice; none of them did. "If I don't, I've met my eyes in the mirror for the last time. Twenty-six women, Mark. Every one of them will suffer what I would have suffered. I can't know that and not even try to help them. I won't."

"You have no idea what you're walking into. Trust me, Lisa. I do know, and this is not a wise move."

She whispered so only he could hear. "What if one of them were Jane? Would you do it then?"

He paled. "That's different. It isn't her and I'm not you."

Lisa placed a gentle hand to his arm. "Honey, they're all somebody's Janes. If not us, then who does this? You can't. Joe can't. They expect us. We have to be in the right place at the right time."

Anger flashed through his eyes, then resignation, and finally acceptance. "You're right. I know you're right, but—"

"You're worried." She cast him a loving look. "Me too." Worry wasn't always a nuisance. It could be a weapon that protected you. One that kept you on your toes, sharp, aware. It could save your skin. "I love you for worrying about me."

"I hate it when you do that." He sighed. "For the record, I'm opposed. I understand, but I'm opposed."

"It's the right thing, and you know it."

"I'm not asking you to do this." Roxy met and held Lisa's gaze. "Actually, I can't let you do it."

Lisa understood that they'd be breaking all the rules. Roxy might even be putting her neck on the line for not refusing. "I appreciate your delicate position—we all do—but we're not asking your permission."

"That's right," Selene said. "Our necks, our choice."

"Ditto." Gwen checked her flashlight. "But I am scared to death, and I seriously need some new batteries."

"You'd be nuts if you weren't scared out of your mind." Roxy nodded to one of her men. "Mini-Mag batteries. Now—and tracking devices." She turned to Mark. "Juan says they're on a very tight schedule because of picking up Amanda in Jackson. If the truck doesn't get moving fast, Masson will know something is wrong."

"That's true," Lisa said. "The whole process is tightly controlled. Orchestrated."

Roxy rubbed her neck. "He thinks the final

location is in Mexico. My boss is working on an agreement with our Mexican counterparts in case he's right."

"We've got to get moving." Lisa stepped closer. "Mark, they didn't fare well tracking Amanda. Don't lose me. Joe, you help him."

"You got it, Lisa." Joe's respect for what she was doing shone in his eyes. "And don't worry. We've got Annie covered. Nora and Clyde are with her, and Sam's parked at her bedside."

"I sent one of the Three Gables guys over too," Mark added.

"Sam sent him back to watch over Kelly—just in case. He's got Annie covered. If Nora doesn't give the nod, no one gets close."

Nora was nearly as formidable as Sam. "Thank you," Lisa said.

Mark wasn't happy; his lips were flat lined. On tiptoes, Lisa pecked a kiss to them. "A long time ago, I had a friend whose dad used to say that it takes a lot of heat to temper steel. I've been thinking about that, and maybe it takes a lot of heat to temper people too—to make them as strong as steel."

"What's your point?"

"Maybe some of our hard things were so we could get the skills and experience and wisdom we need to survive situations like this. Otherwise, we couldn't make it." Lisa swiped her windswept hair back from her face, growing more certain with each word she spoke. "Maybe those tough times were blessings in disguise."

"How can your trials be blessings, Lisa?"

"The same way yours have been for you."

Skepticism shadowed his face.

"Every hardship gave us scars, but it made us stronger and smarter too. We can help others as a result." Maybe even help them help themselves.

"You could end up dead," he whispered and led her off the shoulder into the grass. "This is NINA. Not some half-baked gang of thugs."

"I know." She stroked his cheek. "Just as I know Roxy would try, but without us she'd fail. Those other women won't be spared, Mark. Could you live with that?" Hopefully, he'd think of Jane. Lisa didn't dare raise her name again. He'd put her in a bubble and keep her there for the duration to protect her.

"That's different."

"Why?"

"Because it would be me, not you."

"That's no difference, honey." He was part of her, as much as she was a part of him, and they both knew it.

"But I promised your mother I'd bring you home."

"I can't back down on this, Mark. Any success or failure at it is mine."

"Is there anything I can say to change your mind?"

"No." She shrugged. "Positions reversed, you wouldn't change your mind either."

He grimaced. "Then I'm going with you."

"But how can you help me if—?"

"I can't stop you, but I will not be in the wrong place at the wrong time and see another woman important to me killed. I won't. I'm going."

Lisa opened her mouth.

"Don't bother. You're cute, but not enough to get me to do what you want on this." He clamped his jaw shut.

"Okay." She bit the edge of her lip.

Groaning, he turned away. "Roxy, which one of them will break?" He nodded over at the units holding Frank and Juan.

"Juan," Roxy and Lisa said simultaneously.

"Frank's a Spider. Die-hard, hard-core NINA subcontractor with a long history," Lisa said. "He'll die first because he knows his choices are to die this way or NINA's way, and our way takes longer. NINA isn't merciful. But Juan's different."

"She's right," Roxy said. "We have nothing on Juan, and he's talking a lot already. Frank's got a rap sheet as long as your arm."

"I'll get him." Joe turned to retrieve Juan.

"What are you doing?" Lisa asked Mark.

"I'm stepping in for Frank, and then we'll proceed as planned. That work for you, Roxy?"

"If anything happens to you women, it could cost me a lot more than my job, but, yeah." She

351

nodded. "We'll work out the details on the road."

"Mark, could you get us some fresh air in the back?" Selene asked. "It's stifling and the smell isn't pleasant. We've been miserable."

Mark kicked a deep dent in the side of the truck.

Joe tossed him a tire iron. "Save your leg, bro. Might need it."

Mark swung the iron once and the metal breached. Flipping the iron, he used it as a wedge and widened the hole. The whole process took seconds.

Gwen nearly jumped out of her skin.

Selene stretched her eyes wide. "Okay then."

Joe took back the tire iron. "Sorry for the delay, ladies. He's not typically so slow."

"There you go." Mark offered them a hand to get back into the truck.

Lisa waited until last. "Mark, when I got away to call you, I think Juan watched me do it. He didn't stop me, and he sure didn't tell Frank what I'd done or I'd be dead. Just wanted to pass that along."

"I'll tell the others." He hugged her quickly. "Listen, don't scare me anymore, okay? My heart can't take it."

She smiled and stroked his jaw. "I'm crazy about you too."

When Lisa got inside, Roxy passed Mark an earpod and lip mic. "I'll be in the back with the others. My team will question Frank at the field office. If they get anything we can use, they'll let us know. You work on Juan. We have three unmarked cars following, watching for anyone else who might be tagging along. If you pick up on anything, let me know and I'll relay."

"You handle the logistics," Mark said. "We understand the shipment has to progress to locate the other women. But once you know where they are, these three are done. No discussion."

"I wasn't going to argue the point."

"Good." He shot Roxy a hard look intended to wilt her knees. "I won't lie and say I like any of this. Lisa's been through a lot more than you know, and the other women have had hard times too."

Lisa hadn't yet told him about having been abducted the first time. Yet when he focused on her, it was almost as if he already knew. But how could he? She hadn't known herself until recently.

Roxy stepped back. "If it helps, I don't like the circumstances either. I can't guarantee anyone's safety, but we'll do all we can to minimize risks. Without these women, our odds of locating, much less rescuing, the other women are slim, and there's little chance of success at shutting down the operation."

Lisa shuddered. NINA would have another truckload of women shipped in no time. They had to get to the top of this operation and cut off its head.

"Right now," Mark said, "we get backup in

place and do everything possible to keep the women safe until we pinpoint the others. Then we're out and you take over."

Lisa worried her lip. He was protecting her again, but following her instincts, she decided to tackle his objections one step at a time.

Roxy eyed him warily. "We could fail, Mark. NINA—"

"We will not fail."

"Right."

He returned his attention to Lisa. "You need me or anyone wants anything, tell Roxy or tap the front-end panel three times."

Lisa watched him back away. An agent ran up to him, shoved a file into his hands. "Memorize this, then get rid of the paper."

Mark looked down. "Mission identification?"

The agent nodded. "Full disclosure."

Juan headed for the driver's side of the truck. Mark moved to the passenger's side.

At the rear of the truck, Joe stepped back. "Be careful, ladies. You need anything and can't get to us like Mark said, just wiggle your hand through that busted taillight." Joe let his gaze linger on Selene, then grabbed the door. "The team will catch up with us shortly, Lisa. We're all communicating and we'll be close. You might not see us, but we'll be here."

"Thanks—no, wait." Dutch was still on the loose. "Sam will stay with Mom, right?"

"Kelly and the Three Gables security staff are going to the hospital. Nora, Clyde, Jeff Meyers, and someone with hospital security Sam's personally checked out will be with her until we get back. He'll be sure she's safe. Sam has special skills we might need here. Oh, and don't worry about communications failing. Beth Dawson says she'll do whatever it takes to keep us all linked up." He cocked his head. "Is she really *that* good?"

"She's better." Lisa saw that sparkle signaling interest in his eyes.

Joe flashed her a grin that no doubt melted hearts. "I like smart women."

"She's a brainiac."

"Kind of pretty too, when she's not snarling."

"You can trust her, Joe. Really trust her."

"Got it." His smile faded. "No heroics, okay? Just let this play out so we get a fix on these women. With luck, there'll be no interaction required and Roxy can take over." He let his gaze slide to include Selene and Gwen. "But if something does come up, that no-heroics stuff goes for all of you."

"Don't worry. I'll avoid everything I can." Gwen checked her flashlight for the tenth time. "I'm a bona fide wimp."

"A wimp wouldn't be in your current position, but okay." Joe backed away.

Selene sighed. "You're lucky to have such good friends, Lisa."

Warmth spread through her chest. She hadn't often felt lucky. And only now did she realize how shortsighted she'd been about that. What were the odds of having the exact people with the exact abilities needed in her immediate circle at the exact point in time when she most needed them? A million to one. "Yes, I am. Very lucky."

Joe winked at Lisa and swung the door closed.

This time, it wasn't locked.

Lisa stared at the hole in the side of the truck. About the size of a basketball, it was plenty big enough to keep fresh air coming in—and light. Even with new batteries in her flashlight, Gwen would most appreciate that.

The truck started, then rolled, and soon pulled into traffic. "Here we go," Amanda said.

Roxy pulled a recorder from her purse. "Let's get some statements down for the record. Who was picked up first?"

22

You said we needed to move; we're moving. Now start talking, Juan." Mark angled to get away from the low-slung sun shining directly into their eyes and focused on the driver.

Squinting, Juan pulled down the visor. "I do not dare, señor. I've said too much already."

"You don't dare not talk. Say everything." Mark put a bite in his voice the man couldn't miss.

"You do not understand—"

"I do. Lisa says you saw her escape and go for help. You didn't report it. That tells me you're as much a victim as the women. But if you don't trust me, Juan, I can't help you."

"You cannot help me. I know of these people. They are dead in the soul. No one can help me, señor." Fear burned in the depths of Juan's eyes. "They are evil. *Muy fuerte.*"

Very strong. "We're stronger."

Juan shot Mark a loaded glance. "Then why is your woman in the back of this truck?"

He had Mark on that one. "I made a mistake. I didn't personally verify some information." Not one door but two.

"So you knew they were coming for her?"

"I had strong suspicions her stepfather would do something. I didn't know what, and I certainly didn't expect this." Not until Beth Dawson and his team had linked the tapes.

"Her stepfather did this to her?" Juan made the sign of the cross. "*Puede Dios proteger y perdonar.*" *May God protect and forgive.* "How could he do such a thing?"

Mark had wondered a million times how Dutch Hauk could do many of the things he'd done, but he lacked any answers. To stay sane, he'd taken a lesson from Annie and put those questions on the altar.

Did she have any idea how much their phone

conversations meant to him? His heart lurched. *God, if she has to die, don't let her die not knowing. Give me that much peace in all this, please.* "So who is NINA threatening? You or your family?"

Juan didn't even pretend to be surprised. "*Ambos.* Me with death if I refuse to do exactly what they say without question, and if I fail to act, my wife and children," his voice trembled as hard as his hands, "will be slaughtered."

"I'm sorry." Mark tapped his earpod. "Roxy?"

"I heard." She exhaled on a rush that crackled. "Me too, bro."

"I never thought I would be involved in anything like this." Juan's trembling hands now shook on the steering wheel. "I am a decent man, Señor Taylor. A faithful Catholic my entire life— my wife and children too."

"So how did you get dragged into a NINA operation?"

"I own a boat. It is docked at the marina on the coast east of the estate where I suspect the *hombres* are gathering to buy the women. I fear they have done so before. The men fly in from all over the world. I have ferried them from their seaplanes to the estate, though I did not know then why they were going there." He glanced at Mark. "Masson has *proscritos* watching my family. I have four children. I had no choice."

Outlaws watched Juan's family. "So when did

358

you discover they were selling women at this estate?"

"After Masson brought me to that store to join Frank—I am his relief driver—I learned there that their cargo was the women." He lowered his gaze. "I got sick. I did not know what to do. Everyone at the marina knows about NINA. They are *mala gente.*"

Bad people. "Muy mala gente," Mark agreed.

"A fellow fisherman once denied their wishes. We found his body in three parts. They targeted my family, señor. What else could I do?"

"Got that too," Roxy said into Mark's earpod. "I believe him."

"He's being straight up," Joe said. "No doubt about it."

"What exactly were you supposed to do on this trip?" Mark asked Juan. "Just drive?" That didn't work for Mark. Anyone could drive a truck. NINA had to have dozens of relief drivers.

Juan changed lanes and passed a blue Toyota. When he eased back into the right lane, he answered. "Drive the truck when Frank asked, then after their *event,* I must ferry couples in my boat to their seaplanes. That is all I know, señor."

"So you don't just *suspect* the women will be taken to Mexico, you know it."

"Masson has not said, but given what he told me, I would think nothing else. My boat is there." Juan shrugged. "I assumed I would go to the same estate near my home, and he did not disagree. It is on the coast, so the *hombres* have easy access with their seaplanes. Customs does not interfere with NINA."

That wasn't good news. "Where on the Mexican coast is this estate?"

"Near Tampico."

"Anything else we should know?"

"I have told you all I was told and what I make of it. Masson swore that once I have finished, I can return home and my wife and children will never know anything took place. They will suffer no harm."

"And you won't be bothered again until next time."

"Sí." Resignation slid over Juan's face. "Until next time."

Mark understood Juan's dilemma. With rampant corruption of those in authority and all NINA's power and connections, Juan had been afraid for himself and his family, and no doubt he felt hopeless and lost. Who could he trust to help him?

"Mark?" Roxy said.

He tapped his earpod. "Go ahead."

"My office just phoned on my cell. We've nailed Gregory Chessman."

"About a year ago, I know." He'd been in on that.

"No, in this."

"But he's in jail."

"Yes, he is. He's also up to his crooked neck in this specific operation."

Chessman. Again. The news didn't shock Mark, but it did concern him. If Chessman and NINA could pull off something of this magnitude from jail, what were they capable of doing outside it?

"We've got his cell calls as leverage."

Mark watched the road. "So he's helping you?"

"He has been for a short while. He's the source who told us there were other women involved and that they were random abductions."

That did surprise Mark. He propped an arm on the armrest. "I'm sure NINA will reward him well for that."

"They won't know about it. Ever. We need him."

Interesting. Mark wouldn't have selected Chessman as a likely candidate to turn on NINA.

"We need personal information on Juan's family to get them under our wing."

"Juan, I need your address and your family members' names. Agent Savoy is arranging for their protection."

Juan measured Mark, then gave him the information. He relayed it to Roxy.

"I pray to my heavenly Padre this is not a mistake," he told Mark, his accent thick.

"It isn't. The FBI will secure your family and get them out of Masson's reach. You can't trust a man like Karl Masson to keep his word."

"I realize that. But I have additional concerns."

Juan slid Mark a level look. "Your people will secure my family. This will pass. And then your people will leave. We will return home, and for the rest of our lives, we must watch our shadows to stay safe. NINA will come back."

"Probably."

"What would you do?"

Mark didn't hesitate. "Put my family on my boat and disappear. Start over somewhere else."

"They will just come after me."

"Only if they believe you crossed them. Otherwise, they won't. They have businesses to run."

"We'll help Juan and his family relocate," Roxy said. "Whatever we can do, Mark. He's got my word on that."

Mark repeated the offer to Juan.

He didn't seem reassured by it. "Tell her to secure that aid now, *sí usted por favor.*"

If you please.

"Afterward, she could be fired for allowing the women to continue, no?"

Roxy could be fired. It depended on the agreement her boss worked out with the Mexican authorities and, frankly, on how things turned out.

"Mark?"

"Yeah, Roxy?"

"The field office just called in. Chessman is handling your substitution for Frank with his NINA contacts."

That wasn't reassuring to Mark either. He didn't trust Chessman. He'd helped put him in jail, and this was no time to give the man a chance to bury a knife in Mark's back. "He'd sooner kill me than help me."

"He's got incentive. We'll be okay."

Mark held his silence.

Joe quizzed Roxy and then added his own assurance.

Joe, Mark trusted. "Okay."

"Good." Roxy took a deep breath. "Your code name is Bandit. The mission name is Shifter. There's an authorization code, but Chessman doesn't have it. Karl Masson is Frank's point of contact. If he asks for the code, I'm afraid we're done."

Mark didn't know whether to pray that Masson would or wouldn't ask for it. "So Chessman knows all about this operation, but he doesn't know the authorization code?"

"That's right."

"I don't think he's being honest with you."

"Bet on it. But what can we do?"

Truthfully, not much. Mark frowned and looked out through the windshield.

"Señor, I know the authorization code." Juan swallowed hard, bobbing his Adam's apple.

Mark snapped his gaze to Juan. "How do you know it?"

"Frank said it several times—every time

363

Masson or another called him. Sometimes it was someone else. I do not know who. I did not hear names."

"And you remember it?"

"Sí, I have a gift for the numbers. But I want my family safe and your FBI to handle this so we can stay in our home."

"Roxy?" Mark waited.

"Everything in our power."

Mark nodded to Juan.

"I'm trusting you, Señor Taylor."

"I know."

"*Dios, protección por favor.* Let me do the right thing."

"What did he say?" Roxy asked.

"He asked God to protect him, if He pleased," Joe answered.

Tears brimmed in Juan's eyes. "Alpha 263891."

"Amazing." Roxy sounded breathless. "Write it down."

"He doesn't need to, Roxy," Joe said. "Mark's got it."

Mark did have it. "Looks like we're set. Now we just have to wait for Masson's next call."

Juan checked his watch. "He will phone again at six thirty. When we get near Houston."

Mark hesitated to ask, but he was concerned about Lisa. "Everyone okay back there?"

"Lisa is fine, Mark. We're all fine."

His neck went hot. None of them were fine.

They were all stressed to the max at what had been done to them, who had done it, and what was happening to them now. Stressed and scared to death something would go wrong. But they were thinking steel, and Lisa no doubt was praying her heart out. So was Mark. He couldn't fail her. He couldn't survive another Jane incident.

On a promise and a prayer.

Promptly at six thirty, Karl Masson called Frank's cell phone.

"Juan."

A shiver snaked up Karl's back. "Why are you answering the phone?"

"Did Señor Chessman not call you?"

"No, he did not."

"He was supposed to call you."

"Where's Frank?"

"He got the virus like some of the cargo. Vomiting and the loose bowel. He was going to continue, but Señor Chessman said all the cargo would be sick and a driver would meet the truck in Orange."

"One did, I take it?"

"Sí. Señor Frank left and the new driver is here now."

"Who is he?"

"Señor Bandit."

"Put him on the phone."

"He wishes to speak to you," Juan said.

"Yeah."

"Identify yourself," Karl said.

"Bandit."

Already suspicious, Karl went into full-protection mode. "Mission?"

"Shifter."

"Authorization code?"

"Alpha 263891."

Karl weighed Bandit's reaction. He hadn't hesitated or paused. He was legit. Chessman could have spared Karl some serious anxiety if he'd bothered to phone him, but the man was in jail, and for the sake of appearances, some conventions had to be observed. He might not have had the opportunity.

"Fine," Karl told Bandit. "Drive south on Highway 77 to Victoria." Then he gave explicit directions to a ranch. "It'll take just over three hours. You'll meet a pickup there and then get right back on the road."

Originally the plan called for the truck to stop overnight, but taking on added cargo in Jackson had eaten up too much of their time. The boss had allotted five hours for road emergencies, detours, and traffic. The cargo addition in Jackson had burned up four of them.

"After you meet the truck, you'll be heading south on Highway 77 again. If you're told anything different, you stop and call me immediately." Chessman wasn't taking kindly to

Karl's promotion, and he wouldn't be above setting him up for a failed mission to shove him out and Chessman back into place. "Need anything repeated?"

"No sir. I've got it."

"Fine. Call in once you clear Victoria, and I'll verify your instructions."

"Yes sir."

Karl ended the call and started to dial Chessman, but an incoming call diverted him. *Dutch.*

The man was more trouble than the job was worth.

Unless you need him to take the fall.

The minute he determined he wouldn't need Hauk, he'd activate a plan to take him out. Because the man annoyed him, but also for Annie. The bottom line was he liked her. She was a good woman with really bad judgment. But she deserved better than she'd gotten from Dutch.

NINA won't like it.

He didn't care. She reminded him of Angel. Angel hadn't gotten a chance. Three short months and cancer claimed her. The kids went to live with her parents—he was on the road all the time. He lost everything that mattered to him: Angel and their kids. Seeing them a couple of times a year just wasn't the same. No. If Annie survived, she would get a real chance. She'd earned it.

Angel would have liked that.

Even now, he missed her. A hard lump rose in his throat, sank deep into his hollow chest. His eyes burned, and he blinked hard and fast. He'd always miss her.

The phone rang again. Grateful for the distraction, he thumbed the screen and answered. "Yeah?"

Hauk prattled on for a long moment.

Weary of listening to him, Karl interrupted. "She's alive, but there's been no change."

"And Lisa?"

Karl paused a long second, then told Hauk what he most wanted to hear. "Suffering."

As Karl hung up, the reason he should kill Hauk became clear. Annie made a slave of herself to honor her God and to spare her daughter—something Karl's parents never would have done for him. Even after Lisa left home and Annie could have escaped, she'd stayed and kept her vows. The woman had integrity, honor, and a love of family like his wife.

And that likeness made Annie too good to be stuck with scum like Dutch Hauk.

Karl shifted on his seat. No one had rescued Angel or him, but if Annie lived, he would rescue her. And he would kill Hauk for only one reason.

Because he could.

23

"here's the ranch." Juan pointed through the window. "Why are you stopping here?"

"That's what the man said to do." Mark pulled as far off the shoulder as he dared, then put the truck into Park. If they could get through this transfer, the women would be safe, and their part would be done.

In a cold sweat, he adjusted the mic. "Joe, you prepared if the need arises?"

"Always, bro." A short pause, and Joe added, "Think steel."

"Ditto." Mark typically would. But Lisa was in the back of the truck. *Lisa.* There was no steel in his arsenal when she was involved.

A cloud of dust lifted on the road near the ranch house, and a truck like the one they were in came wobbling toward them. If there were women in the back of it, they were getting one rough ride.

It seemed to take forever, but finally the driver pulled onto the highway and stopped behind Mark. The back ends of the two trucks faced each other.

Mark got out and walked to the rear.

The other driver met him. They exchanged code and mission names, and Mark asked him for the authorization number before he could ask Mark.

After he reeled it off, the man opened the rear door of his truck.

Empty.

Panic surged inside Mark. No way was he letting the women transfer vehicles. "What's the plan?"

"You give me the women and go."

"No."

The man was huge: broad shoulders, barrel chest. His face was pocked with scars, and his forearms, bare from rolled-up shirtsleeves, were riddled with thin white scars. Knife slashes.

"Not my orders," Mark said.

"Just testing you, man." He smiled and grabbed an ice chest from the passenger seat. "Here you go. Stash it in the back. I need to verify your cargo."

Mark opened the door and stepped aside.

The other driver pulled out a piece of paper and glanced at the photos of Lisa, Gwen, Amanda, and Selene. "Who's she?" He pointed to Roxy.

"A bonus."

The driver frowned. "No bonus, man. You follow orders. That's all you do."

"No choice. She spotted us at a stop and was trying to call the cops." Mark squared off on the guy. "You want me to cut her loose?"

"No." He shot Roxy a glare that had her instinctively backing into the truck. "Report it next call."

"Will do." He stared at the white cooler. "What's in it?"

"Does it matter?"

"Not to me. But if it's explosives, I want to know."

"It's not." He sniffed.

Cocaine. "Got it." Mark reached for the door, then swung it shut.

The other driver shut the back end of his truck. "Later." He got into his truck and then drove away.

Mark paused by his rear panel, out of the man's sight. "Everyone okay, Roxy?"

"Scared but okay. Better drive south as instructed. We could be under observation."

He hadn't noted anyone following. "Okay." He tapped the gas pedal, headed down the highway. "Joe, have we picked up a stringer?"

"Negative, but I've got a weird feeling."

"Me too."

"Learn anything on the other women?" Roxy interjected.

Mark hated to say it. He'd have a war on his hands. They'd insist on continuing, and he wanted them out of this. "No."

"What's in the ice chest?" Roxy asked.

"He says it's not explosives. That's all I know, but he sniffed. I suspect it's cocaine."

"I'm going to bust the lock and check it out."

"Don't." Joe responded before Mark could. "We

show up next stop with a busted lock, and you women are dead."

"What if he lied? We could be sitting on C4 or nitro or something."

"Calm down, Selene." Lisa shouted to be heard over the mumbles going on in the back. "We're precious cargo. They're not going to blow us up. They wouldn't get paid."

"Lisa's right." Gwen added. "It probably is drugs. We're worth more alive to them."

"Whatever it is doesn't matter." Mark paused. "We're done. This is as far as we go."

Dead silence.

Finally Roxy responded. "Lisa, Gwen, and Selene want to keep going until we locate the others, Mark. If we hope to damage their operation, you know we need them."

Mark hit the brakes, pulled off the side of the road, and stopped. He jumped out of the truck and then jerked open the back door. He found Roxy and leveled her with a glare.

"We are done. It wasn't a suggestion and I wasn't asking. Human trafficking, death fights, and now drugs? I'm not letting you get them killed, okay? I won't do it."

Joe appeared at Mark's side. "Take a step back, bro."

Mark didn't budge. "X factor," he repeated the team's code to relay an eerie certainty that something had gone wrong, a mission had soured, a leak that could kill them had occurred, and it was time to abort the mission.

"Okay, then." Joe blinked, then blinked again. "We're done."

Roxy opened her mouth to speak, but Lisa stayed her with a hand on her forearm. "Let me." When Roxy nodded, Lisa made her way to the door and then hopped out.

"Here we go." Joe's voice was grim.

"Don't worry," Mark told him. "This time I'm not being led anywhere. I'm keeping my nose."

"Whatever you say, bro." Joe stepped back a bit.

Lisa glanced between the men, then faced Mark. "Honey, listen—"

"No, you listen." He frowned down at her. "We're done here."

"All right then." She looked up at him, cocked her head. The wind caught her hair, half pinned up, half fallen down, and tossed it in the breeze. "We're done."

"Lisa!" Selene sent a charged look at Gwen. "It's our choice too."

"I agree, but Mark is experienced at this type of thing, and if he says we're done, then we should listen to him."

"Okay," Selene said eventually, then shrugged. "Sorry, Roxy."

"Good." Mark gave Selene an emphatic nod. Relief swam through him and he turned to Roxy. "We'll get the next set of instructions, and you can have agents waiting to step in for the three of them. Your people go on; we go home."

Lisa nodded. "Sounds like a plan."

She was too calm. Too agreeable. Lisa Marie Harper didn't behave this way. "What are you doing?" Mark slung a hand at his hip. "Are you pulling reverse psychology on me, trying to mess with my head? If so, knock it off."

Her jaw clamped down tight. "Fine. Then you just answer me one thing." She folded her arms over her chest. "When these substitute agents are in the truck and it stops, and some guy carrying a gun looks in and doesn't see our faces"—she waved between her, Gwen, and Selene —"why isn't he going to slaughter them right there? This one didn't shoot us, but will that next one not kill them?"

Mark's shoulders slumped, and he glanced over at Joe, whose raised brows proved he didn't have a good answer. "They'll be armed."

"Certainly they will," Lisa said. "But as soon as the agents show their weapons, they'll be shot first. If they don't, they'll be dead before they can pull them. So either the next link to NINA is dead or the agents are. Maybe both. And then what happens to those other women? How does Roxy find them? How do they get home?"

He hated it when she did this. Fought him on straight logic. "They don't."

"Which is exactly why I don't have to persuade

you. You see the wisdom in our going on until we know where those women are. We can stop now, of course, and we will if you insist, right?"

"Yes," Selene said.

"Absolutely." Gwen nodded.

Lisa turned back to Mark. Slowly and deliberately, she linked their pinkie fingers. "But if we do stop here, NINA will abduct and ship more women." She expelled a frustrated breath. "I don't want to have nightmares forever about them, Mark. I don't want our life together stained with the guilt of not stopping this because I was afraid."

"You could get killed." He shook their twined fingers loose and clasped her arms. "Do you get that?" He glared at the other women. "Do any of you get that?"

Lisa frowned up at him. "How could we not get it?"

Mark squeezed his eyes shut a long minute, then opened them again. "What if something goes wrong? On operations like this, unexpected things happen. Things out of our control. What if—?"

"You fail to protect me?" she asked softly so only he could hear.

Agony tore his insides to shreds. "Yes."

"I'd rather die trying to stop this for good than live with knowing I didn't even try out of cowardice. I don't fear death. It's life that scares the fool out of me."

Joe started to intercede, but Selene pointed a

"don't do it" finger at him. "The fact is, there are fates worse than death, and we were about to experience them. We know the dangers and risks. We want all of the women free. To get them, we must do this. It's the right thing."

Joe stared at Selene a moment, then swiveled toward Mark. "Forget it, bro. When women team up like this, you can't win."

Mark's sigh heaved his shoulders. "There's still a problem. Juan says Masson doesn't give them instructions on the routine two-hour stops. Frank just knew where to go. I'm supposed to be one of them, so I should know them too, and of course I don't."

"I think I can help with that," Lisa said. "They've all been convenience stores, and unless I'm mistaken, they all belong to Dutch." She turned to Roxy. "Can't you get Beth or somebody to run the records and find his stores along the route?"

"Sure." Roxy looked at Mark. "We're set for a joint effort with Mexico. We're in an observe-and-advise capacity, so that should diminish the risks."

"You know that's absurd."

"We'll do what we must, Mark. Additional resources have been allocated. But that's the official line to avoid tangles on both sides of the border."

"There." Lisa looked back at Mark. "We're good, then."

"Yeah, we're good." He snarled. "But this is not good, and don't think you're going to do this to me all the time."

"Do what?"

"Twist things around so you're leading me by the nose."

She looked at him as if he'd lost his mind. "You're kidding, right?"

"Lisa."

"I said we'd do whatever you thought best."

"Get in the truck, Lisa Marie."

She crawled back in through the rear door and then turned around to face him. "You still adore me, right? You don't much look like it at the moment, but that's just because you're worried, isn't it?"

She seemed pretty worried herself. He kept his tone razor sharp but linked their pinkie fingers. "Quit pushing me, woman."

Lisa smiled, touched her lips to his fingertips, then released his hand. "I adore you too."

How did she do that? His mind turned to mush every time he got close to her. Grumbling under his breath, he turned and was half surprised to see Joe still standing there.

"You'll get used to it," Joe said. "You won't ever walk all over her, and that'll keep you humble."

"Is that what you're hanging here to tell me?"

"No." Pity flashed through Joe's eyes. "Tim called. Mandy's broken off their engagement. She's met a man she can't live without."

"You're kidding."

"Afraid not." Joe swatted at a mosquito on his neck.

"How's he taking it?"

"Pretty messed up. I've got to call him back, so if you want me, stick your hand out the window to signal."

"Sam and Nick are there. Can't Tim talk to them?"

"Not without Peggy and Nora overhearing. Cupid and Rambo need to stay in the dark, at least until Tim quits bleeding. He's talking to Beth."

"She won't let him wallow long."

Joe's eyes lit with interest. "I think I like this woman."

"Hadn't considered it, but you two probably would hit it off."

"I don't know. She's probably too smart for me."

Mark grunted. "She's brilliant. You're not. But balance is a good thing between a man and woman."

"Not cool, bro." Joe headed toward his vehicle. "But I'll let it slide because you're wounded."

"Wounded?"

Joe didn't turn around or look back. "Lisa outwitted you. Bad. You're wounded."

She had and he was. "Tell Tim I'm sorry."

Joe held up his arm and shot out a thumbs-up.

His pride pricked, Mark got in the truck and slammed the door.

Juan wisely kept his mouth shut, and Roxy gave Mark a radio respite; time to lick his wounds. Wise. Otherwise he might take off somebody's head.

He continued south, and when they cleared town, he phoned Masson, who instructed him to go to Brownsville and cross the border into Mexico, then head toward Tampico, Tamaulipas, hanging close to the coastline—Juan's home, as Mark had suspected would be the case. Travel time from the border, Masson informed him, was about four and half hours.

"Got it," Mark said.

"The cargo shipment will be monitored the entire way, Bandit, so don't get any stupid ideas about confiscating it. The world is too small a place for you to hide from NINA."

Easy to answer that honestly. "I never considered it."

The line went dead and Mark drove on. "Roxy, Masson says we're being monitored. Looks like our next big stop is in Mexico."

"I heard."

"What about these other women?"

"I don't know what to think. Chessman swears on the number."

"Unless someone meets us at a store, we're not getting more of them to haul on this side of the border."

"We've got to go with it," Joe said. "My nose is

saying there are more women. This run was too much trouble for just the four of them."

Mark agreed. Grudgingly, he kept driving, stopping at Dutch's stores on the expected schedule. Apparently Lisa's guess about Dutch's stores had been right on target. At each stop, they were expected and encountered no trouble. Why would employees do this?

Maybe they had been coerced like Juan. Or maybe they were paid well to be blind and silent. With people it was hard to tell.

Lisa was right about another thing too. On each of the store windows, Mark saw the two signs: one on human trafficking and one for a lost pet with instructions to call Nina but with no phone number.

In the wee hours, minutes before reaching the border, Masson called with specific border-crossing directions. NINA apparently had friends working for them in that realm too. Though bitter about that, Mark was relieved they had avoided any incident. Once the dust settled in Tampico, the FBI would move in and the corrupt border guards would be arrested.

At seven o'clock Juan took the wheel, and at seven thirty he pulled into the back entrance of a heavily guarded, lavish coastal estate.

The long road was surfaced though sand-slick and bordered by sparse trees, flowering shrubs, and hundreds of pink and white and yellow flowers. Every twenty yards, there was an adobe-type wall three feet wide and six feet high with small cutouts at eye level. The walls were etched with intricate drawings. And rifle barrels protruded through the cutouts.

"Joe, you seeing this?"

"Yeah, bro. Going radio silent for a while."

Joe was infiltrating on foot.

Lisa and the other women stepped out of the back of the truck. All of them were shaking. So was Mark.

At seven forty-five a second truck pulled in beside them and stopped. The driver, a brawny man in his late thirties with short black hair and a spiderwebbed hand, jumped out and opened the back door. "Welcome to your new home. Move it."

Women poured out.

Roxy stepped close and whispered to Mark, "Looks like we found the other women."

Mark stared at them. Arms and legs bruised and battered. Clothing half torn from their bodies. The scent of their fear burned his nose. Most hadn't come easily and it showed. Oddly, the bruises largely were from the neck down. *Bring higher prices at auction.* They were all pretty, muscles well toned. *Good for fighting.*

Mark moved closer to Lisa, providing a shield for cover. Roxy relayed the message about the arrival of the other women to the team.

Lisa stood transfixed by the women. What she was thinking was easy enough to imagine. "You okay?"

"I will be now." She glanced over at the six-story home and paled.

Attuned to her, he felt her strength falter, and fearing her knees would buckle, he clasped her arm. "What is it?"

She darted her eyes, swept the building. "I know this place."

"You do?" How could she? The first abduction. *No. Oh no.* Susan's note ricocheted through Mark's mind. If Lisa remembered, she'd need professional intervention to get through it.

A whimper escaped through her clamped mouth. She jerked her gaze from the expansive home to Mark. Fear flooded her eyes, oozed from her every pore. "Mr. Phen lives here."

Her fear pulsed through him, and while he had no idea what she remembered, he could see that some connections had been made and they terrified her. "Who is Mr. Phen?"

She whimpered again.

"Lisa, who is Mr. Phen?" Mark darted a worried look at Roxy, who'd picked up on the fear too.

A tear spilled onto Lisa's cheek. "The man who bought me the first time I was sold."

24

The phone at his ear, Karl looked into his rearview mirror. The border crossing was fading fast. That was the last huge operational hurdle.

"Yes, I substituted Bandit," Chessman said. "I would have called, but the timing was inconvenient."

"I understand." Just as Karl had suspected. Incarceration had its limitations. "Did you notify Raven?"

"There's no need to bog her down in minutiae. The substitution was mission essential. It's done. End of story. The cargo should be on the premises now."

That bothering-the-boss bit was a backhanded reprimand about Karl's poor management. He let the insult slide. Chessman was still stinging at being demoted. "Excellent." The auction was set for eight o'clock that night. "Do you have an update on the patient?"

"Still comatose."

Alive. Dutch would be glad to hear it. Maybe. Karl was glad to hear it. He kicked the air conditioner up a notch. It was even hotter here than in Seagrove Village. Apparently NINA had remedied its employee gap on the hospital site since Rose's hasty departure. It hadn't taken long. It never did. "I'll notify the client."

"That about wraps this one up."

"Just about." *Sweet. Nearly done and slick as glass.*

"Well done, Karl."

No way was that sincere. Chessman wanted Karl to fall flat on his face so their roles would be reversed again, and only a fool wouldn't know it. "Thank you."

"About that other little matter."

Kelly Walker. Chessman wanted her dead too. She was the reason he was in jail, and the man did hold a decent grudge.

"Won't be long now." The air was still hot. Karl hit the AC again. When he got to the coast, at least it wouldn't be as dusty. He hated dust. He hated heat too. Couldn't wait to get back to Syracuse.

"Excellent."

Essential. Karl frowned. If he removed Walker, maybe NINA would get that artist's rendering of his face off the U.S. post offices' walls. Getting rid of those sketches was a worthy cause.

Chessman cleared his throat. "Still no signs of a memory return?"

Lisa Harper. "None whatsoever. She's been tested multiple times."

"Her buyer will be disappointed."

Phen was a sadistic jerk, and Chessman was right. Phen would be disappointed. He fed off fear, and Lisa's forgetting him would stab his mammoth ego. He'd be determined to make her remember or learn to fear him all over again.

If she were going to remember, surely she would have by now. Either way, she would fear Phen. And Dutch's wishes would be fulfilled.

Lisa would suffer.

Disjointed thoughts swirled through Lisa's mind, memories of this grand estate: the light adobe brick and cold Saltillo tile. Six separate floors, but the first was a type of torture chamber created specifically to incite fear, to satisfy the lusts of deviates. Lisa shuddered.

"Are you all right?" Mark whispered from beside her. "What do you mean, the first time you were sold?"

She remembered it all so clearly now. Being dragged into an auditorium on the second floor. It was opulent and a lot like the one her parents had taken her to for a concert, with a wide stage and a tall, ornate dome ceiling and blue velvet curtains that stretched up so high they seemed suspended from heaven.

But in Phen's auditorium, glimpses of hell came to life center stage.

She tried to find her voice. Gwen, Selene, and Amanda stood behind them. While quiet and watchful, their presence helped anchor Lisa and keep her emotions then and now separate, helped remind her she was no longer the child she'd been, but the woman she'd become.

"When I was seven, I was kidnapped and brought here. A man named Mr. Phen sold me, but I didn't leave with him. I don't know why. I tried to escape, and this little boy told Mr. Phen where I was. He caught me. It took days before I was healed enough to crawl out of bed. My buyer backed out—I was too headstrong for his tastes. He preferred his mates docile."

Amazing, after all these years of remembering nothing, now the details returned, and they were so vivid! "Mr. Phen sold me to a new buyer in the States. A Spider was bringing me to him—I don't know where the buyer was, I never got there. I played sick and escaped. The Spider went into a store, and I shot across the street into a dress shop. A lady there hid me."

"So it was NINA who had you before when you were a kid?" Mark asked, pensive and tense.

"I don't know about NINA, but Spiders were involved." Armed men herded the women from the second truck up the road toward the house. Lisa stiffened. They'd killed her father—and she'd forgotten it. Shame washed through her. How was that possible?

Survival.

"This is what Annie hoped you wouldn't remember." He filled her in on Annie's muddled conversation in the ambulance.

Half-dead, and her mother worried about her.

Tears built in Lisa's heart and lumped in her throat. "Mark, what kind of woman am I? How could I forget this? They killed my father—"

"When this happened, you weren't a woman, you were a child."

He wasn't judging her. Oh, if only she could not judge herself. "I started remembering in the truck—bits and pieces that made no sense. I wasn't sure they were even real. But then the pieces started connecting, and when I saw this place, everything came rushing back."

"Are you okay? Do you need to get out of here? I can take you to Harvey. He'll know what to do to help you."

"I'm upright." She wouldn't lie and say she wasn't rattled. But Selene's words came back to her as they often had when Lisa thought she'd fall apart. *"We don't have that luxury."*

It was amazing how much strength she'd found in Selene. So practical and purpose driven, she had insisted Lisa deal with whatever came and keep it in perspective. The past was past and couldn't be changed. Did she want a future? If so, then she had to deal with the past and put it in its proper place. Otherwise, it would steal all it had and then steal her future too.

Thanks to Selene, Lisa had chosen. She would not become a victim to the past as she had become a victim to NINA, the Spiders, and Mr. Phen. "It's a lot to process, but this is not defining my life, Mark. It's mine, and I want it."

Toward the center of the huddle of people, he shifted, clearly uneasy. "This kind of thing is outside my sphere of expertise, but Susan said—"

"Susan who?"

"Brandt. She left a note, and Peggy found it in your file."

Surprise shot through Lisa. "She knew."

He nodded. "Annie wouldn't let anyone force you to remember. She said God would see to it in His own time."

Lisa would have insisted on just the opposite. But the way things were working out . . . She'd have to think on that later. Now just wasn't the time.

"Susan said you'd need extreme intervention to get through remembering constructively." He paused to study her face. "You seem okay to handle this, but if you're not, tell me and I'll get you out." He narrowed his eyes. "Listen to your instincts. That's all I'm saying."

One of the women in line stumbled. Gwen moved to help her, but Selene jerked her back. Another woman did, and a guard shoved her to the ground and planted his foot on her back.

"My gut is saying nail them."

Pride flashed through his eyes.

"Think steel." She hiked her chin. "Isn't that what you, Joe, and the guys say?"

"Yes, but we've never been in this situation."

But she had. "It's good advice." How could she reassure him? She hated that terrified-for-her look on his face. "I think I've already had extreme intervention. The hardships prepared me for this. So I could cope with what happened then and do what needs doing now."

"But Susan's note said—"

"Collect some fumes, Mark, and have faith. God's in control." Lisa touched his arm. "We just have to get what Roxy needs to shut these people down and lock them up. The Mexican authorities will handle the takedown. Isn't that what Roxy said?"

"In theory, but it never works out that way. We'll be right in the middle of it, and the takedown is always the most dangerous time."

Lisa swept her gaze across the mansion. "The sooner it comes, the better, because I'm telling you, this place is as close to hell as exists on earth."

"I don't mean to beat this to death, but how can I be sure you won't snap? Susan was explicit about the dangers—"

"I won't snap." Lisa leveled him with a look of fierce determination. "I told you, God has been preparing me all along. I'm not a fumes-of-faith Christian here just to serve others, and neither are you. We learn what we need so it's there to protect us. When I was a kid, I was too little and weak to defend myself. Getting away took divine intervention. Now, I can protect myself and help protect the others. Look at me and you see extreme intervention in the form of a doctor trained in self-defense. But the Healer has given me extreme intervention my whole life."

Mark dropped his lids, hooded his eyes. Lisa couldn't blame him for being skeptical, but before she could say any more, men with guns formed two lines that stretched from where they were all huddled to a point toward the house beyond where she could see.

"Line up," a man shouted. "Single file and move through the middle."

Herded through the center between the armed men, they moved into a stone-floored courtyard. More armed men guarded its perimeter, perched on the roof. The overwhelming display of force made it clear that the women were prisoners and if they stepped out of line, they would be shot. It was a common psychological-warfare tactic, but it still had a debilitating impact.

A man walked out and stopped on the stone steps, towering above them, not seeming as large as he had the first time she'd seen him there, though he was a solid six feet and change. His hair was black, his eyes dark in the morning sun, not reflecting light. Trim and fit and tanned with broad shoulders and a thick chest, he stood clothed in a dark suit too heavy for the warm weather. He had to be sweltering, and yet he wore it for effect, down to the proverbial red tie to emanate a sense of power and authority. His message was clear. *I am the master of all in my domain. I am your master.*

Mark moved closer to her and whispered, "Who is that?"

Knowing the horrors the man was capable of, Lisa felt an icy hand slide from the base of her spine up over every vertebra to the base of her skull. All the nerves in her body throbbed simultaneously, pounding out warnings. "That's Mr. Phen."

A group of his armed minions circled the women standing clustered in the courtyard. One guard motioned Mark away, and he moved to the perimeter.

Mr. Phen motioned to the guard standing nearest him on the left. "It appears we are all here."

"Yes sir. All present and accounted for, sir."

Phen nodded. "Good morning. I am Mr. Phen."

No one uttered a sound.

Seeming pleased, Phen adjusted his stance, his legs spread, his hands perched on his hips, his chin lifted to an arrogant angle. "Your situation is this. Your old lives are gone, and you will not get them back. They no longer exist. You are my property now, my shrubs. You are under my complete and total control, and your well-being, your very life, is wholly dependent on my whim, my discretion, and my goodwill. There is no escape. There is no alternative to your doing what I say when I say it. I expect you to follow my orders without hesitation and without fail. If you meet my expectations, you will live. If you do not, you will die."

He paced the span of the ten-foot-wide steps three times, then stopped and faced them again. "If you do not intend to follow my orders, please step forward to the base of the steps. We will spare ourselves and you unpleasantness and kill you now." He smiled. "I daresay we will be more merciful in your murder here than if you are disobedient and force us to kill you inside my home."

His torture chamber made a bullet to the head seem welcome.

Roxy slid Lisa a questioning glance, silently asking if Mr. Phen was bluster or factual.

"Believe it. He defines deviate." Memories washed over Lisa. Memories of rooms with chains on the walls, whips, and wooden racks with huge cranks. Twisted, ugly machines. The faces of the people in them contorted in pain, their screams echoing off the walls. He'd made her watch. Made her see them beg for their lives and then beg to be allowed to die. And then he killed them.

She wept inside, crossed her arms over her chest, and wept for the innocent child she'd been, the horror she'd seen. The poor souls who had died within these ugly walls.

"You okay?" Gwen whispered.

No. No, I'm not okay. She shuddered.

"Whatever you are thinking, stop it now," Selene whispered. "It's over. You survived. Turn it to something good."

She was right. Lisa imagined Mark clasping their pinkies. In her mind, she studied his huge hands, so tender and gentle. Hands that protected and nurtured. Hands that caressed her face and managed to make her feel touched in her heart.

"Better." Selene stepped aside.

None of the women moved.

"No rebels bent on revolt?" Mr. Phen scanned the crowd, and his gaze snagged on Lisa. "Ah, Lisa Harper." He laughed. "It's good to have you back with me again."

Debating on whether or not to let on she recognized him, she opted for ignorance. It had worked with Frank. "Excuse me?"

"Ah, Lisa. They say you don't recall your previous visit to my home. Though brief, I find that impossible to believe. Is it true? Do you not remember your time with Mr. Phen?"

"I daresay that if we'd ever met, I would certainly remember it."

He stared at her a long moment, then his tense face relaxed. "Well. More is the pity, but it's just as well. You're too old for me now, though I will endure and do my best to help you recall."

An earthquake erupted inside her, so powerful

and strong her entire body suffered simultaneous aftershocks and tremors. *Sick. Sick. The man is the worst kind of sick.*

"For now"—Phen returned his attention to the group—"you'll be shown to your quarters. Bathe, eat, and sleep. Clothing will be brought to your rooms later today. Put it on, dress carefully—your future depends on it—and be ready to leave your room promptly at 7:30 p.m." He turned and then looked back at them over his shoulder. "In your former world, it was acceptable to be fashionably late. It is not acceptable in mine."

The threat in his voice was mirrored on his face. He disappeared behind heavy green foliage.

The men started ushering the women, single file, across the courtyard and into the house Lisa recalled as the Chamber of Horrors.

"You're sure you're okay?"

"I'm fine." Lisa looked at Mark, who had appeared at her side. Knowing he'd never believe her, she revised her remark. "I'm fine, I'm scared to death, and I'm praying hard."

Mark looked reluctant to let her go, but if she didn't move soon, the guards would notice. "It'll be okay."

Lisa said it and prayed she was right.

25

Mark planted his feet on the ground and his hands in his pockets to keep from yanking Lisa from the line of women entering the house. "Roxy, you get all that?" He scanned but didn't spot her.

"Already relayed. Wait. Someone is coming. Black sedan. Not sure of the make and model."

He glanced toward the driveway and saw her hunkered down under some shrubs.

Juan stepped closer to Mark. "Señor, a black Lexus is coming. Masson drives such a car."

"Probably Masson," Mark transmitted to Roxy.

"Make yourself scarce. Surely by now he knows about you. Meet the team at the marina to finalize interception plans. Take the truck."

"I'm not leaving Lisa."

"You don't have a choice. Masson can identify you. You could get her killed."

He could. No doubt Masson could tag every member in Mark's old team. Phen might have even been alerted, though Mark doubted NINA would disseminate that much information to him unless they knew Mark was onto them. "My men arrived yet?"

"Ten minutes out," Joe responded.

"What about Juan?"

"He needs to stay and follow his original orders,"

Roxy said. "It's the only way we can cover for him. Now go. Masson will want to meet Bandit."

Lisa stepped inside, and Mark lost sight of her. His stomach sank to his knees. "What do you want Juan to tell him?"

"Say Chessman phoned with an assignment and Bandit left with the truck to handle it. Meet up at Ortego's. It's a locals' café, south end of the marina, away from Juan's boat."

Mark filled Juan in and then looked him right in the eye. "Do what you can to watch over them."

"Sí, señor. I will try." His eyes held his fear of failure.

Mark clasped his shoulder. "Your family is safe now. Do your best."

"Dios willing, I will do all I am able and He will do the rest." Juan lifted a fingertip heavenward. "This, I must believe."

Mark headed to the truck, got in, and cranked the engine. Heat radiated off the dash. "Roxy, you read me?"

"Yeah, I've got you."

"Which direction is the black sedan entering from?"

"The north."

"I'm exiting south, then. Unless you want an interdiction?" Mark would like nothing better than to take the monster down.

"I'd love one, but it's too soon. We have to wait for all parties to get into position."

The buyers at the auction. Pangs of disappointment fell to resignation. Mark knew the drill, and he had been trained to be patient. Patient and persistent and determined. Masson's time would come.

God, let it be in time to spare Lisa and the other women. I can't live with failing a woman again. I just can't do it.

Trust Me, Mark.

Mark stilled. He was tired, scared of failure in ways he'd seldom feared. This fear took him all the way back to his childhood, back to enduring his father's and brother's slurs and blame for his mother's death. Back to that merciless, unshakable guilt that clawed at his soul every day of his youthful life. Then it was easy not to fear failure. He was worth nothing and had nothing more to lose. But now things were different. Now, he had Lisa.

Mark turned the wheel to avoid a pothole. The back right tire clipped it and the truck bounced. He had no illusions. He was flawed—on some things, a train wreck. He wasn't worthy. He had tried to earn his way into favor, been willing to do what needed doing. But down at the bones of it, when it came to faith, he had become a Christian but still ran on scattered fumes.

He'd watched the others at Crossroads. They were the real thing. They had the real thing. Now and then, he believed he had the real thing too.

Other times he doubted and craved what they had. Yet no matter how hard he tried, he couldn't seem to earn his way to it. That special relationship with the Lord eluded him, stayed close enough to taunt him but too far away to reach. He shifted gears, adrift, isolated, alone.

Trust Me, My son.

Love flowed through, warm and welcome and consuming. *God.*

I am never beyond your reach and never away from you. You are Mine, and I am with you always.

Overwhelmed, Mark hit the brakes, pulled over, and stopped. God's voice filled his mind and flooded his heart. His shock melted and an alien sense replaced it: total acceptance, a deep abiding and enduring connectedness never before experienced. And love. Unconditional love. And in it was truth.

Unearned. Undeserved but offered.

Grace. I get it now. Mark hadn't accepted God's gift then. *I accept it. Thank You.*

Humbled and awed, he wept over the steering wheel and, bowing his head, offered a prayer of thanksgiving.

Lisa was right about this too.

Neither of them was a fumes-of-faith Christian, here only to serve and help others. They had believed it, but they were wrong.

God was with them every step of the way.

• • •

Karl parked near the rear courtyard, then made his way into it. The relentless sun radiated heat off the tile. He was hot, exhausted, and elated all at the same time. This shipment had taken a few unexpected twists and turns, but he'd pulled it off. The cargo was in place on time and intact.

He hadn't had time to go back to Seagrove Village and dispose of Kelly Walker yet or take out Dutch—two tasks he relished seeing completed for entirely different reasons—but he had completed his mission. So long as the auction took place as scheduled, Raven wouldn't be inconvenienced, and that was a very good thing for Karl's long-term prospects with NINA and in life.

Considering the added challenges of Taylor's old team, Raven might even feel generous enough to assign someone else to handle the Kelly Walker problem so Karl didn't have to return to the village. Though it would be a personal-satisfaction perk to plant a little C4 at that stupid Crossroads Crisis Center and take out all those jerks at one time, he'd welcome Walker's demise by any means. The Crossroads bunch needed to go. Everyone there knew far too much about NINA. Raven, no doubt, was monitoring that situation and would soon draw the same conclusion, if she hadn't already.

Juan stood at the edge of the courtyard near a clump of spiky bushes planted in vats.

Karl walked up to him, grateful to find a little shade. "Glad you made it. Where's Bandit?"

"Gone." Juan seemed surprised Karl didn't know it. "Mr. Chessman sent him somewhere. I do not know where."

That wasn't uncommon, though Karl would have preferred notice and to get a look at the man. "Any problems to report?"

"Just the virus. Otherwise, none at all."

A weight lifted off Karl's shoulders. That was his kind of news, and just what he'd been hoping to hear. "I'm going to hit the rack for a few hours." Some pungent floral fragrance had his nose itching. He rubbed at it. "You stay here until after the auction, then ferry the buyers back to their planes. Where's your boat?"

"At the marina. Should I go get it?"

"Have someone bring it over and dock it here. They're not to step ashore, so someone needs to follow to ferry them back. It's too far to swim."

"Sí, señor."

Juan took orders without challenge. Karl would remember that for future assignments, not that Juan would be happy to hear from him. But reality would set in. Once NINA tapped a man, he was a lifer. Settling his sunglasses on the bridge of his nose, Karl started toward the house. "I'll be down in time for the auction. Anything comes up before then, come get me."

"Where will you be, señor?" Juan's gaze drifted up the six stories. "It's a big *casa.*"

"Third floor." He hiked his brows. It always had been his favorite.

"Sí, señor."

Stepping under the colorful, striped overhang leading inside, Karl embraced the cool air emerging from the arched entrance. Why hadn't Chessman notified him Bandit was being reassigned? Why hadn't Raven passed Karl the assignment?

An internal alarm went off. Taylor's team was afoot. Dutch Hauk hadn't done anything to neutralize them, but they might have nailed him. He'd turn on Karl in a heartbeat.

Last check the man was still in Louisiana. Karl grunted. Was Hauk there hiding, or was he feeding the Shadow Watchers information to save his own skin?

Better check this out, Karl. Better check this out.

The room was little more than a closet: bare white walls, no window, one door, and a twin bed with just enough room to walk beside it without running into another wall.

Memories of being a child and in a room just like it assailed Lisa, and yet the fear she'd felt then was different. Now, through a woman's eyes, knowing that Mark, his old team, and the FBI were near, she wasn't consumed by it.

Oh, she wasn't foolish enough to fall for a false sense of security or any illusion of being safe. They were anything but safe. Given a chance, to protect its interests, NINA would kill them all. Mr. Phen would be more than delighted to do it.

When he'd hung a man on that rack and turned the crank until the poor man screamed in agony, begging for mercy, Mr. Phen bent down and turned the crank again.

The screaming stopped as suddenly as it had started.

Mr. Phen, in his pristine white suit, walked to the man's head and pressed his fingers to his throat. He paused a long second. Lisa shrank back, as far away as she could get, wringing her hands, her stomach grinding, spots forming before her eyes.

"Oops, I fear that last crank got him." Mr. Phen laughed and turned to Lisa. "He's dead."

She knew what dead meant. Her father had explained it and even took her to the morgue once.

"You see, Lisa? That's what happens when you don't listen to Mr. Phen. You die."

Murder, she'd learned, came naturally to a man who loved to inflict pain.

Given certain circumstances, anyone was capable of murder. Dutch had proven that to her.

Wrapped in a terry-cloth robe, Lisa sat on the edge of the bed, weary from the heart out. How was her mother? How was everyone at the crisis center? No doubt they were all frantic and doing all they could to help her and her mom. Peggy likely had the prayer warriors on duty around the clock too.

And Mark. Mark and the team—how close were they to her now? She imagined their faces—Nick, unsmiling; Sam, his cap tugged low over his eyes; Tim, his head high, pristine and sophisticated; and Joe, cool from the ends of his hair to the tips of his toes, and evidently a little interested in Beth. Then her precious treasure, Mark, so strong and tender. What would they do? They had all sorts of special skills, but would they translate and help them in this situation?

Lisa collapsed back onto the bed and drew her knees up close to her chest. She didn't dare focus on the past or sleep, but the bed felt like the best mattress in the world after all that time on the wooden truck bed. Her eyes were dry, burning like fire. She let them drift closed, just for a second, hoping to refresh them.

Thank You, God, for letting Mark find us and giving us the strength to come here. I'm in so far over my head I can't even see down, much less up. I'm so scared and tired, and I can't afford to mess up. I need courage, strength, and wisdom, God. Lots of wisdom. These women are counting on me.

She turned onto her side, understanding how Mark felt guilty about Jane, and then her and her mother . . . He had to be chewing himself up—and fearful he'd fail them and not be good enough.

Just like her.

Lisa swallowed hard. Peggy Crane always said our timing and God's were different and His was always perfect, but Lisa never really believed it. She guessed that was part of the fumes thing she had going on. Now she knew better. *No matter how this turns out, I know You didn't cause bad things to happen to me, Mom, or Mark.*

Would she be wise enough? strong enough? For the others? For herself?

I don't know. But if it's Your will, I'd like to come through this alive. I could use a break. I want time with my mom and with Mark. We all need it, God. For so much of our lives, we haven't had family. More than anything in the world, I want my own family, and Mark and my mom do too. If that could work out, it'd just be the best. It'd be . . .

Silent tears washing her face, Lisa drifted off to sleep midsentence.

26

L isa? Lisa, wake up."

Lisa cranked open her eyes. Roxy stood beside her bed, dressed in a starched black-and-white maid's uniform. "What are you doing here?" Lisa sat straight up, her voice a stage whisper. "Are you trying to get killed?"

Roxy pressed a finger over her lips. "You have to get up now and get dressed."

For the first time, Lisa noticed a red silk dress draped over Roxy's arm. *The auction.*

"Hurry. You can't be late."

Lisa stood. "Where's Mark?"

"Close," Roxy whispered and helped Lisa into her dress. "You'll go next door to have your hair and face done. I'll help."

"Okay." Sore all over, Lisa turned and lifted her hair.

Roxy zipped the dress. "I checked on your mother. No change, but Nora says the doctor is more encouraged with every hour that passes. Annie's determined to live and that's half the battle."

"I hope he's right."

"Me too." Roxy looked away. "Is Dr. Talbot still at the center? Harvey Talbot?"

"Yes. He's the senior psychologist—my boss. Do you know Harvey?"

"I used to." Roxy avoided Lisa's eyes. "It's been three years since I've seen him."

Something in the way she said it struck Lisa as odd. "How did you know him?"

"Later." Roxy smoothed Lisa's dress at her shoulder. "We have to get moving. You see this pin?" She held up a small crystal pin of three cherries on a gold stem. Lisa nodded, and Roxy went on. "It's a video camera and streams everything you're seeing and saying right to our people. Don't look at it, don't adjust your voice, and don't touch it. Just talk normally. We'll see and hear what you do."

"Okay." Lisa let Roxy attach the crystal pin to her dress.

Roxy stepped back. "Once you're all in the auditorium, we'll move in. We need a diversion. Nothing dramatic. Just something to shift attention. You'll be safest on the stage. Get word to the others to stay there. Lie flat on the floor and keep your heads down."

"Okay. I can do that."

"And what about the diversion?"

Lisa had no idea what to do about a diversion. Her mind was a blank slate. *God, I'm willing, but I need help on that.* "No problem."

"What are you going to do?"

A knock sounded at the door. "Move it!" a man shouted.

Roxy stared at Lisa, waiting for an answer.

"You'll see," Lisa said. So would she.

The makeup room was large and open with salon chairs lining both walls. In a wild flurry of activity, women were having their hair done, their nails polished, their makeup applied. *"A lady never attends a social event without a proper manicure."*

None of the women appeared bruised.

That surprised Lisa, until she remembered concealer could hide a multitude of sins. The gash on Gwen's head wasn't visible. And the bruise on Selene's neck was hidden too. All the women were dressed in the finest gowns, bejeweled, and made up to perfection.

A chime rang.

Silence fell.

Mr. Phen walked in. "Good evening, my little shrubs. It's seven thirty. Are you all ready?"

No one answered.

He smiled. "I'll take that as a yes. Single file, if you please." He swung his arm in a wide arc, gesturing where he wanted them to go.

The women lined up. Lisa lost sight of Roxy but stepped into the line between Gwen and Selene.

Gwen smoothed her hand over her abdomen. "My stomach has so many knots in it, I don't think I'll ever be able to eat again."

Selene looked past Lisa. "You have your flashlight?"

Gwen nodded.

"It'll be okay." Lisa offered them reassurance, though her stomach was in about the same shape as Gwen's.

"What's the plan?" Selene asked Lisa.

"In the auditorium. When everything breaks loose, stay on the stage and lie flat on your stomach. Pass the word to the other women, but don't get caught doing it."

Gwen leaned forward, Selene backward, and the word moved up and down the line.

Gwen was shaking hard. Lisa resisted the urge to say any more to her. She needed to be hyperalert. They all did.

"This way, please." Mr. Phen led them down a narrow hallway lined with doors, Lisa presumed, to more rooms like the one she'd been in, and then down a wide staircase and through the bowels of the mansion to the rear area on the second floor where the auditorium was located.

Inside it was just as Lisa recalled: opulent and cool. She estimated sixty men sat in the center forward rows. All were dressed formally, appearing to be a variety of nationalities and perfectly normal. But they couldn't be normal. Not if they were here.

The women were paraded down the center aisle. The stage loomed ahead, and the closer they got to it and its blue velvet curtains, the weaker Lisa's knees felt and the faster her mind reeled. *A diversion. What am I going to do?*

Nothing came.

This is no time to run out of ideas, Lisa Marie Harper.

Still nothing.

Oh God, please!

Bits of memories converged. Then and now tangled. Her nerves sizzled, her throat tightened, and her pulse thudded a rapid tattoo in her temples.

Gwen's voice carried back. "You praying, Lisa?"

"Oh yeah." *Prayer. That's it. That's it!* "When I signal, copy what I do. Pass the word."

"Got it."

"Selene, did you hear me?"

"I'm on it, Lisa. These animals are ogling us. Can you believe it?"

Unfortunately, Lisa had no choice but to believe it. "Ignore them and pass the word."

As they had done before, Gwen whispered Lisa's instructions up the line and Selene down it.

Cocky and confident and seemingly unaware of anything being amiss, Mr. Phen led them from the front to the right and then up three steps. "Take your card and move along. Move along. Right through there." He motioned to the backstage.

Lisa took her card. The man passing them out had a weapon strapped over his shoulders at his back. She glanced at the card, saw "7," and then moved along. Stripped even of the dignity of their names.

The stage entrance was plain and simple, though the emotions that assailed Lisa on walking through it were profound.

Mr. Phen stepped around the line of women to the front of the stage. Bright lights burned near his feet and overhead. "Straighten the line across the stage now, please."

When they were all in place, he issued his orders. "Number one, step forward and turn."

She did and then returned to the line. He went on to the next woman and then the next. They showed extraordinary discipline and did nothing foolish to provoke Phen.

"Number seven."

Diversion time.

Lisa stepped forward, dropped to her knees, folded her hands, and began to recite the Lord's Prayer.

The other women copied her, dropping to their knees, lifting their voices.

"Get up!" Mr. Phen shouted. "Stop that. Stop it, I say!"

Lisa raised her voice, prayed louder. The others joined and their voices filled the auditorium.

The seated buyers became antsy and then unnerved. "What is this, Phen?" one shouted. "You get religion or something?"

Another yelled, "This is crazy. I'm outta here."

And then another. "Up with this, I shall not put!"

Almost in unison, the buyers abandoned their seats and rushed toward the rear, away from the stage.

When they shoved open the exit doors, an army of Mexican authorities greeted them.

"*Policía,*" the uniformed men shouted. "*¡No se mueven!*" Someone repeated in English, "Do not move!"

Pandemonium erupted.

"Stay on the stage!" Lisa shouted. "Get down on your stomachs and cover your heads!" A woman stood frozen, her eyes as blank as a deer in headlights. Lisa shoved her shoulder. "Down."

The women dropped, some whimpering, some crying, many praying.

Lisa put on her defense instructor's voice. "If anyone comes at you, use your heels as weapons." They were all spiked. "Shoes in your hands— now. Aim for the eyes. You know where to aim your feet. Fight!"

Roxy was on the stage.

Someone jerked Lisa's arm. She turned, lunging toward the man, getting too close to strike. *Mr. Phen.*

"I'm going to kill you for this."

Elbows bent, Lisa thrust up her arms, stomped his foot, jabbed his throat with her pointed fingertips, and followed up with an elbow intended for the same spot to crush his larynx.

He threw himself backward, evaded. "Get her."

Three men grabbed Lisa at once. Something pricked her hip. She jerked away, saw the syringe. "What did you do to me? What was in that?" Outraged, she fought with all she had. Struck the man with the needle, knocked him down. Then lit into another, clipping his jaw with a strong right hook.

Two men moved in and suddenly her head swam. They floated before her in ripples.

Her arms felt like lead, her tongue went thick, her mind foggy. *Drugged. Potent.*

She couldn't break away from three professionals, and she couldn't stop these two.

With each millisecond she grew weaker and weaker until she had nothing left with which to fight. They grabbed her, one on each side, then dragged her off the stage.

Woozy, her senses dull, her thoughts dimmed, grew more and more fuzzy, and her eyelids grew heavy—far too heavy to hold open.

All I wanted was a family, God. Mark, her mother, flitted through her mind.

Don't give in. Don't stop fighting.

She forced her eyes open. Tripping over her own feet, half carried, half pulled, she saw Roxy bent double over some man's shoulder, bobbing with his every step, her cheek banging against the barrel of the rifle strapped to his back.

Lisa's knees folded. Darkness claimed her.

And she saw no more.

27

R oxy, wake up. Wake up."

Mark bent over her, heaped on the grassy ground. Sam and Joe flanked him. Nick and Tim were assisting the FBI, ushering men into buses under Mexican authority and the women into separate ones. The men would be arrested and tried here. The women's statements would be taken, and then they'd be released into U.S. custody and returned to the States. All of the women had been accounted for—except one.

Lisa.

"Roxy," Mark tried again. "Wake up. Where's Lisa?"

She opened her eyes, and they gained focus. Rubbing at her temple, she grunted, as if in pain.

"Are you hurt?"

"Only my pride." She pulled herself to a sitting position, and he helped her to her feet. Scanning, she took in what was going on around her. "Everyone tagged and—"

"Lisa's missing." Mark was losing patience. "You were right by her. Where is she?"

"I—I don't know. She took down—Phen. He was trying to take her, but she had him. He called in backup. I was moving in to help her and—"

"We've got Phen," Mark said. "Where's Lisa?"

"She was on the stage with the others. One of Phen's goons cracked me in the head with something. They were facedown on the stage. Lisa knocked out one of guards and . . . Oh no!" Roxy pulled at the front of Mark's shirt. "It was Masson. Karl Masson got her."

Mark's stomach plummeted. "You're sure it was him?"

"Positive." Roxy clenched her hands into fists. "Where would he take her?"

"Señor Taylor! Señor Taylor!" Juan ran up to Mark, winded, sweating profusely. "Masson took your Lisa." Juan grabbed a staggered breath and then another. "He stole the boat and went to a seaplane. I saw him take off."

Mark fixed on Sam, then Joe.

"Could be anywhere." Joe sounded as grim as Mark felt.

Sam tugged his cap low, shielding his eyes. "I'll see if we can pick up a flight plan or something on them."

"You won't." Mark knew Masson. There would be no flight plan. There would be no trace of Lisa or him. "NINA will kill him and Lisa . . ." Mark's voice cracked and he shut down.

"Think steel, bro." Joe clapped his shoulder. "Lisa found a way to contact you before, and she will again. You know she will."

"Her black belt isn't a match for a seasoned assassin." Dark thoughts and fear swelled in Mark, threatened to take him down.

"She knows that too." Joe snagged Selene's arm. "You stay with me."

"Gladly." She frowned. "Lisa will do something, Mark. She always comes up with something."

"You're right. She will." He nodded. "She will."

"Be right back." Roxy nodded toward her team. "I'm going to get a quick briefing and disseminate the word on Lisa. We'll have everyone looking for her. In the meantime, Mark, you guys need to get

414

back to Crossroads and Annie. After we upset this deal for NINA, you know they'll want payback. She'll be the target."

"Annie." Mark stiffened. "I need a plane."

Joe kept hold on Selene. "We've got Ben's jet. Let's go."

"Roxy, if you need anything from us—"

"I know where to find you. Go." She motioned. "Do you need backup in Seagrove Village?"

"I'll check with Jeff Meyers and let you know." Mark looked at Selene. "Where's Gwen? When we find Lisa, she'll want to see you and Gwen for herself to know you're okay."

Joe nodded at Sam. "Second bus. Pull her off. Gwen and Selene will be with us. We'll have Jeff video in their statements and report their cars stolen, though I expect they've either been chopped up, shipped out of the country, or are resting at the bottom of some lake—maybe dumped in the Gulf as a fishing reef."

"You're probably right on the cars. There's no way NINA would leave them behind." Roxy addressed Juan. "One of my men will take you to your family. We'll get the rest of what we need after you've seen them. I know you're worried."

"Sí, muy worried."

Mark shook Juan's hand. "Thank you."

"Thank you, Señor Taylor. I will pray for your Lisa and for her mother."

"I appreciate that."

Roxy touched Mark's sleeve. "Lisa is resourceful. She took the lead and we all made it. Only she would have thought of prayer in that circumstance, but it worked better than anything else could have. She'll take care of herself too. I won't say don't worry. Only a fool wouldn't. But remember who she is and what she's been through. She'll find a way."

"I hope you're right." Mark took off after Joe, following him, Selene, Gwen, and Sam to the plane.

Lisa awakened to the faint sound of lapping water.

She started, remembered, and forced herself to be still and not open her eyes. The smells were different. Nothing like they had been in Mexico. She took stock, slotted her perceptions. *Wet and humid, not as warm. Tangy. Pungent rotting vegetation, brackish water, and . . . and . . . Dutch's foul cologne.*

Her heart skipped a beat and then sped, banging against her ribs. Wherever she was, Dutch was here. *Dutch.*

That ignited a battle inside her. Part of her wanted to beat him to a pulp for what he'd done to her mother and her, and part of her wanted to hurt him even more. *God, he deserves the worst. Help me control my emotions and keep my head. I need to think smart to come out of this alive. Think steel. Yes. Yes.*

Forcing herself to focus, she blocked emotion and absorbed physical details. The floor beneath her felt hard, slatted wood. It pressed against her hip, her side, and her face. Gritty, and dust tickled her nose, musty and dank. She was indoors but somewhere that hadn't been occupied in a long while. The urge to look burned strong, making her fingertips tingle, but she squelched it and listened. Night sounds. Frogs and crickets. Some nightlife she couldn't identify. A light and humid breeze rustled through the leaves in the distance outside, and lapping water.

She opened one eye, dared to peek, and saw Dutch and another man seated on straight-back chairs staring right at her.

"You can stop pretending you're still out, Lisa." The man's voice sliced through the silence. "I know you're awake."

She opened her eyes and recognized the man from a photo of the artist's sketch Kelly Walker had shown everyone at the center. *Karl Masson. The man determined to kill Kelly. The NINA operative.*

"Ah, I see my reputation precedes me." Masson smiled. "You know who I am."

She didn't dare answer.

"It's all right, Lisa. Your reaction was clear. You know me, though I suspect you didn't know I was involved in your abduction, and you clearly didn't expect to see me here." He chuckled. "Frankly, I didn't expect to be here, so we're both a little surprised."

"Where is here?" Lisa asked. Dutch was tied up, as was she, and Masson knew how to tie to restrain; there'd be no quick fix at getting the ropes loose. It was dark outside and the little room—a fishing camp—was built on stilts above the water. The back door was open. Light from within fanned out. Dead stumps protruded from the water. "I've never been to this place."

"No, it's new," Masson said. "But it's important to you."

"Why?"

"It's where you're going to die." Masson stood and looked down at Dutch, sprawled on his chair. The hems of Masson's jeans were wet, and his sneakers squished, leaving little puddles of water on the dusty wooden floor. "Blame your stepfather. This is yet another of his many sins against you. He's accumulated a considerable list, I have to say." Masson pivoted to look at Dutch. "Lisa might forgive you. I don't. You lied to me. Big mistake." Masson headed for the door.

"Wait." Lisa raised her voice. "You can't just leave us here."

Masson spared her a glance back over his shoulder. "I can do anything I like. I could when you were seven and I can now. I'm not the one tied up."

She stilled, studied his face. Saw it at the window in that motel room, telling her it was time for her to be a shrub—which she now knew was Mr. Phen's pet name for the girls and women he controlled. Saw him crash through the door, shoot her father, snatch her. Saw him look back at her from the driver's seat in the van and peer through the glass door of the dress shop where she'd found refuge.

He was the Spider who had originally abducted her.

"You do remember me." Masson took another step and then glowered at Lisa. "I could shoot you. This place is closed down for winter; no one is around to notice. But you've both caused me a lot of trouble, so I've decided to savor your exits. I am leaving you here. You'll die slowly. You're surrounded by water, Lisa, and if you should manage to untie yourself, you still can't get away. Just wanted to make that clear."

He hitched his pants. "With no food or water, I give you about a week. Plenty of time, Lisa, for you to rail at Dutch for all his crimes." Respect sparked in Masson's eyes. "I've seen you fight. You can definitely take him. I wouldn't mind seeing it, but I have places to go and things to do."

Dutch glared at Lisa, loaded with hatred. "This is all your fault."

Without a word, she twisted and kicked his chair leg. It cracked. The chair collapsed and Dutch hit the floor hard.

Masson laughed. "I do hate to miss this entertainment."

Lisa ignored him. "I've had all I'm taking from you, Dutch. I used to be afraid of you, but I've gotten your worst and it wasn't so bad. I don't fear you anymore."

But he did fear her. She saw it in his eyes.

And maybe that's what God had intended. That Dutch feel what he'd inflicted.

"Impressive, Lisa. He deserves far worse. Who knows? Maybe you'll give it to him before you both die, eh?" Masson hiked a shoulder. "For the record, I would have let you live, but wrecking my mission on that stage was a mistake too big to forget. Still, spare me a kind thought. I did restart your mother's heart to give her a chance to live." He opened the door and stepped outside. "Have a nice death."

He left the door open, which proved one disturbing fact.

Karl Masson felt confident that even untied, neither Lisa nor Dutch would leave alive.

Mark hit the hospital elevator button twice. When the door failed to open, he told Joe, Selene, and Gwen, "You wait. I'll take the steps."

He double-timed it upstairs. Ben, Kelly, Peggy, Harvey, and Clyde stood in the little waiting room. They looked excited, and that could mean really good or really bad news. At this point, he was afraid to ask.

Kelly ran out to meet him. "Annie's awake.

She's talking and everything, Mark—and asking for Lisa."

Relief had his eyes burning. But how would he tell her about Lisa?

He rushed through the heavy wooden doors into the unit. Jessie stood at the hub, smiling. "She's okay?"

Jessie nodded. "Asking for Lisa and you."

A knot in his throat, he stepped up behind Nora.

"Here's our boy." She brushed a firm hand over his shoulder and moved aside so he could get closer to Annie's bedside.

Nora was the only one who called him boy, and it always sounded good. Almost like an endearment. He smiled and gingerly hooked his pinkie with Annie's. "I'm glad you decided to wake up, Annie Harper."

"Mark." She rubbed his hand with her thumb, smiled with her eyes. "Where's my daughter?"

He cleared his throat and tried to keep his fear buried. "She's quite a hero, Annie." He went on to explain all that had happened.

Annie took it all in stride, and he saw firsthand where Lisa had gotten the trait. It was amazing how much like her mother Lisa was. "Masson took her. I don't know where, but I'm betting Dutch is with her."

"Why?"

"He needs someone to blame. Dutch is the logical choice, and apparently he thinks so too.

He's dropped out of sight. Do you know where he'd go to hide out?"

"I don't." Annie paused a long second. "Dutch is a man with a lot of secrets."

Nora blew out a sharp breath. "You can bet he was right in the middle of it, whatever it is. Ain't he the nervy one?" She sniffed. "Having the gall to call my cell phone not three hours ago."

An unseen hand nudged Mark to pay attention to that. "Dutch called you?"

"Sure as spit did. I talked to him myself," Nora said. "The man's got more nerve than sense, my boy. He said to tell Annie he had nothing to do with any of this."

Annie nixed that. "His friend Karl attacked me. He's Karl Masson, Mark. I didn't know his last name, but Kelly Walker showed me a picture the police artist sketched. It was him."

Nora grumbled. "Kelly says he came back here to kill her."

So Dutch had paid Karl Masson to attack Annie and abduct Lisa. "He might have, but if so, that plan's been interrupted. He's got more immediate challenges now."

"Well, that's good news for Kelly." Annie tugged at the edge of her sheet. "But if he's got my daughter, that's not good."

"Where's your phone, Nora?"

She pulled it out of her pocket and passed it to

him. "It's turned off because it messes up the machines in here."

"Turn it on." Annie frowned. "I'm fine without these machines. I am not fine without Lisa Marie."

Mark looked at the number. "Area code 504." He must have used a public phone. Definitely not his cell.

"That's Louisiana," Nora said. "My twin sister lives in New Orleans and that's her area code."

"Where would Dutch be in Louisiana, Annie?"

"He could be checking his stores or down in the French Quarter, I suppose. He likes the *Vieux Carré*."

"He's hiding. He's got Lisa—I know it." Mark couldn't explain it, but he was as certain as if he'd seen Dutch snatch her. "Where would he hide with Lisa?"

She gasped. "Lafitte. The fishing camp!"

"Where's that?"

"Near New Orleans. You cross the Mississippi River over to the west bank. Head down to Marrero and then down Barataria Boulevard to Lafitte."

"Have you been there with him?"

"No, he hasn't been there for a while—at least as far as I know. But I bought him one of those GPS devices and he stored it. I saw it a hundred times. I don't know why he stored it. It's not as if there's a road to the camp. It's on a little bayou—

423

you have to park your car and take a boat to it."

"Is there anywhere else you think he'd be more likely to take her?"

"No. The fishing camp is isolated. If Lisa got away from him, she still wouldn't be able to find her way out of there." Annie's worry shone on her face. "Go get my baby, Mark. You promised. I remember it."

When she'd been in a coma, he had promised. "You heard me?"

"I heard all of it. I know you love her. And I know she loves you too."

His throat went thick. "Annie, I-I—"

"Have faith." She squeezed his hand. "You won't fail."

She had heard and remembered everything. "I might. I'll do everything I can," he swallowed hard, "but I might."

"You won't. I know it."

He glanced from her to Nora, who nodded her agreement. "You won't, my boy. We believe in you."

"We do." Annie sniffed. "Now you go get my Lisa."

"She might not be there. I'll go, but if she calls—"

"We'll let you know," Nora said.

"She's there, Nora." Annie shifted on the sheets.

"I know, dearie. I feel it too."

Mark left the unit and joined the others in the

waiting room. He caught them up on what he'd learned from Annie and Nora.

"We're coming with you." Nick motioned to Tim, who was on the phone. "I think you guys better stay here in case Masson makes another attempt on Kelly or Annie."

Kelly shuddered and Ben Brandt slipped a protective arm around her shoulder. "Do you think he will?"

"Honestly? I think he'll disappear and stay so far underground he'll be beyond the reach of light—at least until things cool down. But he's probably not thinking clearly at the moment so we need to be prepared."

"Some of us should go with you, bro." Joe frowned. "You've got no idea what's going on there."

"Maybe nothing. I could be wrong, and this is NINA, remember? And, well, this is—"

"Something you need to do yourself." Joe got it. Joe always got it.

"Yeah."

"We'll get you an exact location and radio it to you."

"Thanks."

Ben put his cell away. "The plane's waiting, and Mel will have a car waiting for you at the airport in New Orleans."

"Thanks." Mark looked at the faces of the people he'd come to know, depend on, and love.

Selene and Gwen seemed to fit right in. "Pray."

Peggy Crane stepped forward. "The prayer warriors are all over that, Mark. Don't you doubt it for a second."

"Keep me posted on Annie." He turned and left the hospital.

28

"Just stop lying, Dutch." Lisa contorted and finally got her feet through her bound looped arms, so her wrists were in front of her body rather than secured at her back. "You hire NINA to kill my mother and abduct me for a fate even worse than death, and you're going to tell me you didn't have Masson bring me here?"

"I didn't."

Lisa paused to catch her breath and glared at him. "I don't believe—" She stopped midsentence. "You were already here, hiding. You knew Masson would come after you. Why would he do that?"

"After the fiasco in Mexico?" Dutch harrumphed. "You don't think he's going to take the fall for that, do you? NINA lost millions on that botched operation. I paid in money. NINA wants blood. Whose do you think it's going to be? Masson's? No way. That leaves me—especially since you and your Shadow Watcher friends were responsible for the fiasco."

"What's a Shadow Watcher?"

"Spies, you idiot."

"That's crazy." He knew Mark and his team were spies? *Oh no.* "You're blaming me for Mexico? Me?" She curled up her knees, sitting on the floor, and began to work at untying the ropes binding her feet. They weren't budging. Masson tied impossible knots. If she could get free of the ropes, she could get to the drawer for a knife and unbind her hands.

If he tied them, then they could be untied. She studied the knots, then found what she thought was the weakest point to start. "I'm a victim— your victim. You did this, and you're not dropping the blame for any of it on me. You own it."

"You were going to take Annie."

"I still am," Lisa shot back at him. "You've abused her for the last time, Dutch. I promise you that."

"She's my wife."

Lisa gave the rope a hard jerk. The knot broke free. "She's your prisoner."

"I took care of her. She'd have been on the street with nothing if not for me."

"She would have had me. I'm not nothing." The rope fell slack. Lisa began unwinding it from her ankles. "I don't want to talk about this anymore. You twist things. You always did. You're a mean, vicious man, Dutch. And my mom and I are through with you."

"You've always been in the way. Nothing but trouble."

Lisa ignored him and pulled herself to her feet. Stiff and sore, she moved to the open kitchen area and began pulling open drawers, looking for a knife.

"You think you've got all the answers, don't you? Untying yourself, slamming drawers in there. But I'll tell you a secret, Dr. Harper. You'll never leave here alive."

"Watch me." She glared at him over her shoulder. Why wasn't he trying to get free? "Are you planning on dying here?"

He lay still on the floor where he'd fallen when she'd knocked the chair out from under him. He hadn't moved at all. "We're both going to die here."

"No, we're not." She shoved the second drawer closed and then opened the third. "I'm going to get us out."

He laughed. "Right. You're going to give me my freedom. Spare my life. That's rich."

"I never said anything about your freedom." Inside the third drawer she spotted several knives. She reached in and grabbed one, then leaned over the countertop so if her precarious hold on the handle slipped, she wouldn't stab herself.

Carefully, she tipped the knife end over end and then began sawing the rope. "You're going to jail. I'm going to be free—and so is my mother."

"So Annie is still alive."

"No thanks to you. But, yes, she's alive and doing well." Lisa prayed it was true.

"No matter. We'll be dead within an hour, and she'll still be alone." He scooted on the floor to the wall and then shouldered his way into sitting up. "You're out of your mind if you think you're going to escape."

He shifted his weight, leaned back, and grunted. "Such a shame things worked out like this. I was looking forward to getting monthly tapes of you fighting for your life. But knowing you're going to die with me will have to do."

She spun and squared off at him. "I am *not* going to die."

"We both are." His eyes were laced with a knowledge that turned her blood to ice. "Being a doc and all, you're surely not stupid enough to think Masson would leave us here unless he was certain we'd die. He's a professional cleaner, girl. They don't leave loose ends."

She had deduced the same thing, and Dutch had a point. Masson was a professional. One of the ropes binding her wrist sliced in two and fell free. *One down, one to go.* "We'll get untied and walk out of here."

"Hate to break it to you, but you're a lousy listener. We're on a very small island. Islands are surrounded by water. Like Masson said, the only way to walk out of here is if you can walk on water. Contrary to what your mother thinks, you can't. There is no boat. There is no ferry. There are no neighbors. And this"—he pointed to his abdomen—"is no belt."

Belt? She looked over and saw explosives strapped around Dutch's middle. "Did you do that, or did—?"

"Masson." Dutch grimaced. "He's got tripwires rigged all over this place, inside and out. In fact, I'm surprised you haven't already snagged one."

A chill slid up Lisa's back.

Dutch chuckled. "See, I told you. Deader than dirt."

Lisa refused to believe it. "Did you see where he put them?"

"Some of the explosives and wires, yes. Others, no. I just heard them. But it doesn't matter. Here or somewhere else, I'm a dead man. NINA won't let me live."

Lisa tried to focus, to think, sawing at the rope. "You could turn state's evidence. Tell all you know on NINA and enter a witness-protection plan."

He laughed. "You're stupid and insane. NINA members turn up everywhere. Nobody outruns 'em." He blew out a long breath. "I'm dead. And that's a fact."

The rope fell off her wrist. She quickly untied the other piece and tossed the rope onto the countertop, then put down the knife and glanced out the open door to the little porch. They were surrounded by water. "So if I cut you loose, you'll refuse to leave. You've decided to just sit there and die, right?"

"Actually, that's not my plan."

Frustrated, she shoved her hair back from her face and swiped the grit from her hand on her red dress. "Okay, so you've been blowing smoke, trying to get me all freaked out and weepy. I'm not a kid anymore, and I don't get weepy. So spare us both your stupid games and just tell me. What is your plan, Dutch?"

"I'm going to get out of here and blow the place up so NINA thinks I'm dead. Then I'm going to get Annie out of the hospital, and we're going to take off for parts unknown. I plan to live for a long time."

"You're not getting near my mother, but the rest of your plan works for me. Let's go."

"No, Lisa." He separated his arms as if they weren't tied at all. "You're not going anywhere."

Reaching for his side, he pulled out a gun and took aim at her. "Sit down."

Lisa didn't pause to think. She lunged toward the table, using it as a shield, dropped to the floor, and rolled out onto the porch. At its edge, she shot a quick look for stumps, saw none close, and flung herself off.

"No!" Dutch's scream followed her.

The ten-foot drop into the water seemed to

happen in slow motion. She hit the water, sank down, then floated up and broke the surface. The loud splash still echoed through the bayou. Cold water surrounded her, stole her breath. She bumped the soft, squishy bottom and shoved off, heading away from the camp.

The water wasn't deep, four to five feet, but it was likely teeming with water moccasins. Dutch had talked about shooting them off the porch all the time. Were they out in winter?

Having no idea, she grabbed a frosty gulp of air and stared up at the door, thankful she hadn't hit one of Masson's tripwires. *No sign of Dutch.*

Daybreak was coming, and in the sleety gray, she studied the piers beneath the house. One after another was strapped with explosives and charged with tripwires. Everywhere.

For once, Dutch hadn't been lying. And it was a miracle she'd moved inside at all without tripping one.

Dutch still could.

Her heart still careening, she swam out away from the house and tried to get some bearing of which way to go. In the distance, something metallic glinted in the weak morning light. She started swimming toward it—and heard a gunshot.

Forced air streaked past her ear, whistling. Water off her right shoulder splashed. She dove, kicked hard, propelling herself farther away and out of his line of fire. When she thought her lungs would burst, she surfaced and dragged in air, stole a look back toward the house.

He stood on the little porch, his feet and hands oddly bound. He would shoot her like he had the snakes, and he'd had a lot of practice, so he was probably good at it.

Terrified by that truth, she sank low so only her nose protruded above the water.

"You can't hide from me." He took aim to shoot.

She dove deep and swam a jagged path toward that metallic glint.

When she next broke the surface, Dutch was shouting at her, cursing, raging. "I'll kill you! You're going to see what happens when you get in my way, girl. You'll find out just like your daddy did. I hated him and I hate you. You hear me, you sniveling brat? I'll kill—"

He'd killed her father. Killed him because he was in the way. Dutch wanted her mother and to get to her, he had to—oh no. *No.* The Spider hadn't randomly abducted her the first time. It'd been deliberate. Dutch had done it. He'd paid Masson to kill her father and abduct her!

Logic told her to be quiet. Her heart wouldn't let her. All of her fury erupted in a shout. "Why did you do it? You killed my dad! You murderer!"

A memory snapped in her mind. Dutch at the dinner table with her mother and father. Lisa had complained about dressing for dinner, and her mother insisted she be respectful. Dutch was their guest. "You were there. You were at our house. I saw you at our house. You ate at our table."

"Your father was a fool. Taking his money was like taking candy from a kid."

He swindled the money from her father in a Ponzi scheme. "You stole it." She gasped. "You tried to steal my mother, but she loved my father. She'd never have left him for you. So you stole his money and—"

"He left her." Dutch cackled.

Dutch had done it all. Outrage burned like acid, and Lisa bellowed, "How dare you destroy our lives!"

Dutch shot at her again. And then again. Both bullets landed far to her left. He'd lost her, and her voice was echoing off the water; he couldn't peg her position.

His raging turned to a guttural scream that echoed over the water and pierced her ears. She covered them and lurched back until only her nose to the top of her head was out of the cold water.

Cursing her, Dutch moved closer to the edge of the porch. He tripped and fell. Prone on the wooden deck, he fired yet again; rapid-releasing bullets wildly into the air, into the water, hoping to hit her. Water sprayed and showered her face.

The house exploded.

Dutch went flying, his clothes on fire.

Lisa jerked, watched debris fly aflame and

smoke billow from the house. Horror flooded her. He'd hit a tripwire.

She should swim back. She should—she had to—swim back.

The battle to let him die or try to save him was fierce. He should die. He deserved to die.

Vengeance is Mine.

Disappointment hit her hard. She had to go back—or become like him.

Paddling in an arc, she saw Dutch draped on a tree stump, sticking up from the water like a spear. His head hung at an odd angle. His back bent in a way it shouldn't be. The explosives on his body hadn't detonated.

A secondary explosion went off.

Flames shot up into the sky; burning debris fell like rain. Keeping a safe distance, she swam in a wide circle over to Dutch. Still and lifeless, he appeared dead. She felt for a pulse but found none.

In trying to kill her, he had killed himself.

"Lisa! Lisa, where are you?"

Mark. She swam hard toward the voice, toward the glint, and saw it was sunlight skimming over the water to the bank of land and catching on the bumper of a distant car. "Mark! I'm here! I'm here!"

A pirogue appeared at the edge of the fire. Mark sat in it, an oar in his hand. "Where? I can't see you."

"Here!" She waved wildly.

He spotted her. Eating through the water with strong, efficient strokes, he pulled alongside her and lifted her into the boat. "You're okay?" He wrapped her in his coat. "When I heard that explosion—"

"Dutch did it, Mark." She sniffed and words frantically spilled from her mouth. "He's dead. Masson rigged the place to blow. Explosives were everywhere and tripwires. I got free. Dutch made it clear he was going to kill me, so I escaped. He was shooting and shooting at me, and he triggered a tripwire. The next thing I knew, the whole camp was exploding and Dutch got thrown into the water and there was fire everywhere and—"

"Honey. Honey, shh." He covered her lips with his fingers. "Where's Masson?"

"He left." She shivered, snuggled closer to him. Mark was so warm. "I heard the boat. He didn't come back."

Relief shone in Mark's expression. Some of the tension left his muscles.

"Dutch said NINA would demand blood for Mexico. Masson will hide for years." She shivered uncontrollably.

"I heard the shots and was terrified I wouldn't get to you in time." Mark held her close to him, paddled from around her. "I told you not to scare me like that anymore."

Her hair dripping, her teeth chattering, Lisa

smiled. "You weren't too late. But how did you find me? I didn't even know about this place."

He returned her smile. "Annie."

Lisa brightened. "My mom told you?"

He nodded, his eyes glistening. "She's awake, Lisa. She's awake and fine and she sent me here to get you."

Lisa gasped. "She's really okay?"

"Really." Mark blew out a shuddery breath. "And I'm under direct orders to bring you to her."

"Are there any residual effects from the attack? Medically, I mean."

"She's going to be fine." He pulled the pirogue ashore. Two cars were parked side by side. His and, she presumed, Dutch's. "Actually, she's planning on moving into the Towers with Nora."

"No. She's coming to live with me in Kelly's beach house."

"She and Nora phoned me on my way over here. They're going to live at the Towers—Nora shouldn't be alone with her eyes. And you and I are going to live in the beach house." He cleared his throat. "At least that's their version—after our wedding of course, which they're also planning." He offered her a hand to get out of the beached boat. "What do you think about that?"

"I think it's going to take both of us to slow them down. We might need your team to help stop them." Lisa crawled out and stood facing him.

"And for the record, I'm not opposed to marrying you. But I think we need some time to be a normal couple before we start talking about weddings."

"Me too." He smiled, touched a fingertip to her nose. "You've got some catching up to do."

Lisa wrapped her arms around him and kissed him soundly, loving the solid and steady feel of him. "Maybe not as much as you think."

29

"Mom." Lisa burst into tears, stretched across the hospital bed, and hugged her mother.

"Oh, Lisa. Lisa." Her arms were warm, her head burrowed into Lisa's shoulder. "I can't believe it," she said in a trembling voice. "Finally. I-I can't— Mark." Annie reached for him. "Mark, come here, darling."

He rounded the bed and bent low so Annie could wrap an arm around him too. A long moment passed while she sobbed—a moment in which Lisa knew a feeling so long absent from her life: contentment.

"It's beautiful," Tim said, his deep voice gruff.

"Yeah it is, bro." Joe sighed.

Sam sniffed.

Nick elbowed him. "Think steel."

"No way, bud." Sam sniffed again. "This needs to be felt. It's what makes everything else worthwhile."

Nora and Peggy flanked Sam and linked their arms.

Ben, Kelly, Mel, Harvey, and Clyde were there, along with Selene and Gwen, and few had dry eyes. Then gasps of expelled breaths began and the magical moment faded to the thunder of everyone laughing, talking at once, and details of all that had happened were shared, commented on, and digested.

"Excuse me." A woman walked deeper into the crowded hospital room, winding between Nick and Nora toward Annie's bed. Lost in the crush, she raised her voice. "Excuse me."

Everyone stilled.

Tim and Nick moved in, blocked her entrance.

"It's okay." Harvey Talbot stepped forward, looking anything but gentle or welcoming. "Roxanne, what are you doing here?"

Lisa looked at Mark and then at the woman.

"Roxanne?" Mark asked. "Roxy, do you know Harvey?"

"Apparently better than I thought she did," Lisa whispered.

"Um, yes, I do." She looked at Harvey through bright eyes, clearly hungry for the sight of him. "Hi, Harvey." She swallowed hard. "It's been a long time."

"Roxy?" Harvey glanced over to Lisa. "This is your FBI friend Roxy?"

Lisa nodded.

439

"Why didn't you tell me?" Harvey was clearly flabbergasted.

"Tell you what?"

"I'm Harvey's wife, Lisa." Roxy sounded almost shy. "Well, I was his wife."

"You're kidding me." Lisa looked at Mark, and from his expression he hadn't known that tidbit of information either. "Why didn't I know that?"

"I was jealous of all of you and the time Harvey spent at the center, so I stayed away."

"What are you doing here now—at the hospital, I mean?" Harvey couldn't seem to grasp the fact that his wife was in the room.

"Harvey," Peggy said. "You know she's an FBI agent."

Joe told Selene, "Roxy's been working on a human-trafficking case linked to NINA for a year."

"Actually, for three years," Roxy corrected him, then spoke to Harvey. "Since just after our divorce."

Harvey's face turned red. "You didn't divorce me because I neglected you for my work. You divorced me so NINA wouldn't use me to get to you on this case."

"Can we talk about this later?" She worried her lip with her teeth. "Privately would be good."

"Might as well do it now, I'm thinking," Nora said, as interested as the rest of them. "We're gonna speculate anyway, dearie. Best get the truth straight from you."

"Nora, you're heartless." Peggy nodded, adding weight to her claim. "This is about their marriage. They're entitled to privacy."

"Fine. Let everybody down at Ruby's add their little twists on it, then. Because you know they will."

"She's right," Roxy told Harvey. "I'd forgotten about the village grapevine."

"Roxanne, I couldn't care less about gossip. I can't believe you did this to me." A muscle in Harvey's jaw ticked. "Answer my questions."

Looking more afraid of him than of the terrorists, Roxy turned to face her ex-husband. "Yes, Harvey. I got the NINA assignment and divorced you to keep you safe so they wouldn't hurt you or use you to hurt me." She looked down at his chest, as if unable to hold his gaze. "I didn't tell you because you wouldn't have listened to me, and you would have pitched a fit about my taking the job. Speaking of which, I need to share some information with the people here. Now that's all I'm saying about us publicly, and that's that."

"He looks a little too dumbfounded to talk more now anyway, don't you think?" Mark asked Lisa.

"Yeah, he does." Her heart twisted. "We would be too."

"She divorced him. I can't believe it." Mark sent Lisa a loaded look. "Don't you ever think about pulling anything like this on me. Walking out on him for a job? That's crazy."

441

"You know she had her reasons. She protected him too."

"Watch Lisa, Mark. She'll do what needs doing, promise or no promise," Annie said. "Don't glare at me, darling. It's the truth. You've always been that way."

Mark nodded. "True. But what can I say, I love her."

"She loves you too, though at the moment . . ."

Roxy cleared her throat. "Listen up, everybody. We're putting out the word that two people were in the fishing camp and one of them was Karl Masson."

"What?" Lisa straightened.

"You can't be saying what I think you're saying." Mark squared off on Roxy. "Masson is *not* going to walk."

She stiffened. "Just listen to me, okay?" She slid an uncertain glance at Annie. "I'm trying to be consid—"

"I know Dutch is dead, Roxy, but thank you for being careful to spare my feelings," Annie said softly. "Or do you prefer to be called Roxanne?"

"Roxy." She shrugged. "Sorry if I sounded cagey. I wasn't sure you'd been told yet, and I didn't want you to hear it this way."

"Nora told me before Lisa and Mark returned."

"No sense in spoiling their reunion with that kind of news." Nora sniffed. "They've waited such a long time for it."

"Yes, they have," Roxy said.

Lisa was about out of patience. She opened her mouth to demand answers on Masson, but Nick beat her to it.

"Why are you putting out word Masson's dead?"

Roxy swiveled her gaze to him. "If NINA thinks he's dead, they won't look for him. Kelly, you'll be safe."

"While he's breathing?" Kelly said. "Not likely."

"Masson is a survivor," Roxy said. "He knows that if he comes after Kelly, we'll expose him to NINA. If we do, they'll neutralize him."

Kelly gasped and buried her face at Ben's chest. "He'll haunt me the rest of my life."

Lisa swallowed hard. Kelly had lived with constant fear of Masson showing up to kill her. This could spare her that.

"Makes sense." Nick looked at Joe, who nodded.

"Not good enough." Mark crossed his arms.

"It's the only way he'll ever surface, Mark." Roxy sighed. "I don't like it any more than you do. But anything else we do leaves Kelly, Lisa, and the village wide open. He'll lay low, but men like him always surface. When he does, we'll get him."

A lot of thought had gone into this. "Is there more you can't tell us?"

Roxy didn't answer.

Mark scanned his old team. Lisa saw their subtle nods. They agreed with her.

"Yeah, bro. If Roxy says this is best, then I trust her."

"Are you saying that, Roxy?" Mark asked her.

"I am." Roxy looked him right in the eye. "It's not perfect, but it's the best we can do right now."

Mark stared at her a long moment. Resignation settled in his expression. "We'll be notified of any change that impacts us?"

"You have my word."

He nodded. "We'll still have to stay on our toes," he told Ben and Kelly and then looked over at Roxy. "What about Masson's boss?"

"We don't know who that is yet," Roxy said. "You know it's not like in the movies. At the end of an operation, we don't get everyone all wrapped up with a nice bow. We just stay after them and take them down as we can, and we pray a lot in between."

Mark pushed. "Chessman?"

"He's been told Masson's dead. He knows who their boss is, of course, but he'll never reveal that."

Seeing Beth near the door, Joe waved her to him.

"I thought Chessman had crossed over," Mark said.

Beth fell in beside Joe and smiled at him. He

smiled back. Lisa liked that. From her twitching lips, so did Peggy.

Roxy held off a second, then answered. "To an extent, Chessman has helped us. But the minute he tells us the identity of his boss, he's dead and he knows it."

"Wait." Mark lifted a finger. "Juan mentioned Frank getting a call from the boss."

"Did he say who that was?"

Mark hesitated, his eyes glazed as if he were pulling the conversation from memory. "Yeah, he did. Raven."

"Raven." Roxy made a note of it. "Well, that's a start. You guys ever heard anything on him?"

"It's not a him. Raven is a woman," Lisa said. "In the truck, they referred to her as a female."

"They did." Selene nodded.

"I heard it too," Gwen added.

"A woman." Roxy stiffened. "Now that's a surprise."

"Women are as capable of evil as men." Annie tugged at her sheet.

"Ain't that the truth, dearie? My sister Nathara's there in a pinch, but she's mean as a snake." Nora sniffed. "Not at all gentle like me."

Lisa smiled at Mark. Nora was many good things, but gentle wasn't among them.

"Roxy? What about my manager?"

"I'm sorry for not already telling you, Selene. I do have news for you and Gwen. Your manager and, Gwen, your husband, Derek, are in custody. We followed the money and picked up payments from each of them to Chessman. Don't expect them to be a bother any time soon."

"May he die of old age wearing stripes." Selene grimaced.

"That would work for me." Gwen shot a glance at Lisa. "I know. That forgiveness thing. I'll work on it. But right now I'm pretty steamed. Pray for me?"

"Always." Lisa smiled.

"Raven, it appears, will be another battle for another day." Roxy shrugged. "Unless we get lucky and make a connection through Chessman and the payments."

"Something will turn up," Clyde said. "It always does."

"Eventually." Nick tilted his head. "But sooner would be better than later."

Roxy grunted. She hesitated, then spoke to Annie. "I don't know if it's appropriate under the circumstances to express my sympathy for your loss."

Annie gave her a soft smile. "I do love an honest woman."

"Well, I'll get out of your way. I just wanted to catch you up. We'll keep in touch through Jeff Meyers."

"We understand. Thank you, Roxy." Mark turned to Lisa.

"What's that in your hand?" she asked.

Mark opened it. "Our sand dollar."

Her eyes stretched wide. "You carried it with you?"

He nodded. "Everywhere, just like you did."

Annie sighed her content. "It'll be harder to keep track of who has it at what time after you're married."

"You're getting married?" Tim brightened.

"Later, if everything works out," Lisa said. "We need time. So you two wedding planners need to back off. We'll let you know when and if we're ready."

"Pshhh!" Nora blew off that statement, as if the prospective bride and groom had nothing to say on the matter. "They're perfect together, Annie."

"I know and you know. Soon enough they'll know."

Lisa warned them off. "After we have some time together, then we'll see."

"Well, all right." Tim held out his hand, palm up. "Pay up, ladies."

Sam and Nick slapped twenties into Tim's hand. He laughed.

"I know you boys aren't standing at Annie's bedside gambling." Peggy Crane gave them a stern look meant to wilt knees. "Joseph?"

"Not me." Joe held up his hands. "I don't owe anyone anything."

Which didn't mean he hadn't bet, only that he hadn't lost.

"I'm seeing pepper juice in all their immediate futures," Mark whispered to her, clearly amused.

They'd need a tea taster for a month. Lisa bit back a smile. "Just so we know, Tim, what was the bet?"

"Whether you'd ask him to marry you—someday—or he'd ask you."

Mark folded his arms across his chest. "When and if we do decide to make it official, I'll ask her. Until then, I'd say it's a draw."

Everyone started laughing.

Lisa faced her mom. Her eyes were shining, and she looked beside herself, overjoyed. "I expect you and Nora are already picking out wedding colors, but we're not ready for that."

"Of course you aren't, dear."

"So you haven't?" Lisa glanced at Nora, then back at her mother, elated and deflated at once.

"I didn't say that."

"She sure didn't, dearie. I was listening."

"They picked peaches and cream," Beth said from the back of the crowd. "Sorry, ladies, but truth is truth." She shrugged. "And there was a mention of the reception hall at the club too."

"Beth Dawson, I'd be clamming up right about now, dearie, if you ever want to taste my peach cobbler again." Nora bumped into the edge of the bed.

Everyone pretended not to notice. Beth tucked in near Joe. "Protect me. I tell the truth and I've started a war."

"How about coffee at Ruby's?" Joe asked. "I've heard about it and want to try it myself."

Beth nodded.

Joe dropped his voice, then hastily cut through the crowd, pulling Beth along with him. "You're definitely prettier when you're not snarling."

"Thanks." Beth frowned. "I think."

Peaches and cream. Lisa's room at home had been decorated in peaches and cream. Those had been her signature colors her whole life. Swallowing a knot in her throat, Lisa pecked a kiss to her mother's cheek. "You remembered."

Annie sniffled. "You're my daughter. Of course I remember." She deepened her southern drawl. *"I love peaches and cream, mama. I'm making 'em my signature colors."*

Everyone chuckled.

"I like it here." Sam winked at Gwen.

"What's not to like?" Nick asked Sam. "It's hot, humid, and flat. Perfect."

"Man, do you have a romantic bone in your body?" Sam tugged at his cap.

"Apparently he does not." Selene raised her brows.

Sam hooked a thumb toward Nick. "Ignore him. He's a little rusty."

"At what?" Selene tucked her hair back. It snagged at her shoulder.

"Everything."

Selene laughed. Not politely but with gusto.

Nick liked that a lot.

Tim told Mark, "Dead stumps from the neck up."

Roxy stepped over to Lisa and Mark. "I'm grateful for your help. We wouldn't have been able to pull it off without you."

"There'll be more women." Lisa wasn't going to get starry eyed about this. "There's always going to be more."

"Unfortunately, yes," Roxy said. "But we shut down Phen and got his buyers. It'll take time for NINA to build up a network that trusts it again. We got Frank and Karl Masson out of commission, which should help Kelly and Ben sleep better at night."

"We saved thirty women too," Gwen said. "And Juan."

"Don't forget his family." Selene sniffed. "People always underestimate the value of family."

"We did all those things," Roxy nodded, "and revealed NINA's expansion. An imperfect victory, but we definitely won this time."

"We did." Lisa smiled at her mom.

"One crisis at a time, right?" Roxy glanced at Harvey. "Isn't that what you say at Crossroads Crisis Center?"

"It is." Tight-lipped, he looped his arm through

Roxy's. "I've been patient while you said what you had to say to everyone else, but I'm out of patience. Actually, I'm pretty steamed at you right now."

"I expect you are."

"You divorced me, Rox."

She cupped his face in her hand. "And you'll be really mad at me for a very long time and lecturing me even longer."

Anger flushed his face. "Bet on it."

"Wanna yell at me over coffee? I'm thirsty and I guess we have some serious talking to do."

"You guess?" Harvey scowled at her. "You know, it'd serve you right if I refused to say a word. Who would blame me?"

"Not a soul." Roxy moved with him toward the door. "But you promised for better or worse. This has been the worse."

"Don't even—"

"I'm not," she assured him. "I did what I did."

"How could you, Rox? Do you know how miserable—?"

"I do. I really, really do."

As they left the room, Lisa watched the body language between Harvey and Roxy. The sparks were still there. This wasn't over yet.

"I'm smelling a reunion right there."

Lisa smiled at Nora. "I hope so."

"Count on it." Peggy fiddled with her chunky necklace, letting the beads clunk together. "Though we might have to nudge just a little."

"Cupid *and* Rambo?" Nick grunted. "Another goner."

"Yeah, they've all got the look."

"What's the look Sam's talking about?" Mom asked Mark.

"The way I look at Lisa."

"Ah." Mom smiled. "And the way she looks at you."

"Yeah."

Mark didn't even try to hide his feelings about that, which brought Lisa joy that ran so deep she couldn't begin to describe it. Mark was willing to accept love.

Sighing contentment, Lisa watched everyone chatting and laughing, so happy with the way things had worked out. Not without pain and suffering. Not without loss and tragedy. But things *had* worked out. The tunnels in her life had been dark, and some of them had been very long. But God had been right there, preparing her, guiding her, giving her maybe not what she wanted but what she needed to survive even Dutch's deadly ties.

"I'm selling it."

Lisa looked to Annie. "The house?"

She nodded. "I want a fresh start, honey. That's okay with you, isn't it?"

Likely the bad memories there with Dutch outweighed the good ones with Lisa's father. And if her mom knew Dutch had been responsible for

452

her dad's death, they'd be even worse. Lisa had talked to Mark about telling her mother, and they agreed to wait until she'd recovered. It would hurt and she'd mourn again, but she just didn't have the physical reserves to cope with that right now. "Whatever you want, Mom."

She reached for Lisa and Mark. "I have you two in my life. I'm free. What more could I want?"

"Well, you might start with meeting Miranda Kent at the club on Sunday for brunch, dearie. She's been the mainstay for the prayer warriors through all this, and she misses you. It's time, I'm thinking, you start living your life again, Annie Harper."

"Oh, Miranda and brunch. That's a wonderful idea." Mom clapped her hands, setting her IV line to swinging. "I used to love our brunches at the club. And golf. Nora, I haven't had a golf club in my hands in years."

"Don't I know it?" Nora harrumphed. "I can't see to play anymore, but I'd sure like to ride along in the cart now and then."

"We're going to have a lot of fun, Nora. We really are."

Lisa nearly wept. Seeing her mother so excited thrilled her and squeezed her heart.

Mark nudged Lisa, and they walked out of the room and into the hallway. Lisa looked up at him. "We're doing the right thing, not telling her about Dad now, right?"

"We are." Mark stroked her cheek. "Harvey says she's had all the trauma she can handle right now. No added stress until she's stronger."

Lisa touched the placket of his shirt. "That puts my mind at ease. Thank you for consulting Harvey."

"You don't have to thank me. I love Annie too." Mark shifted, tensed. "Lisa, I want to say something to you."

The edge of regret in his tone worried her. "Don't even think about jilting me, Mark Taylor. I'm not ready to get married and won't be for a good while—it's a big step. Nora and Mom are just doing what moms do. Nora's been my surrogate mother, if you'll recall, so I've got a double dose of maternal meddling going on there."

"Jilt you? Not happening, lady." He clasped her hands, pecked a kiss to her cheek, then a longer one to her lips. "They're razzing us more than anything. The truth is, we've never been on a real date. I've never brought you flowers or—"

"You gave me a shell. A beautiful shell and romantic walks on the beach. Remember that first night we walked?"

He nodded. "Nora set us up."

She had. "I so hoped you'd kiss me that night. Then I was glad you didn't because what if you did and you didn't like it?"

"I like it." His eyes glinted.

"Then I wish you had." She smiled up at him, let her fingertips drift down his muscular arms, shoulders to elbows. "I wanted that night to last forever."

"Me too."

"I didn't dare dream you could be interested in me."

"You were beautiful in the moonlight. That was one of the most special nights of my life, and I was pretty frustrated—debating between kissing you and not." He let out a soft chuckle. "If it helps, I almost kissed you."

"Why didn't you?"

"I didn't want you to think . . . I don't know. That's not true. I know exactly," he confessed. "But why didn't you kiss me?"

"I wasn't sure you were interested in me that way, and I didn't want to lose what we had."

"Honey, I've been interested in you in every way since the first time I saw you."

"Really?" Pleased about that, it oozed from her every pore.

"Oh yeah."

She smiled. "I'm so glad. I'd hate to be falling in love by myself."

He smiled back. "Not happening. I'll love you forever, and that's a promise."

Nora's voice spilled into the hallway. "But that's red. Red and orange—peach is too so orange, Annie—clash."

"See why I'm not worried?" She laughed. "Let the matchmakers talk weddings. It'll take a couple of years for them to agree on anything, much less everything. And I have a feeling they'll be recruited to handle a different wedding long before then."

"Harvey and Roxy?"

Lisa nodded.

"That will keep them diverted."

"I am totally crazy about you."

"I'm glad." He kissed her softly, then more deeply.

When their mouths parted, he swayed, looking a little dazed. Right there she decided she needed to keep him that way.

"I can't believe it, Lisa. Things are . . . perfect." He linked their pinkies.

And she was lost. "Absolutely perfect."

"We've made some mistakes, and we were wrong about a lot of things." Mark slid a fingertip down her cheek. "But we were always loved."

"Yes, we were always loved." She pecked a kiss to his finger. Deadly ties might be hard to endure, but from them can spring ties of hope and joy.

Ties of truth and of love.

READERS GUIDE

1. Annie asks God to let her go back twenty-four hours. Have you ever wished you could go back, regretted a decision you made, felt guilty because if you had chosen differently, perhaps another could have been spared a tragic event or being hurt?[1]

2. Mark feels he let Jane down.[2] Have you ever been in a situation where you disappointed another who mattered a great deal to you? How did you cope, survive, and recover?

3. Though Mark's teammates were as close to him as brothers, Mark said that one day he

---

1. To see what the Bible says about these things, you can begin by reading the following Scriptures from the New International Version: "Not that I have already obtained all this, or have already been made perfect, but I press on to take hold of that for which Christ Jesus took hold of me. Brothers, I do not consider myself yet to have taken hold of it. But one thing I do: Forgetting what is behind and straining toward what is ahead, I press on toward the goal to win the prize for which God has called me heavenward in Christ Jesus" (Philippians 3:12–14).

2. "We pray to God that you will not do anything wrong. Not that people will see that we have stood the test but that you will do what is right even though we may seem to have failed" (2 Corinthians 13:7).

hoped to belong to a family of his own, one where he was wanted, not just needed. What are your thoughts on that?

4. Annie stayed with Dutch out of obedience to God, even though she was in an abusive relationship. Have you ever known someone in this situation? How would you counsel her?

5. Dutch believes the key to respect is money.[3] What do you think?

6. Annie wonders why she hadn't trusted God to provide for her. Have you ever felt this way?[4]

7. Lisa is frustrated feeling some Christians get favor, blessings, and peace while she is living on "fumes of faith."[5] Have you ever felt this

---

3. "People who want to get rich fall into temptation and a trap and into many foolish and harmful desires that plunge men into ruin and destruction. For the love of money is a root of all kinds of evil. Some people, eager for money, have wandered from the faith and pierced themselves with many griefs" (Timothy 6:9–10).

4. "Let the beloved of the LORD rest secure in him, for he shields him all day long, and the one the LORD loves rests between his shoulders" (Deuteronomy 33:12).

5. "Do not be anxious about anything, but in everything, by prayer and petition, with thanksgiving, present your requests to God. And the peace of God, which transcends all understanding, will guard your hearts and your minds in Christ Jesus" (Philippians 4:6–7).

way? Mark tells her she doesn't see the big picture.[6] What would you have told her?[7]

8. Lisa feels like she has been sacrificed for her mother. Describe a time when you have suffered hardship or trials for the sake of another.[8]

9. At one point Lisa feels she has been "forgotten in a dark tunnel."[9] Have you ever felt God has forgotten you?[10] Have

---

6. "I tell you the truth, if you have faith as small as a mustard seed, you can say to this mountain, 'Move from here to there' and it will move. Nothing will be impossible for you" (Matthew 17:20).

7. "'My thoughts are not your thoughts, neither are your ways my ways,' declares the LORD. 'As the heavens are higher than the earth, so are my ways higher than your ways and my thoughts than your thoughts'" (Isaiah 55:8–9). "Trust in the LORD with all your heart and lean not on your own understanding; in all your ways acknowledge him, and he will make your paths straight" (Proverbs 3:5–6).

8. "Let us not become weary in doing good, for at the proper time we will reap a harvest if we do not give up" (Galatians 6:9).

9. "Suffering produces perseverance; perseverance, character; and character, hope. And hope does not disappoint us, because God has poured out his love into our hearts by the Holy Spirit, whom he has given us" (Romans 5:3–5).

10. "I say to God my Rock, 'Why have you forgotten me? Why must I go about mourning, oppressed by the enemy?'" (Psalm 42:9).

you ever felt you have forgotten God?[11]

10. Mark said he believes Christ has redeemed him.[12] He knows this logically, but knowing it and feeling it are two different things. Because of his childhood, he grew up feeling that he had to earn love—Lisa's and God's.[13] Have you ever felt this way? How would you advise a friend who is feeling this?

11. Mark believes that everything Lisa has been through had a purpose.[14] What do you think?

12. At one point Lisa struggles with not asking God to kill certain people. She asks for forgiveness instead.[15] Have you ever felt this way?

---

11. "Does a maiden forget her jewelry, a bride her wedding ornaments? Yet my people have forgotten me, days without number" (Jeremiah 2:32).

12. "In him we have redemption through his blood, the forgiveness of sins, in accordance with the riches of God's grace" (Ephesians 1:7).

13. "For it is by grace you have been saved, through faith—and this not from yourselves, it is the gift of God—not by works, so that no one can boast" (Ephesians 2:8–9).

14. "Many are the plans in a man's heart, but it is the LORD's purpose that prevails" (Proverbs 19:21). "And we know that in all things God works for the good of those who love him, who have been called according to his purpose" (Romans 8:28).

15. "And if ye offer a sacrifice of peace offerings unto the LORD, ye shall offer it at your own will" (Leviticus 19:5, KJV).

Dear Reader,

When I was growing up, significant events occurred at the kitchen table. We discussed all manner of things there—shared our troubles, our joys, thoughts, and dreams. We also discussed how our own perspectives can be based on logical and reasonable—even tangible—evidence and still be totally wrong.

Often during the challenges in our lives, we suspect (or fear) God isn't listening or hearing our pleas, even though they are coming from the very deepest recesses of our souls. We get an impression, and it stays with us. And then, with that clarity of hindsight we hear so much about, we discover some new tidbit of information or make some discovery or something happens that we wouldn't even have known about had we not been in the exact place we're in. And suddenly everything looks totally different.

It's hard to walk in faith when we're in one of life's long and dark tunnels. It's easy to feel forgotten and lost and helpless and hopeless.

But we're not.

In God's own time, He reveals that to us, and rather than feeling forgotten, we know that He was right there with us in that dark tunnel, gently leading us to His light.

As we learn this, so too must Lisa Harper and Mark Taylor. I so hope you enjoy their journeys and that their discoveries aid you in some small way or affirm your own.

I'd love to hear from you and invite you to visit me at www.vickihinze.com. Drop me a note anytime with stories of your journey.

Blessings,
Vicki

Center Point Publishing

600 Brooks Road ● PO Box 1
Thorndike ME 04986-0001 USA

(207) 568-3717

US & Canada:
1 800 929-9108
www.centerpointlargeprint.com